THE
INFINITE
NIGHT

THE INFINITE NIGHT

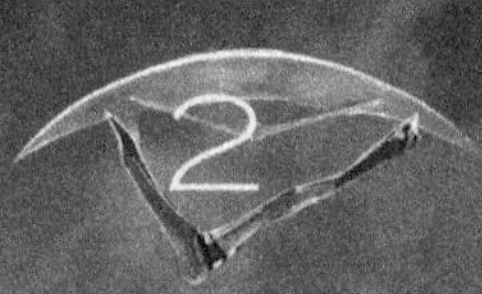

FERMI STATION: PART ONE

JORDAN GRAY

ISBN: 979-8-9917209-3-9
1st edition, 2025

For all the dreamers
who shine their light into the darkness.

Trigger Warning. Look, I did this for me. It's not for everyone, see why below.

- Ableism
- Abortion
- Abusive relationship
- Ageism
- Alcohol
- Amputation
- Animal abuse
- Animal death
- Anxiety
- Assault
- Blood
- Bones
- Branding
- Bullying
- Cannibalism
- Cheating
- Child abuse
- Child death
- Cults
- Death
- Decapitation
- Depression
- Drugs
- Eating disorder
- Emesis
- Emotional abuse
- Eugenics
- Famine
- Fire
- Genocide
- Gore
- Gun violence
- Hallucinations
- Hospitalization
- Misgendering
- Misogyny
- Murder
- Mutilation
- Needles
- Occult
- Pedophilia
- Physical abuse
- Plague
- Poisoning
- Police brutality
- Profanity
- Prostitution
- PTSD
- Racism
- Rape
- Religion
- Self-harm
- Sexism
- Sexual abuse
- Sexual assault
- Sexual harassment
- Sexually explicit scenes
- Slavery
- Snakes
- Spiders
- Stalking
- Starvation
- Suicide
- Terminal illness
- Terrorism
- Torture
- Violence
- War
- Other __________
- Other __________
- Other __________
- Other __________

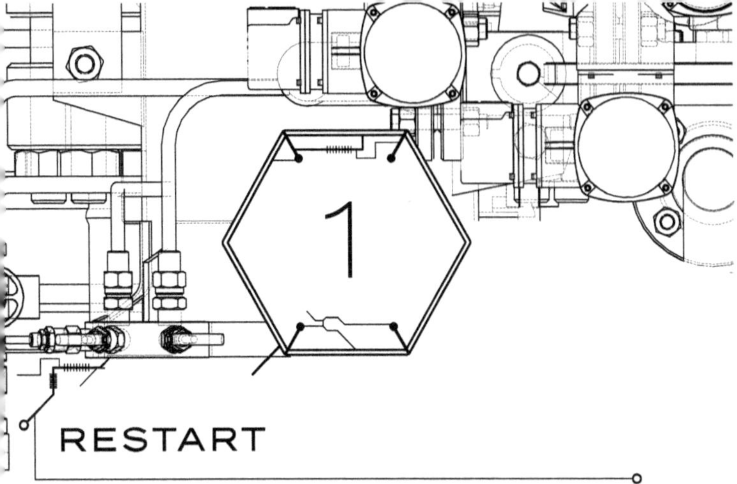

RESTART

522.189.1937, *FTS The Happy Marauder*, Fermi Station Space

I'M KIND OF in a fucked-up headspace, and Scout, the ship's psychologist, suggested I keep a journal… Maybe I shouldn't have stopped…

Maybe it's the nineteen child soldiers who we stuffed back into their boxes.

Everyone, the rest of the crew anyway, is bouncing around like we're big heroes.

I don't feel like a hero…

I don't know if feeding them would have been better than putting them in their boxes.

I don't know if it's about them or me.

They're fucked up.

Fuck! I don't know…

I'm using the same journal as last time. The Door Corp Secure Personal Log and Data Vault with your organic camouflage and all that shit. Shit, I forgot I was wearing this thing with all the work we've been doing.

Anyway, I'll run down the important stuff to sort my mind out. I'll start with a head count, which will be invalidated once we get to Fermi but whatever.

Hello. I am James August Childs.

No. I need to do better than that. From the top.

The Free Trade Ship (FTS) *The Happy Marauder* is a run-about class light freighter. She's the only ship I've been on, and she's home. Go figure that the longest time I've spent in one place since I left the institute is constantly moving. On the documents, she's a mismatched collection of parts, but man, how do they fit together!

If you don't like the technical side of spaceships, go ahead and skip forward a bit cause I'm doing this.

The Happy Marauder's spine is an ion cannon that uses nukes as a loading mechanism. That's some shit that doesn't mean much until you survive it. It's eighteen teratons of directed particle beam and one hell of a way to dodge. If you have no metric, it's like getting hit by a truck.

It *sucks*!

We've fired one volley in the two and a half years I've been here because the maintenance is stupid expensive. It is *NOT* one of those things you can defer maintenance. If that cannon misfires, the ship will become vapor and various forms of radiation.

"What kind of badass drive system pushes that beast of a cannon?" one may wonder. It's from a mobile shipyard… It's rugged and energy efficient, and the parts are cheap. Super cool engines come with super cool price tags, and we don't want that. That being said, it's way oversized for *The Happy Marauder*. It's a joke that she can fly though her own asshole because at emergency thrust, she maxes out at eighty-nine g's. The hull can withstand that for a calculated eight seconds before she disintegrates.

That's some shit I never want to experience.

However, the lifeboat and engineering sections are designed

to break away intact. Then again, we would be flying through our own debris field.

Anyway, here's where my engineering knowledge falls off: The Alcubierre drive, or warp engine, is named after a human who did the math long before the osheran showed up with a working one. A point for humans. However, keeping one running takes a team of humans, so more points to the osheran. The donut of mathematical voodoo that sits around our main reactor and ahead of our drive translates our local mass into a field that compresses the space in front of us and expands it behind us, so we can travel between the stars. The terms *compress* and *expand* are also super inaccurate. It's all energy states and math that my brain can't handle.

Captaining the ship is Gara Vatosh. He's human, if it matters. In combat, he fills the light infantry role. He's the boss—does the briefings and stuff—but I don't see him much. He does that upper management thing where he disappears for a week and shows up with a briefing with projections like he is trying to say "Look! I wasn't fucking off all that time."

Below the captain is Javelin. I think. She's been with him the longest at least. She's a gene-modded human with big ol…wings. And I know what you are thinking.

Her boobs are on the smaller side.

Javelin would murder me or just stare at me with that disapproving glare and unblinking cybernetic eye if she knew I was talking about her body.

I'm too scared to ask her about them, about the wings.

Anyway, she's the ship's purser and backup pilot. In combat, she's a stupid sniper. I have records of her doing quantum physics to Ping-Pong a round around a ship to headshot a high-value target.

Wraith is next in command. I think. He's our ninja spy. On the manifest, he's the morale officer. Which he *does* throw kick-ass parties and cook amazing food. However, day-to-day, he does our readiness scenarios. In combat, he disappears and fucks shit up. For example, he walked around with a measuring stick so Javelin would have accurate data for her long division head ventilation.

Dire-horn is our HR minotaur. He's the ship's lawyer and handles all the contracts and stuff. He, Javelin, and Saluit—I'll get to her in a bit—make up *finance* unofficially. Anything to do with money, you end up talking to all three. In combat, he fills the heavy infantry role with his ridiculous shiny power armor.

Side note: He does fine-dining amazingness compared to Wraith's barbeque. Between those two, we don't need a chef.

I need to learn how to cook…

Piper belongs near the top. They're the pilot and totally look like a murder bot from your favorite time travel movie. They're sweet and dating Shantu. They don't "do combat," and I have no idea what their other responsibilities are besides don't crash the ship. I imagine a lot of math and arguing with Flutter, our engineer.

I'm sticking Flutter here because he doesn't follow social hierarchies, but he's been on longer than Gabe. He's an osheran and the ship's entire maintenance department. He doesn't fight. There's so much to tell there, but I'll cover working under him later.

Maybe.

Gabe is a shoni-vonti—a three-legged, crab-mouthed plant person. He's the ship's armorer. He also runs our machine shop and all the fabrication equipment. He's also in charge of our combat training and qualifications in conjunction with Sergeant (Sgt.) Tok. In combat, he's our berserker because shoni-vonti don't get concussions the way humans do.

Sgt. Tok gets his rank from the Commonwealth Marines. He's on detached duty. Like a foreign exchange thing… I don't know. He's the only one who's getting paid a fixed rate. Sucks for him because all the share crew are getting paid *good*. I get the impression he was brought on, so Gabe wasn't overloaded with training. In combat, he's our small unit leader, so I guess a proper sergeant.

I think Scout might be above Gabe but whatever. He's the ship's lead clinician and psychologist. I don't think of him as above me, more of just the doctor. He's an urglurk, so like a one-and-a-half-meter tall gecko with big veiny elephant ears. He was hired in conjunction with Doc, our praportorian medic. In combat, he's, yeah, our scout.

Scout is biologically fourteen human standard years. Chronologically, he's one hundred and sixty-eight, most of those years having spent in suspended animation. Professionally, for human standards, he's doing a semester *abroad* before a residency program. Socially, he's the wise old man who is helping everyone adjust.

I bring this up because this shit is complicated, and context is important.

Our praportorian doctor is basically a walking starfish who doesn't operate on the same emotional bandwidth as humans. Thus, Scout handles the administrative and psychosocial portion of the job.

This is off topic, but fuck it. This is my log.

A few weeks ago, Doc started stalking Saluit. He was just always in the room, lurking.

To clarify, Doc has two full levels of the ship to himself. What I know about praportorian is they prefer their space brine and sulfur. He doesn't have a need to go to the galley or the gym.

It was very uncomfortable for us. A two-meter-tall starfish dripping water and wedging itself between the stair machine and the bulkhead was off-putting to say the least. They don't have eyes, but the staring vibes were there.

Anyway, Scout figured out that one of Saluit's moles was turning cancerous, and it was waiting for it to… I don't know. Ripen?

Okay. Saluit. She's my… I'm her… We're not dating, but, but we are stuck on a ship together. You get the idea.

Call it a situationship.

I guess she would be the highest of us who got hired from Vanguard City. She's hot, and she knows it. Acts like it. I put her higher than the rest of us because she's our forensic accountant. And don't dare forget *forensic*. In combat, she's standard infantry.

Uvwewe is our anthropologist. Good guy. Another gun on the line. Ryan, aka Turtle Tank, is our environmental tech. He's another good guy and another gun.

They're both human. I just haven't spent much time with them personally. I was chasing my tail, trying to keep up with an osheran on engineering shit.

Lamal was hired after us but is a qualified environmental engineer, so I guess he's above Ryan even. He's a noncombatant and a chinook. Chinooks look like mossy rocks.

Honestly, I forgot he was on the ship because I haven't seen him in months. I need to do better because he's nice and most of the reason why we have habitable spaces, not trapped in our suits.

That brings me to, well, me and Shantu. We're at the bottom because we were the last picks and almost didn't get onboard. Not a big need for articulated vehicle (AV) operators on spaceships. We've basically been playing catch-up due to our lack of formal education and shipboard experience.

Through the genetics lottery, we both were rated for space travel and were bargain bin additions to the team.

We marauders lost both of our drone techs—Alexis and Shannon—and our cybersecurity specialist—Xi.

Shannon's death hit me like a tram… Gym Sock, we called her. I think it's because I was out of the fight when she died. I wasn't there doing something… Holding the line like when Alexis and Xi got their ticket punched.

We all voted to give our dead full shares even though that wasn't in their contracts.

That's us, the marauders. We're not the never-ending supply of goons that super villains always seem to have. We're not even the independent heroes who can do what our government can't because we're not bound by treaties and policies. Mostly, we're governed by our contracts and the agreement that no one must be onboard one port longer than they have to.

The captain has veto authority—which he hasn't exercised with me on board—and emergency command, which saw us through the pirate engagement. So far, Javelin and Dire-horn have been doing their damnedest explaining contracts and the economics of this whole FTS thing, so when we vote on a contract, we understand the risks involved.

It sounds like a great space adventure, but it's mostly being miserable while surrounded by good people.

Shantu's and my real achievements are getting our Class 2 Starcraft Structural Engineers Certifications. It's the equivalent of a bachelor's for most human education systems.

I honestly never thought I would get this far.

Let me explain… On Vanguard—where we're from—I got into some trouble, couldn't conscript, and was relegated to transient labor. I spent every day angry at everyone and everything because I thought I wouldn't amount to anything. But now, at twenty-two, I have done things that *matter*. I am a Marauder, a part of a team.

Side note: I work with Flutter, and if we were the same species, it would have been like a doctor arguing with a high schooler. Maybe a preschooler. We design and run simulations virtually, but the fact I have a working relationship with an osheran is an accomplishment in itself.

I'm not joking. Scout certified me as an osheran liaison. Which is fucking *MONEY*!

I'm proud of these accomplishments though. Really proud. Two years ago, I thought I wasn't going to see thirty. Now, I… We… Shantu and I can retire comfortably.

Instead, we're pledging our shares of the starliner haul to become vested crew. It means we get to go to meetings where the senior crew decide on training schedules and drills. We can have the ship modified with… Well, with whatever we justify. I want to see what the next thing is.

I mean, what else did I not know I can accomplish?

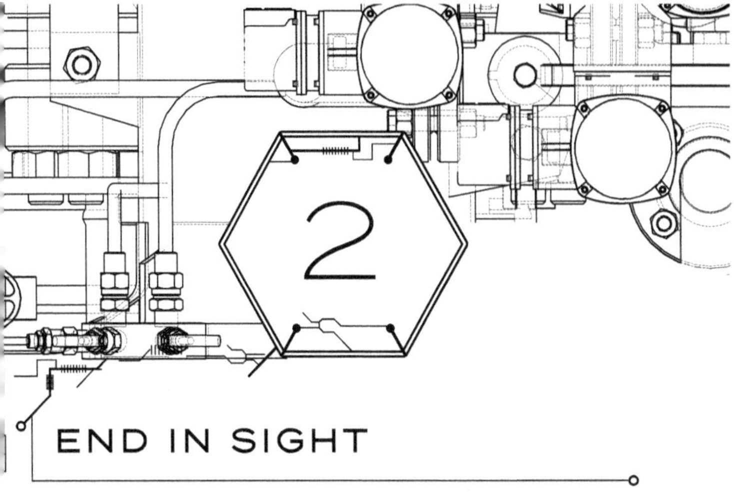

END IN SIGHT

522.246.1930 *FTS The Happy Marauder, Fermi Station Space*

YEAH... NOTHING HAPPENED. I deleted fifty days of exercises, drills, and me reviewing my class modules on starship design integrity and stress management and distributed propulsion systems integration and management.

I need a different specialty.

Maybe that's my problem. The stress and the tests and the reviews looming over me.

I mean, Fermi is right there. RIGHT FUCKING THERE! Less than an hour of a shuttle trip. But we're waiting on a bunch of legal and contracting stuff to be sorted out before we can get on the queue for a docking berth.

The walls of the conference room buzzed an outboard view of the local space as drones, tugs, and shuttles zipped between larger crafts.

The captain started today's meeting with his normal neutral tone that reminded me of a government newscaster. "The tugs from the auction house are almost here, so we can disconnect the starliner. That will close voting for the auction house. Sweep and salvage claims will expire when we transfer responsibility. You have until then to make your final claims. Will-Call Auction House will provide birthing space, security, and amenities pending the sale of the starliner…"

Will-Call Auction House was all but decided. We were just adhering to our contracts and going through the motions. Honestly, we endured the meetings about commodities and other bullshit, so Dire-horn didn't lose his shit.

I love him, but listening to him and Saluit go back-and-forth every time someone wanted to claim something from the starliner made me want to eat my own face. We had to agree on a value based on ship credits, and now, we are reestablishing ship credits versus the Fermi commodities trade. Which will be verified by no less than three different organizations.

SO MANY DOCUMENTS!

I know the captain, Dire-horn, Javelin, and Saluit are doing their due diligence, so we can make our money, but this shit is so FUCKING BORING!

"Next order of business," the captain said, "I have arranged for test and review for when we arrive."

Test and review, if it isn't self-explanatory, is just a lot of skill testing for our individual and collective résumés. We also turn in our mission reports to build an environmental profile for the ship, which is then used to help the brokers and agents types fit personnel and ships together. It's a major pain in the ass from what I'm told. But everything I find tells me if I don't do some form of test and review, go ahead and hang up my space suit because I'm not going to be working anymore.

The captain calmly waited as the bitchfest came and went. It was mostly an acknowledgment that there was still something shitty to do before we went on shore leave.

"Cursory projections have us at Fermi Station for at least

six months for overhaul and refit," the captain continued. "I'm promising, at minimum, one week of uninterrupted R & R following test and review."

"Captain, I officially request two," Wraith said.

The captain looked around the conference room. "Two pending future contracts and training availability."

The placid look on his face and the fact that Dire-horn didn't say anything told me this was already decided in a previous conversation.

"Wraith will be your primary point of contact for testing, and Gabe will be his alternate. If you have any accounting questions, take them to Javelin. Sgt. Tok, Monolith, Tombstone, and Saluit, you are hereby ordered to contact your respective embassies in person on the topic of asylum for our refugees. You must report back before beginning leave. Do not use open comms for this. I do not want the feeds to label us as enslavers or saviors. If they let you use one of their secure rooms, give them the full story. Dire-horn will provide the NDAs."

That was something I didn't know I needed in my life.

Trust.

He covered how the capture of the wandathu starliner would look great on our public record, but we didn't want to have to hide from or fight wandathu bounty hunters every time we went to a bar. So, we had to fill out documents for the ninja-monk treatment.

The ninja-monk treatment is just when a company scrubs our records of all situational data and boils it down to scoring that can be used in simulations. It lets us get credit for our intraship fighting and improvisational engineering without telling the wandathu that we have one of their hulls and are selling it at an auction. It's also soft advertising that we're discrete because we don't give out data on our clients.

There's a professional name for this kind of practice. But it's a stupid-ass name, so I'm calling it the ninja-monk treatment.

I glanced at the status display with our approach vector to Fermi Station. That name, by the way, is misleading. It isn't a station but a planetoid. And every species ever seems to have at least their own nook on the planetoid. Not to mention there are somewhere between one and five hundred quadrillion inhabitants.

Humans, for the most part, live in one section of the three hundred thirty-six spires that give the station its urchin appearance. The one place where the atmospherics and gravity are right, and none of the untold number of other species are *actively* hostile toward humans.

One anthropologist described the station as "a monument to the interstellar age. The seed from which a true galactic civilization will undoubtedly sprout." Yet hundreds if not thousands of religious sects, governments, and self-proclaimed royalty are in varying states of conflict over *their* claim to the station, while the vast majority just go about their business. These ongoing feuds give conflicting accounts of the history there though.

For example, Fermi Station's mass, gravitational, and electromagnetic fields and albedo don't add up. The station's gravity field should collapse it into a planet. The orbital gravity has it as Jovian-sized place, but local gravity in the human areas has it as a little less than human standard. Shit like that.

"Are we not going to talk about the fact we're going to land on a magic planet?" Shantu joked, interrupting my musings.

Everyone ignored him.

I knew morale was tanking, but I hadn't realized it had gotten *that* low. I felt it as much as anyone now. Must be short-itis. As in the end is in sight, and there's little reason to bust your ass with a vacation so close.

The senior crew has been up our asses, especially Sgt. Tok, for last-minute qualifications. We were all a little cranky and sore from yesterday's marathon compartment clearing training.

That being said, if this is what *bad* looks like on *The Happy*

Marauder, I'll never leave. *Bad* where I grew up meant people were getting murdered over the dumbest shit. I'll take jokes not landing every day over that.

Dire-horn picked up his portion of the briefing. "As soldiers of fortune, we are paid to have enemies. So, do not make them for free." His tone had the funk of someone, perhaps the captain's wisdom. "Our docking liaison and I have coded the districts with suggested weapon restrictions. While we are currently granted wide latitudes on the station, we should seek to expand them, not deplete their hospitality…"

"Look, the station is a drunken orgy of different species with a coffee house, a massage parlor, and a rehab for every vice," Wraith added before Dire-horn trailed into some point about honoring ourselves and respecting other species' customs. "If you fuck up before I've had my fill, don't come back to the ship. If you do, I will make it my personal mission to extract my disappointment from your available orifices. Whatever super sapience runs this place won't be able to stop me from—"

"What do you mean super sapience?" Uvwewe asked.

He rolled his eyes and then tossed up a political map in virtual with major trade routes highlighted. The timescale indicated it was for the last five centuries. The various conflicts and fleet engagements gave Fermi Station a wide berth, and major shipping lanes seemed to never suffer an interruption. A shocking number of smaller conflicts seemed to be followed by a surge in traffic.

"This place is the biggest trade hub in the local sphere, and it can take care of itself. We can only infer from effects that someone knows what the fuck they are doing."

Uvwewe smiled at the rest of us so Wraith couldn't see.

"Ugh!" Wraith grunted. "That's not the point. Don't get hit by a transport. Stick to the human-friendly areas and fucking enjoy yourself. We're within range for feed access, so figure it out."

My fling and archnemesis Saluit spoke up. "I need to reach my consulate immediately. I don't see why *I* must go through pass and review."

She always did things like that. Everyone else called it *test and review*, but on her planet, it was *pass and review*. Her planet is better than the uncivilized swine who inhabited the rest of the universe, so it must be correct.

We ignored it as much as we could.

I wanted to say "Stow it, Stripper Glitter!" but didn't. With Shannon gone, Ryan and Saluit had lost the taste for their nicknames.

Dire-horn took the question with all the grace of a trained diplomat. "Saluit, as your contract states, unless you want to forfeit your shares, you are a member of *The Happy Marauder* and will continue to fulfill your role and duties until dispensation."

She was some socialite wherever she came from and had a silver spoon shoved up her ass. Once we came within range of the station, she was advocating for the quickest and, therefore, lowest payout. She got outvoted.

I have no idea why she took a liking to me.

Shantu leaned over, thankfully distracting me from their verbal sparring. "Piper and I are talking about going to pick out frame mods. Do you want to come?"

He's my best friend, but I would really like *some* space between us.

"I'll go with y'all, but I'll wait outside," I answered.

"What? Why?"

"I don't need to know what kind of plumbing you got for your partner," I said shortly, trying to establish some kind of boundary for the millionth time.

"Why? You've seen *my* plumbing," he shot back with an insufferable grin.

I rolled my eyes so hard that it took my whole head with it and came back around. "If I could delete those memories, I would." I sighed. "Look, I'm happy for y'all, but I don't need to be *that* involved in your relationship. I got enough shit rattling around in my head without wondering what features Piper's vagina has and if the extended warranty was overpriced."

"It's not just about that! Piper is going to get translucent skin that flashes colors to convey their emotions. There's a bunch of styling to it, I think."

"Why not a more mobile face?" I suggested.

Shantu shrugged, implying he had made that argument and lost. Then he gave me puppy dog eyes.

Shit…

"*Fine,*" I said.

Shantu, if you ever listen to this, LEAVE ME THE FUCK OUT OF YOUR LOVE LIFE!

"We're opening positions for environmental engineer, drive engineer," Dire-horn continued, listing the dream sheet of personnel he wanted.

I stared at the display behind Dire-horn and tried to make sense of the tableaux. I think someone was getting boarded or space bees were returning to their hive. It looked violent.

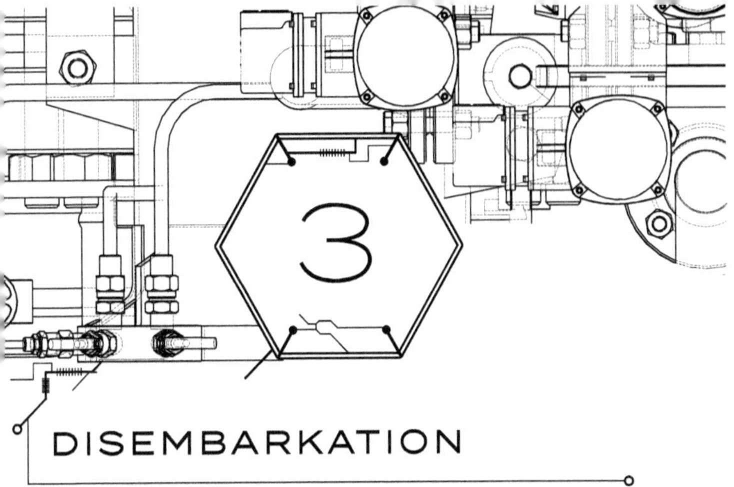

DISEMBARKATION

522.263.0600 *FTS The Happy Marauder*, Fermi Station Space

THE AUCTION HOUSE used a docking swarm carrier rather than traditional tugs. Relative velocity indicators showed our escorts moving away.

Hehe. Sounds like we had strippers.

In the conference room, I was just killing time, lying on the table with the walls set to the external view. It was the only way to really get a sense of scale.

The docking swarm was just a blanket of blinking drives contracting onto *The Happy Marauder* and the starliner. Soft thuds resonated throughout the hull, almost as one, as the drones latched on. More drones assembled their shroud. Think chain-link fence meets monitor. It was meant to fool sensors but be porous enough to let thrust out.

The drone carriers and other escorts transmitted in the clear, and with bright beacons, they blinked that the starliner and *The Happy Marauder* were a navigational hazard. Which is polite for *fuck around and find out.*

Heavy construction equipment got busy disassembling the mounting gimbal I worked so hard to build. I was proud of that thing. This kid who should have died in the gutter had helped design, fabricate, install, and integrate a device that allowed his ship to push another.

I was *pivotal* to our big score. Get it? Pivotal… Gimbals pivot on multiple axes.

I'm sorry I'm down to engineering puns.

In a formal letter, Sgt. Tok announced he had been recalled to the Commonwealth and thanked everyone for the experience. Said he's a Commonwealth marine and will not abandon his duties. Blah, blah, blah. He's in a cult.

Sucks to be him because everyone else can retire if they want.

I would have liked to have gotten him something nice as a send-off. But I was queued for my test and review, and he'd be gone before I could see him again.

Ryan's letter followed his, explaining he was going back to the colony. He wanted to settle down and study the dirt squids because he thinks they could be added to shipboard horticulture.

Not a bad way to spend a career… Trying to make the next big breakthrough.

I need to start making people send-off gifts before we get to port.

Fuck. I need to do better.

The alarm chimed for breaking maneuvers. It was a polite chirp that meant to stop juggling knives, not the angry buzz that meant brace for impact. We were on the final approach to the silvery cloud that was Fermi Station. The lights of millions of ships looked like coalescing wisps of a gathering storm.

I held onto the conference table as we closed with the station. The g-forces made me sway. The wispy lines were now spires tens of thousands of kilometers long and hundreds thick. Blue lines—I could call them trains perhaps—shot up and down at ludicrous speed.

I had to use my feed to stop the image, and still, the structure was fuzzy.

Mountainous heat sinks lifted and lowered onto the surface with demand, like glowing red mechanical tubeworms. Fermi Station was a beautiful living creature. No, not a creature. An ecosystem. Like a coral reef. Something in my brain made me think of steel ships chugging along in a vast blue ocean.

Maybe I had seen it once on the feed.

"Makes you feel like a bug, right?" Shantu asked from the hatch, interrupting my thoughts. "Come on, man. The shuttles are almost here."

We went to our respective quarters to prepare to leave. I took my tet. It's a meter-long piece of scrap metal that had saved my life when I had used it to fight galunkin. Dire-horn had rendered his honors and gave it a minotaur-style woven grip.

Shantu had his pal'loch—the minotaur crescent moon shaped blade designed for leverage to defeat armor.

Dire-horn kept trying to be a mentor figure to us, which equated to weekly dinners where he taught us about his clan and stuff. Even then, Wraith was running a lot of the interference, translating Dire-horn's culture to the rest of us humans, because of the piles of shit that Dire-horn was responsible for as the ship's lawyer.

I'm still unclear on Dire-horn and Wraith's relationship. I haven't worked up the nerve to ask for details. Honestly, it's none of my business.

Anyway, Dire-horn adopted Shantu and me as prospective clan members during the fight on the starliner. There were plans in the books about getting us anointed as herd mates. The minotaur word is ahkochal, literally meaning folded steel. There's a meet and greet and then training. And if we graduate, we can wear clan colors and have access to their banking and economy. Many humans comfortably retire as brokers for minotaur tech.

But that is if Dire-horn ever crawls out from under the pile of legal shit pending for him.

Oh! *Fuck me!*

Ready to have your mind blown?

I had a pending alert.

Social media alert, not incoming fire alert.

It was from Dire-horn's old account that was idling on minotaur servers.

He used to *dance*. Like ballet! He was a ballerina… Balladeer…? Ballerino! He went to college on a *fucking ballet scholarship*. He got his undergrad law degree as a backup if he didn't make it as a ballerino. His whole clan is a bunch of *dancers*. There are videos and articles about how he was going to be the next big thing. How the fuck is our resident samurai and lawyer a fucking ballerina?

Also, he's forty-three human standard, early middle-aged. The equivalent to thirty-one if he was human. Do with that what you will. I'm still dealing with the fact he was a fucking ballerina.

"SHANTU!" I yelled with an annoying scream, even though it was going directly into his head through his ear bugs.

Shantu did not disappoint. He soon slid down the shaft into my quarters, seeming excited for fuckery to spread. I played him the video and opened all the articles for him to read.

"NO! FUCKING! WAY!" He then turned and yelled in my exact tone. "PIPER!"

Piper entered with far less excitement. Their stance was a sassy murder bot. "What are you two knuckleheads up to?"

"Did you know about this?" He put the articles about Dire-horn's ballet career up on the monitor on my wall.

I don't think I've turned that wall on more than once or twice. I do everything in virtual. Or use the big monitor in the galley. Or the walls in the conference room if everyone wants to play something.

"Yeah?" Piper said. "So?"

Shantu grabbed his chest and fell to his knees. "My love, what have I done for you to betray me like so?"

"Really? You know I have shit to do?" Piper's sassy murder bot's eyes didn't roll, but I could feel it in their tone.

He made it a full telenovela. "Does my happiness mean so little? How could you dare deprive me of such joy? Months, years, I wandered in the desert—"

"Shuttle's here," they said, their tone saying they were not having any of it. "Get the fuck off my ship and get to test and review."

I had both hands over my mouth to stop my laughing because I wanted to see where this went.

Shantu thrust his hands up in a dramatic pose.

Piper picked him up by his wrist.

"You always know how to lift me up when I'm down," he said, holding the dramatic tone.

"Seriously? Go." The shiny metal humanoid skeleton's stance then softened, and they hugged.

I got uncomfortable and grabbed the rest of my kit while they were all lovey-dovey in my quarters.

Though soon, Shantu and I were walking off the ship with our sidearms, our minotaur weapons, and a strut to match the expense account attached to a ship.

"It's official. Everyone's scattering," he said as soon as we completed our buddy checks. "The captain, Dire-horn, Javelin, Wraith, and Gabe will be all that's left. Scout hasn't said anything. Doc is already gone, and so is Flutter. Piper's staying, of course."

A record scratch played in my head.

I thought Flutter was going to be in engineering bliss, overseeing the ship's overhaul. The idea of him leaving was just… unimaginable.

"Seems anticlimactic, doesn't it?" I asked rhetorically.

"You want to return to a planetary neural ecology?" Shantu joked.

He was talking about Doc, who was apparently returning to the praportorian mass. However, that works.

"No, fuckstick," I said. "I wanted a party, a celebration, a fancy dinner… Something… It's been a ride, man. Maybe not for Flutter and Doc but for the rest of us. A bit of fanfare for the farewells."

"Say that five times fast!" Shantu almost shouted.

"A bit of fanfare for the farewells. A bit of fanfare for the fare-wells. A bit of fanfare for the farewells. A bit of fanfare for the farewells. A bit of fanfare for the farewells."

"Nailed it!"

Something in my brain sent an error message. "Wait. *Scout* is on the fence?"

"I think it's more of an issue that he doesn't want to sit in the dock for months while the ship gets worked on," he said.

The error message in my head evaporated. "How the hell do you get an itchy foot when you haven't even taken your shoes off?"

"I don't know. Maybe he wants to be around his own kind for a while."

"He's more of an academic than a soldier, so there is that," I said. "Where's Flutter going?"

"Don't know. And he doesn't have to tell us. Piper's losing their shit because who do you think oversees the overhaul now?" He said it like we might be volunteering our time to help.

We transitioned to the air lock. The tramp shuttle was a little more than a drive system on a greasy empty tube. It was pit marked and abraded with years of small collisions. The shuttle used mooring lines, not a transition tube. I took a hold of one of the four line riders and let it pull me to the shuttle.

Inside, we found some cargo netting to lash ourselves onto.

We didn't meet the pilot, just watched the map and vector data change.

The shuttle ride was brief, and it deposited us in a cargo hangar. Warning lights and marking lasers that projected the course of moving equipment lit the hangar. At a certain point, it was a mess because everything was yellow strobes and red markings, and I didn't know what side of the line I was on.

I expected a similar concourse to Vanguard with cafés and information terminals. Not cargo containers.

Oh well.

We stood at the hatch—not even an air lock—trying to figure out where to go without getting crushed by freight. The local net blared warnings and flashed "Unauthorized Area" at us. A lady representing the hangar told us to ignore it and half shoved us toward the passenger concourse.

On our private comms, I asked Shantu, "Are we being smuggled onto the station?"

"Yeah. Feels like it." He shrugged and rolled with it.

"So, we're not going to talk about it?"

"Nope."

We transitioned through a few air locks with various decontamination procedures to the passenger concourse. The concourse must have been a factory at one time because the conveyor belts of the moving walkway looked industrial with questionable maintenance. It now was covered with a writhing mass of people.

It was a strange system where everyone was getting a running start before jumping onto the walkway and grabbing the person in front of them. It seemed to be acceptable to grab onto whoever you could that was going in your direction. People also seemed to keep an eye on each other, so no one fell. If someone struggled to stay upright, the nearest people grabbed onto them to stabilize them.

I already hate crowds. Crowds with moving sidewalks and everyone shoving was an absolute fucking nightmare. I needed to figure out how this works.

I gently nudged a person near me, and he acknowledged me with a friendly enough nod. He then spoke gibberish, and a moment of confusion passed before my feed recognized his words as Old Earth English and translated it into Common.

"I acknowledge you. Or yes?" the translated voice said.

"What's the rules to this?" I asked.

The underlying tone said something about being happy. I'm not stupid, but the translator said, "It is wise to ask. Just tap between people, and they'll try and give you room to move." He pointed at examples of people trying to move toward the faster centers of the walkway. "Be ready to help anyone in arm's reach, or you might get your faceplate broken."

He pointed at someone in a nice-looking suit who was being shoved from the walkway by everyone around him. After giving him a few kicks to the stomach, someone cut the respirator hose that went to his face mask.

"You help, and everyone gets where they're going. You don't, and we'll kick your ass."

What was that expression? "When in Rome, do as the Romans do?"

I played our conversation for Shantu. He took a moment to verify the information with another random person.

I surveyed the area. My local feed showed me the current prices for the air hookups, which were *astronomical*. Pun intended. It was dozens of local credits per liter of air, hundreds for the pure stuff at high pressure. It would have cost me months of work just to refill an air bottle here.

The ambient air had too much carbon dioxide and nitrogen, not enough oxygen to be healthy. Then I noticed how many people *weren't* in vac suits. Everyone who was not in some variation of an environment suit seemed to be wearing Frankenstein abominations salvaged from other bits of clothing or standard coveralls. The locals seemed to be misshapen. Their faces were gaunt, and their limbs seemed disproportionately long. Their chests seemed broader and more barrel shaped.

The number of visible tumors and sores made me thankful for my hazardous environment protection system (HEPS). I had a rough time growing up, but this was a magnitude worse. Maybe it was the overcrowding… But somehow, we were the fancy ones in space suits here.

Weird.

I hesitated to join the other commuters because we out massed most of them twice over, and then our HEPS added like thirty kilos.

Shantu and I synced our location markers, got our running start, and made it onto the walkway smooth enough. We did our best to pull a few others on before we were pinned in with the masses. Having someone's greasy bony ass pressed against me was *not* my idea of a good time, but everyone seemed to ignore each other and mind their manners.

We were just two more bodies on a giant overflowing conveyor belt that stretched farther than I cared to think about. I felt faceless. Overcrowded.

Ugly, dingy lights struggled under all the filth. Dispassionate composite walls covered with directional and emergency information were half hidden under layers of grime. Everything—the people, the walls, the handholds, and the pressure seals—were covered in a uniform soot, which I assumed was all the stuff people left behind—hair, skin, oils, dandruff—held in place by the trapped humidity.

I was glad my suit was sealed.

That makes me feel like a dick.

As we neared our waypoint, we tapped and pushed to get to

the outside of the walkway. Soon, we were a part of a surge of people trying to get off. We collectively tripped and regained our balance in a wave as everyone took steps off the moving walkway.

I found my hand on my tet and sidearm too often for public commuting.

Shantu and I followed lines of people as we passed through a decontamination air lock. The grime melted off our HEPS in a pressure wash filled with intense strobing lights that caused my faceplate to go opaque.

"If this is how the whole station is, let's get a deck of cards and go back to the ship," I commented.

Shantu's tone sounded equally displeased. "Fuck the deck. We can print some."

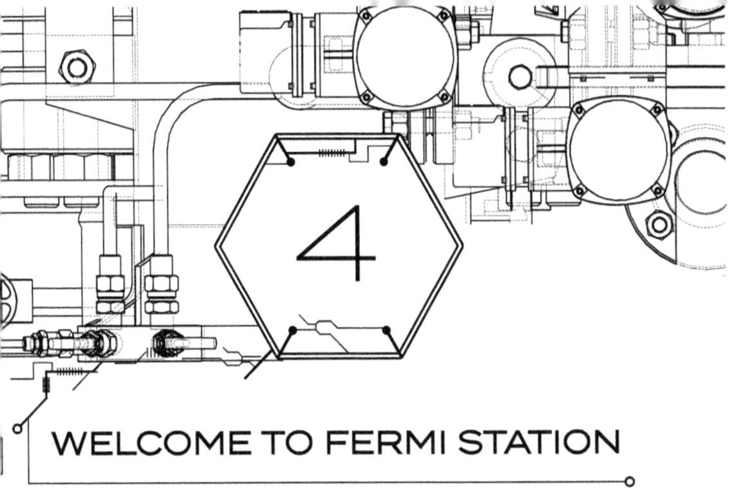

WELCOME TO FERMI STATION

522.270. 0100 Vanguard Block,
Human District, Fermi Station

I'LL SPARE YOU the six mind-numbing days of standardized testing, sleeping, and eating goo from a straw. It was a new height of suck. Just imagine all the indifference of a factory shuffling you along a conveyor, only to have a machine bump you into the next slot. Except that slot makes you retake every test you've ever taken. It was like high school and the DMV had a hate child and made it everyone's problem.

I don't know how many tests I took. I don't *want* to know.

I need to talk to someone about the overlap between the tests. It was like ten bureaucrats wanted the same job but called it different things. I mean, drive systems structural management and propulsion load engineering cover the exact same fucking thing. I'm almost sure they were the exact same test with a different label at the top.

Two days were spent on welding in different environments. Another day was assembling and disassembling different air locks.

I get why Saluit was trying to sham her way out of it. I'm done. I'm not putting any more of that bullshit in my log. Moving on.

Sorry.

"How'd you do?" Shantu asked as I approached him in the lobby.

The lobby was a bland utilitarian affair filled with people screaming at the staff in booths over… I do not care.

"Fucking *awesome!*" I said with way more murder than I meant.

I need to do better. I shouldn't take my irritation out on Shantu.

Wraith, Gabe, and Javelin had stressed how important this shit was for our profiles and how much money we make. Still, the testing was more on my patience than my skills.

"I'm sure you did fine," Shantu said, ignoring my tone. "Let's hit environmental services, so we can get out of these and get a drink."

We pushed our way through the crowd for the queue to the nearest environmental services area. Here, people were relatively clean. There was this odd polished strip where people had cleaned the corridors by brushing up against it with their shoulders. The overhead looked like a vent over the fryers at your local greasy spoon. It was a solid five minutes before I realized we were still in the passageway, not even the waiting room.

The vibe was quite indifferent, patient.

Ten more minutes passed, and we took only two steps forward.

"I'm messaging the auction house," Shantu said, seemingly reading my mind. He gestured into his feed for a moment. "They have their own environmental services." Still gesturing. "We can go…to this station and take a tram to this concierge service." He let out a sharp bark of laughter. "They're asking if we need a security escort. Anyway, this way."

"I wish someone would start something, so I could let out some steam," I said, feeling more violent than usual. "Between the testing center and this shit."

"Coming right up." Shantu sent me a pin for a bar with an open entry fighting ring. He then spoke with his best advertising voice. "A Fighting Chance and Drinks for all your bloody bare-knuckle human fighting needs! They also have on-site medical and every variety of alcohol a human can't tolerate. If you can take five rounds in the cage, you can get a trophy and ten thousand in local credits."

We laughed at the money. Ten grand in the local funny money would *maybe* cover our tab. Drinks were almost a grand apiece. We marauders were trying to keep shipboard credits valued at one for every three to five thousand local. That meant there were large swaths of the human district we couldn't, or rather *shouldn't*, visit because they wouldn't honor our accounting practices.

The trophy was cute though. It was a polymer transparent fist gripping red dice.

"Do you think it's the fact that our leave is here, as in we should be on vacation, that makes these little errands seem like such a pain in the ass?" I asked idly.

"Maybe. I don't know," Shantu answered with an honest tone. He stared off into space, making gestures to his feed. "I feel weird being off the ship and around all these people. Like a step in the wrong direction. Like we're back on Vanguard, and Telex is going to call and bitch at us for something *he* fucked up."

I laughed. Hard. "That's what it is! It's all the people!" I yelled. "I'm all fucking twitchy and moody because I keep expecting some bullshit to start. Fuck, man. I haven't thought about Telex since we left. I would put money on that he either sold out or went under. I felt like we spent half our time cleaning up his messes."

Fermi wasn't the same as Vanguard City.

First, Vanguard City was freezing. Second, the people walked differently.

Here, everyone pursed their faces if I met their eyes. I don't know how else to describe it. They didn't smile, but it was like they were trying to say "Please don't talk to me because I have anxiety, and I'm not equipped for random social interactions. If you do, please keep at where's-the-lavatory level."

The crowd shifted toward dirtier, and I noticed the growing stains of the unofficial bathrooms on bulkheads. The memory of the smell hit me, and I was glad I was still in my HEPS.

"Do you want to go back and buy him out if he's still there?" Shantu asked, bringing me back to reality.

"For what? The satisfaction? No. Fuck him. I'm good," I said. "No, sitting in an office and arguing about percentages sounds awful. You and I are not planet-bound. Retirement sounds like a big ship and a contract that will last the rest of our lives. Maybe Piper will pilot it. You know, with you going steady with a pilot and everything."

"You don't want to have Saluit on this Dreamliner of yours?" he asked.

"Fuckstick."

"Fucknuts!" he shot back. "Come on! She's a *forensic* accountant. Take one for the team."

We were drawing attention as our conversation became more animated. Reactions ranged from interest to irritation. But I didn't get the impression that we were crossing any lines yet.

"She's headed back to her home world, something to do with her family," I said. "I wasn't listening because she pegged the bullshit meter."

"I bet she pegged more than that," he joked.

One of the people pressed against me started moving like they were laughing.

Shantu and I were on a private channel, but I didn't know how much could be heard through our HEPS. The random person could be having their own conversation, and the timing was just a coincidence.

"I would have taken it just so I didn't have to listen to her prattle on about how things are done on her planet," I said. "She was doing that thing where she overexplains it like she's almost lying to herself and needs to fill in all the details so she could believe it too. Fuck! Why did you bring this up?"

"To watch you squirm," he said. "And so you can process it in an entirely unhealthy way for my entertainment."

"Fuck you!"

The random person chuckled again. They were definitely listening to our conversation.

"Want to go to the bar now?" he asked.

"Yes!" The word came out way more like a pouty child who was just offered ice cream than I'd like to admit.

Shantu clicked his tongue as the tram arrived. It was just a series of windowless cylinders covered by the same pervasive grime. No seats. Locals just sat on their belongings or hooked them on the nets that hung from the overhead. Several children seemed to be playing up in the nets. Adults batted at their hands playfully before offering small food packages.

Flashing lights just below the nets indicated the direction of travel and relative speed. A scrawny, shorter man took off his shirt and wiped the grime away to reveal this line's circuit information. He tensed before wiping more of the grime, looking for something.

A second man stood next to the first and struck up a conversation. It continued with gesturing and pointing. Then the second man reached into his belongings and produced a well-worn but intact shirt.

It didn't take long before Shantu and I made it to a stop where we switched trams. The next tram had seats. The seats' restraints deployed and firmly held us down. Speakers chimed three times, and then we left the station with an inappropriate level of acceleration for public transportation.

The deceleration was *worse*.

All the other passengers took the abuse in casual stride, so I tried my best to look unfazed.

"Well, shit!" Shantu commented. "These people know how to get around."

I responded with a grunt, recovering from the deceleration. I was pretty sure gravity had changed. I didn't think to check it.

Shantu and I were the only ones who got off. The corridor out of the tram station switched from the common polymer to decorative synthetic stone flooring with soft instrumental music.

I could feel others looking at us. The guards in the subtle security station watched us. If it wasn't for Sgt. Tok's training to look at every corner, I might have missed it.

Cleaning bots—which were basically overgrown shop vacs— scoured every surface and retreated to alcoves to replenish or whatever.

A guard spoke in a language I didn't understand. They gestured, and we saw the queue for the decontamination stations and followed other pedestrians for our turns.

The wide-open space almost felt criminal after having to climb over people. Well-marked signs and stations advertised air and water. A shiny printer advertised the rates for adapters. Another machine cycled food and drink options.

I didn't have much time to muse on the social-economic disparities when we cycled through another decontamination unit.

Exiting the decontamination chamber, we were approached by what I think was a human. They were androgynous with pale, almost blue skin and a completely hairless head. I could see vascularity through their skin.

Our feed pinged them as our concierge.

They led us to a large green deck with artistically crafted rainbow bonsai trees that were three or four meters tall. People in robes were tending to the trees with simple tools. The juxtaposition was so disorienting that I immediately checked the seals on my HEPS.

All good.

Behind us was all the metal I would expect from a space station. In front of us was a beautiful courtyard that would make some kung fu master proud.

The citrus fruit spanned the light spectrum in an array ahead of us.

"Beautiful," escaped my lips before I could think. I had never seen so much color and order before.

The only blemish to the utopian green deck was a simple sign on the path that read "Please ask for fruit."

It stopped me in my tracks for a long moment while I took in the majesty of hundreds of square meters maintained down to the individual leaf. This was also the longest Shantu had ever shut up without being shot at.

"How little do you have to get laid to keep an orchard more trimmed than my balls," he said, murdering the moment.

The subtle path was almost half a kilometer long and brought us to a pressure seal stylized to look fit for a medieval castle. The hatch opened for us as if we were expected guests. More bald androgynous humanoids wordlessly gestured for us to follow. They ushered us into a three-meter by three-meter room that stepped down into ankle-deep water.

One wall held the terminal and transparent cabinets with all the tools of their trade. Opposite of it were benches with hooks and adjustable hangers.

When I unsealed my HEPS, the smell of antiseptic and algae filled my nose, and my face contorted into a sneeze with the sudden change in humidity. I tried to catch it in my gloved hands, but a tech placed a fabric spatula over my mouth and nose for me to smash my face into.

I gave them questioning faces, but they didn't react. The techs just simply continued doing things with their doohickeys and whatchamacallits.

The attendant politely but dispassionately walked us through the rigorous decontamination procedure. They took samples and fed them into machines as we stepped out of our HEPS. Shantu and I were then hosed down, rubbed with goop, and fed things until the machines decided we were no more a threat to the local biosphere than any other meat bag. Our HEPS got a thorough steam clean and purge as well. The whole time, the androgynous staff circulated, never saying a word but gestured in exceedingly clear ways. I didn't feel the need to talk to them or ask questions.

Surreal.

As we left, Shantu spoke. "Dude, that was weird. Did they all take a vow of silence or something?"

"I want to know how they kept you from talking, so I can bottle that," I answered. "I could get rich!"

"Fucknuts."

"Fuckstick. I wonder if they don't talk because of how many languages come through here."

Shantu gave me a seems-reasonable shrug.

"All right," I said, trying to stay focused. "I'm letting the embassy know we're on the way. Then I have an amazing idea…" I trailed off for dramatic effect.

"Don't keep an idiot in suspense," he barked.

I slowed and dramatically closed my eyes, savoring the moment.

He punched my chest harder than necessary. "Out with it, fucker."

"Super spy!" I exhaled. "We get suits and everything. Wait. No. That'll never work because you can't keep your mouth shut, much less be polite past a drink order."

It was something dumb from watching too many shows, but we could afford nice suits, so why not get one with gadgets built in? Then we could go somewhere nice to eat and drink fancy wine and pretend we belong.

"Fuck you. We're totally doing this." Shantu trailed off into fabricating a bullshit backstory.

I had never seen him smile so big.

We took several high-speed trams to a station near the Vanguard embassy. The facility had simple clear doors with the Vanguard star emblemed on it. We walked over a blast door that was over a meter thick.

"Do you have that spinning feeling?" I asked. "Like you expect gravity to change or the ship to maneuver or something?"

"It's called vertigo, dipshit, and yes," Shantu said. "We've been on the ship for too long. Moving in a stable g isn't normal anymore."

"The ring was spun to two and a half g."

"Yeah, but we only slept in that. We went back and forth all day long."

I pulled the door open, popped off my helmet, and let it drape across my back. The simple lobby had nice but not extravagant polymer furniture. Two doors flanked either side of the reception desk.

The phrase "Who we are is what we do with what we have — Vince Lombardi" stood boldly in black letters along the back bulkhead near the overhead.

A young man, maybe eighteen, acknowledged us. Packard, B. His two chevrons indicated corporal (Cpl.) and Vanguard Fleet Diplomatic Services. Followed by the emblem for the Vanguard Aggregate Forces (VAF) with the emblem for Change of Watch, which showed he was retired. The white with black and red accents uniform looked comfortable, though thickly padded. Cpl. Packard's career badge was a stylized olive branch, and my feed said it meant diplomatic offices. He casually had a submachine gun-style weapon strapped under his left arm and a pistol on his right hip.

The expanded definition of the ribbons on his chest appeared in my feed. There weren't many, a few weapon ratings and other minor campaigns and merits. The Purple Heart jumped out, indicating that he was wounded in action. When I stared too long, the details of the award populated. He was also awarded an academic achievement for completing courses while on convalescent leave.

I shook my head to reorient from diving into my feed. Cpl. Packard was standing, waiting patiently. I smiled sheepishly.

"Tombstone and Monolith, conference room six is available if you're ready," he said.

I shared a look with Shantu. Apparently, our nicknames were our official handles now.

The corporal walked us down a hall and into a room that was heavily shielded with sound dampening foam on the walls. The room was completely dark, but Cpl. Packard pulled a battery pack from his pocket and placed it in a floor lamp that was hidden by the darkness. The illuminated room contained a simple table with four chairs around it.

"Ambassador Nguyen is"—he glanced down the corridor—"here."

An old man of East Asian or Pacific Island descent walked into the room. His uniform was neat and tidy yet well worn. His stack of medals told of a lifetime spent in military service.

"Welcome to Fermi Station," Ambassador Nguyen said warmly. "Your ship must be an autoclave for you to clear quarantine so quickly."

I didn't know what he was talking about. I didn't know how long it usually took to clear quarantine or if that was just something polite to say.

Was he talking about environmental services?

The ambassador's casual stance and sunny demeanor were at odds with his casual fondling of his weapons. His personal defense weapon was on his right side.

Did that mean he was left-handed?

I dismissed the thought and focused.

"How are you doing, Ambassador?" Shantu said. "I'm Tombstone, and this is Monolith."

Cpl. Packard turned to leave, but the ambassador gently steered him into the room and gestured for him to sit with us. The door closed as we found our seats.

My feed prompted a connection error, and I killed it to focus.

"I can only imagine how valuable your time is, so thank you for having this meeting with us on such a short notice," I said as diplomatically as I could.

Ambassador Nguyen seemed to stiffen. "It's nothing," he said warmly. "Got this old garrison commander out of his office and caused some excitement here. You must have had a tough time hauling that big starliner with that tiny ship of yours. Most impressive. Quite a feat of engineering."

So much for trying to keep *that* under wraps. Granted, we were recruited from Vanguard, so they probably verified our identities in eight different ways in the lobby.

I resigned to let Shantu do the talking while I stared at the rack of metals on the ambassador's chest. I felt half blind with my feed off, no longer providing me with information. I wondered if Sgt. Tok was referring to guys like this when he had asked to kill that galunkin commander.

"To answer your question, Monolith, no, I'm not a TC," the ambassador said.

My face dropped because I had tuned out of the conversation. "What the f…" I stopped myself and took a breath. "I'm sorry?"

"Triple C. Command craft critter," he said in hearty humor. He then sized us up for a moment, and his face twisted. "I saw you were from Vanguard. Did you not serve?"

We shook our heads.

His eyes darted between us. "Why not?"

"Sir," Shantu said carefully, "we have a criminal record that barred us from service when we came of age."

The ambassador's face went from confused to befuddled, and he shook his head. Cpl. Packard kept his mouth shut with a placid expression on his face, though his eyes darted back and forth.

The ambassador's light brown cheeks bloomed red. "That's illegal. The Redemption Act guarantees…"

"Sir! That is not why we're here," I said, almost shouting to get ahead of him.

He struck me as one of those people who made things happen with a sledgehammer. Now, because of us, he was out for blood. But I knew the matter wasn't closed by a long shot.

I shot Shantu a what-the-fuck-just-happened look.

Shantu nodded to the ambassador but spoke to the corporal. "Where were you born?"

The corporal glanced at the ambassador, who nodded for him to answer. "Atoll City, Vanguard Prime. Between the elevator and the colosseum."

Atoll City is on the opposite side of Vanguard Prime in Greater Oceanic Gyre. That rotation of the city is harvested for energy. It's supposed to give the most amazing oceanic views.

I've always wanted to see the ocean. I didn't even get to see it from orbit because of the onboarding and safety training.

"Lived there your whole life?" Shantu shot out.

The corporal's eyes kept looking to the ambassador for guidance. "No. CT—"

The ambassador cleared his throat.

"Sorry. Conscription tour. Two years on *The Bastion* and one here."

Shantu focused on the ambassador. "You trust him?" he asked, nodding to the corporal.

"I do." The ambassador's eyes shined, and a slight smile touched his worn lips.

"So, no connection to Packard Interstellar Solutions?"

The corporal's face asked if he was supposed to know who that was. "No?"

I like to think I can tell when people are lying, and he seemed too earnest. Like he was already in trouble for not knowing something he should.

I took a deep breath and took the conversation from Shantu. "Sir, we've come into, uh…" I searched for the right word. "We've come into custody of seventeen child soldiers. We wanted to see if you can do something for them. Give them an asylum or something. Maybe recommend treatment facilities."

Cpl. Packard's face cracked with disgust, and Ambassador Nguyen's face went dark.

"How *exactly* did you come into custody of said children?" The ambassador's tone dripped with righteous venom.

"They were sent to eliminate a colony after a biological attack failed." Shantu nodded at the corporal. "Packard, no offense, but we have reason to believe Packard Interstellar Solutions is behind it. And the colony doesn't want to give quarters to enemy combatants." He put his hands up in an uncomfortable gesture.

The pieces seemed to click into place for the ambassador. "Some loose ends are better left to fray." He turned to Cpl. Packard. "What do you think we should do for these two children of Vanguard?"

That hit an emotional chord.

Children of Vanguard? I didn't know what it meant, but it meant *something* to these two professional soldiers.

Me and authority on Vanguard never really saw eye to eye.

My training and therapies on *The Happy Marauder* helped me get past most of the animosity I held against authority and replaced it with professional understanding and expectations.

But this was something new.

Were they holding me in *high regard*?

Cpl. Packard didn't hesitate. "Substantiate their story and then help in any way we can." After a moment, he added, "In this matter."

"I agree. Cpl. Packard, can you get on that?" the ambassador asked in a dismissive tone.

The hair on my neck went up, and my hand fell to my tet and sidearm. The room was silent as Cpl. Packard got up from his seat and slipped out of the hatch. I gripped my tet's fiber handle and realized the ambassador had been eyeing its handle and Shantu's pal'loch since we had entered the room.

I smiled at Shantu and then at the ambassador.

This was a rare moment where I got something ahead of Shantu.

"Dire-horn, our ship's council, gave them to us," I said, anticipating the ambassador's question.

He studied us for a moment and then let out a breath of disbelief. "Huh… No shit?"

"That's not how you tell the story, dipshit," Shantu said.

"He's an am-bass-a-door," I snapped. "He doesn't need the whole story. He has shit to do." I then turned to thank the ambassador so we could leave.

"No, please," the ambassador said. "I would like to hear the story."

"Fuck…" I said, going boneless in the chair.

Shantu was out of the tube like a missile. "So, there we were. We had just completed a mission with the dillers. They're megafauna the size of a tram car—"

"They're not—"

"Shut up!" He then turned back to the ambassador. "They were at least as tall. Never mind. They had lost their minds by some piece of biotech that either worked or didn't work. We don't really know because the thing slagged itself when we got too close. We think they were there to kill the colonists so someone else could claim the world. Namely Packard and a cult known as The Dawning Flower. We delivered an ecology team and saved the colony, and that's when someone dropped the pod of kids. Wait. I forgot to mention that this one did a coffin drop awake." He slapped my chest with the back of his hand.

The ambassador's eyes went wide, and his mouth opened in dismay. "I remember how beat to shit I felt, all wired on stims. I couldn't imagine doing that awake."

"That's how he got his call sign. He shook that shit off and got to work while the rest of us were sleeping. Anyway, we got the trajectory for their pod and set an ambush for them. On their way down, someone found out they were kids and not a proper strike team, and my main man here—"

"Don't say that," I said. "You're with Piper. I'm single. You're making this awkward."

"Shut up. No, I'm not. *You're* making it awkward." Shantu wasn't even breathing, just spewing words. "Anyway, Monolith here had the brilliant idea to set the kids as priority one defensive targets and to use our point defense turrets to fire ground effect and scare the shit out of the kids without killing them. The colony didn't want anything to do with them and even less with us."

He then went back-and-forth, doing voices.

In an annoying high-pitched voice. "You killed babies!"

In his normal voice. "Would you rather we let them kill you?"

High-pitched voice. "Why would you say something like that?! You're awful…"

"That doesn't explain why a minotaur invited you into his clan," the ambassador said, looking thoroughly entertained.

"I'm getting to that," Shantu said. "On the way back, the galunkin had the starliner painted at us with active sensors. Piper, my partner, managed to flip *The Happy Marauder*, our ship, ass over tits and got a three-round volley right down the throat of the starliner before they could do anything with the return. Piece of badass flying by them. We took a boarding sled and launched quick, fast, and in a hurry. It was during the boarding action. Mind you, this wasn't day one; we had been at it for a while. Anyway, the galunkin were cutting through the deck when he stabbed his thermal blade into the power cell of the cutter. He was on the other side of the deck and didn't really know where he was stabbing. He was just trying to fight." Shantu gets on his feet, acting out the encounter. "He blew up the cutter and almost killed himself. His blade got fused to his HEPS, and I don't know how it didn't breach. The galunkin poured through a hole, and he found that thing…"

I held up my tet and offered it handle first. "Oodak-hulome. One step closer to home or perfection."

The ambassador smiled and ran his fingers over the stitching. "I learned it as: perfection is only found in our future home," he said returning it.

"…and started whaling into them," Shantu said. "By the time I got there, it was an ugly furball. I didn't know what was alive or dead. It was zero g, and everything was bouncing all over the place. I ran my weapons empty on everything that was twitching that was not him. I got to him, and his suit was more of a colander than a pressure vessel, and his hand was welded to his thermal blade that was lodged in the overhead. I didn't want to lose any more air, so I sedated. Dire-horn got there and saw what we did and medi-vaced us. I took some shrapnel to the guts, so we spent some time in the infirmary before we went back to finish the job. That was when Dire-horn rendered honors."

The ambassador tilted his head. "In the infirm—"

"Yes, in the infirmary. Not after we went back."

"You left out your cow lick," I said. My shit-eating smile was glorious.

"No, I didn't. Shut up."

"He was being like this with Dire-horn, so I had Dire-horn lick his face, so he would stop being an asshole. It worked." I beamed.

Ambassador Nguyen chuckled. I didn't know if he was sizing us up or just going through things in his own head.

"Would you like a drink?" he finally asked.

"Yes, sir," we answered quickly.

"Is there anything else we need this room for?" he asked.

We shook our heads and followed him to his office.

My feed started updating when we left the secure room, but I set it to do not disturb and nudged Shantu to do the same thing. However, I watched the ambassador gesture feverously during the short walk through the decently wide corridor.

At his office, I expected a vanity wall. You know, all the shit with him shaking hands with notables and political circle jerks.

No.

His entire office was covered deck to overhead with photographs about the size of my hand. All in an identical format. Like ID cards. They were mostly humans, many minotaur, and a smattering of other species.

I noticed the sheen of one at eye level and stepped closer. Holographic text came into focus over a pretty light-skinned woman with a bright smile.

Tetum, Ashley, A, Conscript

406.334-429.199

KIA, Fleet Action, Lending Expanse

I moved on to a tawny-looking minotaur.

Sure-fist, Conscript

409.203-429.199

KIA, Fleet Action, Lending Expanse

"I didn't realize *that* many minotaur conscripted," Shantu said.

"It is a tradition," Ambassador Nguyen said, offering us each two fingers of an amber liquid in a square glass. His eyes glazed over, lost in some distant place. "If you must spend lives, spend them well." He said it loud enough for us to hear, but it sounded like it was more for himself. He then looked at the glasses and perked up. "Engineering's reserve." He nodded to the half-full bottle on his desk. "What should we drink to?"

"To doing what we can," Shantu said smoothly.

That's a fucking good line.

We tapped glasses and sipped. The spirit was warm but not harsh. I think it was what wood smoke would taste like. There was something in it that made my saliva taste sweet by comparison.

I think I may have found my new favorite drink.

The ambassador's office was just large enough to have two low-sitting couches and a small table that I had to step around. They seemed comfortable enough. His desk was only a shelf that held a physical keyboard and an assortment of snacks. Under the desk, partially hidden by the ergonomic self-adjusting chair favored by the elderly, were the storage brackets for the weapons he was carrying, along with a few grenades.

I had questions about the grenades.

Like…can I have one? It felt weird I didn't have one.

"Single malt scotch, aged in the surviving oak barrels from Old Earth." Ambassador Nguyen gestured for us to sit. "I don't have very many occasions to open that bottle…" He let that statement hang while he took a slow sip. "If you two have been honest with me, Vanguard will be happy to have you home. If I have anything to say about it, aggies will be with you."

We sat in silence for some time. The way he said "aggies will be with you" hung with reverence that I didn't understand. It gave me the warm and fuzzies but like with fire superiority.

Shantu chucked to himself, while I sat uncomfortably. I was pretty sure this was the first time someone's tried to poach us.

That was not true. A Vanguard recruiter tried to poach us during our medical evaluation.

If a ship was losing crew because everyone was getting rich, why the fuck would we leave? We didn't have anywhere else to go. That ship was our home.

That wouldn't be true forever. Eventually, we would lose our space rating and have to settle down. But I'd worry about that shit during our next financial planning meeting.

"First drink off world…with an ambassador," Shantu said. "Who would have thought?"

Ambassador Nguyen chuckled. "Would you be so excited to have a drink with the person from the help desk?" Our faces must have given us away because the ambassador added, "Parts counter?"

"I thought ambassadors like sway nations and end wars and shit," he said with disbelief.

The ambassador guffawed. "That shit is to get children to study language arts," he said between laughs. "No. We aren't any more important than the work getting done. Don't you think Cpl. Packard could have taken your meeting? He's going to be the one making calls and filling out forms with your ship's legal section."

I didn't correct him that the legal section was just Dire-horn.

I felt fancy letting him think we had a legal section.

"He's going to go home to his young wife and tell her all about the mercs who brought in a busload of war orphans from the infinite night."

Shantu and I looked at each other in confusion.

"You didn't see the tattoo?"

We shook our heads. I was distracted by all the medals and stuff.

"Child soldiers…" Shantu corrected.

"Even worse," the ambassador said. "Mercs, hired guns, and soldiers of fortune had the moral fortitude to risk a g-anchor to do what was right when there was no one to answer to but themselves."

A g-anchor is anything that limits a ship's acceleration and maneuvering.

"If an independent contractor, with no obligations, finds another way to deal with that situation, why should I expect anything less from *my aggies* with all of Vanguard behind them?" he asked, seeming to bend reality to his will.

Those poor sumbitches.

I was offended by the way he referred to us like we belonged in the same breath as savages or criminals. At the same time, *his* aggies just got the bar raised on them, and *I* was the reason.

My emotional engine stalled. I didn't know what to do or feel.

"That's the shit that gets me out of bed in the mornings." The ambassador chucked to himself for a moment. "Busload of orphans… The problem, of course, is keeping *The Happy Marauder* and her crew out of it."

"Why is that?" I asked.

"People can't stand missing pieces of a story. If there is a blank, speculation will fill it in."

"As long as it doesn't come to us," Shantu said, sounding like he's trying to be stoic. "Like you said, we're mercs. We can't get bogged down with every charity case that comes along."

The ambassador narrowed his eyes. I don't think he believed Shantu any more than I did. I don't think Shantu believed Shantu any more than I did.

We sipped the warm liquor in our glasses.

"I'll see to it that we stick to the spirit and the letter of the NDAs," the ambassador said.

"What's going to happen to the kids?" I asked, not wanting the kids to go through what I did at the institute.

Pain tore at my soul as I realized what I went through was likely nothing compared to what those kids had already endured.

"I assume we'll see if they have any relatives we can track down," the ambassador said. "If they don't have any, I'd imagine we'd process them into the Institute for Developing Children here on Fermi."

"Heads-up: Tracking down their families might be a no-go," Shantu said. "I know Dire-horn, from legal, is concerned about Packard having a legitimate claim to them."

The ambassador waved at his feed. "I'm messaging legal and ethics." A moment passed while he completed whatever he was doing in his feed. "If we can keep this in house, it's the institute and adoption. That's for the legal minions to work out."

I don't know what I had expected.

I know children are not supposed to travel. The space cocktail causes a bunch of developmental issues. Cryo-sleep isn't easy on their bodies either. More likely than not, they're all going to need long-term care for the rest of their lives.

I should have seen that coming. Maybe I did and just turned away because the kids were Dire-horn and Scout's responsibility, and I had the luxury of hiding behind my new guy status.

"Why do you two look like I've just killed your dog?" the ambassador asked.

For once, I spoke first. "We were raised at the Institute for Developing Children in Vanguard City. I wanted something better for them."

Shantu stared off at nothing, probably reliving one of our traumas.

Blood seemed to drain from the ambassador's face. The muscles in his jaw flexed. His face also turned into a snarl for a moment—like he was preparing for a fight—before returning to neutral. His color returned, and a warmness radiated from him.

He downed the rest of his drink with a smack.

Silence.

There's a silence people can recognize in each other. I don't know how else to describe it. Trauma bonding maybe. Something like "those who know, know not to ask, and those who don't, will never understand."

Ugh. I'm probably butchering that.

The ambassador then took a sharp breath. "I can't make any promises, but I know people. We'll get something worked out."

I believed him. I had faith. I never knew faith until now.

There was a certain type of humility that came with a man his age, one who had moved his mountains. I would imagine he knew what promises he could and could not keep. This person's *something* was worth more than all the reassurance, promises, and legalese in the galaxy.

The ambassador's eyes glazed over, he gestured in his feed for a moment, and then he shuffled his hand in his desk, mumbling, before returning. "If you get a chance, have… What was his name? Dire-horn? Have him take you two to the Sublime Artificer in the minotaur district. I wouldn't recommend you go without a minotaur escort. Be safe and welcome to Fermi Station."

I sent Dire-horn a simple message that outlined the situation. His reply was that he was busy, and he would get back to me.

Ambassador Nguyen shook our hands and gave us one coin each as he bid us farewell.

I walked out of his office, examining the coin. One side was the VAF crest, and the other had the words *Ret. Nguyen, Ca, A.* raised above the admiral's insignia with a ring marking retired. Shantu showed me his identical coin, save for a unique identifier code on the edge beneath a layer of protective transparent polymer.

Oh shit.

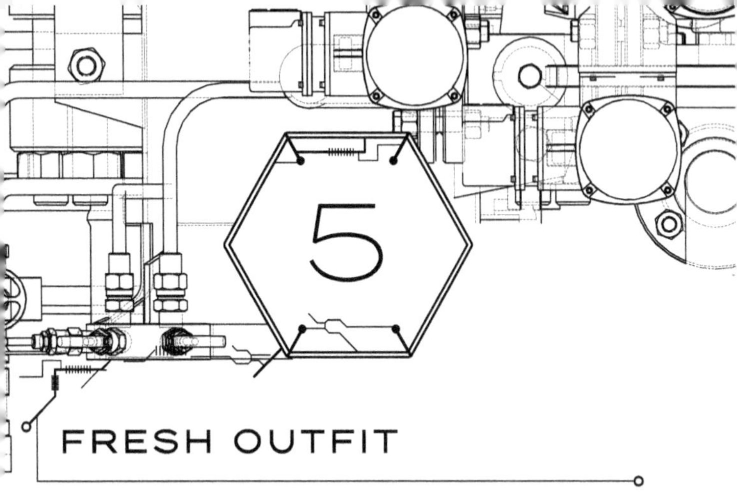

5

FRESH OUTFIT

522.270.1730 Elite-Commerce Block,
Human District, Fermi Station

SHANTU AND I left the Vanguard embassy to embassy row. I think we had come in through the back door or something because we left through a much larger, busier lobby with help desks and people circulating with their duties.

Embassy row was centered around a huge lake with a fountain. Two or three dozen governments flew flags around the atrium's perimeter. It was easy to forget that I was hundreds if not thousands of kilometers from the surface on a spire when looking at the wide-open spaces and beautiful scenery.

Vanguard might have the ugliest building out of all of them. A simple transparent facade let light into the lobby. It was like the office buildings from everywhere. The only thing they had going for them was the fresh garden, which grew corn, beans, and other things. A few gardeners tended to the plants with almost loving care.

Across the pond, the khanate embassy stood, glaring in annoying gold, silver, and purple. Guards stomped their feet and manually opened the grandiose castle-style doors.

"That fuckery right there is why Vanguard revolted." Shantu pointed at the announcer who was yelling names of who was coming and going.

"Vanguard didn't exist yet," the gardener said. "Vanguard was supposed to be the first fleet for them."

I didn't realize how old the lady was until she gave a world-weary sigh and sat on her small box of gardening tools. She seemed fresh out of fucks to give.

"The khanate wouldn't turn into *that* for another two hundred years. But I suppose you're right."

Shantu and I looked between the two embassies while she sized us up.

This lady was saggy levels of ancient, and yet my survival instincts were popping up and screaming to not fuck with her!

"Your accent… You're from Vanguard City," she said.

"Yes'm," Shantu answered.

His attempt at casual courtesy told me he was feeling the same thing.

"How are things there?" she asked.

"Things seem to be turning like they always have. We're mercs, ma'am." He was dialing up his Vanguard City charm. "We're just doing a favor for some passengers, so they can get on their way."

"That's good, that's good," the old gardener crooned. "Good to know folks will still look out for each other. Time's a-comin' that good folks'll have to see folks are good to each other."

"Whatcha mean by that?"

What the shit is this? I didn't say it, but this wasn't the way Shantu normally talked.

"Khanate up ta sommin'," she said. "If we were on a planet, I'd say there was a change in the winds. More than the usual nonsense."

History lesson time!

Somewhere in the twenty-first or twenty-second century, the

osheran made first contact with humans. They were fleeing their home world ahead of another species called the swarm. They picked humans up along the way and transported us to the opposite side of the galaxy.

The osheran dropped humanity on a planet the settlers named Ziwa… That part I know.

Movies and games have really gone wild with the genre, so I'm iffy on fact and fiction.

Anyway…the Vanguard Fleet was supposed to be the usher in the new age of independence from the patronage of the osheran. It went real bad—hundreds of millions dead bad… At the time, it was like sixty percent of the population.

That planet is dead now.

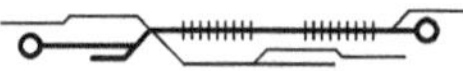

The osheran gave us a perfectly good planet, and we broke it. Not uninhabitable. We broke it, and it's still reconsolidating. I don't have a straight or official answer…but the top three theories are: One, antimatter weapon. Two, relativistic impactor. Three, upper tier bitch slap.

I think the prevailing theory is that the antimatter production facility happened to be over a natural fission reactor. It's the only way the math pans out. The planet was rich in fissionable materials, after all.

In the scramble to not die, humans roughly split into three factions. If ruling the universe is a human destiny, the khanate is your jam. If you think titles are stupid and that people need to shut the fuck up and get some shit done instead of bitching, you might make some friends in Vanguard. If you want to step away from the same cycle of human shit, go to the Commonwealth. You might just find whatever it is you didn't know you were looking for there.

My thoughts returned to embassy row as the osheran shot in and out of their second- and third-story openings, avoiding foot traffic all together.

Flutter didn't have this much space on *The Happy Marauder*. That might've been why he left. He needed to have space to *fly*.

The osheran darting around embassy row was a sight to behold—even against the other flying species. The winged ones, gliders, and gas bags didn't *dart* the way the osheran did. They were impossibly fast, bordering on teleportation. The gas bag species were sometimes dragged along in their air wake, taking longer than the others to recover.

Shantu and I slowly walked, mostly watching the flying species. I didn't know what they all were, but it was lovely to watch them.

The adjacent shopping district was jarringly different. We transitioned from an air lock to a quaint small town with wide walking streets divided by trees and benches. Overhead was a display of a sky with birds and clouds.

A vague memory from my Earth history classes started to surface but got stuck halfway. The theme was supposed to be pre-information or preindustrial… Artesian maybe? Anyway, all the staff wore similar brown coarse threaded clothing. Linen, I think it was called. They had light button-up shirts behind darker ties, which were all tucked behind a vest that matched their pants.

And we were in our abused HEPS that were held together by patches.

"Motherfucker, traveling in this place is like doomscrolling," Shantu said.

"Right?" I said. "Like do we have to get a matching outfit for every level we visit?" I turned off my feed and pointed at the Ye Ol' Tailor Shop.

"This is going to be so fucking spectacular," he said, skipping his way to the shop.

The door was painted to look like wood, but there was a pressure seal built into it. I pushed it open, and it jingled a bell.

The shop smelled like wood, and fabric-y wonderfulness hit me. Vertical bolts of fabric and those mirror alcove things lined the walls.

Three racks were the only interruption in the dark carpeted interior. One had khaki suits, one had not quite black suits, and the other had abyss black suits. I guessed those were the only three colors allowed to be purchased in a hurry.

Shantu's HEPS glove dangled from his wrist as he ran his hand over one rack of suits, disturbing their perfect spacing.

Near the racks, a mannequin, one for each style of suit, stood. The khaki one was in a casual walking pose. The not quite black one had its hands open as if it was explaining a concept. The abyss black one was in a regal power pose with exposed cufflinks and one of those pocket square things.

"Casual, business, formal?" I asked Shantu.

He made a how-the-fuck-should-I-know face.

I wandered over to the mirror alcove thing and looked at my HEPS. It was scorched more than I had realized. These really were at the end of their useful lives, and we were just beginning ours.

Man, reality is getting flexible. My struggles seemed distant, like a book I had read or something. Like my life could change as easily as changing my outfit.

It feels like yesterday I was jumping off a highway overpass to avoid getting robbed, and now I'm looking at fancy suits.

These suits represented vehicles, homes on Vanguard. More money than Shantu and I would have made in both of our lives, even ignoring our reduced life expectancy.

Here on Fermi, they were an errand, not even registering as an expense.

My attachment to my first space suit severed when the

mirror's interface activated. A warning banner at the top flashed with a message that the readings were incomplete due to my HEPS. I ignored it, looking at the specialty features: ID blockers, fragrance dispensers, woven ablative armor, reactive armor, holdout weapons, and hazardous environment support.

I held up my tet and found the menu to catalog it as essential equipment. Instead of doing the same with the other mirror, Shantu shoved me and generally got in my way, making an ass of himself for no reason.

"Fucker, you can use the other ones," I snapped.

"Yeah, but then I wouldn't be in your way," he replied with way too much energy to be in public. He quickly splattered my outfit, rendering it in lace and a moving pattern of pink and purple swirls that drew attention to my crotch.

I tried to shove him out of the way, but he set his weight and held me back with one arm. I shifted my weight, pulled him off balance, and swept his legs the way Wraith had trained me.

"Dick," Shantu forced out as he went sprawling across the shop's open space.

"I understand you would like phalluses on your outfit," the driest, most disinterested voice said. "Would that be stylized or anatomical?"

I looked over. A short, rigid balding man stood nearby. He wore a suit with the proper measuring tape draped over his shoulders.

He had just appeared. There was only one door I could see, and we had already come through it.

I shot Shantu a look to tell him not to be an asshole and offered him a hand up.

Shantu took it.

I turned back to the tailor. "Apologies," I said, trying to match the tailor's tone. "We were looking for something in the current fashion that wouldn't stand out during our time on the station."

"Excellent idea, sir," the tailor said in that tone that meant it was an automatic response, and it didn't matter what the fuck I said.

He gestured toward the mirror, and it bent to his will. Three suits appeared almost identical except for the number of buttons. The color options were dark blue, dark gray, and not quite black. He took a moment to show the different options variations of lapels, tux, and tails tie and handkerchief combinations. Each one rendered my reflection, editing out my HEPS. I didn't get a chance to really appreciate them before he moved on.

"If your wish is to be seen but not noticed, this is where we are," he continued.

While he did that, I checked the feeds and the local public cameras. There was no shortage of people wearing similar suits along with various hats.

"Now, I see you have an item that needs to be incorporated into the outfit. Would it be too much trouble to ask for your preferences regarding said item?"

My left hand instinctively went to my tet. The piece of scrap metal sat in a hoop with a small tension snap that was easy to latch and release in a quick motion. The position of the holster kept it from banging around in zero g's and kept the shaft pointed at my knee.

I tried to match his tone and cadence with some success. "I would like my tet to stay on display and functional. The pistol can find a more subtle home."

I missed the days when my rhino was the only weapon I needed, but it was still in the armory on the ship.

"As well as it should for a person such as yourself," the tailor said, but I didn't know if he was insulting me or not. "What other features would you find important?"

A memory of Gabe showing me how to print clothes on the ship rose in my mind. I had been scared that I was falling into some trap that would turn me into an indentured servant, but his happy-go-lucky demeanor had put me at ease and helped turn the ship into a home. Now the ship was home, and we were taking a vacation.

My first *real* vacation.

Fuck! How far have we come?

"We need as much life support, armor, and scan blocking as you can cram into one of these suits without changing the inseams," Shantu said. "Our top priority is to be sexy without shouting that we need attention because we're compensating. Then we need life support. We're worried about vacuum and toxic threats. Caustic and radiation are low on the threat spectrum unless you know of some events that we need to know about. Then the stealth stuff."

The tailor didn't even acknowledge him at first. But after a moment, he gestured to Shantu. "Is *this* of importance?"

His tone was so flat—a baffling indifference—that I didn't know what to do with it. I wondered if he was a construct.

Shantu spoke up again. "What the failing air lock is that—"

"Yes." I spun on Shantu to keep him in line. "I didn't tell Javelin you're coming." I turned back to the tailor, whose face was still placid.

Shantu switched gears and spoke in a mocking tone before I could do anything to stop it. "It seems we have skipped introductions. Tombstone and Monolith of the FTS *The Happy Marauder* at your service."

I nudged him. "Dude, just let the guy do his job, so we can get on with it."

He feigned ignorance, but I ignored him.

The tailor did not react, just continued with his process. "Indeed, you are. Do you have plans that would require outfit coordination?"

"No, sir," I said, trying to smooth over any insults Shantu had given. "The only plans we're looking at is to drink at an open fighting venue."

"If there is nothing else to add, I will begin." He gestured at the mirror, and I received a prompt from my feed for medical information.

I selected external dimensions and range of motion from the options list.

"Externally, the outfit will display any color or image of your choice, defaulting to charcoal to be with the current fashion, of course. Gloves will be integrated to the jacket hip pockets like so."

The preview looked like someone was digging into their pockets for change, and the motion sealed the thin gloves to the jacket.

"Sir, this portion of the sealing process is most critical."

The preview shifted to show how the hat connected to the jacket with interlocking sliders stylized as stitching in the collar and lapels.

"Sir, I must inform you that this is for emergency use. These features will not replace, well, rugged apparel." The tailor glared at my worn and patched HEPS, probably wanting them out of his pristine store.

I started a live feed so the crew could chime in if they wanted. I got a few thumbs-up and no major warnings. Dire-horn wanted clothes in minotaur-style robes, but I ignored that.

"Our premium soft armor is rated at a thousand joules per centimeter," the tailor continued, "before separation at a less than ten percent degradation rate."

I cross-referenced what he said with weapons and found it would stand up to most pistols. I would be turned into putty because of the drag effect though, but it was better than nothing.

The tailor went on about environmental tolerances for the suit, which was considerably narrower than my HEPS. It would have the devices for a false identity installed, but we would have to set up the alias.

I pinged Wraith about the aliases.

Oh, and I did opt for the fragrance dispenser. I went with a scent called mahogany cabin, which was not too sweet and kind of leathery.

The tailor complimented me with an "excellent choice," but when Shantu made his selections, he kept getting odd words like "unique" and "interesting." Eventually, he caught on and asked the tailor for a suggestion. He's now wearing Ode du Sandalwood.

The dark polymer shoes we got were a style called oxfords and supper fluffy and comfortable, even with the magnetic array. They were like walking on pillows.

Shantu and I changed and dumped our HEPS into boxes provided by the shop to be delivered to *The Happy Marauder*.

"Come on, man," Shantu said, dancing around me. "Don't you feel sexy?"

I just wanted to blend in and not draw attention to myself. But I made an effort to indulge him. "Want to go to a dance club instead? Since you're feeling so sexy?"

"I love where your head is at!" he all but shouted. "Here are the problems I see though: I'm hungry and sober, and Piper is on the way, and they don't care for dancing." He tossed up a finger with each reason.

I tried to hide my relief.

"And someone—not naming any names other than my own—leaked to the crew that you're going to fight."

"For fuck's sake," I said much more dramatically than I felt.

"Come on! Who would you rather have in your corner other than Wraith or Dire-horn?"

"The whole point was to get *away* from everyone."

Since I'm being completely honest, I am looking forward to

the fight because I haven't been working out after being stuck in a testing center for six days. I need exercise. I never thought working out would become so much a part of my routine that I would miss the absence of vigorous exercise, but here I am.

I miss Gym Sock.

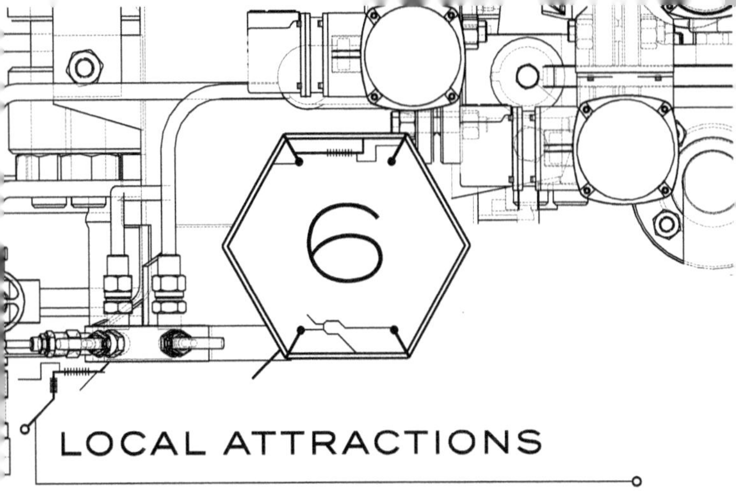

LOCAL ATTRACTIONS

522.270.1900 Entertainment Block,
Human District, Fermi Station

SHANTU AND I decided to get something to eat before going to the bar. The stop would also give the other marauders a chance to rally.

The café we picked had a double-decker booth layout that could be reconfigured for party size. The ceiling had a track for the waiter drones to deliver meals and then bus and sanitize the tables. The algae tanks that made up the bulkheads gave the place an oscillating multicolor hue and a fish tank smell. The floor was a simple grate with water moving underneath.

Scout, Piper, Gabe, and Wraith all responded to the dinner invitation. The captain, Javelin, and Dire-horn declined.

Scout was the first to meet us there. "Thank you for inviting me," he said, crawling into his seat like a toddler.

"We're glad you could make it," Shantu said. "We were afraid you were going to jump ship before we could see you again. How did the kids make it out?"

"Honestly, I don't know. The Vanguard Fleet medical people

took over, and I left. They did find some irregularities in the cryo-pods. I was never qualified to induce cryo-sleep, so I am relieved they are going somewhere more equipped." His big ears wafted slowly, indicating relief for the urglurk.

"Yeah," Gabe said, sliding in next to Scout.

Gabe hooked his massive rear leg over the back of the bench, taking up space in the next booth. His front legs occupied human leg space. He simultaneously looked like he was lounging and hunched over.

"Patron, would you like us to remove the back panel for your comfort?" one of the staff asked Gabe.

"Nah, I'm comfy," he said. "Why will I damage it?"

I stopped paying attention to that side of the conversation because Scout said, "We took our losses, but this time, I really feel like we did a good job. Who really comes back with a bus-load of orphans?"

We marauders shared a chuckle. That joke, no matter how many times I heard it, made me feel like I mattered. If I didn't do anything else in my life, I did that.

Wraith gently pushed Shantu into me, so he could share the bench. He wore a nondescript suit that looked a lot like ours. "If you're in a good mood, check this out."

He tossed up the current bidding on the starliner into a local workspace. It was in the trillions of converted credits, approaching a quadrillion. A big bite of that was going toward maintaining *The Happy Marauder*, but it was still going to be one hell of a payday.

I shared stunned looks with everyone, which turned into broad smiles. We didn't scream or dance around the table because Wraith glared at us though.

"Check out who the highest bidder is," he said.

It was the Vanguard Fleet Resource Center.

"What did y'all say to the ambassador?" Wraith asked.

"Mostly, he was happy we weren't in trouble, seeking asylum," Shantu said. "He was floored when I gave him the whole story."

"Anyway, excellent work. But before you get too ahead of yourselves." Wraith got up and slapped us both on the back of the head. Hard.

"What the fuck, man?" Shantu said for us.

"Don't give your name and ship out here. I've already fixed your IDs. You can still be Monolith and Tombstone, but the whole 'of the ship' advertises that you are worth billions, dumbass. If you get taken prisoner, you better hope I'm drunk because if I have to rescue you, I'm going to have you scrubbing thruster nozzles with your dick so hard you're going to become related to the ship."

We took our ass chewing quietly because he was right.

"I like the suits. Good move to blend in," Wraith said so suddenly that I didn't realize the ass chewing was over.

My feed alerted me that he was sending us the profiles with our aliases. I clicked through the acknowledgments for the false identity.

"Ambassador Nguyen gave us these and said go to the Sublime Artificer in the minotaur district," Shantu said.

I presented my coin with his.

Gabe held out a hand, and I let him see mine.

"It's a tradition in human militaries," Wraith said. "Commanders' coins are tokens to say good job to their subordinates. It's like a letter of recommendation. If he's saying go somewhere, you'll probably get the five-star treatment and maybe a discount."

"Awesome," I said.

"Side quest," Santu chirped with enthusiasm.

Scout picked up the conversation. "What's everyone's plans for leave?"

"Nothing," Gabe said. "I am going to do as little as possible. There is a green deck where I'm going to get paid to sleep. I'm going to do my best to induce a frack via high radiation and overindulgence."

"So, you're literal when you say you're going to eat until you explode?" Shantu asked.

He flared his crab-like maw in his version of a broad smile. I threw some table bread at him just to watch him snatch it out of the air with that bear trap of a face.

This is what I wanted.

Leave.

I didn't have to worry about how much I eat because a training cycle might make me puke it up. No physical training through a hangover, while Sgt. Tok yelled and then punched me in the face.

"I'm going to try to do the same thing but with more sex and less skin peeling," Wraith said.

"Lucky fuckers," Piper said, joining us. Their voice had adopted something more feminine. They wore their going-out space suit that I hadn't seen since we had left Vanguard. "Yours truly don't get a proper leave because I'm the point of contact for the overhaul."

"Piper, no. You're better than that," I said, not letting their change in personality slide. "Do not sully yourself by altering your personality profile to be closer to Shantu. We can barely handle the one fucker. Two of you, and we're fucking doomed."

The table broke out in laughter.

I looked at the menu displayed in the table. Something inside me still hurt as I spent years of wages per item. Shantu and I glanced at each other as we made our selections.

"Don't worry," Wraith said, sotto voce. "We're billing the auction house for room and board while the starliner is up for sale." He then spoke louder. "Go crazy. But take the spacer supplements, or it'll destroy your stomach."

Gabe was ordering like crazy with his industrial strength metabolism.

"Wraith, where are you staying?" Shantu asked. "Because I do not intend on remembering my own name by the end of tonight."

Genius bit of foresight.

Food delivery reminded me of Bullet Casing that my life used to revolve around. Each food item arrived in its own stackable container. I, being against the wall, was stuck returning the containers to the track.

Wraith amended his hotel reservation to include us, and we took a moment to swipe through the acknowledgments and confirmations.

"Monolith, what the hell are you thinking, trying to cage fight?" Wraith asked, catching me off guard.

I nodded to Shantu while stuffing a fried crab puff thing in my mouth.

Gabe snapped his maw at me as I took another one from his pile of plates.

I gestured that I was the one stuck handling the food containers.

"And you let him?!" Piper yelled at me.

I tried to say, "Yell at him! I didn't do anything." But...crab puff.

They are awesome by the way! If there's a reason to travel, it's food.

"Why not?" Shantu said. "Seeing you get your ass kicked on the first day of leave would be great! Come on! It'll be good for you too. I know you and Saluit were completely unhealthy, and you need to get all that aggression out, or I'm going to have to deal with you being bitchy all through leave."

Everyone stared at me now.

"Have y'all lost your motherfucking minds? You're agreeing with *him*!" I said with disbelief.

"You see, it's like this." Wraith pushed Shantu against the table to grab me by the neck.

I tensed.

"You can fight," he continued. "I've seen to that. You're a nightmare in that AV of yours, even drunk and concussed. However, you're a bitch when it comes to Saluit. And this is a new place! I think it could be good for you to come from a place of strength. Get a video of you holding your own in the ring out there."

Fuck it. What I'm doing isn't working.

Piper chimed in. "We don't have a medic on staff. If something serious happens, you're going to be paying station prices for medical care."

"They have on-site medical," Shantu said.

Wraith and Scout looked at each other, seeming to silently argue about who was going to speak.

Scout lost. "Does it say *free*? Mention the quality or even the kind of services?"

Scout and Wraith stared at Shantu while he desperately gestured in his feed.

When the air in the conversation got awkward, Wraith said, "The bartender probably has a first aid kit and maybe a bot for suturing."

Gabe shrugged. "Wraith can patch you up."

He gave a menacing chuckle. "You know I specialize in un-healthcare, right?"

"Let me get a trauma kit before we go to the bar," Scout said.

"What does your species do for recreational intoxicants?" I asked Scout, trying to get Wraith distracted.

I think Scout smiled. His ears perked and waved, and he wiggled in his seat. Close enough for an urglurk.

"OH! We call them crunchies. They are most delicious." His professional persona was slipping with excitement. "They are dehydrated arthropods coated with flavored calcium that is injected with the venom of"—he made a screeching burping noise, and my feed provided the translation—"predatory insect.

I will enjoy them after your fights because I do not intend on remembering my face." He didn't even seem to notice us anymore as he was lost in his feed, no doubt shopping.

"Wraith, are you taking the night off with us or what?" Shantu asked.

I could almost hear him praying for a positive response.

"I'm already off," Wraith said as the drone waiter placed a beer in front of him.

"Honey, are you okay with babysitting the squishy organics while we get ourselves into trouble?" Shantu batted his eyes at Piper and gave them an overexaggerated smile.

They pushed his face away playfully. "Only because you admitted you're squishy."

Appreciation went around the table as the food arrived. Gabe fed things into his physics-defying face. Food just disappeared into his head.

Scout was much more refined with a meticulous little ritual, dipping his two-pronged fork into some sauce before stabbing the crispy nugget of whatever.

When Gabe finished devouring some kind of bone with a disturbing crunching noise, he said, "Did you check the lineup and the rules for the fight? You want to fight in a spacer only class."

I looked at Shantu.

"Fuck," he said.

I quickly checked my feed. "I'm in a baseline human class."

I wondered if the aneurysm mesh had deteriorated yet.

I glared at Shantu.

He shrank back.

"No, you can't fight there," Gabe said around a whole baguette, surprisingly clear.

"You've had a spacer cocktail," Scout added. "All the drugs and treatments we gave you when you came onto the ship… You're considered augmented now."

That never occurred to me. I wasn't just human anymore. I didn't feel any different. I only vaguely remember reading the stuff on my treatments for travel.

"You went through the dockworkers' concourse, right?" Wraith asked but continued before I could reply. "The skinny, frail-looking humans are usually the only baseline you'll find out here. They don't last long. Thirty is old for them."

"What? Why?" Shantu asked.

"Think about it. If you have money out here, the first thing you do is get the spacer treatments, even if you don't need it. Better food, living conditions, medical care… That's why the expression is *shit floats.*"

I felt bad for the people who live short lives on a space station while paying ridiculous prices for air.

"Take either a mercenary class or an unmodified one that says something about the spacer cocktail in their description. Don't do anything that says modified or augmented. Those are bloodbaths." Wraith gestured with his cheese-covered carb injection.

It came way too close to my face, and I managed to take a good bite out of the cheesy bread.

"Hey!" he barked.

"That's for calling me a bitch," I said around a mouthful of deliciousness.

He tossed the remainder onto my plate and helped me get into the right class.

The bar was a good twenty minutes away on foot.

"It looks like my prize is twenty percent of the winnings for every match I participate in," I said. "Oh shit. There are a shit ton of gambling options." I closed out to find everyone waving at empty spaces, clearly placing their wagers.

"I'm putting a thousand credits that you're going to enter the ring," Shantu said. "The lowest they go is even money."

"Tombstone, you fucker!" Wraith barked in his commanding

tone. "I'm putting everyone down as his entourage. Mono, confirm it. Someone just put a big bet against it."

I did as he asked.

Wraith, officially my coach, was slotted to be in my corner. "Gabe, I need your durable ass to just hang back a step and follow like you're going to do a hit. I'll add you to his corner after we get to the venue. Humans should be shy about fucking with a sho-ni-vonti, but you stand out." His voice then turned on all of us. "Eat up, everyone. We're moving in five. Scout, you're in the bag." He pulled out a backpack, and Scout happily hopped into it.

Apparently, that's a thing.

Three humans in suits and Piper did not stand out, even if one of them was carrying an urglurk in a backpack.

We made the short walk without incident.

A Fighting Chance was a better bar than I expected. The dim lighting drew my attention to the fighting ring—which was a well-lit sphere—above the bar. Right now, it contained two skinny humans basically slap fighting. I was not impressed with their performance. All around, there were rows of seats with the flip-up style food tables broken up by normal bar tables and stools. A few good-looking bartenders circulated between patrons.

Wraith spoke to the bouncer and let Scout out of the bag. Gabe followed shortly after.

"Man, for a fighting venue, this place is dull," Shantu said quietly.

"It's the middle of the workday around here," Wraith said equally quietly as he led us to a table. "Besides, this is the bottom rung. No one gives a shit about these fights."

I noticed Scout's eyes shining in the dim lights but didn't say anything because I didn't know if it was insensitive to his species.

Shantu had no such composure. "Holy shit, Scout! I can see the entire universe in your eyes. It is *magnificent*. Like looking at the face of infinity. I think I understand God and creation."

Wraith thankfully smacked him upside the head and ordered a round of drinks. I, however, received a fruit cocktail, which is bullshit.

Options for my ring configuration opened at the one-hour mark, and I placed them in order, starting with a wide cylinder and a cube. A sphere with the hemisphere and inverted hemisphere being my last choices.

The bar started filling up when I was notified to come to the small dressing room in the back. Wraith joined me and produced a box for my contact lenses for my feed, and I was relieved. I can't lose those. I removed them, placed them in the fluid-filled container, clipped my bracelets to the outside, and stuck the ear bugs into the slots.

My eyes felt strange, free of information that had been continuously pouring into my vision. I could see shadows for the outlines of the icons and the map. I was tense as I changed into simple black shorts and used the gloves and foot wraps provided.

I stretched vigorously, trying to warm up and to deal with the nerves.

"Any words of wisdom?" I asked Wraith.

My face hurt, and one of my cheeks swelled. He had back-handed me hard enough to split my lip. I could taste blood in my mouth.

"There! You've been hit," he said. "Now you don't have to worry about getting hit again."

"Fuck, man. Why are you in my corner? The point was to stop getting my ass beat by you!"

"Shut up, and don't kill any of these scrap trollers." He checked my gloves and foot wraps. "Don't aim for their heads. Let them tap out unless they look military."

"We're all wearing bar-sponsored shorts… How do I tell if they're military?"

He pointed at his dark brown eyes. "Look at me! Just take it easy. This is a bar scrap, not combat. Everyone goes home today. Got it?" He shoved the mouthguard in my face. "Got it?!"

I nodded.

The walls were disorienting uniform white. My depth perception glitched and gave up because I didn't have any cues to tell where the walls and floor were. I wobbled on my feet with vertigo. Eventually, I took a deep breath through the piece of polymer in my mouth and danced around, trying to get a feel for the gravity.

"This guy is a merc," a voice from the opposite corner said. "Look at that build, that face."

I looked down at my belly. The weird gut I had was gone. There was a good layer of fat, but I saw the muscle behind it. How about that? I wasn't that skinny kid from the gut anymore.

"Up to you…" A pause. "All right. Be smart. Fight defensive and tap out if you get your bell rung."

Wraith came over a different speaker closer to me. "We need you to dial it down because we try to keep the ship at two g's, and the locals live at like 0.8 g."

I tossed a thumbs-up because I didn't want to talk around the mouth guard.

The other fighter descended his stairs, skinny and long limbs. DING! DING!

My opponent tried for a quick punch combo, but I easily batted his hand away. We really were at different levels.

I fainted a jab, swept his legs, and then fell on top of him in a full mount. He guarded his face. I took his left arm and rolled into an arm bar with fast but steady pressure. My opponent tapped out on my leg. The ring flashed red, and a buzzer sounded, announcing the end of the fight.

It was too easy. He didn't have the technique or the strength to defend himself.

I bounced off into a crouch, waiting for a cheap shot. But the fighter was slow to get up. I offered him a hand and patted his shoulder. He gave me a polite nod as he exited.

"Okay. You are the defending fighter," Wraith said. "You have ring control. Your choice of audio, shape, color, and brightness. What do you want?"

"Can we go translucent and let me hear the bar?" I asked. "I want to know what shit Shan… Tombstone is saying."

"A false image is the best I can do. We're almost a deck above the bar."

I gave him a thumbs-up.

A distorted false image made it feel like I was standing on glass in the middle of the bar, and I could see the other patrons.

"You're a bitch!" Shantu shouted at me.

I returned the appropriate rude gesture.

The next fighter and the one after that were equally unimpressive. The one after that charged down the stairs into a flying punch. Ribs broke against my foot as I snapped out a front kick.

The fighter crumpled into a heap, gasping into a fit of whining. No hate. I've made worse noises.

I just don't know how else to describe it. High pitched, not quite crying, and struggling to breath. *Whine* is all I have.

Full disclosure, Wraith had caught me with a liver shot once, and I had shit myself. I have a pretty good idea of the pain the other fighter was in.

Wraith, in rare praise, complimented my form and stance. I stood back when medical personnel entered the ring to remove the guy.

The fighter after that had dark skin and a heavier build. He was lean; I could see individual muscle striations. He bowed at the hips, showing off his flexibility but keeping his eyes on me. I copied his bow the best I could. I offered him a fist to bump, and to my surprise, he tapped it with his and retreated.

A respectful start to the match.

His stance was bouncy and loose. I moved in, keeping my weight on my back leg to guard my balance and energy. He danced away with a probing kick.

There was going to be a lot of this. Xi would do this because I was twice her size. She would wait for her opening and take advantage of some commitment in momentum.

But since I had ring control, I might as well use it.

I fainted a front kick and turned it into a spinning back. He had to dive to clear my kick, committing his momentum in one direction. I spun into an ugly leap and tackled him to the ground. Fists, elbows, and knees pounded me as we fell. He lacked power or leverage.

I clasped my hands around him. He squirmed as I took more and more control. Sweat made our bodies slick. His nails raked my back. He lifted a knee, trying to find purchase. But my experience in zero g exerted itself, and I wrapped my body around the bent knee and got my legs under, ready to launch myself.

He tapped out with a drumbeat.

I bounced off the fighter. We repeated the bows and fist bumps, and he respectfully departed.

"We have a break, while they find another fighter." The stairs descended, and Wraith brought out a stool and a squirt bottle. "How are you feeling?"

I couldn't help but laugh. "Good."

He waited until I took a swig from the squirt bottle to slap my head. The electrolyte juice came out of my nose as I laughed. Someone tossed a towel down the stairs for us to clean up the mess.

The ring flashed green, a warning that another fighter was ready.

Wraith left with his coach stuff.

That was when *she* entered the ring. Lean and mean looking. She was half a head shorter than me with zero g shoulders. Her jet-black hair was pulled back into a tight braid. She had dermal patches poorly covering the armor hard points protruding from her dark skin.

We touched gloves and circled each other.

She did not fuck around for long. She kicked my thigh hard.

Sgt. Tok taught me that if I took too many shots like that, the leg would give out. I closed to deny her that kick again, and she launched into a flying knee. The knee that forced me back to maintain balance. If it had connected with my face, the fight might've been over.

She whipped her hand around into a backfist that cut my eyebrow, barely touching the deck.

I was guarding, but I did not have control of the fight.

I gave ground. Her flying knee twisted into a solid back kick to my stomach. I grunted with a hit and caught her ankle out of reflex. She tried to kick free, but I took the opportunity to solidify my grip. She hopped, probably trying to set her weight for a head kick.

That was what Shantu would have done.

I let go of her foot so she couldn't use my hands for leverage and struck her thigh with my elbow.

We crumpled into each other.

When we hit the deck, the smell of her filled my nose.

She found an opening to nail the side of my head with a powerful punch. I grappled for a full mount, but she managed to push me off and get control of my right arm.

I rolled and gripped my hands together to guard from a complete armbar.

She hesitated. I saw the fist that didn't fuck up my face.

I don't think any human on *The Happy Marauder* has missed that opportunity to punch me in the face.

Instead, she twisted and disengaged into a feral roll. I copied her roll to get my feet under me.

She closed with a series of jabs and hooks.

I sacrificed my balance to kick her stomach. I felt the air. Then I kicked off my plant foot for a follow-up spinning back kick. It connected.

She let out an angry grunt.

I landed on my chest.

My knees twisted in a painful angle as she scrambled up my back, raining blows anywhere she could. I threw feral elbows to keep her from gaining too much purchase. I then bucked my hips and sent her flying over my head.

She held on to an arm and tried to knee me in the face. I rained down hammer blows, ruining her nose. She managed to get a hold of my neck and pulled us into a headbutt.

No one wins in a headbutt. It's a stupid-ass move.

So, I did it again.

By this time, we were both so sweaty that we might as well be two worms in dirt.

"Can we call it a draw?" I offered, struggling to breathe around the mouth guard.

"Sure," she answered, not half as winded as I was.

I rolled off the feeble mount I was attempting. We lay on our backs for a few more moments.

"Good fight." I lifted my fist for her to bump.

She bumped it.

The ring buzzed yellow, giving us a draw and ending the match.

Wraith helped me to my feet, and when I noticed no one came to help her, I offered her a hand up. I didn't say anything between the exhaustion and the blows to the face. We ascended our opposite sets of stairs.

I took a quick shower. Scout patched me up, I replaced my feed, and I joined the group back at the table.

"You feel better?" Shantu asked.

"Yeah… I do actually," I said honestly.

He didn't even acknowledge me. "Did you get her name?"

"What the fuck is wrong with you?" I asked. "When is a fighting event the appropriate place to hit on someone?"

"My dear friend, *every* event is the appropriate place to hit on someone," he said, and Piper pulled away from him. "When you're single."

They relaxed.

"Babe, can I go get her for my socially inept friend here?"

"I'll do it," they offered, and affection oozed out between them two.

I made a heaving face. "Please no…"

"No one asked you," Piper said, and they left.

I turned to Scout. "What just happened?"

"We have collectively decided you are no longer qualified to manage your own relationships after Saluit," he answered.

"When the fuck did this happen?"

"While you were showering. Wraith said you didn't ask the dark female fighter for her name after the match."

He and I had a professional distance, but I loved the amphibian's candor.

Piper brought her over, and I buried my face in my hands.

"I'm Takakoa," she said politely. Her hair was dripping water down her back. Her tone shifted to hostile when her eyes landed on me. "Wait. Is this some kind of kink shit?"

Scout's ears perked, and Gabe went rigid.

I tried to shoot everyone an I-told-you-so look. "So, it was rude to try and hit on you after a fight? It sends the wrong message?"

She jerked her head back in indignation. "What? You're going to fuck up my face and not even get to know my name?" She held that pissed off face for a moment longer before it failed, and she smiled. "No, I don't think it's rude."

"What…?" I mumbled out of pure bewilderment.

"You never know someone until you fight them." She sounded so strong and sure of herself.

I was scrambling with my confusion.

"See! We told you!" Piper said with all the gusto of a commander. "She seems nice."

"Fuck me…" I muttered. "They're already giving me hell for not hitting on you, and now I'll never hear the end of it."

Takakoa laughed, and it was beautiful.

Chomp, chomp, chomp. This is me eating crow. Whatever crow is, I'm eating it. *Chomp, chomp, chomp.*

"What's the deal here?" she asked. "Three humans, three non. Really close. Mercs?"

We collectively nodded.

"In that case, I am Gunnery Sergeant Takakoa Houston. VAF Garrison Division. Fermi Station Outpost."

"I figured you were either military or a merc," I said, "because you fight like you know how to kill but…was holding back." It was supposed to be a compliment. I don't know if it came out that way.

I also wanted to steer the conversation away from the fact Shantu and I were from Vanguard.

"Tombstone and Monolith are both from Vanguard," Wraith said, throwing me straight under the bus.

He also triggered Shantu into one of his wild retellings. It was painfully awkward… I ordered her drinks and more food because I didn't know how to stop Shantu when he did this.

Takakoa's face twisted into an ugly snarl. "Okay. No! I call bullshit! If you think your dick is big enough to take a coffin drop awake, you can shove it up your ass! Do you know how many people wash out of aggregation because of the pod failure training?"

Her tone drifted between a sergeant who's going to PT me until I die and an angry woman who's about to throw a drink in my face, the two kinds of people I didn't want angry at me in one. How about that?

"Five days? Fuck *off*. And let me guess… The mission records are classified. That shit might work on the civilians around here…"

I looked at Piper for help, but they seemed just as shocked, slowly shaking their helmet. Shantu's face was apologetic. Neither of them was of any fucking use.

"I get that you have your love bot, and you're trying to gas up your friend so he can get laid, but—"

Piper stood, ready to fight. "What did you call me?"

"Kids, kids, we can settle this so easily." Wraith put himself between Piper and Takakoa. "Tombstone, Monolith, the coins."

We placed our coins on the table near her.

She looked at them and then gestured in her feed for a moment. "These were given out earlier today." After a moment, she added, "I have a friend that was telling me about some refugee kids?"

"Seventeen." I took a deep breath and held it.

I didn't know if she was going to leave us or fight us. What was worse was that I didn't know which would hurt more.

"Sorry about the love bot thing," she said. "I thought this was a setup."

I let out my breath.

"It was but for *him*," Piper said. "He's useless with women."

Bless them for not going into detail.

I caught Scout's shiny eyes darting between us while he popped a bug into his mouth like we were his private soap opera.

"You got a good idea of the shit we've been through," Shantu said. "Tell us about the scars I saw."

She lifted her shirt. A thin scar outlined a chunk of her abdomen. "One kidney and half my bowel when an AP round went right through me and hit some armor behind me. I was a conscript then. Void jumper didn't even acknowledge me. Just jumped out of his armor, took his weapons off the bracket, and kept fighting. His armor scooped me up and got me to the med bunker."

Scout lifted a finger to show an invisible scratch. "I caught my finger on some metal."

We laughed.

"Decompression cost me the arm. A grenade cost me the leg. Still have the grenade."

"Wait. Start over," Gabe said.

"I was young, just starting out with the Urglurk Border Patrol." Scout switched to his native language, and the translator took over. "We shot down a smuggler ship. When it exploded, weapons and ammunition hit my ship. A grenade severed my left leg. Shrapnel punctured my suit, and I had to seal it. Was my misdirection funny?"

"How fucked up are you?" Shantu asked.

"Very," he slurred, waving around a crunchy before popping it into his mouth with his ears waving.

"That's called burying the lead," Wraith said. "I don't know if you're going to remember this, but what you did there is called burying the lead, and you did it very well." He patted Scout's head.

"Okay. Good," Gabe said. "Because that sentence was a roller coaster, and I wanted off."

That ignited belly laughs.

The evening went exceptionally well. Some other people joined us, and I couldn't tell if they just wanted to be a part of the party or were xenophiles.

Then Takakoa hit me with this. "Why did your friend have to come get me?"

I froze, a strider in headlights. What the shit do you say to that? Moreover, what do you say to that when you have a slideshow of your own ineptitude when it comes to relationships flashing in your brain?

Nothing. You say nothing. You shrug.

"You're sticking with it's rude?" she asked.

"And clearly, I am wrong, so I would love to hear your perspective," I said, abandoning all sense of dignity.

She gave me the side-eye. "Sarcasm?"

"Situational awareness. Survival instinct."

Her side-eye turned into a bright smile, her dark skin blushing. She seemed to gather her thoughts for a moment. "You don't really know someone until you fight them."

I asked the obvious question because she was leaning into me now. "What do you know about me?"

"You can hold your own in a fight. You're not any more brutal or vicious than needed. You don't have anything to prove."

I stood because I was so nervous and started stretching to hide that I was shaking.

"Is that the tree pose?" she asked.

"Yeah." I twisted my face. "I didn't stretch enough, and you… Fuck if you didn't give me a run for my money."

She joined me in the awkward stretches in the middle of a bar. We did our best to respect the other patrons' space.

Yet Shantu then stared at me with his goofy fucking face that had a weird mix of pride and drunkenness. Piper was right next to him. They didn't really have a face, just a visor that reflected everything in the bar. But they might as well as have had his expression.

"Why are they staring at us?" Takakoa asked.

"Because they're fucking creeps." I grabbed a handful of napkins and threw them at them.

The bouncer stepped up to us. I had a momentary panic because I thought I was in trouble for throwing napkins.

"Sir, ma'am, your winnings." The bouncer presented us with

a pad that had menus of both digital and physical items corresponding with our matches.

Gabe shouted, "LOOT BOX!" and reached for the pad.

The bouncer jerked it back and took a step back.

He almost fell over but caught himself. "LOOT BOX! LOOT BOX!"

The chorus of people joined his chant.

I nodded to the bouncer and mouthed that it was okay. I then took the pad, and Gabe gave me one final cheer.

"Take all physical items," Gabe said. "Take the items that only give material breakdowns with no cataloged description."

I shrugged and navigated the menus.

Takakoa followed suit. "Can we trade? I have limited allowances."

"Yeah. Sure."

She acknowledged the option and completed her forms. We then drank and ate, swapping war stories.

I learned that the area catered to the Vanguard installation nearby, which made sense because we hadn't walked too far from the embassy. Plus, this bar was basically full of off duty Vanguard military at this point. The VAF are also aggies due to the intense training called aggregation.

The young conscripts were mostly curious about the nonhumans and mercs because it was the biggest distraction from their grind. Gabe and Shantu were eating all the attention up, butchering songs.

This—*this*—is what it's all about. The best times.

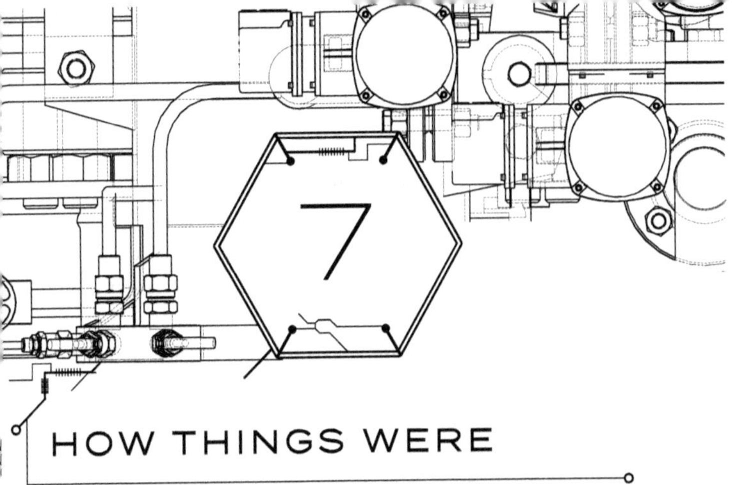

7

HOW THINGS WERE

Unavailable Context Modified

I KNOW VIRGINITY is important to some cultures. I don't get it for humans.

For the species that have significant biological changes as part of their reproductive cycle, sure.

Like the hydra, think sea anemone. When they mate, alpha and beta genders fuse to make a new gamma. Sometimes, they go crazy and self-destruct. I mean, no one's perfect. For the most part, gammas make up the bulk of the hydra economy and infrastructure because their nesting behavior manifests the same as a human setting up shop.

When they manage to attract a seasoned delta, the warrior gender they became an epsilon pod in effectively die. Metamorphosis directs biological resources away from higher cognition and toward producing offspring.

There's a shit ton of chemistry involved, and it's fascinating.

Okay. I'm avoiding the reason I started this entry.

I've gone over this a lot with Scout.

I have fucking issues, especially when it comes to sex and relationships. That's why I'm rambling on about a species I watched a documentary on versus dealing with my own shit.

I'm surprised I've managed to get this done with Takakoa next to me. But this is important, and I need to sort this out in my head.

I'm not sure what intimacy is. I thought it was just a polite word for sex.

Cameron was her name.

I was too young.

She was younger.

At the time, I was getting mean, aggressive, and defensive. I thought it was better to get into an ego fight than suffer any slight. Looking back, maybe it was puberty, the environment, or both.

I had just gotten in a fight with a guy named Ben. I don't remember having any real problems with him. Looking back, we could have both been having bad days or succumbed to social pressures.

Cameron hurled insults after Ben. I remember thinking how unnecessary that was since the fighting was over already. Then she hung on me and kissed me.

Adults broke everything up.

I was the talk of our cohort for the next few days. That was when Cameron attached herself to me.

I thought I was the king of the institute.

I remember her face. Cameron was the first girl to look at me with an excited smile. It drove me crazy. I wasn't used to positive attention at the time. I remember the hollow feeling of trying to play it cool while trying to hide how uncomfortable it made me.

I don't remember much besides how exciting it was to sneak around, hiding from the adults making plans, to do things we weren't supposed to.

Cameron and I slithered into the dark space between the walls and the massive curtains that separated the stage and the auditorium. It was dark and safe with the pressure of the curtains providing a barrier between us and the rest of the world.

I kissed her, and she kissed me back. She sucked painfully on my tongue. I thought she was going to cut that webby bit on the bottom.

I pulled away, and she dropped to her knees, undoing my pants.

That was not what I had meant.

I wasn't ready.

That didn't stop her.

She wasn't gentle, and I didn't like it. She scraped and scratched me with her teeth.

That didn't stop me from getting aroused.

I had this idea of what a blow job should be like. The guys in the videos seemed to be enjoying it. I was not having the same experience.

Was there something wrong with me?

Was I broken?

It hurt too much, and I pushed her head away from me. She flopped onto her back, squirmed out of her pants, and pulled me into her.

I unceremoniously slid into her and thrusted like I had seen in the videos.

Cameron arched her back and bit her lip. One hand gripped her breast while the other went down to rub herself.

I liked seeing her boobs and the way everything moved.

But nothing…

Maybe if I go faster?

She grabbed onto me, painfully bit into my shoulder, and whispered, "Right there. Right there."

She finished with a squeak of a moan.

I didn't.

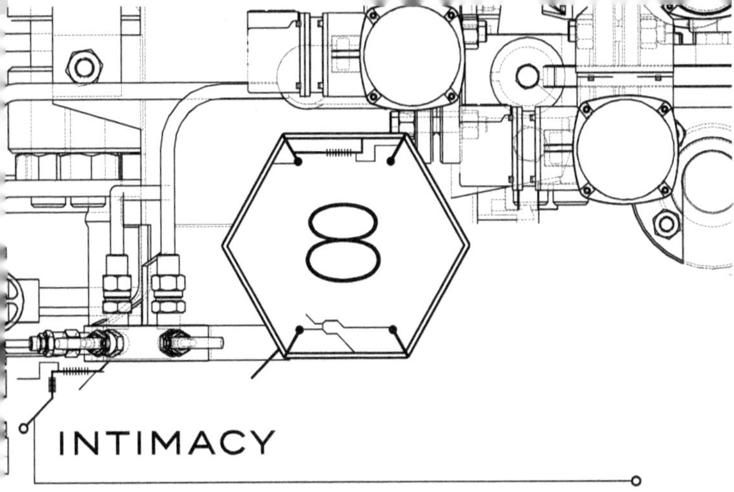

INTIMACY

522.271.0122 Entertainment Block Human District

I'M WIDE AWAKE because I can feel a shift in me. It's a revelation, an epiphany. I am not the same person I was hours ago.

That's okay because I don't want to be.

This may be a fleeting moment in both of our lives, but it feels like the tiny course correction here, now, is when it matters.

I should be able to talk about this stuff. Why can I articulate pain so easily but not pleasure?

Oh right. Trauma.

The evening, our evening anyway… I didn't know what the locals were on as far as schedule.

Anyway, our time off was going great. I don't know if the marauders in attendance were the life of part of our own party. Really it didn't matter. We were having a great time. Jokes were landing. Playful banter was staying playful. War stories were interrupted with enthusiastic off-key singing.

Takakoa looked at me during one of those renditions. "I really want to kiss you right now. I'm feeling it."

"I really want you to kiss you too."

I was drunk, all right? Don't judge me.

She snort-laughed into my face before resting her forehead on my chest. She came up for air after her laughing fit, looked me in the eyes, licked her lips, and leaned in for a kiss.

I've been tased and hit with eighteen gs and a maneuvering baffle. I've donned my HEPS with the air literally ripped from my lungs during decompression training. I've reassembled weapons in industrial washing machines.

I've been strapped into a box and had all my bodily functions forcefully overwritten for days on end. I've survived situations where the only option was to stay calm and endure.

None of that hit me this hard.

I was paralyzed.

I couldn't breathe, think, or exist.

I was everything,

I was nothing.

I was a transcendent apotheosis.

It's the name of the big religious moments in shows where someone either gets high or breaches some holy threshold and communes with their god or ancestors or whatever.

Suddenly, all those romantic comedies with the music and over-the-top production for the first kiss weren't so stupid and overdone anymore.

The moment lingered long enough to calibrate my reality before all the mechanisms that kept me alive this long started interfering. The spy, the heist, and the horror movies played in my head, painting me as the mark because I was vulnerable, ignorant. I was an easy mark with wealth ready to be taken.

I didn't care.

That kiss was instant addiction, pure chaos. I knew how empires got built and how people descended into madness.

I was a coin flipping in the air, set in motion by my creation.

I decided how I'd land.

I understand how dumb this all sounds.

All that from a kiss?

Fuck you if you think this is dumb, but this was a life-changing moment for me.

Insecurities and hypothetical people don't matter because this does.

These moments should matter more than all the shit I've been through.

The only not traumatic and emotional moment I can think of is the man from the top side gun range who taught me how to shoot. He treated me with respect even though I was gutter trash. He was kind in a cruel world.

I wish I knew his name.

How's that for an emotional audit, Scout? Oh shit. Awesome sauce. Scout's ears are heavier than I thought. They are kind of meaty like a wet sponge. They're also cool and velvety soft. He smells nice too. Sugary, like coffee creamer but with more earthy tones. That's the best fit I could come up with.

Anyway, Shantu started losing the fight with gravity. Scout climbing on everyone like a cat in heat, draping his ears over everyone in range, was our cue to leave the bar.

On the short walk to the hotel, we passed a royal blue gas bag things. Wraith grabbed it by one of the tentacles. Then he proceeded to lick the tentacles one by one, smacking his lips like he was grading the flavor.

I tried to use my feed to identify if it was sapient, but my gestures were fucked.

"WHAT THE FUCK!" I yelled at Wraith when he bit two meters of tentacle off the creature.

Wraith drew in a deep breath and blew into the tentacle, and the creature inflated while dipping with the loss of buoyancy. He seemed dissatisfied with the flavor of the tentacle and returned it to the floating jellyfish. The remaining tentacles passed the disconnected one up to an orifice.

"It's fine," Piper said, using Scout's ears to smack Shantu in the face. "Wraith just blew into that kallownin, so it will produce nitrous oxide."

I lost it. "He just blew a jellyfish for drugs."

That joke hit hard, and people started taking turns with the creature puffing on the creature.

"Does it hurt them?" I asked Piper.

Takakoa laughed into an answer. "'Scripties end up in the infirmary all the time for fucking that up. I never had the ovaries to try it."

"How bad is the sting?" I asked.

She shrugged. "Can be fatal if you fuck with them but mostly irritating. There's translators. It's a chemical, tactile language. I've never seen someone rawdog one before."

"So, he didn't hurt the thing, and we're cool with this?"

"Fuck if I know. If it gets pissed off, this'll be the weirdest pillow fight I've ever been in."

The mood was jovial when we landed on the couch of the hotel.

Takakoa and I were content watching the absurdity of people puffing on the kallownin. The ventilation kicked up to stabilize the atmosphere, dropping the temperature.

I, in a moment of clarity, ordered a medical bot from the hotel to make sure no one over did anything.

"Smart," Takakoa said, holding eye contact with me.

My feed would have alerted me to cardiac arrest, but I felt it.

I couldn't keep up with the dancing, the activities, the displays of affection, and the emotional breakdowns that were happening in front of me. Takakoa and I were a small harbor of peace, watching the chaos of all the lives in front of us unfold.

That's something else I've never had.

Peace.

I've never got to disconnect and just let things happen. I've always been scrambling for position, trying to get the girl or trying to numb the pain.

Takakoa shifted her weight to lean against me, sliding her arm under mine and interlacing our fingers. She snuggled into me against the almost violent environmentals doing battle against the number of bodies in the space.

I imagine the ventilation would be refreshing if I was dancing with all these people.

This, sitting on a couch and watching people have their myriads of experiences without interference or participation. In a crowded room with deafening music and chaotic flashing lights. I had my tiny bubble of peace with a partner.

The effects of the drinks were waning, but I was comfortable and felt no need to reup.

The party wound down, and as quickly as things took off, we were left with only the spindly humanoid housekeeping bot that was fixing up the living room area.

Ho-kay. Here we go.

This is important, so get it on the record.

She, Takakoa, kissed me passionately.

I wish I had read those romance books some of my former crewmates were into. Maybe then I would have the words.

Takakoa pulled herself onto me, and I lay back with her approach. I didn't feel pressured or forced, nor did I feel in control either.

Her kisses were a conversation. A peck was a cute little anecdote about what she liked. Her tongue sung of her desires. Gentile bites screamed about her passion.

She left my mouth to take kissing steps with her lips across my cheek and to my neck. Her hot breath in my ear made me squirm as I rose between her legs. She let me know she knew by pressing her hips into me before lifting them, freeing me to adjust. It felt approving, comforting, accepting, and safe.

Her fingers in my hair told me to kiss her the way she kissed me. Her weightlifting callouses gently pulled at my hair.

I took in her sweet earthy scent as I kissed her across her cheek as she turned her head. She let out a soft breath of pleasure and pressed her chest against mine.

I ran my hands up her back. Scars reminded me that the stories she told at the bar were real.

Takakoa didn't tell me this, but I understood it all the same.

Her scars were a choice. They were badges of honor for every trial she had survived.

Just like mine.

We were the same.

Her hard points warned me that battle was in her bones. She was more a professional soldier than me, and that was okay.

That was a decision I didn't have to make tonight.

She sat up, pulling her shirt and bra off in a smooth motion. Her breasts fell free, and callouses above and below them told me how much time she spent in armor.

I sat up just enough to kiss her stomach while she straddled me. She arched her back, allowing me access.

I cupped her breast, licked before sucking, and twirled my tongue around her nipple. I could feel faded stretch marks that had become permanent creases from unyielding compression of armor that I had never seen.

Takakoa came with a manual in the form of changes in her breaths, her hands on me, and her kisses.

I rolled her onto her back, wanting to know every part of her body.

She lifted her hips, inviting me to pull her shorts off. I gave her feet a little tickle and was rewarded with a beautiful little giggle. I kissed my way up her thigh. When I reached her lips, I licked gently, barely disturbing her hair at first. I barely touched her with my tongue, teasing, as she tried to wiggle her hips into my head.

Frustrated, she grabbed my head, pushing her clit into my lips.

I used the way she had kissed me on the mouth as a template of how to kiss her down there. Her hands and hips guided me.

The fragrance of the soap the bar had provided lingered, and her natural scent was starting to come through.

I honestly can't tell if she was any sweeter than other partners or if this was just the first time I wasn't lost in my own head.

The absence of my normal anxiety was a drug unto itself as I worked her clit with my lips and tongue. My thumb replaced my tongue as she lifted her hips, telling me where she wanted me to focus my attention.

I gently slid one finger into her, finally receiving the message. Her grip on my hair guided me to what she wanted.

I laughed into a raspberry on her clit because the move of the rat piloting the chef flashed across my brain.

She sharply pulled away in a violent convulsion, wrenching my head back from her vagina. My fingers remained inside her, reporting the waves of her orgasm.

Gently, she pulled my fingers from inside of her to lick them clean.

We switched places without a word. Without awkward fumbling.

My breath caught as she took me into her mouth.

My anxiety and insecurities evaporated as we repositioned pillows for maximum comfort. Takakoa's body was warm and silky between my legs. She squirmed, pleasuring herself and letting out moans around me.

That sent me wild. As I neared my peak, she seemed to intensify her efforts to match me.

In the heartbeat before climax, she forced her head down,

using the tightness of the back of her throat to send me plummeting over the edge.

The feeling of her swallowing made me cross-eyed. I convulsed as the dumbest giggle escaped me.

I floated, paralyzed and enveloped in a warm blanket of euphoria.

Neither of my brain cells were shaking hands right now.

Takakoa's lips were sweet and cold with a sugary drink when she kissed. She maintained the kiss as she took position on me.

She pulled my head into her chest, and I cupped her breast to suck at her nipple. I switched sides to balance out the pleasures.

Takakoa yipped when her nipple piercing caught between my upper teeth.

News flash: Only her left nipple was pierced.

She forced my face into her breast to keep me from pulling away.

I'm not proud of this, but it seemed funny at the time.

She had a firm control of my head with one hand and was trying to work the piercing free with the other without putting too much tension on the sensitive nipple. I thought it would be fun to fight her fingers with my tongue.

I don't remember doing any drugs, so I don't have that excuse for my behavior.

I lucked out when she flicked my tongue instead of getting frustrated or angry with me.

The distraction served to reset me.

Freed, she held my head in place, looking into my eyes, as she slid, dripping onto me.

I imagine my face was mirroring hers as we represented opposite sides of the same well-balanced equation. Her mouth was open, and I think every muscle in her body relaxed, taking me in. She did it slow, deliberate.

I felt seen, studied.

I felt like I mattered to her.

This wasn't transactional. This wasn't a negotiation.

This was intimacy without words. I was there for her, and she was there for me as we worked together for each other.

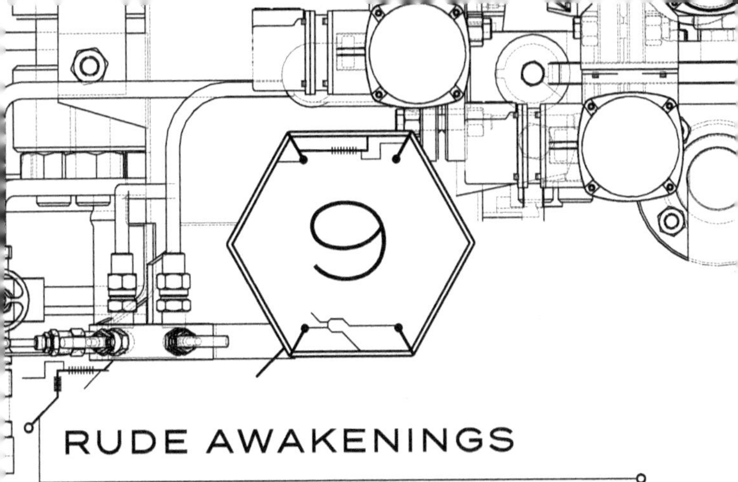

RUDE AWAKENINGS

522.271.1100 Entertainment Block,
Human District, Fermi Station,

I WOKE UP to the smell of rendering fat or perhaps chemical electroplating. Maybe burning plastic?

Regardless, it was awful and alarming.

I did a quick survey.

Takakoa and I were tangled in the nice plush triangular portion of the common room's sectional couch. Her hair was a poofy mess, free from the hair ties that now live around her wrist. Those ties and her feed were the only things she wore. Round bits of chrome protruded from her shoulders and pelvis that I could see.

I tried to remember where the other hard points should be based on movies and shows. I pet her hair affectionately and felt one behind and above her ear.

Hard points don't matter. THIS! This is what matters. This is what I need in my fucking life! A good night's sleep and to wake up next to someone I'm actually excited to be around.

Someone I wasn't afraid of the conversational minefield I would be wandering in if they woke up, and we had time alone together.

Comfortable.

Content.

Takakoa's firmly conditioned body and cybernetic hard points were deceptively cuddly. I did *not* want to get out of the bed…couch.

But what the fuck is that *smell*?!

At the far end of the couch was a foyer/office area that had a standard exit sign. To its left, talking heads moved on a screen, reporting their version of the news. A thoroughly emptied wet bar had its own alcove set at ninety degrees. A dining room was at the near end of the couch, to my left. I assumed the kitchen was behind the wet bar.

Takakoa lifted her head with the same alarmed confusion plastered across her face.

I was close enough to see the glint of her feed.

Minotaur honor code. I can't pronounce the real word; Shantu can. Anyway, I'm supposed to protect my guests with my life. And I really like this guest.

Given that she was a trained soldier with cybernetics, she could probably do more with the pistol than me. I handed her my sidearm while retrieving my tet.

The safety clicked off.

Tet in hand, I slid off the couch bed and gestured for her to look around the unknown corner of the foyer while I investigated the kitchen.

The vibe of the room changed as she quickly and silently stalked along the back of the couch. She gave me a thumbs-up, and I quietly walked toward the dining room.

If you've ever shared space with a predator, you know the only reason you're not dead is because it didn't feel like getting up to separate you from your life. That's the aura radiating from Takakoa.

Where the fuck did all the warmth and safety go from that woman?

I quick-peaked the corner and saw Wraith, naked, opening cans and putting them into a Crock-Pot. The newest addition gave off a strong smell of ammonia, making my eyes water.

I gave Takakoa the thumbs-up and relaxed.

Tension evaporated from the room. I could feel it the same way the environmentals kick on.

"Wraith, what the fuck are you doing?" I almost yelled. "Please tell me you're making a bomb."

I averted my eyes from his swaying erection.

I don't know why *that* was the sensible explanation to this scenario.

Takakoa put her hand on my shoulder to peek around me while hiding herself behind me. The press of her body against mine got my attention.

Wraith giggled. "Oh, something much more exciting!" Each word was a spider crawling up my spine.

I shivered uncontrollably.

He ladled blue goo from the Crock-Pot into a bowl of ice water. He snatched a gob of whatever from the ice bath and slapped it onto his body repeatedly, leaving bright purple splotches with a lime green outline.

I looked around to make sure my eyes weren't broken because of the overwhelming cacophony of color using Wraith as a battleground.

I tried to shake that image out of my head.

I found the hotel room's control panel and activated the ventilation in the kitchen. I then requested a housekeeping bot.

Finally, I looked at the room assignments and found mine. I gathered my things from the common room floor and headed to my room.

Takakoa followed.

We passed the lavatory, which wafted the stench of heavy brine. It was a writhing mass of slugs and tentacles with some humans in the mix… The gas bag thing was bobbing nder the shower. Honestly, I didn't look too closely. Splashing and giggling, mixed with moans of pleasure, echoed from the room.

Takakoa lingered, but I grabbed her hand to keep her walking.

My assigned room had my HEPS lying on the dresser with a basket of snacks next to it.

I thought I had sent the space suit to the ship.

Her eyes were wide, and she was covering her mouth with her hands. "Did you see—"

"Nope!" I said over her. "Don't need to. Don't want to. Whatever was going on in there was not my business. I've already seen too much of that."

The dresser was across from a comfortable-looking bed with six pillows arranged in a triangle. Who needed *six* pillows? It had a bright blue throw blanket at the foot.

"You ever know anyone for a long time and then learn they're not the person you thought they were?" I plopped down on the foot of the bed and wiped my face with my hands, trying to get the image of Wraith's erection out of my head.

She exploded with laughter, making me jump. "Did you just walk in on your parents?"

I looked at her like she was going to eat my head.

"Like when you were a kid," she continued, unhindered. "You walk into your parent's room because you had a bad dream or something. But instead of your parents comforting you, you find yourself eye level with your dad's asshole while he's plowing your mom." She laughed so hard she snorted.

I didn't understand what was so funny. Was she insulting me?

I stared at the basket of snacks, appreciating the plastic weaves. It had been colored to look more organic.

I then gave her a deep side-eye. "I was raised at the Vanguard City Institute for Developing Children."

The mirth drained from her face. "Oh shit. Wow, um, fuck, uh, okay. That is…why…you're not…laughing. Shit. Fuck. Uh, I'm sorry. Let's shower, and we'll talk."

She clicked the safety on and returned my pistol to me. I placed my weapons on the dresser before following her into the shower. She took her time adjusting the temperature and smelling the provided soaps.

Takakoa's voice then took on a gentle, patient tone. "Remember last night when we were joking about the fucked-up things we do in combat? Like your teammate rigging up a thruster in a corridor?"

I nodded and smiled.

I didn't feel like smiling, but I was trying to get there. "Like your teammate using video game stickers and trash cans to trigger point defense."

She pulled some soap from the dispenser, sniffed it, and began affectionately lathering me. I knew she was trying to get me to relax, which made me more tense. But I had to pretend to because I knew she meant well.

"Exactly," she said. "So, most people I have met have trauma like that growing up, where you learn that the people caring for you are still people. As a child, seeing my parents being intimate was disgusting and traumatic. As an adult, I realize their relationship has endured, and that's something special. We don't have that shared trauma, and in fact, you might be going through it for the first time. I'm sorry if I made you uncomfortable. I want you to understand that."

I relaxed with the sincerity of each word.

We embraced, and everything was going to be just fine. We just held each other, occasionally rotating to let the water run over our bodies. The shower seemed unusually quiet without the vent pulling the air down.

We finished showering and wrapped ourselves in the robes the hotel provided.

She nervously poked around the hotel room, looking through the furniture and amenities. "What's with the suits?" she asked as she opened the wardrobe.

"Those are all the clothes I have on the station. Honestly, I feel naked outside my HEPS." I tapped the helmet for emphasis. I then stuck my hand into my new hat, and it deformed so I could show her the visor section. "Makes me feel better that I can button up."

"Oh, that's nice. You still look like you're going to tell me that I owe docking fees."

"Seriously though… Do I blend in?" I asked.

"Yeah. Just need a pad glued to your hand, and you'll find yourself getting bribes by the end of the day."

Something from my class about interpersonal communication told me that since the tense moment had passed, it was okay to talk about personal stuff.

"Thanks." I took a deep breath. "Look, you're awesome. Help me out here…"

She smiled bright teeth with that thank-you-shoulder-shrug thing people do.

My feed alerted me that our loot boxes were waiting with the concierge. I gestured to dismiss the notification.

She seemed to be patiently waiting for me to continue.

"Can you…"

Can she what? Stay in this room with me until we both die of diabetes from room service because that's how I want to spend the rest of my life?

That's stupid.

"How long have you been on that ship?" she asked.

I had to think about it. "Tw-two and a half years… Vanguard Standard."

"Same crew?"

I nodded. "Plus, the kids. And we lost a few to the galunkin."

"That's fine. I'm asking about turnover, the revolving door. You know, people coming and going all the time."

"The bar and the elevator I used to work at were like that," I mentioned.

"What happened with the kids?" she asked.

"They were trained by some company to be suicide soldiers. Had explosives in their vests and… You would have to talk to Scout for the details, but I know they were in rough shape. I was busy doing other shit. I know he put them back in the pods, but he did not seem confident. He kept reminding us that he's not rated to induce cryo."

"Right, right, right. Shit. Sorry. Someone was talking about that last… Anyway," she said, talking so fast. "I was going to say that I get it. You've been on one ship with the same people for two plus years. In the VAF, each ship becomes its own little town—crackheads, mayors, and everything in between. Each deployment is different because you can reinvent yourself. One of my conscripts became a one-man band. First time out, he gets mocked because someone caught him humming to himself while doing scut work. Terrible deployment for this kid. Second time out, like nine months later, he bursts into full-blown show tunes at the top of his lungs. They're terrible, but he has confidence. Everyone loves it and even sings with him. By the end of his conscription, he was doing concerts in the hangar. You know who that kid was?" Her voice was doing that thing people did when building to a massive reveal. "Eric Danik! The Electric Dance himself!"

She was really good at telling the story, but I had no fucking clue who she was talking about. I tried to make a *wow* face.

It didn't work.

But she didn't let it phase her and spoke in a bland voice. "Massive singer who went supernova three years ago. My point is that a new station is a fresh start. What we have is a fresh start. You're cute… The synth, what's her name?"

"Piper, and use they/them. They don't use gendered language or anything that implies they're a copy. Synth, AI, android, and bot are all no-go. Inorganic, abiogenic, silicate, and variations are okay because they're descriptive."

"Copy. Piper told me that you had just gotten out of a rough relationship. I have my own baggage. So, I'll handle *mine*, and you handle *yours*, and we will try to manage *us* like adults."

The concierge chimed at me again, and I dismissed it again.

"Do you need to get that?" she asked.

"It's the concierge. The delivery guy is waiting," I said. "I thought we were on something important."

She waved a finger at me, and it landed on my nose. "That's sweet, but what delivery guy?"

I pulled the message up. "From the fight." I selected the deliver-to-room option and alerted her.

She stared out while she had hers diverted here, so we could open them together. I dressed in a fresh suit, while she pocketed her undergarments and put on the clothes from the night before.

In the living room, I opened the door for the delivery. A white-scaled creature, from between the two drones, stuck out a pad for me. It exploded in green gore before I could really get a good look at it.

I leaped away and tripped over Scout, who had fired a scatter gun from between my legs. I took two more steps back before spinning to land on my hands. "WHAT THE FUCK!" I yelled at him.

"Not a delivering person." He had abandoned his scatter gun and was on his back, writhing and holding something in his hand.

"Is that your…" I started to ask but then aborted because his hands were in his crotch.

"Yes," he answered quickly. "First, you sign. Then take you."

The gunshot rapport had summoned everyone into the living

room. Wraith was in his full kit, rifle up. After a quick sweep, he relaxed and checked the corridor.

Shantu asked, "Scout, why is your dick in your hand?"

"I … Gravity collision," Scout said.

Wraith paused for a moment before his helmet retracted. He laughed before scooping up Scout. "Come 'ere. You did good." He put Scout on the couch, got the urglurk a first aid kit, and treated his *injury*.

Did Wraith get that rainbow vomit shit all over the inside of his armor?

Takakoa gently put her hand on my shoulder and viewed the carnage. She glanced at my confused face. "Rodolfo, slavers and drug dealers. They aren't allowed in human districts because they like to stab everyone in sight with basically super heroin. Can you see if the hotel will clean off our crates before we bring them in?"

"Why are you so chill about this?" I asked, not nearly as calm.

She shrugged. "They take people. I use retrieval operations to get the new guys bled in."

Her casual business-as-usual tone was more alarming than Scout almost blowing my balls off with a shotgun.

Alarms for weapons fire rang outrageously late. The hotel manager profusely apologized from the door panel, promising free services for letting a rodolfo past security. The clean-up team arrived in biohazard gear at a sprint. They hosed the corridor with a bleach solution and vacuumed it up. When the cleaning people cleared out, two security people stayed behind.

Wraith appeared, wearing a bathrobe and one of those elastic swimming caps. Thankfully, he had cleaned off the kaleidoscope of surfactant biohazard.

"Hey, Yolanda. How's Martha and the kids?" Wraith asked.

Security person number one, in the matte black sealed armor, stiffened at the not-so-subtle threat. They casually dropped their hands near their sidearms.

He shifted his tone to a friendly mob boss. "Look, not my style. I'm a carrot kind of guy. That school you're looking to get Jean-Pierre into might have an opening just for him."

The strong deep feminine voice came out positively *dripping* with suspicion and on the verge of violence. "What do you need from me for this…*arrangement?*"

"Nothing really. I just don't want any more *incidents* for me and my friends." His emphasis implied there was more that happened at this hotel than what was on the brochure.

Wraith glanced down at Scout, who was massaging some goo onto his member. The smell of tea and nail polish filled the room.

Wraith looked back at Yolanda. "We're on vacation, and I don't want to have to worry about anything."

"No sketchy shit?" they asked, popping the seal on their helmet. Her helmet liner left her hair a tangled mess that she brushed away from her skeptical face.

"No sketchy shit. To make my expectations clear: Keep the suite cleaned when we go out and make sure nothing goes missing. We will be having the occasional drunken orgy, but everyone will be consenting adults, and I would like your help verifying, seeing as you probably know this station better than me. Do you think you can do that for us?"

Yolanda's face went from an angry scowl to resting a bitch face. She nodded and put her helmet on. There seemed to be a restrained argument.

Security person number two left in a silent huff.

She then removed her helmet again with beads of sweat on her brow and upper lip. "I'm getting people I can trust on this. Some people are going to be pissed about the scheduling…but that's none of your concern."

"No, it's not," Wraith coolly said. "Let's take care of some things so I can get back to my vacation."

Takakoa and I sat in the dining room, unwrapping a sausage egg and cheese with Texas sauce breakfast bagels while watching Wraith work.

I enjoy real food!

Wraith brought up the company website in a local workspace and made it public for everyone to see. He then went through the list of security personnel for our wing. Selected Yolanda's profile, which had a link to her public social media profile. From there, he selected the post about the school and brought up the admissions form.

Yolanda buried her face in her armored hands.

He gestured at the form. "Yolanda, if you would."

He highlighted sections with personal information that disappeared as she completed them. We couldn't see what she typed as she worked in virtual. She stopped when she got to the document's payment portion, and he took over.

"There you have it. Four years paid in full," he said.

Her stony face cracked with motherly love.

"Yolanda," he said, "I need you to stay in the moment and do your job until you can get relieved."

Her face quickly hardened. She stuffed her helmet back on her head and straightened, seemingly awaiting orders.

I felt guilty for sitting on my ass, eating, while someone else worked. I contributed to the situation by giving her a food expense allowance while she guards the hotel room. Generous but not extravagant.

She looked over the delivery drones before letting them in. They were a little more than pallets with omni wheels. My box was twice the size of Takakoa's, which was stacked on top.

We soon finished our food and retreated to my suite. Shantu, Piper, and Gabe promptly invited themselves in, just behind the delivery drone.

"What the fuck? No!" I shouted. "Get the fuck out!"

"Were they this rude on the ship?" Takakoa asked.

"No. But we spent a lot of time trying not to die. Now that we're in relative safety, everyone has decided to become ass-holes." I turned back to them. "Get the fuck out of my room!"

"All right, all right," Shantu said. "But can you please open the box in the living room? The suspense is killing me. Please?"

When I agreed, they finally left. I rubbed my face and took a deep breath.

"I may have asked this before, but what's his deal with you?" Takakoa asked.

"We grew up together at the institute. We've been stuck together, and it has really worked out so far." I gestured to the nice hotel room. "He's a dick who never shuts up, but he's a good guy. He's dating Piper, the pilot. So, now, I get twice as much shit."

"Right… I remember her saying something about wanting a woman's opinion on something. Fuck… There was a lot going on last night. It's pretty fuzzy." She chuckled.

"They," I corrected again.

"What?"

"Piper wants to be referred to as *they* in Common," I said, sounding like Shantu. "They don't get all butthurt, but they don't like their gender being a consideration in their identity. They have many opinions on various cultural matters, and they can put out the flashlight at a half million kilometers, so I tend not to argue."

She turned the corners of her mouth down and nodded.

"They also got two follow-up shots while dealing with eigh-teen g's of recoil."

"We take care of our stick jocks on the ground too." She started dressing and checked at least two pistols and a knife.

I smiled at the hardware and the fact I had sex with this woman.

We ignored the noises coming from the communal bathroom

as we went into the living room. The housekeeping drone was making its rounds nearby. A maintenance bot was replacing the stove that looked like it had been melted by boiling acid.

"Nope. Not asking," I said, and Shantu chuckled, clearly having similar thoughts. "Do not need to know. Do not want to know."

Shantu spoke in his game show host voice. "Now, gentle beings, this is what fighting in a bar until you can't anymore will get you in life. Let's open the boxes and see if anyone shit the bed. Let's see who *really* won in this. James"—he gestured toward me—"if you would start us off."

Takakoa looked at me. I think that was the first time she heard my first name.

Right on top was my trophy. It was heavier than I had expected. I held it up to the cheers of my friends. With the trophy, I had an invitation to fight again and my fight scorecard, which gave me an official ranking.

It was 123,041 in case anyone was wondering. I don't know what to do with that since I have no intentions on becoming a professional fighter. It did update my professional profile though.

I waved Gabe over to help me identify the rest of the items since the labels were strictly mass composition. I held up a bag of small cylinders, and he poured the whole bag into his mouth.

"Hey!" I yelled.

He spit the cylinders back into the bag like a machine gun. "Batteries. All depleted. I can put them into the fabricator as medium."

She offered him a bag of metal bits.

"Steel bearings with lubricant. Raw worth," he said.

I pulled out bags of soil. The live bacteria and moisture made it worth ten times their material weight. She found two live grenades and four broken rifles that could be salvaged to make one working one. But she didn't really want them. She took the grenades though.

I wanted the grenades…

The bottom third of my container was a mangled drone. The design suggested light manufacturing. Its power cell had ruptured and mangled the internals. In the voids below the container were several chunks of scrap and a sophisticated-looking component the size of a thick book with wires and connections hanging off it.

I held up the device, and Piper and Gabe stared at each other.

"That's a kernel," he said. "You're holding an abiogenic being's brain. I don't recognize the structure, but it is a kernel."

"Do we hold a funeral or plug it in and see if there's someone in there?" I asked. "I'm not being rude. I'm just trying to understand what to do."

Piper looked shaken.

Gabe ran to his room and came back with a tool bag. I closed the lid and placed the kernel down on it gently. It had scuff marks from being handled like scrap and having a drone bounce around on top of it.

I looked at all the structures, and none of them made sense to me.

Gabe worked his magic with his various instruments. He also threw up a shared workspace for us to view and explained that there's a weak electromagnetic field with a frequency that implies electrical conduction. The seemingly random peaks and valleys implies something is running in there. I tried to convey what we were seeing to Takakoa since she wasn't tied to our common net, but I didn't understand half of what he was talking about.

Piper didn't have a face, but I imagined they were sullen. "If there is someone in there, they're likely psychotic. Sensory deprivation for years at minimum. If they're not initialized, we might be looking at autonomics."

"I would like to get it checked out. Where or who do we talk to?" I asked them and then turned my gaze to Gabe.

They just shook their heads at each other.

I looked around the rest of the team, but they all shrugged like we were deciding between burgers and pizza.

I pinged Wraith, and he turned it into a video call. I don't know what I saw, but I didn't want to see it. I shut my eyes, which made the image clearer, but I found the command to go audio only.

The lavatory door slid open. "What?!" he yelled while grunting.

"We have a kernel. I want to get it checked out." But I had to yell it at him twice more over the splashing and hissing noises. I then lowered my voice for everyone around me. "He was right here like five seconds ago…"

Naked, he slid into the living room, dripping water and other liquids. The concoction I saw him preparing now covered him from head to toe. His eyes were red, and his contacts were glowing green. He wavered on his feet, making his erection sway.

Shantu noticed. "What are you on?"

He smiled. "Life!" He then looked the kernel over without touching it and addressed Gabe. "Harmonics?"

"Irregular. No noticeable degradation or cycles," Gabe said. "If it had regular cycles of activity, it could be a sign of psychosis. Irregular cycles of low-level stuff are a sign of autonomic functions. It may not be actualized."

"Right," Piper agreed.

"What the hell does that mean?" I asked.

"Kernels are often integrated into larger systems to act as subsidiary intelligences, like fire control and point defense," they said. "It needs to be able to make decisions on the fly but doesn't necessarily need to be sapient if the master intelligence is functioning. It's more like a baby that won't grow up unless it's forced to. Not like a human baby either though because it can remain stable or dormant."

Shantu and Piper looked at each other.

"Do you want a baby because this is how you get a baby?" he said with a mischievous tone.

The collective *what the fuck* went around the room.

He plowed forward, heedless of the offense he was giving to nearly everything in the room. His feet danced as he pointed and sang. "A man and a woman love each other very much. He puts his wing wang in her hoo-ha, and if they're lucky, they make a bouncing baby. But instead, these two violent vindicators wanted to play pull the punches, so the progeny was provided via the post."

The room exploded in laughter. I covered my face with my hands, and Takakoa snort-laughed next to me.

"I hate you," I said to him.

QUIET MOMENTS

I GENTLY PLACED the kernel in my room's safe and set the combination to today's date.

Since I won't forget today any time soon.

I turned to Takakoa. "So, this is my life, and I don't know what normal looks like, but I'm pretty sure it doesn't involve finding computer babies in scrap boxes."

She looked at me, deadpanned. The tears of laughter still wet on her cheeks, lessening the effect. "I've been an aggie for six years," she said like it explained everything.

I didn't challenge the sergeant face. I knew it well. Usually, Sgt. Tok gave it to Shantu, and I was caught in the crossfire.

I gave her an uncomfortable side-eye. One that said "I've seen you naked. You're not my sergeant, but I don't want to make you mad because I want to see you naked again. However, please don't treat me like one of your subordinates."

That's a lot to say with one look, and I don't know how much went through.

When her face relaxed into something human, I asked, "I have roughly two weeks of leave. What does your schedule look like?"

Her face softened, almost apologetic. "I have to be on post in thirty-six hours for a training and integration conference. Then I think I can carve out some time."

I smiled and nodded enthusiastically.

"What the hell are you?"

I dropped the smile. I don't know why I look around the room in situations like this one. Like there will be a subtitle out of frame that will explain it to me.

"You fight hard, you're not xenophobic, you don't seem to be threatened by me, *and* you don't have a weird kink about it," she said.

I fight hard because that's all I did growing up. Now, I have training in both how to kill and how to pull my punches, so I don't harm a teammate.

I'm not xenophobic because humans have historically been my problem. They're the ones who abused me, robbed me, and lied to me. All the species that showed up at my various jobs endured my staring with grace and were polite and professional at least. Humans would lie to my face to try to get me to fall into some conversational trap to get free shit.

In the gut, everyone does two things: fight and fuck. I want something more. Honestly, I'm glad I didn't get a kink about it. I've seen too many drug-addled psychos whose reality consisted of seeking the next stimulus.

No thanks. I want my sex to be cuddly and safe.

Does that make me weird?

Side note: Can someone please explain to me the topic distribution in porn? It's weighed in a very peculiar manner. Is it targeting the whales? You know, like the games that suck unless you spend ridiculous amounts of money. Are the people with a very particular taste funding the content?

"Uh…" came out of my mouth while all that shit raddled around in my head, preventing me from forming actual words.

"Most men have a massive chip on their shoulder when fighting women," she said, while I watched her dark lips form the words. "Or they go too far the other way, and they get aroused by it. You don't really fall into either category."

I shrugged. I didn't like the focus on me. "Really? Like they get hard from your mean back kick?" My face screwed up as I rubbed my stomach, remembering the kick.

"You have no idea the amount of kinky shit that goes around the fleet. I had to go through a few fucked-up relationships before my dumbass learned how to spot the signs and—more importantly—set boundaries. You, I don't know what to do with you. Because you'll punch me in the face but almost run in terror if I wink at you."

"That's because your wink hits harder." I smiled, hoping it wasn't going to backfire.

As I got lost in her eyes, a range of emotions danced across her face. First was the reflex offense from the fact her punches didn't hit hard. Then it was understanding and all that came with that. She leaned in to kiss me, and my universe was swallowed up.

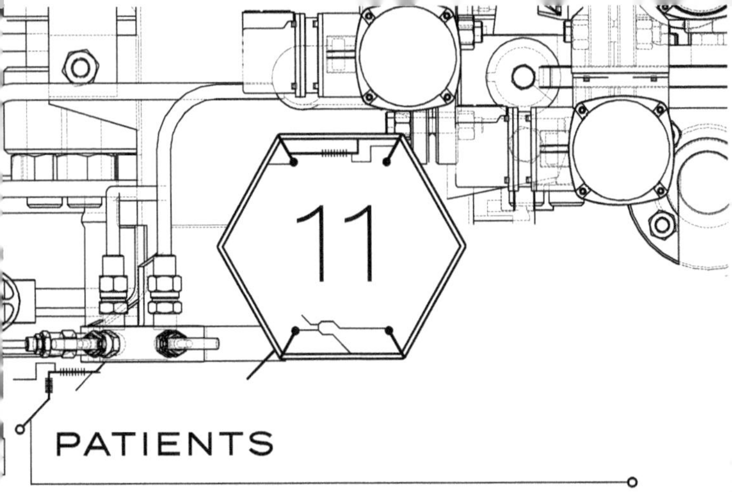

PATIENTS

522.273.0900 Entertainment Block,
Human District, Fermi Station

DO NOT MESSAGE her! She's at work!" Piper had me wrapped up with their hypermobile limbs and hydraulic grip.

Shantu "helped" by "tripping" and "falling" on me.

The three of us had fallen off the hotel's couch, sprawled across the living room. "Oof" was the noise I made as his weight forced all the air out of my lungs.

"Stop struggling!" he yelled at anyone but me. "This is for your own good!"

I didn't have a chance against Piper's machine body, which could rip me limb from limb if they wanted. He was actually in their way with his belly flop on me instead. Next thing I knew, he was feebly struggling to get my feed bracelets off while rubbing his crotch and ass in my face. I took the only option left, which was to bite the fuck out of him. He kneed my face in his pained struggle to get off me.

Piper took advantage of the distraction and hit the release on my bracelets. My feed went dark.

I, resigned to my fate, stopped struggling.

Shantu complained while pulling up his athletic shorts to expose the bruise filling in where I had bit his inner thigh. He swatted my head like I was a disobedient pup. "No biting!"

I was too busy laughing at the bruise with Piper to be mad.

While shuffling to get his coffee, Scout looked at us disapprovingly and muttered, "I am going to write a dissertation on adolescent clinging stress management because of you two… Three. Perhaps the effect on adaptable sapience."

"What the shit is this?"

The icy voice of death triggered my instinct to stand at attention.

"Lovely for you to join us, Javelin." Piper met her ice with their warmth. "Breakfast or beer?"

"Beer," she said like she could refrigerate it herself.

They nodded to the dining room while going to fetch two beers. The bottles had the crimp-style lid that needed either a tool or violence to open. Javelin chose violence.

"James seems to have found himself a partner," they said, launching into my gossip like I wasn't there.

"Bitch!" I said.

They threatened to crush my feed bracelets in their grip.

I tried to look as sullen and as apologetic as I could.

Shantu laughed. "You done fucked up now!"

Javelin was quiet with only her disapproving grunts. But them treating her like one of the girls was freaking me out.

"Go." Piper waved at me. "The adults are talking."

Shantu nodded for me to follow him. He still had a smirk on his face, even while he rubbed my bite on his thigh.

"What do you know?" I asked, sotto voce.

He matched my tone. "Scout wants Piper to include Javelin in our shenanigans."

"But? The fuck? Why?"

"Between the losses, Wraith and Dire-horn fighting with the

captain, the kids, and everything we've been through, she's done it ten times already. She and the captain have been the only permanent figures on the ship." His eyes took on an annoyed look, and he took on Scout's informational tone. "In the interest of unit cohesion. Blah, blah, blah. She needs downtime to be safe with friends."

"So, we're stuck with her…"

"Yes, and if you say something like that in front of her, I'll smack the shit out of you. If Piper doesn't do it first. So, suit up. We're going out."

"You just wanted to say *suit up*."

He smiled. "Uh-huh."

Leaving the hotel, I was still expecting an open street and a sky. The lobby was nice, but when we walked out, there was another corridor when it should be outside. Why have a lobby where there's no traffic flow for street level? There's no street level. We're in the middle of a giant office building or a beehive for that matter. It's disorienting!

These corridors were clean with an army of bots and robust environmental systems. Everyone's clothing was clean and in good repair. There was enough space to get through without touching other people but not much.

Javelin, who could cut deep with her ever-present look of disdain, had wide eyes darting all around. She kept reaching for her sidearm and then pulling her hand away. Frightened? Piper had a hand on her shoulder, steering her through corridors.

I get it. I don't like being around this many people either, but this was something worse. Trauma maybe?

Piper did their best to keep Javelin's attention with shoptalk about the ship refit. I couldn't dodge people and keep up with the conversation.

The locals… Fucking weird! I'm the foreigner, and *they're* the locals.

WHAT! THE! FUCK!

I used to be the one who would get mad at porters from starliners. Now, I'm the off-worlder… Stationer…? Yep. Not unpacking that…

Anyway, the locals were fascinated by Javelin's wings. The double takes lingered a little too long to be polite but not long enough to warrant a response. I watched them give sheepish apologetic smiles before finding somewhere else to put their eyes.

I made a show of looking bored on the tram. Maybe my chill would help her find her chill.

Shantu tossed me a file with Piper's new design. Their endoskeleton was getting wrapped in a heated polymer with lights. The meeting today was going to be for them two, so they could decide on the textures and define inputs.

"It is more of an organ transplant than a paint job," he said.

"This is a big deal for y'all, isn't it?" I asked sotto voce.

He nodded.

That was the thing about Shantu. The bigger the deal, the less he said. Nothing meant everything.

I gave him the I'm-here-for-you nod.

A dopamine drop hit my brain, and I smiled at my friend. I've never had the presence of mind to recognize a neurotransmitter release, but this one fell over me.

This is what love looks like.

All that big ceremony shit is for narcissists, political alliances, and sellers. Real love is my best friend and our pilot trying to bridge the gulf of biology. It's people trying to become better versions of themselves together. Anything else is bullshit.

Javelin stood there next to Piper. She might as well have been naked instead of wearing light powered armor that connected to her prosthetic limb. Scared, in an unfamiliar place, and surrounded by strangers. She didn't know how to ask for comfort or reassurance. Rules and regulations replaced the emotions that betrayed her time and time again.

I know exactly why she didn't trust emotions. She had been conditioned by abuse to not, and that lesson was hard learned and reinforced by betrayal. The details didn't matter.

But to me, it was like looking at myself without Shantu. I could have gotten there so easily... And Scout knew it. That was why Javelin was here with us.

Fucking crazy that I am mentally healthy enough to see what was wrong with others.

Scout, if you ever get to hear this, thank you. I get it.

All that shit aside, I wanted to share this moment with Takakoa. Because looking at Piper and Shantu, I wanted that to be our future.

If not her, then someone.

I want someone to figure out *life* with.

I'd be lying if I said I wasn't jealous of Piper and Shantu. At the same time, I was happy just to see it. Too many people miss these moments.

I basked in the moment, fully aware the four of us were crammed into a tram surrounded by strangers with their own shit to do. That tram ran through one section of one spire that encompassed all of the human-friendly area. That was not even accounting for the other three hundred thirty-five other spires or the main body of the station.

"That's why we're bringing y'all," Shantu said, his voice rousing me from my musings. "Piper's on their third frame since they came aboard. Javelin has recovered their core twice. The last time, they almost decompiled. Javelin sat and talked into a microphone for two weeks, not knowing if they were going to come out of it. They think getting an elective mod might be good. Like make it all worth it."

"Decompiled? The rest I get."

"Brain death. Imagine being stuck in your own head with no connection to your body."

"I know exactly what that's like," I said.

"The coffin?"

We drew the attention of some of the other passengers because Shantu didn't know how to be subtle.

"Yeah," I said.

"Out with it."

"Have you seen the meme about we're really some tapioca hallucinating our lives?"

Shantu nodded.

"When I woke up, I wasn't down for very long. I felt the initial launch. I freaked the fuck out. Then I remembered the briefings and thought that if I could just stay calm enough…I'll survive. I didn't want to die like that. Don't get me wrong. There was a big part where I freaked the fuck out with all that shit in me. I don't know who really knows this, but it's *so loud*. Like louder than a shuttle. And it makes your bones hurt. All of them. Like a jammed toe but everywhere, over and over again." I tapped my temple. "I made an AV cockpit in my head and treated my body like I had a status board. At first, every alarm was going off, but one by one, I installed green, yellow, and red lights to make sense of it."

His eyes were wide, and his face was blank. He didn't blink for way too long. "You just blew my mind."

Piper had stopped talking as Javelin just stared at me.

I did my best to keep my eyes locked on Shantu, pretending I didn't notice. "Want to know the trippy part?"

"Yeah," he said.

"Don't think about breathing."

A moment passed. Then he said, "Well, that's fucking impossible."

I walked him through how I organized my body with the

controls and the display inside my mind cockpit, gesturing in the open space between us. "Breathing is pretty front and center. There's a weird deliberateness you have to do to not look at the controls. Look over at the left arm. What do you think that burning sensation is? Oh, my heart rate is slowing but pounding. Must be something to get my blood pressure up." I closed my eyes, sinking into the memory of it. "That pain is more of an itch…and I'm peeing now." A bit too far into the memory, I almost wet my pants.

"That's insane!"

"Insane is trying to stay calm when a machine is inflating your lungs with ramen noodles."

"Ugh… Yeah, that stuff was so gross," he said. "I swallowed a bunch of it. Comes out like it goes in. I just showered. Didn't bother trying to wipe. It just smeared."

"Disgusting," I said a bit too loud.

Some of the passengers were exchanging looks and whispering about us.

I gave no shits. Let them have their story to tell.

"You think that's gross?" he said. "I had to steam purge my water filtration because it clogged it up."

"STAHP!" I turned my head away and waved at him like he was giving off an odor instead of talking about it.

We changed trams several times, having to seal up twice to pass through nonhuman areas. On the longer haul tram, we got stuck with a polite being, who happily hung from the overhead a good portion of the time. It was a bardo. Think grasshopper in a space suit that's three or four meters long. I couldn't make much out through the armor it wore.

It didn't take long before we realized we were stuck with an old person on the tram as they regaled us with stories of their two hundred twenty-five children.

One every other year for all of Vanguard history.

Wild!

We asked them about an environmental engineer, but they weren't on good terms with that kid. Worth a shot.

"Nope! Abso-fucking-lutely not!" I yelled at the blinking pink and red neon sign that advertised adult novelties.

"Come on… It's for research," Shantu said.

I turned to Piper and barked, "You took my feed so I wouldn't see the destination, didn't you?"

The space suit looked chastened if such a thing could make sense.

I backed up and folded my arms in flat refusal. If that wasn't enough, I planted my feet and leaned against a post that looked like a Roman column to drive the point home that I wasn't going in that place with them.

WE NEED BOUNDARIES!

The post stepped away, and I stumbled. I looked up and found markings on the post's armor for security. Shantu and Piper ran away like children caught somewhere they weren't supposed to be. Javelin was half dragged along by Piper.

"Pardon, sir," the post grumbled in a clearly synthetic voice.

"Shit! Sorry!" I said, quickly following the leg up to the person towering over me. I didn't know if I was talking to a drone, a vehicle, or a person. "I thought you were decor."

"Thank you," they replied. They radiated bashful, flattered energy.

Not what I meant, but okay.

That was when we got to talking. I'll spare you the awkward back-and-forth as they worked their feed through different Common dialects until we got something close to Vanguard Standard.

The linguar—what the post is—are four meters tall and like ten long. They're on the human emotional and environmental spectrum, despite looking like a fallen tree walking on its surviving branches. They like their g lower, their CO_2 higher, and their oxygen even higher. However, there's plenty of tolerable overlap between humans and linguar.

Linguar train their limbs for specialized tasks. They only have so much power running their spaghetti brain, so if too many limbs grow, they get bunched into groups and end up looking like a fuzzy caterpillar thing with no fine motor control. I thought my life decisions were rough, but I don't have to decide where and how many of which limbs to keep. However, I learned the optimal and fashionable number of limbs is three to eight.

The pointy end of the fallen tree holds a slit that marks their vent, which is their mouth and their butthole. Their digestive system is complex, and they have significant conscious control over it.

I think the linguar considers explaining the happenings of intestines small talk. I didn't understand most of it because of translation issues and my desire not to know.

For lack of a better expression, human communities are pet colonies in their homes. A barn cat is the best example I can think of. Just don't irritate the homeowners and use the bathroom appropriately, and you can stay. Might even get treats.

I wish I had known about this growing up. I might not have gotten in so much trouble and saved money to get to a linguar world.

I wanted to know how fast they could move and how much firepower they could absorb. And I wanted my feed, so I could look this stuff up instead of idly wondering and not asking because I'm pretty sure asking "how do I kill you" is rude in most cultures.

Sorry. That was how I spent a couple of hours trying not to think about the conversations happening in that *store*.

The district felt like a shopping mall and a parking garage. Well-lit, hard surfaces with stores lining the corridors. Tons of more species than our classes ever taught us about.

It was weird though. I kind of went blind to all the novel sights and sounds. I stopped trying to make sense of what was going on. Without my feed identifying everything and letting me dive down a rabbit hole of new discovery, I just vibed.

I was in a coral reef or a rainforest. Life swirled around me, a riot of color and sounds. This was a place of patience, if not understanding. There didn't seem to be any offenses given or taken. Just a harmonious flow in the chaos.

I enjoyed chatting with the security person, watching a district do its thing.

For the love of every shining star, Piper came out of the store, fuming. I didn't know how I could tell. Maybe it was the way they walked.

I smiled.

"Shut up!" they snapped, walking past me.

Shantu wouldn't meet my eyes. Javelin looked at me for help—like I knew what the fuck happened in there.

We made a quick stop to pick up some food analyzers from a locker. They looked like wristwatches with a quarter meter-long flexible needle that we could stab into our food. We also could program our preferences on top of the basic tox screen. I didn't get mine because Piper still wouldn't give me my feed back.

The lab for Piper's frame felt sketchy as shit when we walked there. We took turns out of the main thoroughfare and into a winding back alley. Which made me extra nervous.

"Are you taking us back here to cut us open and sell us on the black market?" I asked as the corridor became filthier, and the lighting failed.

"No. Relax," they said, *finally* handing me my feed hardware. "It's all for show." They kicked a garbage bag, and it spun, showing that it was a foam prop. They nudged it back into place.

"He goes by," Javelin said with an uncomfortable sigh, "the Ascendency. He's the oldest full body prosthetic. The only known survivor from before the Human Civil War."

I reinitialized my feed and found it air gapped. No connection. Great.

We entered a large compartment that was being reconfigured from a cafeteria into a lounge with couches and a coffee table by overhead cranes. Beyond that was a terminal with an impractically large screen, where someone was playing a stylized shooter with lots of flashing colors and explosions.

The player rose and waved with frantic excitement as they crossed the distance between us. The avatar died on the screen, and a teenage boy gave Piper a warm hug. The kid had a dark mess of hair and a bright smile.

Some of the hair caught in Piper's suit, and the boy winced.

"What? You have sensation from your hair?" They sounded like a giddy child.

The Ascendency peeled his scalp back to show a metal dome that looked like theirs. "Do you want hair?"

"Ugh, no. I need more flair than fucking with fibers. I have a challenge for you. Something no one's done. This is Tombstone." They gestured.

"I know…"

"Don't be rude," Piper snapped like they were chiding a child. "This is Tombstone, my partner. His best friend—or brother, for a lack of a better word—Monolith. You know Javelin."

"Right!" But his eyes were on Shantu. "Can I see your pal'loch?"

Shantu pulled it from his back, flipped it, and presented the handle. The Ascendency snatched it and flicked it through the air with inhuman strength and grace. His pal'loch was ten kilos of metal.

"This is not a minotaur weapon. Are you a fanboy or something?" the Ascendency asked Shantu.

Shantu stiffened and said flatly, "A minotaur forged it; therefore, it is a minotaur weapon."

"Printed on the ship?"

"Yeah."

"I won't hold it against you then." The Ascendency returned the weapon and turned to me. "Your tet please."

I offered it to him handle first. Because apparently that was what we were doing today.

He swung it around and seemed unhappy before returning it. "That needs some work."

"As do I," I said, returning to the minotaur tradition of never stop working on yourself.

"I have a challenge for you," Piper said, resuming control of the conversation. "I want tactile sensation based on him and her. I want Monolith to act as a randomizer."

The kid smiled. "Oh, that *is* a challenge."

Piper tossed up a local workspace, showing their new configuration. They would have an undergrow mapped to a human emotional color wheel.

But I quickly grew bored as Piper and the Ascendency talked technobabble about sensors and feedback.

I was going to adapt Piper's frame to become a mass of walking dicks and balls. However, I got lost in the doodling.

I was also irritated that I didn't have access to my feed. I wanted to message Sheila and see how her day was going and send her stills of what was going on here. I wished they would have at least let me set my status to away.

"Piper, I like this," Shantu said, hovering over my shoulder.

I was fucking around with filigree patterns, experimenting with all the ways I could make them move and dance. Mostly, I was trying to be out of the way as Javelin lent her expertise as both a woman and someone with prosthetics. But him putting the spotlight on me made me feel like a kid showing macaroni art to the parent I never had.

He shoved me to take my seat on the couch. The couch had space for six to sit comfortably, but he just wanted the spot preheated by my ass. I relented only after the appropriate amount of wrestling.

He attached emotions to the patterns I was playing with. Anger to the little pointy triangles. Rage pulsed those into stabbing spikes. Happiness made the filigree wave into vibrations. Sadness made the filigree look wilted.

Piper looked at Javelin, who gave the slightest smile.

It was the first time in two years that her face showed something other than contempt, scorn, or irritation. Even unconscious, she looked ready to murder someone.

Seeing Javelin smile was a wash of relief over my soul that I didn't know I needed. I imagined it was like that moment fathers have when holding their newborns and waiting for them to take their first breath.

I don't know what I'm talking about.

I met Shantu's eyes, and he was *not* having the same moment I was. Somehow, he made the filigree rubbing flourishes together *suggestive*. He smiled the biggest shit-eating grin I had ever seen him with. My disgusted face must have told him that he nailed whatever he was aiming for.

He gave me a giant bear hug and pinned my arms down. "I love you, man!"

"Ugh!" I shouted. "Get off me!"

He kissed my cheek before releasing me. Piper laughed, Javelin scowled, and things reset to default.

Piper abandoned their project to make mine the primary. "Think you can do it?" they asked the Ascendency.

The Ascendency nodded in slow contemplation. "Let's use the filigree for your eyebrows and lips. If you want to slide into the human spectrum without falling into the uncanny chasm, you'll need expressive eyebrows."

I tried to place the eyebrows. It wasn't going well. They looked wrong.

Javelin actually understood the tools of the program. She got the eyebrows and lips aligned appropriately, not too perfectly.

"This is good. I like it. I have never seen this before. It's Eldar meets *I, Robot*. You're getting the ears," the Ascendency said, adding the ears. "How many piercings do you want? Never mind. You can sort that out."

The view shifted, and data about their inner workings expanded. The Ascendency collapsed. I only made it one step before he spoke from the overhead speakers.

"Leave it! We have work to do. Okay, okay. Here we go!"

A drone-dolly thing lifted the body—shell?—or whatever and removed it.

The workspace then expanded like in a movie about cyber-security. Everything was in code with overlapping menus and warning prompts.

I turned down my feed's opacity and tapped Shantu. "Do you think all the stories about wizards and stuff are actually about this shit?" I gestured to Piper and Javelin.

He laughed and dug deep for his narrator voice. "The princess brought their companions…"

"Warrior companions," I corrected.

"Warrior companions after a long and arduous journey with many hard-won battles."

"We had *two*."

"The starliner was a campaign."

I turned the corners of my mouth down but nodded to yield the point.

"Before the wizard—"

"Wait. Is it a wizard or a god? You know, disembodied voice, use of avatars…"

His eyes tried to look at his eyebrows, the human version of a loading screen. "Spirit of the temple," he said in a normal voice. He then cleared his throat before going back to his narrator voice. "The princess brought their party before the spirit of the temple…"

If I knew Shantu, he would avoid a Pinocchio reference that would torpedo his relationship.

"…which would give them the tools to speak the language of their new companions and unlock the beauty within."

"Wait. Piper's getting boobs?" I asked.

He smiled like the giant child he is. But then stuck out his lip and pouted. "I don't get to pick them." He dropped the act before I smacked him. "I do get to pick the texture of their skin though."

"You were doing so well when it was about communicating," I said.

His face turned distraught.

"What?"

"Scout tells me I'm high risk for rejection for mods."

"What…?"

"After the drop, Scout went over everyone's records with a fine-tooth comb. I'm a bad candidate for implants. We couldn't get the halo thing to sync. So, it fell on Piper to become more expressive outside of VR. Even then, they can't do it at the same pace. Think of text messaging and scrolling through memes to find the right one."

He had mentioned his frustration on the communications front but hadn't talked about his medical stuff yet. We really hadn't had the chance because we were running around and putting out fires constantly on the ship.

I searched my messages and found the one he was talking about. It was marked read, but I had forgotten about it. There was a list of drugs I was resistant to. Something about my mu receptor. Scout had attached suggested alternative drugs and what went right and wrong from my surgeries. From what I could tell, I was a pain in the ass to sedate, and they had to get creative.

Anyway, after way too long, because Scout is *thorough,* I found the clinician interpretation of assessments from my predeparture medical screening. The assessments also said I was a poor candidate for implants. Apparently, it was not that uncommon for spacers but rare for the general population.

"Huh… Me too," I said, reading some of the linked documents. "Scout wants us to get cloned, so we have replacement organs. Super freaky… They won't have a brain."

"So, here's the deal," the Ascendency said. "I can set this up, and you can run it like an avatar and figure it out yourself, or I can slave the whole setup to autonomic."

"Slave it," they said without hesitation.

They met Shantu's eyes, and silent words passed between them.

I knew that look. Shantu was smitten.

Ugh.

"If I do that, there may not be a coming back," the Ascendency said. "It'll—"

"Don't mansplain my body to me," they said. "I knew what I was doing when I came here. That's why I came to you. There's no one else I trust to do the work."

"All right, all right. No need to get testy."

They started to talk about embedded polymers, and I knew what was on the menu and wanted no part of it.

"Nope, nope, nopety, nope, nope," I said, starting for the door. "I'm happy for y'all, but I'm going to be somewhere else."

"There's a gaming pod, you prude," Shantu said. "Go check out while we have all the fun."

Piper slapped him upside the head.

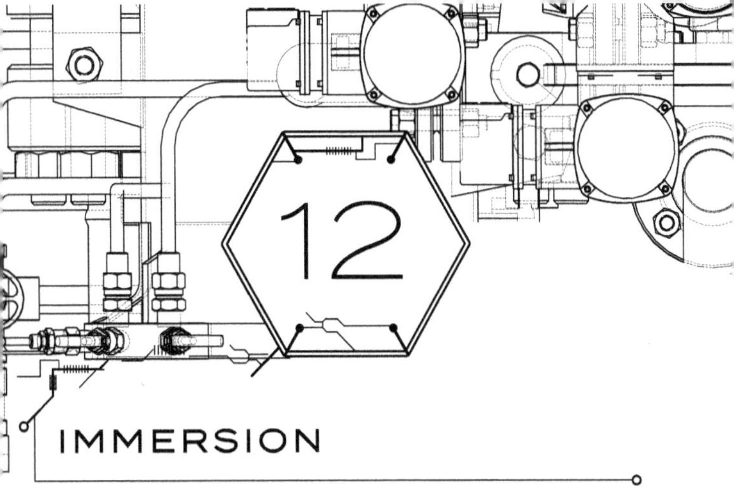

IMMERSION

522.276.0500 Undefined District, Fermi Station

I **EXPLORED THE** gaming pod as they got gross. Right now, it was a fancy gaming chair with feedback with gloves and boots. I wouldn't call it a pod because it wasn't enclosed.

I selected the game *The Trenches of Metal and Magic,* a steampunk fantasy shooter that's title card had a wizard blocking a tank shell with energy from his hands.

My feed blocked a bunch of features before I found the right setting for gaming mode.

The game started with breathtaking cinematography, explaining the discovery of aether channeling that led to an arms race and the clash of the Allied and Central powers. I went back and watched it again. It was an immersive flight through the magical breakthrough and how it was supposed to unite humanity in a new age of wonder and discovery until the two opposing ideologies.

The Central powers represented technological progress and industrialization. The Allied powers represented a return to nature and how the aether could be used to enhance organic life.

It was a ride through discovery, investigation, experimentation, and implementation in every field of science.

I canceled out of a menu to watch the cinematic again before starting the character creation, which sat me in a barber's chair with the dehumanizing tradition of shaving one's head on entry to military service.

I didn't spend much time crafting my avatar. I just picked something that generally looked like me. Each time I changed a feature of my face and build, the barber walked in front of the mirror to avoid me watching my avatar mutate in real time.

...

Javelin cut the power to the gaming rig.

...

I deleted like forty hours of me screaming at NPCs and other players in the game.

...

Supported by my ferret familiar, I was arguing with tree-people over the morality of escalation and provocation in a war. I don't know if the tree-people were a player faction or a part of the main story arc.

"What the fuck?!" I barked at Javelin as she ripped the goggles off my head.

Her stone face held no reaction to my outburst.

She pointed to a spot on the deck, where I was to stand at attention. She didn't yell, scream, or order me to do physical training. She just stared at me.

That was worse, and I wish I could explain the anxiety racking my body as she stood silently. I wished she would punch me in the face, train me, and berate me.

I'll talk to Scout about it.

Javelin held me at attention eye to eye. Almost nose to nose with me. Her cybernetic eye moved with mechanical muscle mirrors to her organic eye.

My heart ached for her.

My understanding of cybernetics was at the show level and some curious searches through the ship's library but no formal training. So, take this with a grain of salt.

What does that mean?

Anyway, muscle mirrors were supposed to be uncomfortable but significantly shortened rehab time by keeping nerves active. If my memory was right, they were supposed to be used for less than three months.

What was she waiting for?

There should be a facility on station that could do her surgeries.

I stood at attention nose to nose with Javelin, and behind that wall of ice and disdain she radiated was fear.

I could smell it.

Fear of the unknown kept her clinging to familiar pains.

Who was Javelin without her rifle, without her duties to the ship?

An image entered my head. A little bird. A little girl. Small and alone. Broken wings dragging behind as she trudged forward, destination unknown.

That little girl carried something in her arms.

Something precious.

Something valuable.

Something important.

My curiosity reached out for what was in the little girl's arms.

Feral RAGE swiped at me. Images of lions, bears, and other mighty beasts charged at me with wild abandon.

Panic pulled the ejection handle in my mind, and I slammed back into my body with a beeping of my HUD alerting me of heart rate and blood pressure changes for both me and Javelin.

Javelin and I had triggered combat protocols with our physiological changes.

As I'm getting this down, I checked my feed. It looks like I was waiting for a proper smoking. That is not the experience I had.

I'm not going to confirm my experience with Javelin though because she mauled the shit out of me in that scenario.

Anyway.

Piper pulled us from that nebulous place of emotional secrets.

They shined in a golden prideful glory. Their filigree waved and vibrated, letting me see their happiness and excitement for the first time. Their eyes, eyebrows, nose, and lips made it increasingly difficult to not see a beautiful woman.

There was that thing though. She—THEY—were naked.

I don't know how or why Shantu and I are so far apart on this.

I was taken aback by everything that was Piper.

They walked up to me and hugged me. They were warm and smooth, almost silky. "Thank you, James," they said. "You've helped complete me."

I melted.

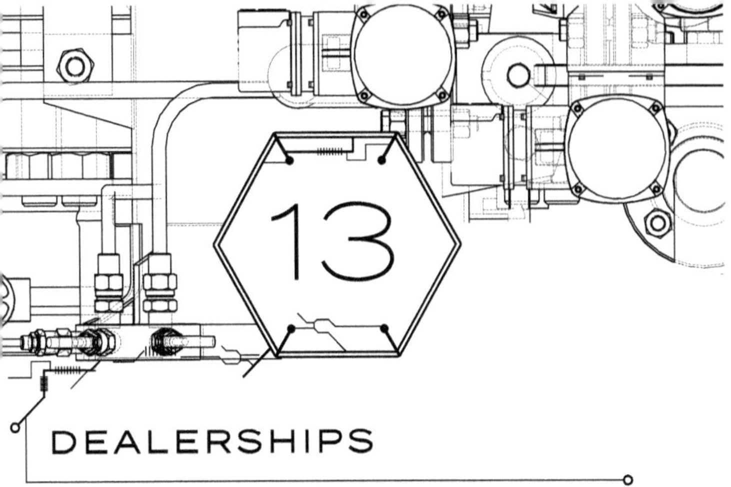

13

DEALERSHIPS

JAVELIN SENT SHANTU and me a message that we had to be at an armor dealership in less than an hour.

Rude as shit!

No "Good morning." No "Hey, this is short notice."

Just "Be here." And the location.

Shantu and I got dressed in our spiffy new suits and scrambled to meet her at Steadfast Armature Service Center. She declined to answer any of our questions about why it was so important to get there right fucking now.

"I have transport enroute," she messaged, not acknowledging our complaints or protests.

The cab we took was this super-weird-crab thing that crawled through maintenance corridors. It used a specialized lock to enter a fluid line. I think it shot a big eel thing with a rapid-fire weapon. I couldn't really tell. When it exited the fluid line, it launched missiles at some kind of hive structure. Greenish fire flashed. That should mean copper burning in an oxygen environment.

I don't know.

Shit happened too fast, and we were in the armor dealership, getting pestered by salespeople before I could process getting shaken like a bug in a can.

Why does every dealership have off-white floors and glass walls? I thought Telex's was nice because it was clean and shiny. Now, here I am hundreds of light-years from Vanguard, and it's the same shit.

I don't know how to express how disappointing it is to be on a magical-fucking-space-urchin-hive-planet-city-station and walk into something so underwhelming.

I just got out of a crab that shot missiles at… Bugs…? Yeah, I'm going with bugs. I didn't see what was in the hive thing. It looked like it was made from that expanding foam stuff. But now I was at a dealership!

This was stupid.

What made that hive? Why did it need to get shot with like ten missiles?

I did love the distribution pattern though—with its even spacing, symmetrically opposing impacts, and coordinated detonation.

Someone named Rodger greeted us. "Good morning. Coffee?"

I was not excited to share DNA with this sales critter.

He was younger than me but not by a whole lot. He had this nervous excitement of someone happy to have their first job. My read on him was that he was sticking to the script in lieu of experience.

There was a gulf between Rodger and me.

A portion of my consciousness isolated the gulf and put it in the background. I knew he wasn't a threat. Even if he was armed, I was reasonably confident I could disarm and subdue him without injuring anyone.

Around the sales floor, the only real threat was some lady with smartly dressed security following her around nearby in another cubical. Her security looked ready for business, not twitchy but professional. She wasn't the eye candy she pretended to be was the *real* threat though, the classic femme fatale.

And that woman triggered every alarm I had.

—HAZARDOUS—

—STAY THE FUCK AWAY—

—NOTHING GOOD WILL COME FROM MEETING HER—

Rodger didn't have those alarms. His eyes kept drifting over to her. That poor sumbitch.

Monitors around the showroom showed Steadfast armors getting abused in both combat and industrial accidents as displays of durability. The floor models silently cycled through firing positions.

I hated Rodger unfairly because too many of the salespeople at Telex's were the predatory douche canoe who commission-based jobs attract. It was more of a question if he would develop the cutthroat attitude needed to survive in sales or move somewhere that was a better fit.

Javelin's stoic nature made me realize that today might be the day he finds out if he wants to stay in sales. What information did she have, and why didn't she want Shantu and me spoiling the surprise?

Shantu and I took our coffee mugs and politely drank, while she translated our combat profiles into our armor order and a training curriculum. Was this how rich kids felt when their parents took them to get their first car?

Mommy Javelin buying us new clothes for school… Hehe…

Javelin, if you hear this, please don't kill me.

Fuck that! Don't go through my shit! This is private! Scout or whatever psychologist follows him are the only people with privileges. So, fuck off!

I'm sorry. Don't kill me.

Anyway, Rodger's office had just a few transparent walls separating us from the rest of the sales floor and the identical offices. He had a plant and a picture of a cat on display. He also had an assortment of toys and other schwag proudly displaying Steadfast Armature emblems.

I hid behind the provided coffee mug, afraid to speak.

"Clarify something for me, Rodger," she said, turning his name into a vulgarity. "Is this facility operating inside Vanguard or the minotaur jurisdiction?"

What the fuck?

Our briefings explained that Vanguard and the minotaur governments had a porous border that created wealthy districts that benefited from overlapping infrastructures. From what I understood, both governments looked away because it was good for commerce and relations.

"Why do you ask?" he asked.

She pulled up the End User License Agreement, which had dense provisions about safety and maintenance. She then pulled up a lawsuit between The Huntsman Group and Steadfast Armature. The headlines were about Steadfast remotely disabling features of their armor behind a paywall.

"We are from a free trade ship," she said. "Our flight schedule does not allow for time-sensitive updates nor maintenance at an authorized facility."

Rodger pulled up present packages for maintenance plans and other things that would multiply the costs of our armor.

"I'm going to stop you right there," she said with menace.

It took every gram of discipline to not shrink away.

Rodger didn't have that discipline and noticeably flinched.

Shantu had a large smile on his face. The same one he got when he was watching sports, and someone did a big play.

I still don't sports-ball.

"If you can't authorize whatever executive package your actual executives get for their personal protective detail, you need to get me someone who can," she said. "Let me clarify. We need armor that has the bios completely unlocked. No access by your company through the firewall unless we are specifically authorizing it. No ads, no demos, no data gathering…" She went through so much legal shit and loopholes that it spoiled my desire for armor.

Why would you buy armor from a company that would remotely turn it off during combat if you didn't pay for their subscription services? Oh, right. Because they all did it.

The real money wasn't in the armor. It was in letting it take a bit of damage and charging the absolute most to get it fixed.

Javelin was citing cases where people were killed because of that shit.

"I-I need to get my supervisor," Rodger said, sweat beading his forehead and upper lip.

Let's see how much you like sales, Rodger…

A connection error prompt appeared in my feed.

"Just who the fuck do you think you are!" a yell came from behind two security people.

Shantu moved first. He leaped like a spider monkey, putting his feet onto the transparent bulkhead and pulling security person number one into the tiny office before they could raise their weapon.

I don't know how to explain to people who haven't *been there* with people they trust. They do something, and you go with it. They fire, and you fire in the same direction and figure out the target afterward. You roll with them, even if it's off a cliff.

I dove into security person number two, sending us sprawling out of the little sales office and into the main showroom. In the fray, I landed my tet in their armpit, prying through the armor plates.

"MOVE AND DIE!" I barked in a voice I had never used before.

It was the command voice that Sgt. Tok used, strong and authoritative. Almost like he was shouting for me. I had never *COMMANDED* anything like that before, especially with someone's life hanging in the balance.

It scared me.

A circle of startled salespeople and clients parted around me and my pinned security person, almost illustrating the range of my will.

Then everything was still.

I met both private security people's eyes as I swept the showroom for more targets. I might be able to get one but not both.

My tet was in the sweet spot under the security person's left arm. Blood was dripping from where I had pierced the armor. Any deeper, and it would hit the pumping pipes, as Sgt. Tok liked to put it. If they tried to bring their left arm down, they would drive my tet into their own heart.

It was weird. I held this person's life in my hands, and all I could think was: NAILED IT!

"That's who we are," Javelin said coldly. She had a well-built person by their throat. Her mechanical fingers dug into their neck muscles, careful of their windpipe.

The man wet himself.

"Anyone dead?" she asked us.

"Negative," Shantu said.

"Are you okay?" I asked the security person I was on.

Flicked their wrist, discarding their sidearm, and gave a thumbs-up.

I then shouted to Javelin. "Negative!"

The security armor could rip me in half, but now it held its user hostage because of me and my tet.

My feed had shifted to a HUD again, and I released a breath

I was holding, noticing how little my heart rate changed in this life-and-death struggle.

If the roles were reversed, I would have crushed my head with this armor and taken my chances with bleeding out.

"What is all this?!" a man shouted, pushing his way through the onlookers.

My pistol sight found an older man with a similar suit to mine. He stopped when he seemed to notice I was aiming for his head. He held his hands out to the sides, not up.

Peculiar.

"What is it you want?" the man said, his composure steel.

Javelin waited a beat before answering. "To buy some armor."

"Sh-she attacked me." The well-built person was on the verge of tears.

"Hush now. The adults are talking," Shantu said in a loud whisper.

"Why are you holding my employee by the neck?" Ol'Steely asked.

"Sh-she's threatening us," the well-built person said.

Javelin and Ol'Steely seemed to ignore him while studying each other.

"Our feeds were cut, and armed security personnel interrupted what should have been routine negotiations," she answered in a straight-to-the-facts tone. "We responded to the threat level appropriately. Furthermore, your other employee refused to answer jurisdictional questions, meaning there may be no governing body to whose laws we are subject to."

"I apologize for any inconvenience." Ol'Steely shifted gears with amazing precision. "You said you're here for armor. Just so happens that we specialize in it. Maybe my office will be a better venue."

What *the fuck* is happening?

"Feed first," she said.

"Sir!" the well-built person shouted.

Ol'Steely kept his hands out as he approached them. "Where is it, Mick?"

Javelin locked her eyes on Ol'Steely and stood as rigid as a statue against the big well-built person struggling. Ol'Steely ruffled through their pockets, tossing items onto the floor. I saw a vape and two pistols among them.

The guard I was kneeling on knocked on the deck and pointed at their back with minimal movement.

"On your back?" I asked.

They nodded.

"Javelin," I called. "Uh, little help here."

"Tombstone, help Monolith," she ordered.

Ol'Steely raised his right hand into a fist, I assume ordering security to stand by.

"Nice fucking hit!" Shantu said to me before addressing the security person. "Can you lock your armor down?"

Our answer was whirrs and clicks.

It took both me and Shantu straining to roll the guard enough to get to the tablet in its socket on their back.

I gave it to Javelin, who put it in Mick's hand. The device unlocked, and our feeds reconnected. She took a step forward, so Mick landed on his ass when she released his throat.

"Stand down, lead?" Shantu asked.

"Stand down," she ordered.

"Medic!" I shouted.

A compact white bot pushed its way through the crowd of onlookers. I pulled its tablet, and my feed translated the symbols into Common. I tagged my tet as a penetrating foreign body.

The bot popped my tet out with mechanical violence before disassembling the torso armor. It cut through the liner, and a pair of beautiful pink breasts appeared. I hadn't realized the guard was a woman. Not that it mattered.

Tits, however, were distracting.

The med bot thrust tools into the security person's chest and flushed the wound before closing it. It stopped asking the security person if they needed additional medical care before informing them that they're overdue for a reproductive health screening.

Shantu laughed. "Do you want a Pap smear with your thoracotomy?" He turned on me. "Wait until I tell Takakoa about this. You were inside another woman!"

A small chuckle circulated through the crowd, and the tension began to release.

"I'm sorry," I told the security person. "He's an asshole."

I didn't know what made it through the helmet because they didn't respond. I hoped the bot gave them pain meds.

"Zoe, go to medical. Mick, stay right the fuck where you are," Ol'Steely ordered. "Where's Rodger?"

"Right here, Mr. Jones," Rodger answered from the corner of his office.

"What happened here?" Mr. Jones asked.

I like calling him Ol'Steely.

"Sir, they didn't want a maintenance plan or a-any subscription, and the lady said something about bios, and I didn't know what she was talking about, so I pinged M-Mr. Mick."

"I was monitoring him from my station, and she brought up the Huntsman suit," Mick added.

Ol'Steely pinched the bridge of his nose and scrunched his face in a way that aged him twenty years. "Mick, you're fired. Talk to personnel."

"You can't fire me!" Mick shouted. "Do you know who my father is?!"

"*Was!*" he barked. "He's retired. The Huntsman suit is all anyone is going to talk about until the next disaster takes the limelight off us. The fact your response was to bring in security

instead of addressing their concerns means you don't have..."
He took a deep breath and looked around.

"They as—"

"What was your plan, Mick?!" Ol'Steely's composure slipped into frustrated yelling. "Hold them? Execute them? Then what?! What happens when the rest of their merc buddies come looking? This one has a pal'loch. He's friendly with the minotaur! You're a danger to yourself and everyone around you. Effective immediately, all your access and privileges are revoked pending an investigation for your termination."

"You can't..."

"I *have* to. You can't arrest people for wanting to bargain. Who do you think buys our armor? Mercs, miners, and military. They all have people who do research for anything we've done wrong so they can get a better rate. That's why I've written pricing guidelines." He sighed and turned to other security people. "I don't know why I'm wasting my breath. Get him out of here."

The other security people dragged Mick off.

I liked Ol'Steely. I got the feeling that if we were being belligerent, he would have had us splattered. However, he took the best option presented.

Ol'Steely gestured for us to follow him. I cleaned the blood from my tet and followed him into his office. His transparent bulkheads overlooked the showroom floor. The large office was comfortable, decorated with small models of armor. Competing for the space were photos of company events and I assume his family. He hung his jacket on the back of his plush office chair and fell into it, rubbing his neck.

A big white and orangish-brown dog appeared from behind his big wooden desk.

HE HAD A DOG! HE HAD A FUCKING DOG! I had never seen a dog in person before...

"Okay. I need to reset before we continue," Ol'Steely said. "I'm getting lunch. You're welcome to join me, or I can message you when I'm done."

"Is that a dog?" I asked, unable to contain myself.

"Can I pet it?" Shantu said. He pushed his pal'loch toward me while falling to the floor.

I looked around to find a place to put our weapons and found Javelin

Ol'Steely seemed taken aback by our rush to disarm in the presence of his furry companion. "S-sure… Just have a seat, and I'll send her over to you. Her manners aren't the best though. She's just getting past her puppy stage."

Shantu and I plopped onto the seats like the excited children we were.

"Go say hi, Chelsey," he said to the dog.

Chelsey pulled a rubber squid thing from under his desk with her mouth. She then darted over to me, pressed it into my lap, bounced back, and barked.

I looked at him and picked up the squid. She darted over to me again and snatched it. The squid made a squeaking noise as she shook it violently. She then ran around the desk twice before taking the squid to Shantu.

So, Chelsey ate like an hour, maybe two. If you don't know, dogs are super soft, and if they lie on their backs for belly rubs, it's the best thing ever.

"How would she do in space?" I asked.

The way Javelin and Ol'Steely glared at me, I might have interrupted something important. But I didn't care. I was playing with a dog.

"If I ever had to travel with her, she would do the journey in a pod," Ol'Steely said. "Tell you what, let my marketing—"

"No," Javelin said, cold. "Despite today's events, we try to keep a low profile."

That was that.

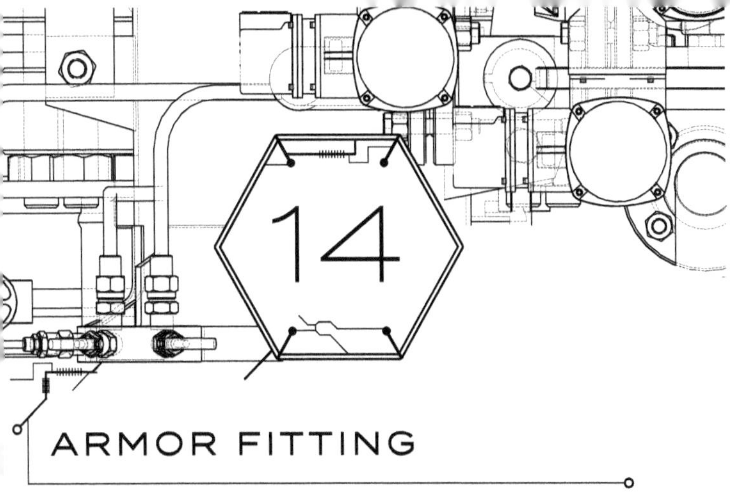

14

ARMOR FITTING

THE ARMOR FITTING area was just a different level of the Steadfast facility. It was not as badass or as exciting as the movie montages make them out to be at all. Maybe it was the lack of theme music and editing.

The level was a gym-meets-hospital-meets-garage centered around a big obstacle-course-jungle-gym thing. The deck was that shock absorbent matting found in every weight room. A blue track of the same material served as a separation for equipment stations.

Some equipment I recognized from Telex's, and some I didn't. There was the expected assortment of material-shaping tools: drills, grinders, rams and vices, and whatnots. Everything was fancy with vacuum hoses and lights. The other equipment was specialty for armor, and I could only speculate at their uses.

There was an air of danger on this level, like working at a construction site. It made me painfully aware of how squishy humans were.

At least it wasn't that off-white bullshit from the sales floor.

Getting armor is a process that's not just a transaction though. There's a bit to it. Here's what I learned:

Step one: Get your biomechanics measured. If the armor doesn't move around right, it can snap your head off your shoulders. That's really important.

In the provided leotard, I emerged from the small changing room, and Shantu exploded into laughter. "Keep laughing, fuckstick," I snapped. "You're next."

"Dude! I can see every wrinkle of your balls!" he managed to sputter between laughs.

I looked down. The material was thick enough to only show an outline. The outfit was light and formfitting but not constricting. Just enough support to not feel naked.

"You're going to taste yours." I chased him into the small changing room while miming kicking him in the groin.

The tech person nearby gestured to an alcove with a pair of wide-open boots.

I stepped into the boots. They clamped down and adjusted to my feet. The alcove then assembled a measuring exo-frame around me with fast-moving robotic arms. The arms presented gloves that locked the exo-frame at the wrists. The helmet used inflatable pads around the jaw and crown to secure my skull.

"Okay. Take a lap," the tech person said before I could inspect the frame.

Shantu managed to slap my ass around the frame. After a few strides, the exo-frame calibrated, and the extra weight vanished. I did a lap on the track, getting passed by people further along in the process, and came back to our tech person.

The tech person went down their gambit of situations—standing start to sprint, walking to sprint, run and jump, roll, lie down and get up...

"Think Sgt. Tok would yank power cells and make us run in these?" I joked to Shantu as he finished his exercises.

"Good luck," the tech person said. "They're eighty-five kilos. The final has your armor at two-ten, give or take. Another twenty for the riot shields."

Shantu looked at me. "He'd definitely make us do laps in them."

The tech person looked stricken. "Well shit… That's a completely different drive system." They fervently tapped on their pad but then smiled.

Shantu and I exchanged slightly irritated looks.

"I didn't mess it up. It was in your initial order but didn't get passed along."

Shantu and I simply stared at them.

"Mostly, we sell two styles of drive systems. Integrated, which lock down with power loss. They're more durable but harder to repair. They're also safer because you're not at the mercy of how you fall. On the other hand, we have clutched, which disconnects the drives from the actuators. They're easier to repair but can't take the same punishment that the integrated systems can."

The tech person offered us bottled sports drinks and beamed with professional pride.

"*It fits* just isn't good enough. We make armor that will fit you if you're stuck in it for a year with no support," they continued. "If you have to walk twenty or thirty thousand kilometers across a planet to get to a crash site, we're the ones you want."

"What if I get fat?" Shantu joked.

"Then take your hover chair here, and we'll get you back into shape," they answered without humor. "We have projections of your ideal combat size." They tossed up renderings of us that were only a hair bulkier than we already were—a far cry from the ideal superhero body I was expecting.

"Ha!" Shantu pointed at the seventeen percent muscle mass gain for my glutes. "Even the computer knows you don't have an ass!"

I ignored him. I was in good shape, but I didn't think I was that close to anyone's ideal shape. However, I wasn't the skinny kid who was told to go around obstacles anymore.

"Really? I don't have to double my muscles and shed all my fat?" I asked.

"No," the tech person said with a shrug. "That's not really healthy, and your caloric needs would go through the roof to maintain that kind of muscle mass."

Step two: Get to training. In the best armor, with all the features in the galaxy, you still need to learn how to use it. If you don't, you're a danger to yourself and everyone around you. The same as any other piece of equipment, I suppose.

The tech person used the same alcove to swap us from the measuring rig to the adjustable training exo-frame. It was a polymer version that was weighted and balanced to mirror the armor we were getting.

Once we could safely move, we were cut loose to play. The rest of the day was spent playing dodgeball with balls of various densities and other games that help relearn how to move.

"Why the fuck didn't we have this on the ship as a zero g exercise?" Shantu stood on one hand with his foot in a virtual sphere.

"I'm hearing you're looking for those training credits." My arms shook as I tried to change hands in this inverted moving version of Twister.

"Why not? Aren't we going to be senior crew?" He fell but popped back into it.

We moved on to these little plastic puzzles, and the tech person walked us through how to set the dynamic force application settings. Long story short: It was another process we needed to learn.

This exercise in frustration was the difference between picking someone up by their uniform and ripping their heart out of their chest. It took time to learn as well.

The movies where they just jump into armor and conquer the world were such bullshit.

The tech person got relieved at some point, and I missed it, but I'm going to treat them as one person. Anyway, they got through the checklist, and we were green lit for another training floor.

We knew Dire-horn was in the loop because he was making us sign a lot of documents for the showroom *incident.* In return, we were given a maintenance station for our armor with all their cybersecurity stuff removed, and there were a bunch of intellectual property agreements to it. The gist was we could not sell it for two years, and only people who signed an NDA were allowed to service the armor.

No one ever talked about the amount of documentation that went into what we do. *Everything* was documented. I understood the logic, but fuck, it was tedious.

Anyway, Dire-horn appearing in his workout tights was *not* on the agenda. I thought he was still on the ship with the captain, arguing over work rates, material costs, and all that shit. Not *with* the captain but on his behalf in meetings with contractors and whatnot.

"I have come to introduce you to the dynamic phalanx," he announced from behind us.

"What the shit! What are you doing here?!" Shantu hugged one of Dire-horn's arms. "You missed it! He stabbed some chick in the tit—"

"It was the armpit, and they were security," I snapped. "Don't tell people I go around randomly stabbing other people!"

"Doesn't matter. They were being dicks. They got the drop on us *in armor*!"

"It was that light secur—"

"Shut up! It was fucking awesome!" He worked the leotard up to show the bruise filling in around his shin.

"Did you have too much sugar today? What the fuck?"

We kind of spiraled from there as the tech person stared, wide-eyed. After Dire-horn managed to wrangle in Shantu, he made us watch a short educational video on the basics of dynamic phalanx.

Yep. Like the Romans with their shield walls. Except now, it was with all the bells and whistles of modern combat—point defense, ECM, active camouflage, and so on.

The ablative armor had a shield that was a meter and a half tall and had a few slots for gadgets. The real decisive advantage was the distraction. Human, minotaur, and a few other species liked to "feel with fire," where they engaged inappropriately.

Let me explain it like this. Imagine two squads of ten with equal strength. One had a two-person phalanx, and the other had a heavy weapons team. The squad with the heavy weapons would overcommit to defeating or pinning the phalanx. That, historically and statistically, would cost the heavy weapons team's victory.

According to Dire-horn's video anyway.

During the video, I saw him trying to be subtle with his gestures as he worked in his feed. I would be lying if I said I wasn't disappointed that he wasn't really here. I could hear bits and pieces of his side of the conversation, his bass rumbling.

Intellectually, I knew his conversations swayed millions and billions of credits and set the pace for the overhaul of *The Happy Marauder*. Emotionally, I wanted him to get off his feed or go back to the office.

Eventually, Dire-horn surfaced into reality as we practiced against bots with polymer analogs. "Hold your ground against a superior foe," he roared as he sprinted into a flying kick.

If you've never been run over by a bull and lived to tell the story, you haven't lived.

A background app in my brain alerted me that he was probably feeling the frustration and irritation that I felt going through test and review. On top of that, there was the weird twitchiness that came with new environments and circumstances. Except he didn't get to go to the bar with us and blow off some steam.

"That all you got, HR minotaur?!" Shantu roared back.

What kind of idiot provokes a minotaur?

Dire-horn had separated Shantu's shoulder once in training, and since then, he had been more careful around us. Which just pissed Shantu off because it wasn't good training.

I appreciated not getting injured during training.

But as I looked around, I was pretty sure I saw some training people gesturing like they were placing bets on us.

"Again! Force must be met with force!" Dire-horn said, trying for a stern teacher, but it wasn't landing. This was the same guy who set up our wills and went over our contracts with the patience of a preschool teacher. He air-dropped his training curriculum. "There is more to learn that *they* won't teach you." He growled at the dealership's training staff before leaving to crawl under the pile of shit he was responsible for.

"Thanks, Dad!" Shantu yelled after him. "Glad you could make time for us."

I knew he was sincere.

The training staff resumed their program. All the good refreshers—breach and clear, repel, eliminate, extract, defend, escort and secures… Because we were different *breeds*. See what I did there?

I'm tired. Leave me alone.

522.281.0800 Steadfast Armature,
Undefined District, Fermi Station

Shantu's and my final challenge was to assault a village with an unknown layout and kill the militia warlords with minimum harm to the locals. A thin veneer for a test drive.

We shared irritated looks as the tech brought out polymer analogs of our armor. We knew the spiel, even if it was a suit of power armor and not a forklift. Shit, normally, we were the delivery guys who trained the customers on how to use it. It was weird being on the other side of the conversation.

This training room was printed polymer with a uniform dust that limited sensor range and gave everything a sandy slide. Shantu and I put on our professional faces while the tech person gave us our safety briefing.

The tech person then left, and the village rendered as some bland post-apocalyptic-desert-punk thing. I did my best to lean into the exercise, aware that someone was probably monitoring the tightness of my sphincters for my company profile.

Our map populated, and the village was centered around a spring, where water and food were rationed out by the local government. We held position in the nearby hills and observed. We fast-forwarded a day in under an hour. There wasn't a time restriction, so we were allowed a limited ability to simulate time passing with the showrunners having master control.

I don't know if it was the simulation procedurally generating random details or the showrunners rewarding our patience, but the time spent in observation yielded pay dirt. In my head, there was a person in a booth somewhere who just wanted lunch, and we were keeping them from that.

The pay dirt was a man who had been beaten and thrown off a roof of what we assumed was his home. The militia proceeded to loot the structure, fighting over a raggedy mattress. The victim survived and crawled away to a shack that looked decimated by an explosion or something. We designated him priority one contact as we observed the militia.

The militia sported salvaged mismatched armor that was roughly attached to labor exo-frames. They all had these half-meter missiles, unknown design and capability but no launcher.

"Do you think those missiles are self-guided or have a master controller?" I whispered to Shantu.

"I don't know," he muttered. "Let's assume there's some form of target designator. I'm afraid they came from a larger ripple fire point defense. Anyone in the village can be ordered to throw the missile, and it'll track and crater us."

"Worse. Their sensor packages are on, and they have much more surveillance than it looks like."

Shantu and I went full turtle, covering our shields with simulated sand while leaning on Sgt. Tok's and Wraith's cover and concealment training. We then crawled on a flat, smooth surface, trying to pretend it was the desert and not a polymer deck.

It was hard to keep my head in the game with the sound of plastic grinding across metal.

Couldn't they have done a cityscape, so the sounds made sense?

When Shantu and I got within audio range, the armor simulated building a language profile. Once enough cornerstones were found, it concluded it was Japanese.

The simulation paused, and a prompt filled my vision. It was an acknowledgment that all cultural simulations were not meant to harm anyone, and it was our fault for not filling out the parameters of the simulation. Blah, blah, blah. Don't sue us if we hurt your feelings.

This should have been done when we *entered* the simulation.

"Dude, let's go for broke we-are-the-holy-fist-here-to-smite-the-usurper kind of shit," Shantu said, his voice low.

I knew he wanted to make a show of it. I let him take the lead on contact.

"Do not raise any alarms or look any further for your salvation, good sir," Shantu said to our priority one contact. "We have been sent from the stars to bring unholy justice upon those deserving wrath. We know not the location or what forms it inhabits. It is our way to find the broken, lift them up, and let them guide the hand that will fell monsters and beasts. Those who would abuse their fellows."

The man chatted on, giving directions for the compound and about the militia symbols.

I tried to stay in line with our mission parameters. "Spread the word for those who wish to be spared the reckoning to come. Make sure they find themselves ready to defend their fellows. Give succor to those who cannot fight and give hope to the children."

"Succor? Really?" Shantu asked privately.

"Sounded good, right?"

I let him keep talking while I went over the map and planned a route during evening prayers. But that went to shit when the NPC ran into the local pub and started spouting off about angels.

I was pretty sure the game runners were fucking with us because they were bored.

The village freedom fighters flipped shit and thought a spy had infiltrated their network. The warlord's militia saw the runners and started mowing down the locals.

"Dire-horn's whole point was that these shields were distracting. Let's get to it," Shantu said with a shrug, his tone a jarring juxtaposition to the chaos around us. He then maxed out our external speakers. "We come for you, tyrant!"

Vibration packs shook the simulated armor. Our real armor would use the shields and chest plates as external speakers.

I took the left side because after my time in physical therapy, I was almost ambidextrous now. Throwing with my left was still weird but well above offhand minimums.

Shantu and I held our point defense in reserve for grenades and missiles as we rushed to the villagers' aid. Our shields absorbed the fire, and our HUDs filled with target data. The fake vibrating rifles and the smooth terrain made the whole simulation too easy and too fake.

"Dire-horn's soft, at least in training," I told Shantu. "Sgt. Tok would have had the missiles self-targeting. The militia used them as grenades, which were completely ineffective. And Gabe would have given us a juggernaut to fight at the end—just for the satisfaction of a boss fight."

Shantu didn't hesitate to open the feed to Dire-horn. "Dire-horn, I don't feel like we're being challenged."

Dire-horn snorted and gave us his honking laugh over the call. "Good. Because this is not training. This is *shopping*. These scenarios are for children whose parents want them to exercise during their video games. Every tree services its own roots."

What the fuck was he talking about?

15

NORMAL THINGS

OKAY. SO, THERE is a *huge* gap in my knowledge base. I've always thought the thing where people browse clothing and accessories while talking and imagining situations was just shameless product placement in movies.

It's a thing!

Takakoa and I spent *four hours* looking at dresses. She looked amazing in everything, but it seemed fun for her to try everything on and not buy anything at all. I aimed to act like the suave partners in shows who were happy to play cheerleader.

We were walking up and down the department store's racks with slight variations on the same shit I didn't understand. The value of items seemed to fluctuate without reason besides tags that said Sale or Limited Edition. It was pointless when I could fabricate comfortable clothing on the ship.

I guess not everyone had that option.

She would mention how beautiful the dress was and then complain about how the mass and volume didn't allow for her berth. "Seriously… I'm an aggie. You met me in a sports bra and shorts because I don't go to places that need dresses." Her tight braid was in the process of being freed into a majestic mane of jet-black fluffiness.

I dialed up the charm to eleven because this was her idea. "It's not about you. That dress needs you to fulfill its full potential. Otherwise, it's going to drop out of grad school and start stripping because she's mad at her father."

"You know I strip…" she tried to joke but couldn't hide the twinkle in her eye.

"Oh shit. Are you on the clock? What do I owe you?"

She laughed and hit my chest with the back of her hand.

Success!

"All right. Far enough," she said. "We do need to meet in the middle somewhere…" She flicked my hat and gently tugged at the lapels of my suit before pulling me in for a kiss.

"If you're asking for a suit, I know a place…" I said.

She smiled, but then her expression faltered. "I need to be honest. I checked up on you."

I raised an eyebrow, more curious than offended.

Her eyes defocused as she dove into her feed. "James August Childs. Born 500.08.15.2150."

"That's not accurate because that birth date was assigned to me at the institute. I didn't have the money for the teeth thing, where they find out your date of conception and your real birthday."

We migrated to a quieter corner of the clothing store. I wanted to check my manual for counter surveillance tools, but it didn't seem appropriate.

"Oh, I see the footnote," she said. "Childhood, blah blah blah. Emigrated in good standing to the FTS *The Happy Marauder*. Guild registration code, blah blah blah. Platinum class credit, nice. Ambassador Nguyen for the transfer of seventeen orphans."

I smiled. "What I'm hearing is that you're looking a gift horse in the mouth."

"What does that even mean?"

I remembered the rabbit hole I went down one day. "The expression used to be 'don't look a gift horse in the mouth.' The dental examination of burdened animals was used to gauge age and health, usually in barter. To do so with a gift animal was rude because, you know, it was a gift. Anyway, without reading into it too much, you're a smart, cautious woman."

In my head, I was whirling with scenarios. How serious was she? Was she…*the one*?

"You're not offended?" she asked warily.

I shrugged. "Should I be? We met at a brawling bar light-years away from Vanguard. Seems sketchy enough."

She seemed to accept it.

There was a long, awkward pause where it felt like neither of us knew what to say.

"Okay," she said like she was ending a trade negotiation. "You're not enjoying this. Let's get you some normal clothing and a backpack environment suit."

THANK THE STARS! "What the fuck is normal? I think, statistically, normal here is working the docks while suffering a hypoxic brain injury." I winced as the words left my mouth because of how insensitive they were.

Saluit was in the back of my brain, telling me how much of an asshole I was. I never did anything right around that woman.

"I don't understand decorative fabrics as social advertising," Takakoa said. "Maybe I've been in the military for too long."

"Fuck! I don't know," I exhaled. "I like the colors and textures."

"Yeah, it's something me and my mom…" A long moment passed. Her face then lit up with a bright smile. "Did I tell you how I got my name?"

I shook my head.

"My mom was in labor and all messed up from the pain drugs. She kept yelling, 'TAKAKOA! TAKAKOA!'" She snort-laughed as her eyes got lost in the memory. "Takakoa is a character from her favorite book series. She has a whole set of throw pillows but an extra one for that character. My mom wanted to bite onto that pillow because it didn't matter if she ruined it. My dad thought that was what she wanted to name me though. If you knew my dad, he wasn't one to argue. I was supposed to be Naomi. It wasn't until they were checking out that they realized what had happened."

It was that point in movies where I should share some equally funny anecdotes about my childhood. But I didn't have any. And I didn't want to get any of my trauma on her.

I politely laughed and did my best to hide how uncomfortable it made me. "That's awesome," I said through a forced smile.

"That's why I'm a Black woman with a Japanese name," she finished.

Thankfully, she didn't seem to notice my discomfort. The moment passed, and I got a few new casual outfits. The new clothes weren't as comfortable as the stuff I printed on the ship. But they were popular and middle end, so I didn't stand out.

The backpack space suit was neat though. I could reach back, pull the helmet over my head, and slide into the suit in a few seconds. One long fastener ran up the left leg like a wet suit and attached under the helmet. Not a huge fan of all the straps that keep you from puffing up like a marshmallow…

Once that was done, I tossed the local map between us and filtered out stuff I didn't want to do. One activity caught my eye. "I know one *normal* thing I would like to do." I selected a kinesiology clinic that offered massages.

Takakoa gave me a suspicious side-eye. "If you want to see me naked, that's not the right way to go about it."

"What is the right way?" I blurted, clearly not thinking with my brain.

"I think you know," she said in a sultry voice.

I did not. That was why I had asked…

I smiled anyway. "Have you ever had a massage?" I opened the kinesiology clinic, allowing her to look through the services menu.

"Not a professional one. I feel like everyone I've dated has tried that as a prelude to sex though…" She seemed like she regretted the words for a moment. "There's always someone, usually the med staff, setting up shop, but people get weird on ship."

I didn't press the issue. "Well, if you don't like it, you can pick the next thing we do."

She brightened. "Their menu looks more like a doctor's office than a whore house, so I'm in."

We went to the spa-pital. Soft green and blue tones were color coordinated with comfortable art. The place had a way of making my eyes drift around the room to appreciate it all. The faux wood paint had people in various yoga poses, and the medical art was simplified diagrams of medical items or their various evolutions over the centuries. They were winning at making a lobby not feel like a waiting room.

Takakoa opted to have us stretched out by physical therapists before the massage. We were led to a comfortable-looking room that mirrored the lobby, save the four padded tables. We changed into the provided pants and shirt. The soft white material had a nice silky texture to it.

"On ship, if we can, mind you, we stretch each other out before getting into our armor," she said. "The numbers say we get between ten and thirty percent better performance in combat conditions." She chuckled as two bald but friendly looking therapists arrived with some flimsy white boards. She leaned over and whispered. "This place is legit. They have bitch sheets."

"What now?" I asked because her smile was setting off alarms.

Not danger alarms. The new-guy-is-going-to-whack-himself-in-the-face-because-he-doesn't-know-what-he's-doing alarms.

One therapist asked, "What would you like your stop word or phrase to be?"

"Excuse me?" I looked between them and Takakoa.

"Our stop phrase will be 'I'm a bitch,'" she said wolfishly.

"What? No."

The therapist who spoke shrugged and pursed their lips. "Sir, it should be something that you would not say on accident. However, it shouldn't be something easily forgotten."

"Whose side are you on anyway?" I asked.

"Sir, as a matter of survival in uncertain times, side with the woman."

"Fine." I pointed at the polymer board. "What's the bitch sheet?"

The therapist's eyebrows came together and seemed vexed.

Takakoa fell into snorting laughter. She leaned against the table with her hand over her mouth, trying to suppress her snorts.

"Sir, I do not know what you are referring to," they said.

I tried to look at her for help, but she was too busy trying to control her laughter.

"We are medical professionals, not servants to be abused," the other therapist said, turning for the hatch.

"He's talking about the muscle strain monitor," she said between laughs. "We, in the VAF, call them bitch sheets because if you're not bitching, you're not stretching hard enough."

Everyone froze for a moment. The looks of understanding between her and the therapists almost made me leave. However, the tense moment passed, and the therapists slid back into their professional personas.

The therapist's work quickly taught me a new language in profanity. They stretched and pulled and wrestled me in ways no human was meant to bend, ignoring my protests and waiting for a chime from their gadgets. Takakoa seemed to be getting a harsher treatment but only growled and grunted, cut by the occasional laughter when I tried to summon a demon to destroy everyone.

"This is how people get kinks," I said while the therapist tried to pull my shoulders out of their sockets.

"Eh?" she grunted.

"Ow wow ow ow ow ow— Like urgha." I was steadily learning the difference between my body's painful limits and mechanical limits. "I am enjoying your laughter, but I am not enjoying making you laugh. I do not want the association."

After the therapists left, Takakoa and I lay there, looking at the multilayer overhead that gave the impression of looking up through the leaves on a sunny day.

A long moment of silence passed before she spoke. "I like what you said. I didn't even feel the PT. That's why I went quiet."

I didn't know if she meant physical training or therapist. Not that it mattered.

"I don't want a kink." Her tone was neutral, declarative. "I think I'm ready for a real relationship. No pressure on you, that is. But I'm tired of this immature, sham-shield shit that I won't take from my people."

I had no idea what the fuck she was talking about.

She glanced at me. "But for some reason, I'll take it in a relationship…"

When the pause stretched out too much, I asked, "What if I want the pressure?"

"What?"

"I mean, what if we give this a fair chance? You and me…"

She scoffed at the idea. "You're a merc. You chase the money. I'm an aggie. I go where I'm needed."

"Okay then. Treat this as a live fire exercise."

She gave me the side-eye. "What does that mean?"

I didn't have an answer ready, so I deflected. "What do you want it to mean?"

"Uh-uh… I'm on the verge of a personal discovery in my life, so you're going to have to do better than that."

Challenge accepted!

"I don't think either of us have had"—I threw up my hands for the quotes—"a 'real, healthy relationship.' And Scout tells me that transparency is the basis for any relationship…"

"Wait. The lizard guy with the big ears?" she asked without a hint of bigotry.

"The urglurk, yeah."

"Scout, the urglurk," she said in the way someone does when they were trying to get something to stick to their memory. "And he's giving relationship advice why?"

"He's our psychologist. As part of our contracts, we have to attend EQs."

Her blank face told me to explain.

"Expanded qualifications. It's a lot of *get better or get off the ship.* He does a lot of training on interpersonal communication, which keeps us from murdering each other in the long stretches."

"Didn't he fall on his dick the other morning?" Takakoa asked.

"Yeah. He landed on his dick. To save me from a slaver posing as a delivery person. So, be nice." My tone was more threatening than I intended. I tried to bring it around. "Anyway, I was saying that he says the pillars holding up the roof of a relationship are communication, boundaries, and compromise. I bring this up because I keep thinking about his lessons when I talk to you."

She screwed her face up. "You're relying on classroom education for a relationship?" Her disapproving tone was a backhand to the face.

"Like you, my previous relationships are *no-ot* something I should use as a guidepost. I'm trying to do better. I may have a lot of work to do, but if this has a built-in expiration date, why not get our money's worth?"

She seemed to be considering that when the massage

therapists walked in. They dimmed the lights and asked us to undress to our levels of comfort. They then asked about scents and pressure level. And…out I went.

I don't know if the massage was good or not because I passed out. Like lights-out-motherfucker passed out. A bot woke me with a voice that said to vacate the room.

"Did…did they drug us?" I said, extra groggy because no one was yelling, no alarm was blaring…

The memory of my first and only other massage surfaced. It was years ago, on the Vanguard City Space Elevator. Shantu and I had just gotten hired on *The Happy Marauder*, and we got our first real massage. He must have been holding a fart in his gut the whole time because when the massage therapists left, he let out the longest, loudest fart to ever come out of a human. I had retaliated by babooning the life out of him.

"What's going through your head?" Takakoa asked.

I explained, and she glared. I froze.

But before I died from holding my breath, she burst out laughing. "Sorry… I'm thinking of a similar story. Back when I was on the script, the conscript, I got extra duty for popping a guy with a towel and sending him to the medic. He screamed like he was dying. Okay. Before I continue, first off, I was aiming for his ass. Second, I had my towel wound just right, and third, he did that thing guys do when their balls stick to their leg. That long step. So, he comes out of the shower, and I see my target. During my windup, he takes that weird step, and instead of hitting his left cheek, my towel wraps around his leg and clips his balls. He ended up with a testicular torsion."

There's nothing better than a good big belly laugh… Well, maybe dogs.

She smiled, and it lit up my world.

16

MEETING THE FAMILY

TURNS OUT, I get antsy and weird if I don't keep to my exercise routine. Some—Scout—would call it anxiety with a dash of PTSR. Piper and Shantu tried to get me to stop my pacing and fidgeting during breakfast, but it turned into a shouting match.

I should treat my friends better when they're trying to look out for me…

Scout intervened, calmed everyone—mostly me—and explained I was under stimulated. This was part of our decompression. I needed to learn how to downshift from active combat and survival to clearheaded business calculations.

I was a hair away from being assigned as Javelin's shadow, to get training on business math, expense reports, contracting, and all that shit. But someone must have told Takakoa because the invitation to the VAF fitness center rescued me from that fate—until the end of leave when we were expected to take on additional management duties anyway.

Takakoa waited for me at the large transit air lock to escort me through the checkpoint into the VAF facility. The air lock was giant, for several trucks at a time. Drones darted around the vehicles. The nearby convenience store drew in foot traffic for people getting their vehicle or cargo inspected.

We transitioned away from that area and to the foot traffic corridors. There were still more people than I liked. The hustle and bustle of base life, I guessed.

The Vanguard base was clean, well-lit, and ventilated. Fruiting green walls surrounded the lavatories, the kiosks, and the vending machines. The smell of machine oils fought with the soil and the plants.

The distracting horticulture delayed how long it took me to notice the looks. It felt like I was in the wrong neighborhood, and I just got caught dealing.

"Why is everyone eyeballing me?" I whispered.

"You're not VAF, a lanky, or on the script," Takakoa said. "You walk funny. And you're with me..."

What the fuck did that mean? Was this some taboo?

"Lanky?" I asked.

"The skinny locals. Only call them that if you want to start a fight. Also, motherfucker is a compliment here, if you didn't know. Means you can satisfy a woman," she said flatly like she was giving a safety briefing, and I was a fresh recruit.

The bulkhead of the corridors we were traversing had displays for local award winners and upcoming events, along with the regular emergency information. No propaganda or those shitty motivational posters.

The movies totally lied about what a military base looked like. No people running in formation, chanting. If there weren't so many matching uniforms, I would think it was an upscale neighborhood...or a cult.

I pointed at some art. "Is that..."

"Sculpted with fléchettes. Yeah." She seemed irritated by it.

A piece of metal had been painted and then shot so that the paint flecked off. The mural was maybe two by three meters. It was of a dragon attacking a mountain village. Meteors rained from the sky like they were going to hit between the dragon and the village.

I thought it was awesome, but I kept that to myself.

She kept walking, while I kept getting distracted, wanting to linger at the variety of arts. My feed gave me data for each piece. There was a bowl of fruit that bordered on a sculpture because it was several centimeters thick with paint. Then a naked woman in the middle of some ballet jump viewed from the back that looked like a black-and-white photograph, but it was hand drawn with graphite on cellulose.

The pieces that were not a part of the bulkhead had armored shutters unobtrusively framing them, as well as purchase information. Most of the proceeds were donated to theater orphans.

"What's a theater orphan?" I asked bluntly.

"It's an NPO who—"

"NPO?"

"Nonprofit charity."

"What's the *o*?"

"Organization. It helps rebuild the places we smash. It's run by matygoi. Sweet, sweet, fuzzy things. Like a koala but almost completely incapable of violence." She laughed and seemed to get lost in a memory. "The couple I knew were known as Dickfart and Chlamydia."

Before I could ask about the phonetics of their language, she pressed forward.

"They don't have a sense of personal identity. So, some asshole gave them those names. The worst part is that they seemed to like them because it made us humans laugh. They're so sweet..." She laughed some more.

A kind-looking man with the same buzz cut everyone had in the Vanguard area approached us at the gym's entrance. She stopped in her tracks and stiffened.

"Gunny, how long have we known each other?" the man said in a severe sergeant's voice. His face didn't match his projected demeanor. He had too many smile lines, and his face didn't take to the scowl he had.

I could feel a joke coming.

"Sir, you were my gunny when I joined the unit," she answered flatly.

"I haven't ever seen morale this high." He took a moment to glance at me. "Whatever you're doing, keep it up. I won't keep you." He then walked away like he had left the stove on.

What the shit was that about? Did I just get Daddy's blessing?

Takakoa beamed, threw her arm around my waist, and steered me into the gym. The place was what I expected—free weights, standard exercise machines, donut track that simulates various gravities with harnesses and suits, and a wind tunnel for freefall training.

Midway into our routine, the sparsely populated gym started filling with mostly humans, a few minotaur, and the occasional other species I didn't recognize. They whispered about. She seemed to have noticed the whispering and knowing glances before I did though.

I thought everyone was just being polite and keeping the conversations low. But she stopped mid-set and slammed the bar back onto the rack before popping off the bench. She spun around—like she was deciding who she was going to kill first. Her face twisted into an ugly snarl. I hadn't seen that yet.

She was not Takakoa right now. She was GySgt. Houston.

The busy gym went stone fucking quiet. Even the ventilation decided to shut the fuck up.

GySgt. Houston's murder face landed on a target. "La Roux, you have twenty seconds to tell me what the fuck is going on before I revoke the birth certificate of every pile of meat in here and then refund their parents for the calories spent to make you all."

La Roux was a well-built ginger whose flushed exercise face turned pale.

An olive-skinned woman with the same short hair stepped forward and spoke up. "You cross the line, Gunny." She nodded toward the entrance.

Someone had taken pink glittery paint and wrote in artistically embellished cursive.

Lover's line, GySgt. Houston and the merc.

Shame washed over Takakoa's face as she looked at the footprints of glitter we had tracked all over the gym. "That's why the major was talking to me…" she muttered mostly to herself, I think.

Someone opened the air lock, and the kind man walked in with a shit-eating grin. "This is a first for you, Gunny. Let us know where you stand," he said with passion and vibrato and… pride maybe…

"First off," GySgt. Houston said, projecting her voice around the room, "which one of my aggies missed their calling to decorate princesses' rooms with that much glitter?"

"Only the best for *the gunny*." The deep voice came from an exceedingly huge, flat-faced dark-skinned man.

I briefly wondered if he was gene spliced.

"How the fuck did you do that with those bear claws you call hands?" Takakoa asked, and a soft round of laughter circulated. "And who the fuck is Jody?!"

The laughter cut abruptly. Tension clamped down like a bear trap.

"Major, would you please explain what's going on here to my merc."

Dozens of people stared at me. I wanted to run out of the room. I couldn't though… I like Takakoa, and I wanted to impress her. So, I thought about what Shantu would say.

"I have a name," I said like I was making a speech.

She spun on me with a twinkle in her eye peeking out from behind her sergeant face.

I held my ground…and my breath.

"Yeah. I know what they call you. *Monolith.*" She turned on her aggies. "And do any of you misaligned strands of DNA know how a merc gets a name like Monolith?"

Dramatic pause.

"You get it by doing a coffin drop without sedation and then getting right the fuck to work."

That was not what I meant, but okay.

I also knew what bashful felt like. I hope I didn't show it. I just tried to stay still and let Takakoa, GySgt. Houston, do her thing. I was not going to interrupt her while she had her sergeant face on.

She let the collective *holy shit* die down before moving right along. "If any of you lactose intolerant shit britches are Jody, get the fuck out of my sight before I reach down your throat, pull out your soul, and use it as an anal catheter. For him." She pointed.

Glances went to the biggest, hairiest man I had ever seen. If he didn't have a human face, he could easily be mistaken for a minotaur…or a bear.

A brief tussle broke out elsewhere, and someone was literally thrown out of the gym. I couldn't see it, but I heard the wet smack of a body hitting the deck. GySgt. Houston lifted her chin with approval.

What the fuck was that about? I stayed put and pretended it was a Tuesday.

The kind major put a hand on my shoulder and pulled me to the sidelines of the forming circle. "Jody is a name originating from Old Earth militaries. It's for the person who fucks your partner while you were away on military duty. They're lower than kiezel worm shit. What's going on here though is when an aggie is too distracted by their new partner to notice their name written on the deck in glitter." He gestured to our artwork. "It's our duty to remind said aggie that their attention is lapsing, and they need to decide what kind of balance they want to strike. If it's not serious, the couple runs away, and that's that. If it is, you get something like this…"

I took the major's confiding tone as an opportunity to ask, "What am I supposed to do?"

"It's not a formal thing. Some commanders don't like these traditions, but I think it brings my people together. Gives them something to talk about other than the grind. If anyone asks, this is a combat skills training exercise."

I laughed.

Three people were circling Takakoa, taunting her.

A light-skinned fireplug of a woman flashed her chest at Takakoa. "Come on, Gunny. You know you want another pair of tits in your life!"

The distraction let the biggest, hairiest man sucker punch Takakoa in the jaw. She rolled with the punch, straight into a scary uppercut into the third person. She then spun into a high hook kick to the woman's shoulder.

Mother of fuck, she was fast and hit hard!

She could have mauled me at the bar but didn't.

Unbridled blows rung out as GySgt. Houston turned into a feral animal on her own people. The first woman went down, and I could see a gap where the humerus had separated from the glenoid fossa. Ugh… Someone pulled her to safety while two others stepped in and tried to even out the odds.

I wanted to know if she was augmented or gene modded or what because she was defending her space against others who were four or five times her mass. She was a ferocious berserk gladiator in gym shorts and a sports bra.

In my head, she was a lion fighting a pack of hyenas.

GySgt. Houston's grunts were working themselves up into a frenzy, shouting taunts. The other grunts seemed eager to be the next victim, circulating in and out. It was like they all wanted to take a punch if just to say they survived the Great GySgt. Houston.

The only restraint I saw in GySgt. Houston's brutality was that she didn't aim for the head.

"Can I get in there?" I asked the major.

He shrugged. "Your funeral."

Time to be awesome!

I jumped into the fray by sweeping the legs of the person who's back was turned to me. I barreled into a second person, and a murmur of approval went around. I wasn't going to swing with the brutality that GySgt. Houston had, but I wasn't going to let her go at it alone either.

When I made it to her, GySgt. Houston's aggies erupted into cheers. They didn't seem interested in winning but in taunting us with sexual overtures. They were more groping and grabbing than a solid spar; however, they would land a blow in any opening.

GySgt. Houston, however, was fighting like she wanted blood from everyone in the room. She liver shot one and smashed another's knee as payment for their trespasses.

The thigh kicks and probing punches were quickly wearing through my self-restraint as I threw one person into another. Before I could lose my temper, someone pulled me off my feet, and the fray turned into a dogpile of squirming bodies as the aggies dry humped us into submission.

Someone called an end to it, and we untangled our bodies with the occasional gripe as someone got something stepped on.

Takakoa and I were on the mat soaked in sweat, panting with smiles and chuckles.

The kind major offered me his hand and pulled me to my feet. "Good show." He looked around the room full of aggies who were as giddy as school children loose in a candy shop. "You be good to my gunny."

He then punched me in the face.

I came to in the dim lights of an infirmary, sick bay, hospital, or whatever you want to call it… The medical facility. Thank the stars, the lights were dim. I reached up to try to remove the docking clamps trying to crush my skull.

A medical person stopped my hands. They had the same Vanguard haircut everyone in this facility had. "I'll give you something for the pain in a moment, but first, what's your name?" he said with a high lisp.

We went back-and-forth with noninvasive questions until my patience ran out. Which took all of twenty seconds. They gave me the good stuff, which made my brain shrink into something that'd fit my skull.

The brain fog made it hard to tell how long it took before I noticed Takakoa in a chair next to my bed. She was trying to hide a smirk but was failing miserably. Her face was shiny with a trans-dermal patch, the fake skin stuff, on her cheek.

I wanted to be mad, pissed even. Maybe it was the drugs, but I asked, "What's so funny?"

"This is going to be one hell of a story." She snort-laughed. "Merc walks into a bar, thinks about dating an aggie, and wakes up in a hospital. Merc thinks about working out with an aggie and wakes up in the hospital."

I didn't end up in the hospital after the bar, but I wasn't going to ruin the joke. "All right… I get the point. I'm not an aggie."

She was still laughing. "The good news is I have an at will three-day pass. I'll take it as soon as you're cleared to leave. I think Major Jenkins is apologizing. Besides, I need to spend the day sorting some things out before I take the time. Anyway, I have to go. Love you." She kissed me and turned to walk out but paused at the hatch as if she just realized what she said.

My brain didn't hesitate. "Love you too!" I practically shouted before she could leave my room.

The medical person looked annoyed.

But I smiled at them, basking in the new glory of my life. "You hear that? She loves me!"

Completely unfazed, they said, "Sir, I have to complete my cognitive assessment. How would you describe your reaction to recent emotional stimuli, as compared to subjectively similar stimuli?" The last part of that sentence was a particular struggle for them.

I felt like Shantu's banter was coming out of my mouth. "You're killing my buzz… Are you kidding me? This is the first time I've had a stimulus like this!"

17

I THINK I'M BETTER

522.285.1347 Life Support Block,
Human District, Fermi Station

TAKAKOA AND I were walking down a green deck with a false sky. The catwalks were stylized to look like a pier. Rice grew in perfect rows, shadowing the techs who ran the equipment. Floating harvesters chewed through the crops. It poured products into two separate boats. I assumed one with rice and the other with byproducts.

This was awesome. I had seen images of Old Earth, where people lived in places like this. Lived simple lives of honest labor.

People lined the edges of the pier, fishing and waving at inspector drones to see if they could keep their catch.

I was giving Takakoa the lowdown about how Shantu and I met and grew up, going from job to job with a scarlet letter on our lives. I didn't feel like I was doing a very good job because I kept getting distracted every time someone pulled up a fish.

"I'm not good, but I think I'm better. I feel different. Do you know what I mean?" I asked. "I don't know if it's having good people in my corner who would rather die than quit on me or what. During the mission, everyone stopped complaining. We complained nonstop during training. Then the noise was gone. Missing. Like the ship's reactor."

"That's good," she said. "That's really good. Don't underestimate how complaining can bring people together. Shitty food. Stuck in armor, smelling your own farts…"

"You fart? In your armor?" I asked.

She gave me a suspicious side-eye. "As a lady, no, I have never farted. As an aggie, no shit."

I looked at the deck. The wood print was worn through in places, exposing the transparent polymer.

"We shit liquid when we seal up," I said. "That's what I mean. I don't have an actual turd for a day or two."

"Oh!" Her face brightened. "Yeah, that's one of the qualifications for pathfinder. You have to tolerate the stuff they put in your food and water. Do you get those gross food pellets?"

"Yeah… We were fighting for days. I was sleeping in position because I couldn't leave. Weapon in hand and everything. In theory, we could be in our HEPS indefinitely, as long as we replace the filtration medium."

"The suit in your room was a HEPS!"

I found a place on the handrail next to a group of avid fishermen having an animated conversation about bait. A few meters below the pier, the schools of fish gave larger creatures a wide berth.

"The one with the real helmet, yeah," I said.

"I thought it was just a shitty space suit. No offense, but it looked secondhand."

"Yeah, it's been through it. At this point, I'm surprised it holds pressure. It's more patches than anything else. I'm going to hang onto it though. It's the first thing that was really mine, you know? OH!" I bounced. "I'm getting armor! Steadfast! Javelin, maybe Wraith, would do shit like this. Set up this whole thing where we came in when one of the supervisors was hungover, so he would lose his shit. I ended up stabbing a security person."

"What? Slow down!"

I did, and she did her snort-laugh when I told her about Shantu's Pap smear joke.

She hugged my waist and leaned her head against my shoulder, coming down from a good laugh. I could smell the stuff she puts in her hair. I had learned the style was called cornrows, and she liked doing it herself while she put on old war movies or documentaries, even though it took her hours.

I loved that smell.

"You know, aggie armor is usually a generation or two ahead of what's commercially available," she said like she was trying to recruit me again.

I liked the fact she wanted me closer, but I didn't like giving up *The Happy Marauder*. It felt like a betrayal. "Did you always know you were going to go career?"

"Hell no!" She was dangerously close to her sergeant's voice but brought it down. "I thought I was going to reinvent the boutique braiding industry."

I struggled with the image. "Really? That was your life goal?"

"Don't look down your nose at me!" she snapped without venom. "I had it all figured out. I was going to have my own place in the Atoll City Galleria near a coffee shop or a dress shop. I really wanted it to be a dress place, me, coffee shop. I saved my conscription money to go to hair school. My parents even said they would help me out with a loan to get started."

I looked around to emphasize my point. "I take it you didn't follow through with those plans?"

"I lasted four months before I signed up for the VAF. Spent a year in remedial training and conditioning before I could aggregate."

"A year?" I asked.

"I thought I had lost too much conditioning with my time off and pushed myself too hard and blew out my knee. Surgery and physical therapy set me back a bit. It's funny, you know. Average people recycle two or three times."

"I thought the VAF was tough, but the injury rate is that high?"

"Injury rate is one hundred percent," she said. "You are not an aggie until you bleed aggie. But best to find your limits in training before an enemy does."

"I think that's why Dire-horn has taken a shining to us." I started to explain how the newcomers were punching bags, playing catch-up for the first few months.

"That right there!" She pointed at my hand.

I had this habit of rubbing my right hand, feeling how the flesh was different. There were callouses from conditioning, but the texture between my two palms were noticeably different. It wasn't a scar, per se, but it was a reminder of the starliner.

"It matters when you have your stories to tell! After training, when I got my unit, that's how people warm up to you. Swapping stories about torn muscles and broken bones or that thing they couldn't get." She chuckled. "There was one guy… We called him Wanderer because it took him six tries to get through the land nav." Her tone shifted from jovial to neutral. "Anyway, mercs make it through here and there without a recycle. They have experience, so they know how to commit and get shit done. A kid making it through all the training evolutions straight out of first term conscription. Mm-hmm… We look at them like they were railroaded if we didn't already know their names from high school fall or something."

Fall is a sport I'm super vague on… The arena is a bunch of nets and fans. There is a disk, but I don't know much else.

I don't sports-ball.

"What?" I asked.

"As in someone had a track laid for a smooth ride through

training. The biggest thing I've seen is someone in personnel adjusting the schedule to make sure a particular probate was going to be paired with the right trainer. Training prep is one thing. This guy had a network where trainers were qualifying people for him. He made a lot of money but had to flee to the Commonwealth. There's a bounty on his head…"

She sent me the information. Small amounts were crowd-sourced from the VAF with a grudge, but it was pocket change.

"I'll send this along," I said, "but from what I've seen, we'd only accept this if he was looking for a way off planet, and we were parked on the docking ring. That's what we've done before." Inside, I was super worried she was trying to get me into something I didn't want to be a part of.

"No worries! I just wanted to show you the guy. Read the article when you get time. The comment section gets hilarious pretty quick."

"I think if you're worried about people leaning on the scales, you're doing all right, but what the hell do I know? We take care of each other and mostly do insurance jobs because that's where the money is."

"Insurance?" Takakoa asked, sounding skeptical.

"Yeah. Where do you think brand-new colonies or terraformers get military support without armies of their own? Investors protect their investments and hire guys like me to shoot brain-damaged megafauna."

She laughed.

Fuck! I love spending time with this woman.

18

GOING SWIMMINGLY

TAKAKOA AND I were exploring a wild deck where a biosphere had been integrated to serve as large-scale water, air, and food recycling. The brief bland description was that undersell and over deliver things that people who knew they did a good job pulled off. The heat from the deck below created full weather patterns.

"Who the fuck names this stuff? Do they hate their lives?" I gestured to the prompt that identified "Radiator Water Reservoir Number 3' 4.83 x 10^15 L." I closed the window in my feed as it populated more statistics.

The water gently lapped the sandy shore. Mangroves had been cultivated to make every few dozen meters feel like a private beach. Children chased each other and their adults between the semiprivate alcoves. Other groups seemed content with fishing and drinking.

Did the fishing poles have something to keep them from hooking a kid, or was this a teachable moment?

"This is a beautiful fucking…" I was suddenly aware I couldn't see the end of the water. My body froze, and my breath got caught in my throat. I had only felt that kind of panic when fighting—usually right before Wraith chokes me unconscious.

My body said FUCK THAT NOISE!

"…but I can't swim," I said after way too much time. "I've never been in a body of water bigger than a bathtub."

Humans are not made to swim. We have hands and feet meant for walking and even climbing.

The sounds of children playing nearby tempered my emotions.

Takakoa giggled. "I should have known better. Vanguard City is on a *mountain*. If it makes you feel better, we don't have to go deep." She waved at the drone that placed chairs, an umbrella, and towels a few meters from the shoreline.

I chuckled. "I had to come all the way to Fermi to finally get a day on the beach…"

"Strange times we live in, right?"

The sand was coarse and warm. I knew the lighting above was artificial, but I had to really look to see the cells in the array. It was so high up that clouds rained kilometers away. The crashing waves called to me. Like something in my DNA had awakened to tell me this was what humans were supposed to have in their lives.

I wanted to feel the rain. Even if it was artificial. I had never felt rain…

"I've always wanted to come here but never found the time," Takakoa said.

We turned back to the ocean that acted as a giant cooling reservoir. She handed me a bottle of gel that repelled the wildlife in the water.

Was it wildlife if it was captive on a space station?

"Only put it on the hair you want to keep," she said, stripping down to her shorts. "There are shrimp and fish that'll eat all the hair off the rest of your body."

I followed suit and tried not to be too obvious that I was appreciating her body. Her hard points stuck out of her skin like metal pearls. There was the smallest bit of callusing at where the metal would meet the flesh.

I actually was looking for a good excuse to not get in the water, but I wasn't coming up with anything.

I put a light coat of goo on my head and face. She spent considerably more effort massaging the gel into the tight braids she wore.

Afterward, she tossed a bottle into my lap. "Eye drops so your contacts don't get itchy." She then sprinted into the water—without warning—until she tripped and splashed, falling with a childish giggle. "Come on! It's great!"

SHIT!

Time to be awesome…?

I tentatively stepped into the water. It was clear, and I saw fish, shrimp, and other critters dart out of my way. I wished I knew more about wildlife…

I felt stupid as a dozen children wrestled, and their adults threw balls and drank out of a floating cooler. I just wasn't as comfortable with being submerged.

My feet inched forward a little more than knee deep when something touched my foot. I made a warrior's battle cry and faced my foe.

I did not…

Screaming, I fell, face-planted the water, and inhaled a bunch of it. When I surfaced, I coughed, but it turned into a half retch. You know when you cough so hard that it almost makes you throw up?

I could feel people looking at me.

Takakoa got me to my feet with pleasant reassurances. I wanted to yell and curse at her. I was scared and angry and embarrassed. Somehow, I couldn't frolic in the water like these kids…

I had never felt so out of place in my life.

"There, there…" Her warm tone was loving, but then she almost barked at me. "Straighten up and take a deep breath." She then turned to the nearest family. "It's his first time swimming! Let him know how good he's doing!"

A couple of the kids circled, trying to share insights into aquatic activities.

"AIRMAIL!" someone yelled, and a fist-sized object splashed next to me.

"Come on," she said in her calm sergeant's voice, authoritative but not loud. "Hands up over your head. Breathe deep."

The kids' guardians wrangled them away from us with apologies. I was only vaguely aware of the exchange, distracted by my coughing. My respiration struggles kept me from losing my temper.

I burped up some water.

She plucked a can that bobbed in the water and took a swig before offering it to me. "Strawberry… Beerish? Here." She turned the corners of her mouth down approvingly while offering me the can and promising that it would help with the coughing.

19

WORK CALLS

JAVELIN CALLED, AND I ignored it because sleep is better.

Shantu called and spoke with excitement. I tried to get him to calm down, so I could understand what he was saying. But…I ended up hanging up on him.

Takakoa stirred next to me. I snuggled back up next to her.

I know the movies always have the men on their backs with the women draped over them, but you know what? I like being the little spoon! And I don't give a fuck if it makes me less masculine. I like fresh air and not a face full of hair. I like to have her squeezing up against me from behind with her knees under my thighs.

That shit is lovely!

I don't give a fuck. I'm not snuggling to fight off the cold in Vanguard City. I'm not pretending to be asleep to avoid awkward conversations. I feel safe, and Shantu's not farting on me. I enjoy it *immensely*.

This is the best sleep, bed, everything!

My feed rang again, and I silenced it again.

Fuck it. I was on vacation, and that sounded a lot like work stuff.

This is so comfy. I dozed off again.

"Aren't you worried your captain is going to maroon you here and take all the money?" Takakoa mumbled into my neck. She must have felt me gesturing to ignore the calls.

"No. Ship's down for heavy maintenance," I said.

She opened her mouth to reply but sprung out of bed instead. At the same time, "EMERGENCY" flashed in my feed.

"Leave's canceled. Grab your shit," Wraith said in a call. "I'm on the way to clear out the hotel." He disconnected.

My feed updated with combat protocols and the sitrep. It then shifted to a HUD, and I belly flopped into an ice cold bath of adrenaline. Every neuron in my body lit up with the sick feeling of life-and-death combat. I didn't know if I was going to puke, shit, or piss myself.

Takakoa cupped the side of my face and waited until my eyes focused on her and not my feed. "The VAF is mobilizing. Take this packet. If you're working for me, I will rip your jaw off through your asshole. Otherwise, watch your ass. I haven't seen enough of it yet. I love you!" She gave me a rough, short kiss before diving into the closet and slipping into a light kit she had stashed there.

I accepted the file. The encrypted Vanguard file read "For Official Use Only."

WHAT THE ACTUAL FUCK?!

She pulled a rifle I didn't recognize from the closet. "Tell Gabe I'm taking this, and thanks."

I grabbed her arm and spun her around before she stepped out of my room. I then pulled her into a deep, passionate kiss. "I love you," I said, holding eye contact.

If tomorrow wasn't coming, I would have wanted better than a hurried kiss.

She melted for just a moment before hardening into her sergeant face. Then she was gone.

I hesitated between my HEPS that had served me so well and my new suit. I decided on the suit because the HEPS was heavy and bulky.

My HUD populated as team members came online. I synced my weapons to my feed and adjusted my settings as Scout talked.

"This is a large-scale operation across the human district," he said. "The baqua are seizing warehouses and storage facilities. It looks like they're being given lower priority targets while the khanate are actively annexing manufacturing, refit…" He hesitated like he was assessing the situation in real time. "It looks like they are taking the smaller private facilities."

I glanced at the time stamps on the data feed. Nothing was more than a minute old.

All right. History lesson, kids.

Remember when I talked about the civil war that led to the creation of Vanguard? The khanate is what the rest of humanity decayed into. The baqua was the late agricultural preindustrial sapient species that got enslaved. Just like the people who formed Vanguard didn't want. It wasn't all done at once, but they got there.

Dire-horn took over the team channel. "I have a representative from the VAF. Verified."

"Soldiers of fortune," a voice said with a comically thick Vanguard City accent. Every bit *the good old boy* the government wanted. His icon populated to say he was a lieutenant from legal affairs. "You're at the top of a list where we're going to honor the standing contingency contract provisions, in lieu of negotiations. Now that that's out of the way, I'm authorized to brief you." His customer service voice evaporated. "First and foremost, no combat is to occur outside the human district. That includes air locks. They will be fought and controlled from the inside. Venting debris from air locks must be avoided—even at the cost of personnel." He dropped the official reading. "If debris disrupts space traffic, the current human population will be removed from the station."

"How?" I asked, still checking my gear and buttoning up.

"We've seen irradiation, sublimation, and even a spire severed from Fermi before. It doesn't matter. Vanguard, and you as an extension, will not be the reason humanity gets purged from this station."

"Understood."

"Very well." His voice turned back to its mission brief cadence. "I want to be clear. This fight is already lost. Keep your exit strategies current. You do not want to get left behind. Our projections show that the khanate will do something stupid if we push them too hard. That stupid thing will likely cost every human their presence, and the station might even get us purged from the local sphere. The politics of a refugee population is a different department, but we're here for two reasons. Primary: Information. We need hard information on how the khanate fights, their supply chains, and their leadership structures. Secondary: Make this station as costly as possible. We are investing in privateers because you are not hindered by our tactics, equipment, or doctrine. We're not stupid enough to think we have this war thing figured out." He paused. "I have a request pending to have you link up with the Havok Section. I'm sending the link to Councilor Dire-horn. It'll have your point of contact and integration details. Any questions before I move on?"

What the fuck was the Havok Section? But I didn't ask.

No one said anything for a long moment. Dire-horn eventually thanked him before allowing him to sign off.

The captain then issued orders like target shooting.

WORK CLOTHES

522.293.1357 Manufacturing Block,
Human District, Fermi Station

SHANTU'S AND MY orders were to rally enroute to Steadfast, get our armor, and report to the VAF's Havok Section. We were ordered to not get bogged down in anything, including engagements or rescue operations, before reporting in.

Our briefing packet explained that Havok Section is the VAF team assigned to coordinate mercs, so we didn't shoot each other. We were to avoid the main conflict to look for targets of opportunity, intel, and high-value targets.

I ran out of the hotel as the contact briefed us. It sounded like Vanguard had been preparing for decades, even influencing local infrastructure to meet their ends.

Why was the battle lost if they had decades to set the stage?

Not my problem.

Gabe, Scout, and Dire-horn were barred from direct conflict because of standing treaties. Piper didn't receive that order because they wouldn't have listened anyway.

Man, I would have liked to have Gabe next to me in this fight though…

The captain, Javelin, and Dire-horn were going to be busy working out a deal to get us off the station because *The Happy Marauder*'s propulsion was down, and her life support was our ticket off the station.

In theory, we could wrap her in stasis-passenger modules and carry a few million people.

The corridor to Steadfast was a fucking madhouse. I neared a crowd of lenders, recruiters, prospects, and everyone else who suddenly wanted high-end equipment right the fuck now.

"So much for the follow-on training," I said jokingly, pushing my way through the crowd while Shantu handled the check-in.

Steadfast Armature had lines out the delivery doors with people screaming and making promises, while others respectfully waited their turn. Security patrolled in the display models of their most advanced armor, along with mules that were stylized to look like vicious animals.

The park, the food court, the foyer, or whatever you wanted to call it was now a waiting area for foot traffic. An assortment of food vendors and other people migrated through the less than orderly crowd, offering their goods.

"If you're going to buy armor, put it to work with Halcyon Corp," a generic announcer's voice boomed while recruiters answered questions and guided people to the kiosks that followed the recruiters around.

Another kiosk started adding their noise to the cacophony. "Protect your investment with a Bungee protection plan. All makes! All models! Take care of it all with a Bungee plan!"

My nerves frayed. They were too close. I could smell them. Colognes and perfumes made their fears and anxiety float like oil in water. Sweat beaded the office minions' foreheads.

Two people blocked my way, screaming about how important

they were and who depended on them. Such fucking yuppie clichés with small dick energy.

"Do you know who I am?" one yelled at another. "I did forty billion credits in contracting work with them! Now, get the fuck out of my way before I have them cancel your appointment!"

"Shut the fuck up!" the other yelled back. "You're in the queue like everyone else! If you touch me, my firm will seize everything you've ever laid your eyes on—even your grandchildren."

I didn't want to turn up the noise canceling and lose situational awareness. So, instead, I scanned for a security minion to notice us. One gestured Shantu and I over. The guards quickly kept people from trying to casually follow us.

We neared the entrance, and the heavy power armored head displayed an image of a smiley face on the solid faceplate's matte background. Others joined me, and we pushed our way through.

Someone grabbed my wrist, but I elbowed their face. I quickly checked to make sure I still had my feed bracelet. They were secure. I couldn't look back to find out who or why they were touching me.

Shantu and I fell into a little cohort of other appointments and erupted from the crowd through the security personnel. Stressed technicians called our names, ushered us through the industrial beehive of people, and led us straight into our individual changing rooms.

I found my name handwritten on the thin transparent vacuum packaging of an armor liner. The liner was the normal matte gray of unadorned spacer ware. The seal had a sticker that identified the pull, hidden on the shoulder. It felt dangerously thin. The thighs had almost invisible pockets with patches and sealant tubes. This suit had smaller pull rings for amputation, instead of the bananas from my HEPS.

I still don't know if I should have amputated my hand when I welded myself to the starliner's overhead. Shantu might not have taken shrapnel to the guts if I had.

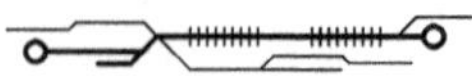

Anyway, this model was sealed with a zipper from the hip, across the back of the shoulders, and down the other side. I couldn't dive into it like my HEPS. That worried me that I couldn't button up during decompression.

I struggled with the extended use plumbing more than I am comfortable talking about. That I *definitely* couldn't do during decompression.

My feed synced with the wrists-to-elbows screens as I slid my arms into the sleeves. The screens were there if we had to disable the wireless features of my feed. They populated basic environmental information in subtle plain text.

When I sealed the suit, my feed prompted me with the standard acknowledgments and warnings. Then the suit's interface and features, like environment and status, came online, and menus folded into tabs under my mini map.

My HUD zoomed out and displayed on my visor instead of my eyeball via the contact lenses. The start-up menu had prompts and settings for me to cycle through.

I just left everything on default and closed the menus.

Almost at the same moment, the changing room door opened, and a harried-looking technician held open a bag for my clothes. I hesitated as I verified the shipping data. Everything was getting sent to *The Happy Marauder.*

I wanted to wear the suit more… I was just starting to like being fancy.

I dumped my clothes and kit into it and held onto my tet and sidearm.

"Sir, if you want that sidearm, you can't take delivery today," the technician said, sounding annoyed.

"Show me the kit," I said.

He rolled his eyes and looked more annoyed before leading

me down the corridor of the changing rooms. We passed through a heavy air lock, and when the opposite door opened, the sound of heavy weapons fire reverberated through the bulkheads.

Turrets actively scanned the corridor from overhead. Heavy monstrosities of armor flanked either side of the air lock, really pushing the limits of what could fit through a human hatch.

A crowd waiting to transition to the air lock parted as much as they could, and the technician walked at a difficult pace to match. He dodged other technicians escorting their groups. We transitioned into a crowded factory floor not meant to handle the amount of people.

Was this what a fléchette felt like in a magazine?

The factory noise triggered sound dampening on my feed. I could still feel it rattling in my bones though. It was the slamming of mechanical safety locks, high-speed motors spinning up and then shutting off, and conveyors rattling as they moved their goods. Rows and rows of power armor sat in vertical conveyors that looked like belt-fed ammunition.

It was comforting once I knew what they were. Things doing what they were supposed to be doing.

We pushed through the crowd until someone vacated a station and slipped into the booth. The technician gestured into his feed for a moment before typing in a code on the control screen. He then had me place my hand on the screen to confirm the process. He stepped clear and held open the bag.

A long awkward moment passed while we listened to the machinery cycle until my armor appeared.

I noticed the station I was in was covered in scanners, sensors, and other measuring apparatuses. This was a quality control station, not a delivery. However, it got me into my armor…

Points to Steadfast for adapting with the times.

I wondered what the normal process was. Did they celebrate and give you a little certificate for completing the course?

The ugly helmet was all hard angles. It stood staring at me like a testament to an unyielding rage against curves. I knew this philosophy was for angle of deflection, but it was ugly as shit. Like an early Earth tank.

The gloves wouldn't fit in the trigger guard of my little pistol. I sighed.

"If you can't be safe, be dangerous," the technician said with a smile.

I eyed the accompanying racks—double tap with bolstered armor, duel pistols sized for the armor, shoulder turrets, forearm blades… And the giant slabs of hull plating we were going to be using as mobile cover.

"My fuck!" I said in excitement.

The technician pushed a button. The armor spun on its pedestal, and the back opened. "Uh… Where is it?" He waved into his feed, gesturing at what only he could see. He then handed me a clasp with a metal ball that would connect my tet to a socket at the armor's beltline.

I attached the clasp, placed the tet in its socket, poked at the armor's deflated gel liner, and then stepped in. It was like stepping into a hug in a crowded room. The armor closed, and the gel padding inflated. My heart rate launched, the memory of my coffin drop resurrecting in this casket of metal and gel padding.

The utter darkness and adamantine isolation introduced me to the void.

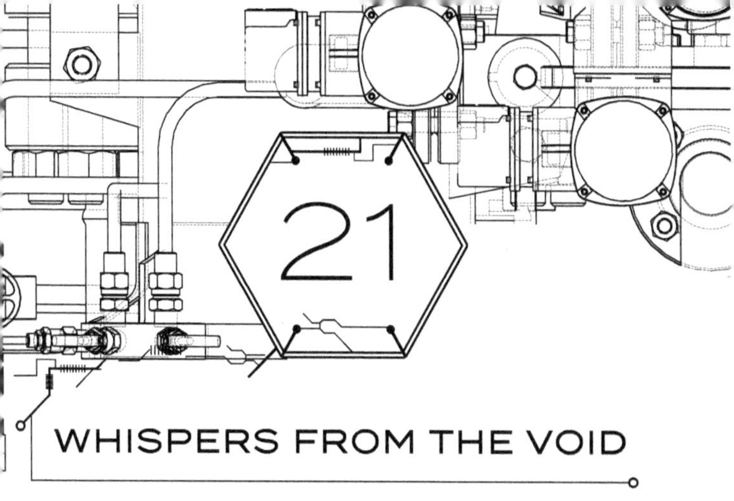

WHISPERS FROM THE VOID

YOU WILL KNOW me," the void whispered.

My mind shattered into millions of pieces. I was blind, deaf, numb, and suffocating. Lost in a place between the stars and the atoms.

The voice echoed from a distant star that would never be. "James… Monolith…"

There was a…presence. An omnipresence.

I was staring at the gulf between the galaxies that was crammed into a pill and shoved down my throat.

I was nothing

I was everything.

One by one, the circuit breakers of my feeble human mind blew. I was only vaguely aware of my own existence.

"Hey, fucknuts!" someone shouted. "If I have to come down there, and we lose our AVs because you didn't check to make sure your environment was set to human, and you're tripping balls because you're huffing methane or something…I'll never forgive you."

Really? That was the shit that brought me back from a communion with the universe?

Fuck my life.

My heart pounded in my ears, and my breathing was ragged. I would have busted my ass as everything spun, but the unpowered armor held me in place. My vision cleared from a pinpoint.

"That's it. Long deep breaths," Scout said. "Now, do we need to break the armor to get you out?"

"No, no. I'm good. I'm good," I said, trying to stop gasping for air. "I think I had…panic attack… The coffin drop…" I steadied my breathing for the most part. "I'm good. I'm good. Thanks, Scout."

An incoming call added to the vertigo. The call window opened.

"My apologies," the technician said. "I should have told you the Mark 27 Gladiator Armor would be unpowered upon entry. From this position, flex your pecs like you're trying to hug someone."

It took me more than one try. It was a very deliberate movement, easy enough but not something done on accident. With the armor powered down, the mechanism—at my biceps and across my chest—released latches in the back, and I had to push it the rest of the way.

The technician pushed it closed like the trunk of a car. "The default emergency doff command is 'shed, shed, shed.' The movement assistance mechanism will over torque connections until the whole thing falls apart."

I also had the option of setting my auto-holster-backpack thing to eject, retract, or self-destruct weapons and ammunition. I set it to retract. If things went so wrong that I was shedding my armor, I might want every round and watt available.

"All right. Don't move, or you'll cut my fingers off." The

technician pulled safety plugs from the armor and made the final connections.

It booted, and the technician took two steps back.

While the start-up menus flashed, I received a hurry-the-fuck-up text from Wraith.

Shantu and I were soon among dozens, doing a live fire armor calibration run. We ran on the top of poles that were meters apart and were at varying heights while shooting at moving targets. It was straight up like a ninja traversing the tops of bamboo poles. I mean, the poles were wider than my foot but still…

If we weren't following the person ahead of us, I would have argued that I needed to work up to this. The armor did the work though. It maintained my balance and adjusted my targeting.

It was over soon enough, and I looked back, going *did we just fucking do that?*

Yet they soon shoved us out of the air lock without so much as a *have a nice day.*

What should have been weeks of training and equipment familiarization was a waypoint eighty-four kilometers away, toward the spire's exterior on the edge of Vanguard territory.

I was examining the map when my peripheral devices updated, and the air lock spit out a mule—a drone that had ammo and supplies, a light printer, and tools for maintenance. The thing didn't have a head. It just had two lifting hard points, an eye loop, and a shackle with a polymer rope tightly securing everything. The overly mobile limbs were the rugged things I would expect for a military supply drone. Above each limb was an angular protrusion where the point defense turrets lived.

The windows flashed as my inventory updated. Our food, water, ammo, batteries, and med kits were all sitting in a duffle bag that sat on the platform for the multimedia printer. Somewhere under the bag was a printhead and multi-tool on arms, but I couldn't see them.

Dire-horn folded us into the Vanguard battle net with a myriad of acknowledgments and nondisclosure agreements. I don't know why they have a special name for it. It's just a feed but for combat.

I was pushed into a vehicle access corridor, where guards kept the vehicle lanes clear. People in armor used the vehicle lanes to leave without dealing with the crowds.

"All right… JanSport. How the fuck do we get there?" I said, trying to plan a course through the station.

I checked my feed and looked up at the news and streams from along my route. What a fucking mess. The current feeds showed a loss of connectivity and service interruption expanding around khanate territory in a sphere. Massive factories were already shut down, liquidated, or moving off station. Workers were rioting when they found security personnel keeping them from their jobs and equipment. Others were looting or just trying to get home. The normal security contracts had been abandoned for more lucrative deals.

"It's a fucking mess," Shantu said, appearing next to me with his mule.

I nodded, lifted my gauntleted index finger at him, and flexed it, firing an imaginary weapon into the overhead.

For the uninitiated, that's a joke saying the only way our weapons are going to be safe from here on out is if they aren't in our hands.

I set my weapons to active, set my turrets to return fire, and set my sensors to active. A few guards turned to face me, their sensors probably painting me in retaliation. But I kept my double tap down.

Shantu and I ignored the people on the other sides of the guards as they offered riches, sexual favors, and everything imaginable, begging us for our armor or services.

"Let me know when you are ready," I said as Shantu gestured to his feed.

"Yeah, yeah," he said. "I'm going through the settings."

"Can you not do that in the middle of the crowd?"

"I don't want to leave the guards until I have a chance to go through this."

"All right… I got your back."

"I know. I'm doing yours too." His voice told me he was focused though.

I walked around Shantu while he stared off into cyberspace, twiddling his fingers. My mule followed me in the laps.

Some asshole slipped through the guards and tried his luck to get into my duffle bag. But the asshole had his sternum crushed when it…mule-kicked him.

He was in a nice business suit with expensive natural weaves. That suit might be worth more than my armor. What the fuck was his deal?

"All right. Come on. Time to go," I told Shantu.

"Okay. It's good enough." He shared his updated settings with me and handled his weapon. He had added a virtual rearview mirror to the top of my HUD, and it felt natural to glance at it.

Security said they would handle things if we left now. We took that offer.

We took off down the vehicle lanes. It was odd, hitting vehicle speeds while running. I was in the air more than I was in contact with the ground. The bulk of the armor gave me traction while propelling me.

I don't know where I'm going with this. I just don't want to think about the desperate people we just ignored.

"Ha! Imagine trying to fit that fat guy in my armor," Shantu said jokingly.

I didn't know what guy he was talking about. "How common are adjustable armors that can fit anyone?"

He was starting to pant. "They're cheap as shit, and no one likes them." He then did a recruiter voice. "Join us and get this pile of shit that fits the legal definition of powered armor. They use labor exo-frames and hot glue some metal and call it armor."

My ears popped as my armor adjusted to the pressure and flow of atmospherics with my exertion.

We soon made it to the local tram hub. A recent firefight had blown out a section of the bulkhead, and the train had derailed, mangling itself and the passengers. Survivors of the incident were helping each other with lights from their handsets. My HUD flashed with electrical warnings.

"Find a junction box and cut the power," Shantu said.

"Are you stupid?" I didn't mean to be so harsh.

A local junction box would kill the lights or environmental systems, not the tram's high energy.

Shantu seemed taken aback. "Right… Linear motor, uh, sonic pulse." He pulsed his acoustic sensors, which showed pipework in layers throughout the wreckage.

"What's the insulation factor on these armors?" I asked, moving rubble to access a power conduit.

"High industrial. They're built for boarding actions. Why?" He dropped the same panel from above.

I pulled one of the main power leads from its mounting brackets, careful not to rip them from the switches they were wired to.

"I see… What's your plan to bridge them?"

I hadn't gotten that far yet. I looked around and pointed at a metal bench. "Shoot them with a laser on the lowest setting and see if we can melt the shielding without cutting clean through."

Shantu hung from the overhead with claws from his gauntlets digging straight into the metal tram tube. I looked at my hand and saw where the claws were built right into the ends of my fingers. I flexed my hands and pretended to be a tiger. The claws snapped out with a *shink*!

AWESOME!

"Focus. Hand me something more conductive," he said, letting his power cables hang from the overhead.

I looked around, found a temperature control unit, and stripped out the radiator. With my armor, the tubing felt like twine.

People had stopped moving to watch or record what we were doing.

Fuck. I didn't know what to do.

"GABE!" I called out on the team channel, using a petulant child tone to bother everyone but him. I explained our plan to short both sides of the tram.

"Stand by." After an uncomfortable minute or two, he came back. "Vanguard says to do what you can when you can, and they'll have your back. Just keep your sensors on."

"Gabe said we're good!" I said to Shantu.

"Why did you call him?" he asked.

I tossed a thumb over my shoulder to the growing numbers of onlookers.

"Oh… I thought it was because we don't know shit about trains."

I shrugged, drew my rifle, and aimed at the radiator tubing, setting it to low-power-cutting mode.

"This is going to arc pretty good!" Shantu yelled over his external speakers while gesturing for the people to get back. "It's going to be loud and bright!"

"Get on with it!" someone yelled from behind their handset.

"You heard the man! You're on the clock." He turned, and we synced our firing.

BAM! BAM! My cameras cut out, and my armor flickered to a false image. My HUD stayed active as my cameras reset.

Whoops.

Our mules shook like wet dogs with their system checks. The electrical arc probably just bricked everyone's feeds and any other electronics they had on them.

The details of the arc displayed on my HUD.

I looked at the cowering crowd. Most looked like they had just gotten first-degree burns from the flash before the breakers tripped.

With our mules, Shantu and I peeled away the tram car's thin metal and polymer hull. Making our way through the mangled tram car wrapped in metal and composites made everything feel so unreal. My sensors warned of a toxic atmosphere and cooling temperatures.

Capacitors discharged the last remnants of their energy into the passengers' charred bodies.

The charred bodies pulled up a memory I didn't want. Shantu and I were teenagers. I don't know where we were coming from or going. But I remember the pop that echoed through the gut.

The next thing that hit us was the smell. Burning meat. Human meat. It was not the same as burned food.

I don't have the words. It's almost painful, primal.

There's a visceral memory lingering in my senses that won't forget that smell.

The person in the memory had tried to scrap a hot conduit and paid the price. The body was a smoldering ruin of melted clothing and burned flesh. The bones of their forearms and shins had exploded, and holes had been burned across their torsos as the electricity had found its path to the ground.

I could smell the memory across time, looking at the similarly charred bodies in the mangled tram car. The tram car's superstructure was largely intact while the inner hull had been shredded by unsecured bodies and belongings.

The life support equipment and its internal batteries was what killed most of these people. Their electrical safety devices were bridged when the sudden deceleration slammed bodies into them. Some discharged their stored energy in devastating arcs. Other batteries exploded, filling the compartment with shrapnel and fiery toxic gases.

Fate has a profound sense of irony.

I knew the tram car was covered in blood and gore burned into place. And somewhere deep in my soul, I was thankful my memory was spared those images.

Until Shantu turned on his lights.

The scene was a beautiful apex of macabre. Blood, either burned or fresh, covered everything I could see. The narratives of momentum were cataloged with every streak and smear. I tried my best to not absorb the murals painted by the final trip through time.

Shantu's silence was louder than the lost souls here.

Steadily, we transited from one compartment to another. It wasn't one but *four* separate trams, each with several cars, that had collided. The last few cars felt like a sick joke because the passengers were largely unharmed.

My HUD highlighted and notified me that it was transmitting body profiles. Icons drifted as my armor scanned and logged feeds and other identification devices to help with the profile. Some of the casualties could be sleeping or unconscious if my armor wasn't displaying "No Detectable Life Signs" in my HUD.

The toxic atmosphere warnings kept me from wandering too much.

It took a moment to adjust the information flow to a more subtle outline and fewer icons. To distract my brain from the awful I just went through.

Intellectually, I understood the lack of environmental systems in these tubes kept most people out of them and thereby making them the quickest route with the least likelihood of trouble. However, I kept waiting for a flash of light and getting splattered across several kilometers.

Maybe I've watched too many movies.

The false image of my sensors did make it feel like I was in an old black-and-white movie though.

"Heh. Fuck that Clothain design seminar tomorrow," Shantu said out of nowhere.

Clothain is the absolute bottom tier of low budget design. They're common with mostly automated shipping. We were trying to pad our training schedule with shit we didn't know but should. The fact it had an open bar and buffet might have influenced our decisions.

Some habits are hard to break.

It took a moment before I realized he was likely looking for anything to talk about beside the mass grave we had just crawled through.

"Free booze though!" I said, but my heart wasn't in it.

"We already get free room service and a free hotel. And that shit is awesome!"

"I still feel like we should know one of the most common ship designs."

He laughed. "That's bullshit. Piper warned me that if we didn't set our own training schedule, Gabe and Wraith would."

I laughed too.

It was forced bullshit, but it was better than thinking about how many people might be stuck to the outside of my armor.

"It looks like we're going to go on the job for more explosive training." I tossed my thumb over my shoulder at the mules with a duffle full of explosives each.

He laughed a bit more real this time.

Our sensors alerted us to weapons fire. It was kilometers out, and the weapons report was giving us clear acoustic data.

We were approaching a habitable terminal where a steady stream of people were transiting to the tube. Most were armed with at least a pistol. They were using feeds and visors with lights to move around. We turned on our helmet and gun lights to match and took turns in close front-back formation.

The armor had its own twitch where it would adjust my

footing when I was walking backward, making it feel like I was nervous or overloaded on caffeine.

Groups had dug in, setting up turrets and stacking debris as ad hoc fighting positions, while they looted the containers and defended their vehicles.

An explosion gave me pause before I entered the hub from the public transit corridor. Locals screamed and ducked for non-existent cover. I changed my armor to passive sensors—or dark mode.

When I looked out from my menus, I saw at least two squads of lightly armored personnel ushering lines of people to keep moving. The mismatched armors reminded me of salvage hounds and improvisation.

Local militia?

I lifted the barrel of my double tap to the overhead in a friendly gesture. The turrets on either shoulder should be plenty of discouragement.

Movement ghosts recommended Shantu and I lock shields and fire while moving.

I dismissed the helper tool.

"OLLIE! SHIT! GEDDA ODE OF DIS!" one of the local ushers said, noticing us.

My turrets offered firing solutions based on weapon threat ratings. The wispy dotted lines showing a firing order made images of civilian casualties play across my mind. Hundreds would be dead in seconds if we loosen our grips on our weapons in this confined area.

"Oi, 'ou 'ere fer da loot?" the largest set of armor in the lead said.

It took me a minute for my brain to process that he was speaking a bastard version of Common.

"Nope," I said. "Just passing through."

"Why not? Plenty a go around, innit?"

I knew the type. Any agreement had a big fucking hook in it. I didn't want to be part of this shit.

"I'm on the clock," I said simply.

"I wouldn't be expect'n no planet sider to be fight'n for my home, now would I?"

I think he was asking a question… But it felt like a threat with hints of fear.

"I ain't got no home. Just places to be," I said, reaching for the thickest Vanguard accent I could do.

The big man seemed to relax.

Shantu followed. "If this is your home, you don't want the khanate as your new property managers. I don't have to like y'all as long as we're shooting the same way."

The man bellowed a laugh. "Ha! The khanate are coming, an' there innit' enough guns on the station to stop them. It an' 'bout stoppin' em. Not worth arguing about who skims the top, but we need to let 'em know not to cut us to the bone."

The militia murmured their approval.

I nodded. "Tell you what? I'm headed up the shaft one way or another. If it helps you and yours, I don't mind expending some ammunition on the way… Maybe I'll make a mess of the situation. A mess a smart man can do something with."

A lull in the sporadic weapons fire grabbed my attention by the throat. Everyone drifted off into their feeds.

"Oi!" The big man hollered at the others. "Mercs a-comin'. Let 'em pass."

22

PUBLIC AFFAIRS

522.293.1945 Manufacturing Block,
Human District, Fermi Station

WHEN SHANTU AND I cleared the blackout area, I pinged Dire-horn and Javelin for my fragmentary orders, and she sent me a Sgt. Dewy as my point of contact and my area of operation with the general objective to kill khanate and break their shit.

My area of operation was an elevator shaft. It consisted of six three-hundred-meter-wide hexagonal elevators arranged around a seventh. Each elevator had multiple drive systems, and each could move each car independently.

Our feed linked with the Vanguard Conscript Corps.

Note: I had been referring to all of Vanguard as the VAF. I see that's not right. I thought the VAF meant everyone. I was wrong.

But aggregate means *to combine and form a whole.*

Oh well. No one asked me.

The conscript corps made up the bulk of the ground and logistical force. The Vanguard Fleet had ships and all the technical specialties. The VAF, the aggies, didn't do logistics. They hit and flip.

Takakoa should have told me this stuff. But no. My dumbass was too busy falling in love and shit and missed a chance for a lot of shit to get cleared up.

This is bullshit!

Also, as a gunnery sergeant, she oversees anywhere between one hundred and seven hundred people, depending on the way she organizes her forces. No wonder she was so patient with me.

The area feed populated, and a message went out with our armor and mule descriptions. My HUD highlighted the conscripts with blue friendly silhouettes, along with virtual lasers based on where their weapons were trained.

"MERCS! Coming through!" someone yelled at the local sentries.

My waypoint updated to Sgt. Dewy.

Shantu and I slung our weapons and climbed over more wrecked tram cars. We were looking at a few hundred meters of kill zone. At the far end were spotlights that saturated my sensors. Despite their filters, I could only see a small contingent of conscripts. We kept our turrets pointed up and our hands out and empty.

He opened a private channel. "If they don't hit us in the collarbone, I think we could take them all out. If it came to it."

"Good to know," I said. "Why are you bringing this up?"

"I'm just saying our helmets and chest plates are made for this. Take a knee and return fire, and we are at like eighty percent odds to wipe the whole squad."

"Cut it out. We're not going to shoot conscripts today."

"I know. I'm just—"

"STTHAAP."

The conscript armor was light, just ceramic plates. Life support and I assume some communication gear. He was right. We could probably maul them in a fight.

The forward guard was bobbing his helmet ever so slightly

like he was talking to someone and pointed down the tunnel. We walked down the tunnel. Vanguard Conscripts had dozens of hardened fighting positions built into the approach with powered down equipment and weapons.

My confidence in fighting them bottomed out when I saw the concealed recoilless rifles and staggered explosive penetrators. It wasn't about holding the position. It was a fucking *trap*.

Most of the visible sentries were preparing decoy fighting positions with disposable turrets and spare armor. The turrets were just double taps on tripods.

We let them be, and they barely glanced at us as we walked by. Wire mesh hung from the overhead like curtains. My feed identified it as the stuff used to reinforce ceramic armor.

"What's with the mesh?" I asked aloud as we continued down the tunnel.

"Sergeant says missile defense," a random conscript answered. "They can't get around all the way to the rear. Missile hits it and swings into the overhead. That's what the sergeant says anyway."

I thanked the conscript and continued down the tunnel. It gently curved the way tram tunnels do. Someone used explosives to cut a shortcut through the bulkhead and to a garage for trucks. We followed a down ramp, passed a med tent, and tried to not look at the casualties.

We found a man sitting on the ground, stabbing his kit with a screwdriver. He looked rough. He pulled off his helmet and threw it onto the ground as tears poured from his face. The helmet bounced while he stood and walked in circles.

"Uh… He does not look okay," I said.

"Don't be a bitch. Just come sit down," Shantu said. He then stepped forward. "Sergeant Dewy?"

"What the fuck do you want?" the sergeant said between sobs.

"You're our point of contact. If you need a moment, we can come back."

I retrieved his helmet.

He took in a long centering breath. "I just got my whole platoon wiped. You sure…"

Shantu stepped into the man's face. He was taller by half a head because of his armor. "Were you where you were supposed to be, doing what you were supposed to be doing?" It was as much of an accusation as it was a question.

Shantu's an artist with bullshit, I swear.

Sgt. Dewy's face twisted into rage. "Command sent us into that fucking slaughter…"

I thought he was going to take a swing at Shantu, armor or not.

"Yeah? Did you run?" Shantu asked. I think he was clenching his jaw into a fake gruffness that wasn't his normal speaking voice.

Sgt. Dewy threw out his hands and spun. "We're here?"

Apparently, this garage was the objective.

Shantu retracted his gauntlet, showing his liner gloves. Amazing how much that brings down the threat factor. "Then it'll be an honor to work with you." He offered his hand.

Fucking magic.

Sgt. Dewy appeared to be coming to his rational self when he looked at Shantu's hand protruding from the armor. He drew in a long breath before taking it. "Sorry. This is my first command."

Shantu held up a hand. "I recently met Ambassador Nguyen."

I missed what conflict Sgt. Dewy mentioned at first, but he kept going. "He's a legend! What—"

"It's not important why I was there. *What's* important is that he makes it a point to spend lives well. If you fucked up and waisted a life, learn from it, so you can do better next time. If command thought you fucked up, you wouldn't be our local liaison. Let's get to work."

I handed Sgt. Dewy his helmet.

On our private channel, I said, "Where the fuck do you come up with this bullshit?"

"What the fuck was I supposed to do?" Shantu said. "Give him a hug and tell him everything is going to be all right?"

I didn't take the bait.

Sgt. Dewy took a moment to pull himself together and shared his briefing packet. Our assignment was to work with the locals to assess threats and assets. Known threats were the khanate and their baqua cannon fodder.

I needed to look up more on the baqua. The information packet said they were behind on sensors but made up for it with low tech smoke grenades and lunge mines. Then I needed a bachelor's course on contingency options.

"Are your orders always this vague?" Shantu asked.

Sgt. Dewy chuckled darkly. "This isn't a corps op. This is the VAF. This is what I get for thinking I could be an aggie."

"Come again?" he asked politely.

"I tried out a year or two back. They sedated me and tossed me in a flooded shuttle after I spent the day climbing cliffs. I freaked out and bit the rescue diver. I can't swim, you see. No warning. No training. I thought I was going to drown when the helmet started filling with water. They can kiss my ass if they think I'm getting within a hundred kay of that shit. No, sir. Anyway, corps orders are clear, concise, and to the fucking point. Not this vague bullshit."

All the time spent discussing strategy and tactics in *The Happy Marauder*'s conference room started paying rent for the space in my brain.

I put my fist out for a bump. "Explains why we're here. Show me to an aid station or something where the locals are gathering."

He led the way between trucks full of gear in standard shipping crates. A few ad hoc fences kept the civilians from the conscript corps' gear. A single printer was spitting out polymer bunks.

I hated the part of my brain that was like "Oh, this looks like a disaster movie."

No shit!

Time to be the hero then… I guess.

Fuck it…

I turned on my external speakers and set my mic to a public address. "You tell me this is your home."

The sound of my voice echoing through the corridor made me uncomfortable. When people turned to face me, I tried to think of something clever. But nothing came. So, I just kept talking.

"You tell me you don't care who calls themselves boss or what orbit they come from as long as you can get on with your lives. The baqua are coming, and they call you *food*. They call you meat. They call you protein. There's only one way to change their minds." I unnecessarily manually cycled fléchettes, and my mule practically pounced on the discarded round. "Be dangerous. I need a coordinator because I'm not getting eaten today."

I'm really glad no one could see the horror on my face behind the armored helmet.

I did not like public speaking.

"Really? Eaten?" Shantu commented on a private channel.

"You want to take over?" I asked.

"No." He laughed. "I want to see what other gems our magnificent orator produces. Then I'll take over."

I turned to walk through the hole between the corridor and the parking structure. My armor started getting pings for calls and messages.

Sgt. Dewy said, "We got a hit. Follow me."

I overexaggerated looking at my wrist, attempting to compensate for the bulk of my armor.

"You look like an idiot," Shantu said.

I felt like one too.

The militia leader was a tall wiry man in a jumpsuit with a conscript helmet and plate carrier. He tapped his helmet for the get-out-of-your-feed gesture to those near him. "Oi, you really on about fighting here."

I looked at Sgt. Dewy. He had his helmet interior lights on, so his face was clear. He nodded.

"Stick around and find out," I said with a challenge.

"Aye!" the militia leader said. "I'll be around. Meet Mitche1!-Oh-One."

The militia leader pushed a kid with nontactical light powered armor. He was a walking concert of lights and drones. He didn't have a weapon on him. Just a confetti cannon and a projector array. Thank the stars for my helmet because I was making the what-the-fuck face.

"Oh-one?" I asked, trying to be civil.

"Yeah," the kid said. "Like mark one. The first. The original. Anyway, let's get it." He tossed a pocket drone that centered on his face, and his voice took on an infuriating amount of energy. "Fermi Station! It's yo boi, Mitche1!-Oh-One, streaming live from where most of you live and work. That's the maintenance levels of car gamma. Shout out to my floaties up there at the top of this same elevator being brave AF. We're going to show you the respect you deserve by doing something with it. I'm here with the Local 546 Transporters Union POC, Lucas McCloud. Mr. McCloud, what do you have to say to the 4.6 billion people who will be at ground zero of this clash?"

McCloud—the militia leader—looked uncomfortable in front of the drone but held his stance. "Aye! I have something to say about it. I say if they want a free port, a free port's what they'll get. Free ports'll always belong to the porters. Let's see how long it'll take them to learn that."

His accent made the whole interview sound like poetry.

Mitche1!-Oh-One gestured, and the drone centered on his face again. "No better way to put it! Now, I need every hacker, every dev, every drone jock, and all of you magnificent motherfuckers to start raising the rent around here. Special shout-out to Abstract Arms for supplying me with this sick-ass armor." He played some upbeat music and danced, striking vibrant poses to show off his armor. "Mitche1!-Oh-One, OUT!" When he snatched the drone out of the air, it was like the character he was playing went with it. He was wide-eyed and seemed unsure of himself. "Mr. McCloud, are we really going to war?"

"No, laddie. War's come to us. Your mam and wee siblings live, what? Ten, fifteen minutes from here?"

I didn't like the calmness of his voice. It was the resolution of a man who had decided his fate.

"Me and the lads are going to buy them time to get going. You know me. I don't know shit about the feeds. We need you to get this going if we're going to have any chance."

The kid nodded.

"What do we do now?" McCloud asked me.

"Sergeant?" I differed.

Sgt. Dewy put up a finger and turned away while he talked with someone in his helmet. He turned around before things got awkward. "Mr. McCloud, there are some useful public transit sites nearby. Could you get the word out?"

He seemed uncomfortable talking to Mitche1!-Oh-One directly. It wasn't a glamorous awe-inspiring speech. It was a guy talking to another guy talking to a kid. Everyone was uncomfortable.

"Vanguard Conscript Corps are coming to you." McCloud relayed to Mitche1!-Oh-One. "We want to seal everything within two compartments of the shaft. Priority one: Make sure everyone has their own air. It looks like the atmosphere is going to get bad down here."

Gabe called Shantu and me. "Easy money. Mission accomplished. The logistic gurus are coordinating with the locals, and they like what they're seeing on the socials."

Mitche1!-Oh-One launched into his high-energy shout-out persona for the drone complete with a mixtape. "Forget that heroic last stand bullshit. Survive today. Fight tomorrow!"

McCloud turned from watching the kid and stared at me. "Get that boy out of here the moment things go sideways. He's my son, you see. I never told him because I wouldn't be much of a da to him. I knocked his mam up, and she kicked me out when she found out. Smart one, she is. Found herself a good man and got right along with her life. If I can be a da to him now, I gotta keep him breathing. That's not nothing."

Piper appeared in my feed as an active call. I gestured for a moment and put two fingers to my helmet to show I was on a call.

"James, what the fuck are you doing?" they asked.

"Uh, let's see," I said. "I'm organizing a resistance and setting up for an ambush. While planning for asset denial and a fighting retreat. Speaking of which, where the fuck is local security?"

Their tone lightened up. "No heroic last stand bullshit?"

"Ha… The kid just said that. Anyway, no. Just waiting on my ride out of this shit show."

"All right. I'm an hour-plus out. Twenty if I start running people over. I have a trauma pod and your AVs." They then launched into a mission brief on expected tactics.

I stopped them though. I had seen this one before. It was the same data we had covered on the ship. I even did the follow-up reading.

It wasn't really a reading. They were audiobooks and helper tools while I was welding and assembling shit for days on end.

That society is so fucked though… I bitch about Vanguard, but fuck! The khanate conscriptions aren't optional, and you must bribe or blackmail your way into the regular infantry. It's the taboo standard to threaten, fight, or fuck your way to the top.

"You ready for this?" Shantu asked, probably after just having the exact same conversation with Piper but with more affectionate overtures.

"Should I hang it up and try for some content creator revenue?" I joked.

"Negative, dickhead. The asshole is full. Seeing as that kid is putting his money into local HEPS and portable shelters, we might want to keep any finance talk quiet though. Anyway, let's get to it."

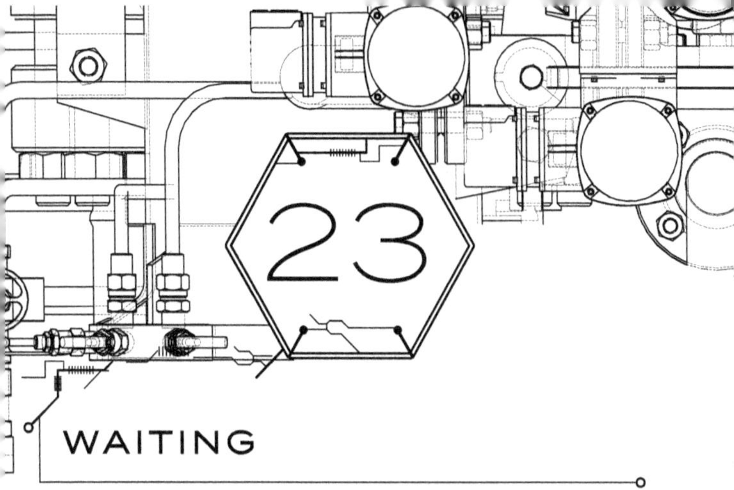

23

WAITING

SHANTU AND I weren't allowed to move forward until we got a software patch. I didn't know shit about the cybersecurity front, but I trusted Piper.

We watched sergeants barking order into chaos. The parking garage's atmosphere quickly shifted from refugee camp to boot camp as trucks with weapons and body armor arrived.

I had to give it to Vanguard. They organized and armed the locals quickly.

Vanguard painted the walls white to use projectors to give briefings on what to expect. The briefings were no bullshit, no promises. They were getting a crash course in small unit tactics and first aid.

Sgt. Dewy asked us to run interference, so he could do useful things like talk with the streaming kid and keep his subordinates from having any fun.

"Lookie here, Ms. Ochoa," Shantu said, interrupting the lady who was pestering Sgt. Dewy.

The tall lady looked offended to be in sealed armor. "Alderholder Ochoa."

What the fuck is an alderholder?

"Alderholder Ochoa," Shantu said in a diplomatic way. "I don't know or care about the history of this place. That triumphant last stand bullshit will end up getting a footnote in history like The North American Creek War. Unless you have resources, I suggest you start paying attention to these briefings."

He was actively quoting an alternate history series about if The Alamo was won, and Texas became a world power. It went off the rails somewhere around season six. By season ten, it was a comedic caricature of itself, centered around peddling its merchandise.

"I am an alderholder!" she shouted, clearly missing the reference.

Maybe the show was only big in the Commonwealth.

"Very well, Alderholder." Shantu reached out and snatched some passing private. "Private, this *alderholder* needs a kit. Can you see to that please?"

"See to that?" I asked on our private channel. "What the fuck? Are you a knight on a quest for your lord-shit?"

His shoulders bobbed as he struggled to keep up his facade.

I started gesturing and pointing like we were in a feed. I waved the private over and whispered to him. "We're just keeping her from bothering Sgt. Dewy until our ride gets here. Unless Ms. Twat Face decides she wants to take about twenty percent off the top and dedicate it to growing a backbone, she's not going to need the kit."

"Why are you doing that with your hands?" the private asked me.

"If she looks, she'll see me going over the details of her kit."

He showed me his wrist pad that displayed a code for a private channel. "Are you mercs?"

"Yeah."

"What's it like?"

"I was on a beach yesterday. Or was it the day before?"

"I get it. When your sleep gets all screwed up, you don't know what day it is." He told me a story that I didn't listen to because I was watching Shantu just sandbag the shit out of this lady.

I had a solid view of the interactions with my rear camera. I gestured to the private to look over my shoulder. "She's so mad!"

"I need to impress upon you the burden of responsibility..." the lady said.

Shantu's helmet lifted, and his shoulders slumped. If he wasn't wrapped in a couple hundred kilos of ceramic and metal armor, he would have looked like a moody teenager complaining that he couldn't go out on a weekend or some other shit from sitcoms that I didn't understand.

Really? *Impress*? Why the fuck is this lady speaking like a politician? Be a person! It works better.

He stiffened straight up.

"This is going to be good," I said to the private, and we turned to watch.

"Alderholder Ochoa, you *were* some kind of administrator," he said. "*Were*. And you've had the misfortune to outlive your usefulness. I say this because if you were useful, I would have been sent to find you. Now, I have been asked to watch the kiddie table, so the adults can get some work done."

I laughed because Mitche1!-Oh-One was on the young side.

On cue, Shantu calls the kid over. "Do you have a use for Alderholder Ochoa?"

"Who?" Mitche1!-Oh-One asks as the kid stepped over.

The alderholder looked incredulous, spinning up for another self-important rant, when Shantu steps between the alderholder and Mitche1!-Oh-One. "Thank you, Mitche1!-Oh-One. I'm sorry for interrupting your work." He then turned back to the lady. "Your coveted position no longer exists, Ms. Ochoa."

He caught her wrist as she tried to slap him. A man in powered armor. She tried to slap a *man in power armor.* His turrets targeted her, but she just tried again with the other hand.

She tried to slap a man in powered armor *twice.*

And the closing actuators on his helmet were enough to decapitate someone!

Yes, I read the manual. Go me!

Shantu locked down his weapons. He then gently placed his foot on her chest and pressed until the linkage from her unpowered political environment suit failed, and she landed on her ass.

I was laughing so hard that I almost had tears in my eyes.

In horror, the private slowly looked back and forth from the woman to the pair of arms Shantu casually held. I think it took his brain a moment to catch up to the fact the woman was unharmed.

"Ms. Ochoa," Shantu said, "I recommend that if you wish to speak the language of violence, you become fluent. Take this as a warning to improve upon your behavior." He dropped the arms of her environment suit in her lap.

She hugged them for dear life as she scooted away on her ass.

I used my external speakers to chirp. "Way to disarm her!"

He shook his head because I was totally spoiling his badass moment. He then switched to the private channel and asked, "Remember that twat who would make fun of us, but if we ever said anything back, she would cry and tell on us?"

"Paddy? She would make up shit like we were trying to grab her nonexistent tits." I tried to remember it all, but the memories felt so distant, like a story told by a stranger.

He shrugged. "That sounds right. Always talking. Always needs to be the center of attention. Nonstop lies. Anyway, this is what she would look like as an adult."

The private piped up. "Who was that lady?"

"The kind of bitch who shows up to a funeral and makes it all about her," he said with so much malice that it killed my laughter.

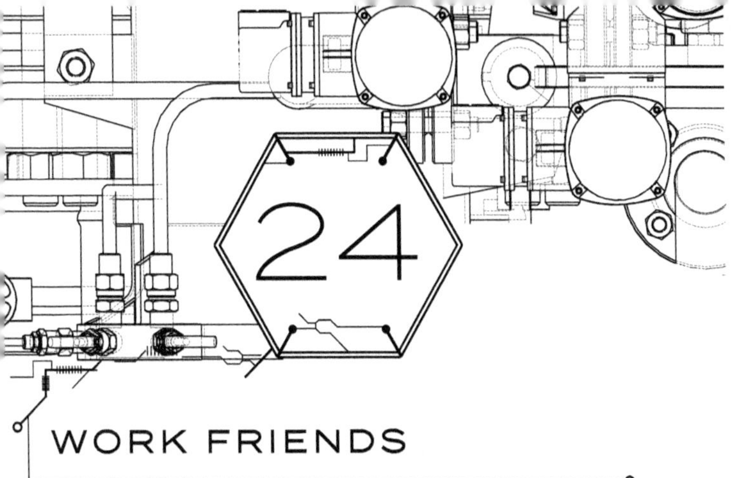

24

WORK FRIENDS

PIPER SENT SHANTU and me updates on delivering a trauma pod to the conscript corps. Volunteers were already staging it as a makeshift hospital. The hospital was centered in a middle-scale housing area with redundant environmentals.

According to Piper, the corps was trying to be as hands-off as possible, assigning locals to take over the project and act as intermediaries. If any corps people were there when the khanate arrived, it could be considered a legitimate target.

Piper glazed over some violence, where I think they killed a gang that tried to take advantage of the situation. I winced when I realized that if this was in Vanguard City, I would have probably been in the gang that had gotten killed.

"A Piper going to do what a Piper do," I said for no reason but nerves.

"Shut up, James, or I'm going to override your switch to make your AV dance," they snapped.

I tried to match one of those annoying offended voices. "You wouldn't dare."

Their voice took on a dangerous tone. "Do you think the person who has managed to create a relationship with the biggest shithead to come out of Vanguard wouldn't?"

"No?" I said with negative amounts of confidence.

Jovially, they said, "You would be right, but I will whoop your ass myself if you keep this shit up."

"I just want my AV… We haven't had them since we got here."

"I know. And while you've been playing grab ass with your aggie girlfriend, Shantu and I got them refitted because we love you. I want them saved for a second wave counterattack. Before you try to argue, we need to know what they're bringing to the party. Speaking of which"—their voice took on a high-pitched creepy tone—"they're here."

Every one of hundreds of mercs I could see in the parking-garage-loading-dock area stiffened right along with me.

In an ordered storm, everyone scattered to their respective positions around the elevator. Jamming missiles covered point defense in a scorpion style that filled the stadium-sized shaft. The electromagnetic field saturated the area so heavy that static washed over my visor.

After a long moment, distant thuds and booms reverberated through the bay, triggering my acoustic analyst and giving me an x-ray view of the elevator's super structure.

The term *metal rain* came to mind.

The initial salvo destroyed sixty percent of the corps' decoys and shredded every soft structure on the elevator's surface, along with all the native monitoring. Toxic warnings filled the feed as metals and composites burned.

Piper caught up with us at our rally point near one of the decon air locks. I was surprised they wore the exact same armor as Shantu and me. But before I could come up with a three musketeers joke, they introduced Dr. Selig. His doctorate was in computer science, not medicine.

"I'm here for signals analysis," he said. "The Commonwealth and Vanguard are putting bounties for the info sector front. She—excuse me—they… Ms. Piper…"

We let him struggle while we examined his kit.

He wore heavy environmental armor. It didn't have all the combat-oriented bells and whistles and half our mobility, but he didn't have to worry about seal failure. He had an electrophoresis cleaner unit that would drop tech samples into an air gap bag. The tool kit on his chest looked equally rugged. On one shoulder, he had a circular saw, and on the other was a smaller oscillating saw. Everything seemed secure with heavy duty clips and that black sandy-oily tar stuff they use for chemical resistance.

"Commonwealth?" Shantu nodded to the heavy rail pistol.

He nodded. "Did four standard years, turned out, and got my PhD in data storage, transmission, and analysis. VersiTronics are popping the umbilical. I couldn't just run away, you know. I've lived here for almost fifteen years. How can I look at my kids and grandkids and tell them I didn't do anything when I could have done something? I used my contract to get them out. My wife is over at Greenway Plaza. Vanguard promised to get us off station if we helped. So, what do you need?"

"What do *you* need, Dr. Selig?" Shantu said with a tone of authority.

Dr. Selig flinched but found his metal. "Any piece of data storage you can find. Put it in the gel. I may not be seventeen anymore, but you won't have to worry about me. Trust me."

Javelin sent over a packet that outlined criteria for keeping Dr. Selig and his remote team alive. Someone else was in charge of the remote team. We were all getting paid based on things like samples analyzed, risks taken, and results produced. The document went into excruciating details that I didn't care about. The rest of the packet gave details about his contingent role to the team and risk criteria.

Piper was in charge though. That shit was their problem.

"I appreciate you asking instead of telling us. As long as you understand this is the front lines and that we can't make any promises." I extended my hand.

He hooked my thumb and brought our palms together in the Commonwealth fashion.

"We're mercs, Dr. Selig. We have no authority over you," I said, ruining Shantu's fun. "You do your job, and we'll do ours. I wish we had prep time, but…here we are."

The ground thumped as the sound dampening icon in my HUD appeared. The second and third rounds turned the top of the elevator into a burning nightmare. Sensors in the shaft showed chemicals and oxidizers mixing to keep the flames going.

"Next, we're not calling you a doc," Shantu said. "That right is reserved for medical personnel in combat situations. Will tech do?"

"No, yeah," he said. "Ye-yeah, no. I think tech will do just fine. I wouldn't want anyone coming to me for any medical advice. It would not go well at all." He chuckled nervously.

"NOPE!" I shouted at an inappropriate volume. "Sorry, Tech. From here on out, it will be affirmative or negative. That *yeah, no, no, yeah* shit has got to go. Understood?"

"No, yeah. Affirmative. It's just…" He prattled on about how this conflict came out of nowhere. Yada yada.

Eventually, he quieted when our waypoint changed to a different air lock beyond a mass of Vanguard personnel and equipment. The four of us ignored the attention we were getting by being the only ones moving as we made our way to our new rally.

Things were uncomfortably quiet, aside from the shelling. I could feel the tension as hundreds, thousands, and millions of people were having the same thought—wondering if we were all going to die here.

Common doesn't have the words…

I looked it up. The word *zeitgeist* is the best I can do right now. The summation of the collective unconscious ideas, beliefs, and feelings.

The elevator's freight entrance was ominously cleared of pallets and shipping containers that should be filling the space.

FUCK!

This was a lift, but the locals called it an elevator… I, for the record, maintain that because humans don't maintain a large enough presence on the spire, much less the station, this is just a big ass lift.

I explained it on our local channel.

"What the fuck is wrong with you?" Piper asked.

"No, he's right," Shantu said. "It's not an elevator unless there's a significant change in elevation."

"Is this what you're thinking about when people are dying a few hundred meters away?"

"Yes," I said. "Between that and if a few meters of composite fail, we get to watch a few thousand conscripts get incinerated around us, I would very much like to think about anything else."

"Common isn't my first language," Dr. Selig said, "so you're saying, like, equipment lifts fall into the same category as the ones in buildings…"

The conversation went sideways, sprinkled with Piper's annoyed chidings. I wondered if any human feet had ever been in this corridor before, considering most freight traffic was automated. I really hoped they had that figured out because my imagination ran away with the mayhem caused by one of those massive self-propelled containers barreling through all the people standing in its way.

Our fragmentary orders updated. Dr. Selig, Piper, Shantu, and I were going in with the first wave of mercs and other specialists who had armor rated for the environment and the willingness to test it.

The waypoint was a tertiary secondary containment air lock getting constructed by the corps, while aggies staged on one side of the air lock and mercs on the other. Waiting for the order to transition.

We found our place with the mercs.

I felt like an impostor next to all the hardware walking around. In a way, it was like high school, and I didn't have a table for lunch. We had the punk freaks, whose armor was an expression of their individuality. We had the rich kids, whose armor sparkled with the latest and greatest.

I got hit with a case of the giggles. "Hey, Shantu. If this was high school, would the aggies or the modders be the jocks?"

"Ooh," he said. "Tough call. Modders would be track-and-field because each one is only good at their one thing. Aggies would be fall because it's all teamwork."

"All right, New Kids on the Block," Piper said. "Front of the line. We're going in first."

We walked past drones painting the deck. The markings and navigation lines were the same standardized ones: red and white for medical, green for supplies, black and yellow for mechanical, and so on.

"Does this make us the cool kids?" I asked with nervous enthusiasm.

"Fuck yeah!" Shantu said. "We're the badasses."

It felt like he was working himself up for a fight.

We were going to meet behind the maintenance bay. There wasn't a shortage of Steadfast armor there, but none of them looked as bulky or had the tower shields that we did.

Maybe we were special.

The Vanguard Conscripts and drones scurried back and forth, organizing the chaos and shouldering the logistical burden. The influencers and reporters stood out like the pox because they were very animated while the martial people waited at their gathering points.

I laughed and shrugged when a construction drone assembled a pallet rack, and people almost immediately climbed in and seemed to start napping. I guessed sealed powered armor eliminates the need for bedding. The ground vehicle corridors were getting portable air seals and turrets installed.

We waited…

And waited…

An icon changed in my HUD from red to green. Shantu and I parked our mules with the guards to protect the duffels of supplies. Conscript guards stood aside and saluted. Which made me uncomfortable. I didn't know what to do in return, so I just followed Piper through the air lock.

The other side of the lock was where forklifts and tugs were stored between elevator car transits. It looked like it had been converted to do maintenance somewhere along the way. The vehicle lifts, workbenches, and equipment showed years of use but not abuse. Some lifts had been repaired by a skilled welder, just never repainted. The organization was neat and obvious: Tools were on their racks, and components in various states of repair were on their benches, waiting for their workers to return.

I didn't think that was going to happen.

We received a Vanguard-coded friendly ping before four more mercs transitioned to the air lock. We formed up with Piper in the middle anyway. One of the other mercs wore armor that was so large and heavy that it had to duck and turn sideways to join us.

My sensor readings were that they were a reliable rugged model, a generation or two behind ours.

In a briefing long ago, Wraith had told us to trust our guts since our sensors could be spoofed. My gut told me these people were as high strung as we were. But springs were ready to snap because we didn't know each other.

The other crew kept their weapons pointed at the overhead while maneuvering around. I took it as a sign of respect. They settled in, and everyone minded their manners.

I checked the feeds and found that the khanate had a support carrier parked at a dock near the top of the lift…

Yeah. I'm not letting that go.

But at the top of the lift, drones and personnel were dropping ballistic munitions. Not the orbital bombardment stuff, the indirect ground fire. The video showed some personnel in a khanate HEPS just pushing the artillery shells down the hole like they were throwing garbage down a chute. A moment or two later, we listened to the explosion.

The fourth round was all chaff and flares. Our cue…

The external lock heated, and the atmosphere was replaced with argon. My ears popped, and my heart pounded. I listened to metal creaking and moaning with the rise in temperature.

I changed my alarm setting to armor threat. I wasn't going to be around a safe atmosphere for a while.

"Seals check!" Piper barked on a proximity channel that echoed aloud.

The window to shut the external lock before someone was cooked in their armor would be short.

"Good!" I rang out, followed by Shantu.

The other mercs checked in on audio.

The heavy door cried in agony as it parted. The inert gas blew out in a puff of ash while thick toxic smoke filled the compartment, setting off a whole host of new warnings.

"So…this place or go back to high school?" Shantu asked on an open channel.

"Shit. I must be lost," someone from the other crew said. "I thought third period started in two minutes."

My armor's acoustic sensors cut through the black smoke, allowing me to watch the garage get mangled with centuries' worth of corrosion in heartbeats. Paint and other coatings peeled and flaked or melted and dripped. Vehicle lifts and the overhead gantry sagged as if too old to support their own weight. Chemical containers exploded, and glass shattered. Infrared warned of fire torrents where some surviving conduit was pumping oxygen into the bay before a system shut it down.

"I'm pretty sure we just voided our warranty," I said to no one.

"Actually, no," Piper said flatly.

The ambient temperature was beyond death and into combustion ranges. Hard swirling convection winds made me take a step to steady myself. Some weaker materials just evaporated as if they were never there. Seat cushions, polymer tools, and batteries degraded into piles of unrecognizable debris. So many things I thought of as sturdy or even dangerous had disintegrated.

I questioned the wisdom of being out in the first wave.

The next big shock was the subtle vibration of my armor. While I watched the vehicle service bay get decimated, I failed to notice the utter silence or the loss of signal icons. The armor had stabilized itself against the wind with an almost gentle swaying motion. The sound dampening was locked in safety mode as it harmonized against dangerous acoustics.

The other mercs had disappeared into the fiery torrent, off on their own mission.

Shantu and I formed our formation in front of our tech with Piper brought up the rear. We sprinted to the biggest pile of welded garbage in the immediate vicinity. The salvaged vehicle hulls, chunks, and metal were disturbingly pliable.

The first thing we found was a turtle, a ship point defense cannon mounted on wheels with a fast-acting heavy armored shell. We tagged the location for the next group.

We were like rats looking for some perfectly cooked meat in a dumpster fire. That's the best way I can describe our mission.

A whining noise vibrated my back, reminding me that I was only as comfortable as my armor functioned.

Piper flipped off the turret. "No see. Blind. Hear one. Mute. Sky. Hold hand. Now. Hand fix. Time. Useless punch here."

Change of plans. They want us to find some aggies and have them run this turret.

I spun in a quick circle, looking through the haze of overlapping false sensor images for another merc band. I jogged, leaping power-assisted bounds, to the nearest silhouette that resembled powered armor. Speed over stealth. I announced myself by using both hands to form a *V*, *A*, and *T*, which—according to our briefing packets—would keep me from getting shot.

I really hoped whoever I was approaching got the same packet.

Granted, I had target lock on before they seemed to notice me.

The visible figure kicked something, and two others quickly rose, raised their weapons, and then pulled them skyward.

The merc gestured for me to come closer. Our communication range was down to a few meters, but the merc team soon pointed me in the direction of a Vanguard damage control team.

Turns out, it was a Vanguard *Fleet* damage control team because I wasn't having enough trouble keeping track of shit as it was. But anyway, their mule was a stout sumbitch. More of an elephant or a diller. I guessed it was built for emergency ship repairs.

Bonus: I got a new certification in hazardous atmospheric welding. TIGER! Right. It was really TIGRR—tungsten, inert gas, and refrigerated radon. Refrigerated is a relative term.

Their big ass mule bent decking into place while me and the five-person team used hand welders to seal it.

Even in the middle of a shitstorm, I still managed to level up. AWESOME!

With their current objective completed, they were willing to come to the turtle. Dr. Selig, Piper, Shantu, and I watched over the damage control team while they got the turtle operational.

"Piper…" Shantu said.

"NO!" they snapped.

"But—"

"We don't have a shuttle that can handle that thing."

"Okay…" Shantu let out a defeated sigh.

"Besides, your AVs are more capable."

The atmosphere in front of the turtle's point defense thing vaporized in a clear pocket that collapsed upon itself. Lightning danced from the barrel down to the shield before grounding out through the anchors near the tracks.

Weapons fire played in my helmet.

The sound was a default clip that I recognized, but the speaker in the helmet attenuated the sound for direction and distance. Shantu stood on a hill of scrap metal, firing his double tap in rail only. I switched all my weapons to match his settings before running to join him. The armor jerked, adjusting my footing.

I ignored the action.

When I got near Shantu, our armors synced, and a hostile red shadow appeared behind a hill with a three-plus tag. I felt nauseated with a vibration through my chest. My vision doubled. The turtle was firing, and the sound dampening system rattled my soul out of my body to protect my delicate hearing.

Piper joined us. "Turtle is secure," they said through static. "It's not mobile, but that's not our problem."

Two new mercs plopped down next to us.

Who the fuck were these guys? Their armor was rounder, but I didn't bother to read the make, focusing on the threats.

"Are you engaging them?" one merc asked.

"Yeah," Shantu barked. "We got shields. Get to our inside and wait for us to give you a gap to shoot through."

That put Piper behind them if they tried anything.

The baqua were dead before we had a chance to split their fire and give the two newcomers a chance.

Intellectually, I knew the baqua were enemy combatants, and they would kill me if I gave them the chance. Still, I didn't like watching them writhe in pain as their seals failed, and toxic gases consumed the meat inside their armor.

That could be me…

Nearby, a small group of baqua were paralyzed with fear, watching their comrades burn next to them. My sensors modulated all too quickly. I could see their dog-lizard, like a velociraptor with jowls, bodies in false color, translucent layers at diagnostic levels.

I read their histories on implants, replacement organs, and scar tissue. I looked at their double hearts and a device, presumably a kill switch, between their hearts. The sensors said a bunch of shit that I don't remember, but the kill switch stuck.

"Get Tech," I ordered.

"On it," Piper said.

Shantu and I slammed our shields into the ground, trying to provoke a response. The group wasn't firing. My best guess was that we were out of their sensor range in the swirling fuck storm.

Dr. Selig barreled into the fear-frozen baqua group, grabbed one by the head, and fired into its neck joint with his hand cannon. Shantu and I followed, ripping weapons from the baqua and making the most out of their hesitation.

He fired again and again into his target's neck, and with a violent jerk, the armor failed, and the creature inside was bathed in flames. He threw the helmet, head and all, into the gel part of his backpack. The rest of the squad flinched, and their seals failed as well.

We did the work. Got the bits we needed.

It was awful…

Dr. Selig's backpack had eight articulated arms that operated inside the gel and quickly extracted the data storage components from their armored housing. The arms were even smart enough to use a chunk of armor or bone to push other pieces out so they wouldn't be damaged by the infernal caustic environment.

The two other mercs left without so much as a happy hunting… I don't know how much they watched of what we did. A part of me hopes none of it. Another part of me hopes all of it.

Without warning, my armor jerked me to the side. A pile of armor hit the ground in a mangled mess. Dead and dying baqua fell toward us with no decent arresters of any kind—no parachutes, no gel pads, and no braking thrusters.

Just THUD.

The armor jerking me out of the way with the force of a car accident was jarring to say the least.

Shantu started singing "It's Raining Men" by the Weather Girls but didn't get far before Piper interrupted him.

"Too much," Piper said flatly.

"Sorry."

"Yeah. 'Though I walk through the valley of the shadow of death, I will fear no evil. For thou art with me; thy rod and thy staff comfort me,'" Dr. Selig said with no introduction.

"Who's with you?" Shantu asked.

"Ancient Earth religion. Christianity, I believe. It was their prayer for times of hardship," he answered. "I read about them in college. It seemed appropriate here."

"We're not in a valley…"

"I didn't take it as a *literal* valley as much as a scary fucking place." The fact my acoustic sensors showed a shifting image of his skull through his armor really made his point. He had an implant on his right eye. "I mean, they are dropping lost souls on us."

"What the fuck are you talking about?" I snapped, perhaps a bit too harshly. Maybe watching his jawbone move was disorienting.

"The baqua," he said. "Their whole civilization was hijacked and drug addicted. According to my human history, this led to the Vanguard War for Independence."

This conversation was taking place in a blast furnace where the only thing keeping us alive was the fact our armor could heat sink a reactor.

"What?" I asked. "I thought the Vanguard War for Independence happened before the first worlds were settled."

"No, they were settled," Piper said. "Well, early days anyway. The Vanguard Fleet was the first generation of human warships produced. That's why the osheran left. The next ten years led to the Great Exodus."

"What now?" Shantu asked.

I wasn't participating in that conversation and circled our parameter, folding up a shipping container like it was made of wet cardboard. Static arced from me as the harder particles swirled by.

"I need to have the curriculum adjusted to include more history," Piper said.

"I thought y'all were from Vanguard?" Dr. Selig asked.

Shantu, as quick as ever, ran with Piper's setup. "Technically, sure, but most of our education is aboard ship."

He was completely bypassing the orphanage and our time in corrections. Granted, our two years on *The Happy Marauder* had earned us the equivalent of bachelor's degrees, mine in spacecraft structural engineering and his in spacecraft subsystem networking.

"We're working on our master's in engineering."

"Spacers, right?" Dr. Selig seemed satisfied. "Why stay? I mean, if your ship is just out there, why not get on it and get away from…"

An air battle ensued overhead, strafing our position with debris and laser fire.

Piper answered. "Good ports are hard to come by. If the khanate succeed here, it won't be one. I don't know how many human ports will take a khanate trade agreement to avoid invasion. I'm wondering if this is going to be a repeat of The Green Worlds Annex."

"The what?" Shantu and I said together.

A battle sounded overhead like gods fighting in the sky. My sensors filled with flashes of winged creatures mauling each other with laser backscatter.

"They said The Green Worlds Annex," Dr. Selig said.

They laughed. "They're asking what I am talking about. Anyway, before the khanate adopted their unified title, after the Vanguard War for Independence, The First Worlds were in economic shambles with widespread famine and disease. In the Commonwealth, it came to be known as The Royal Flight. Pejorative considering it led to the influx of humans to Commonwealth worlds. Anyone looking to rebuild after the Vanguard War for Independence went to whatever colony they could, and they brought their politics and religions with them. Until they started the same shit all over again."

"Fair enough. I'm Commonwealth, so everything is written to hate the khanate. Which seems to be accurate…" He made a show of looking around.

"Okay. That's it. Is anyone else freaking out by watching a skull move in his helmet?" Shantu said.

"No. I'm not a wuss," I said. "It is weird though."

Dr. Selig made a show of feeling his helmet. "Wait… You're looking at my skull right now?"

"Yeah. You have an implant in your right eye," I said.

"There should be a setting for it to render my skin…"

"Yeah, I found it," Shantu said, "but the warning said I could miss concealed weapons and whatnot."

A local connection available icon blinked on.

"Piper?"

"Isolated only," they replied.

The local connection was run by the teams below deck, letting everyone know that they were down there, to not shoot them, and that they were going to have the oxygen feed shut off in about five minutes. Then some stuff about bandwidth restrictions.

"Hope this doesn't get us killed." They released our logs and sensor reports.

The damage control team replied with "What the fuck am I supposed to do with that information?"

I closed the window because I knew where that was going. It wasn't their job, but we had bandwidth clearance for check-ins.

"Tech, keep an eye on this and get out," I said. "Your armor isn't rated for what comes next."

"What comes next?" he asked.

"Shattered tears…" Shantu answered for me. When Dr. Selig didn't respond, he continued. "It's based on the Prince Rupert tear. Look it up. Melt some ceramic and drop it in a coolant. The teardrop shape that comes out has an extremely hard body and a brittle tail. Snap the tail, and the whole thing explodes with more force than most moderate explosives and has no residue. The body is nearly perfectly transparent, so it scatters lasers, and it's hard enough to resist most rail fire because of how dense it is. They're designed to rupture seals just like yours in environments just like this."

"They are going to use them to cover their ground forces," I added, remembering the briefing packet. "Glass rain the size of basketballs and weighing almost three hundred kilograms will saturate point and air defense. I don't expect these to survive." I tapped my shoulder turrets, and they retracted into their housing like scared pets.

Piper was busy manually porting over map information from our isolated comms to our shared HUD. I turned my isolated comms off.

My ears popped painfully as the ambient pressure dropped. The sound I was accustomed to was suddenly gone. A wave of nausea washed over me. The winds shifted, and the temperature plummeted. The audio filters didn't screen the moaning metal as it contracted. The turtle covered its barrel and sensitive components and locked itself down. The occasional loud BANG rattled me.

"Get Tech back to the turtle," Piper ordered.

Shantu and I holstered our weapons to shove-carry Dr. Selig's heavy armor back to the turret emplacement. There, we propped our shields up and waited.

The first bang knocked the wind out of me. I felt my bones being slapped by the shockwave. The following slams were so disorienting that all I could do was relax and wait.

I was still being raddled out of my body when Piper's voice pulled me back in.

"Plasma snap!" they said. "Weapons free! Tech, stay in the hole!"

Shantu and I left our shields over Dr. Selig.

Plasma snap is a misfire for the shattered tears. The shrapnel turns into plasma, and if you're not within a meter of it, you're fine, save maybe going deaf. The effect has something to do with ambient temperature, pressure, conditions, and something. I don't remember.

The snaps came with the thick black rain I was emerging into. Chemical sensors warned that it was an active corrosive slurry of a bunch of changing shit. I didn't bother reading the details beyond the lethal threat.

Weapons fire consistent with khanate inventory appeared on our sensors.

Piper ordered us to go dark at the top of a mound of scrap,

which was melting in the corrosive rain. We found depressions that would hide our silhouettes. Our acoustic sensors had active stealth that could, in theory, give false images back to unmatched sensors.

The fact I was comfortable wrapped in environmentally controlled armor made the flashing and noise feel like a rave.

What the fuck was wrong with me?

Note: Unpack this with Scout. There should not be this much emotional overlap between engaging with the enemy and public ridicule for social ineptitude.

I have issues, but I'm working on them.

Back to worrying about shit that will kill me. I worried that even if the acoustic active stealth worked, the snaps were producing enough radiation to give us away versus the pile of rapidly softening metal we were on.

A red threat arrow appeared overhead. Its acoustic signature was a khanate's braking thrusters. The massive thing touched down with a heavy thud. Heavy electrostatic fields pushed the chemical fallout away. The shoulder turrets were larger than my rifle. Its arms were massive plasma cannons with barrels I could stick my leg into. The racks of missiles across its back were enough to siege a city.

Things in my brain snapped into place. The shadow below the shoulder turrets was massive. I could get a grenade into those plasma cannons. The exposed articulation was asking for a thermal grenade or a blade. I wanted to glare at Piper for not letting us have our AVs.

This thing was stupid.

It was one of those pride pieces. All fat, no muscle. We had briefings about these monstrosities. I don't know why looking at this engineering abortion pissed me off so much.

It took one step, and my acoustic sensors detected speakers in its feet to amplify the thud.

Then it hit me. I was irritated at this overengineered pile of shit because of my time at Telex's. It was one of those concept-driven pieces that should have been aborted after the trade show or at inception. It was built to empty the accounts of unsuspecting traders. These walking facades of engineering competence were held together by paywalls, maintenance plans, and recalls.

They were never meant to be functional; they were built to look good while nothing worked, and the owner was blamed for not buying the ultra-premium platinum package.

I now had the chance to get retribution for all the hours wasted on the phone with a call center while they told me the part couldn't have failed even though I was on day three of a thirty-minute bit of recall work ordered by the manufacturer.

I gave a little kick and rolled downhill, taking as much trash as I could with me. The big mech made an amplified metal noise as it spun toward me. It was off target, looking at the other trash.

I hate this fucking thing. Its existence was an insult to me and my AV.

I could feel Shantu cheering me on, and Piper scolding me.

But my leap was perfect. I killed the gyroscope on impact. Drove my tet right through it. Claws out, I held onto the mech and drove my thermal sword into the primary power bus before it hit the ground. The whole thing went limp.

It wasn't fast or clean. It took some time to get through that much armor. But we got it done. The impression I got was that the pilot didn't know how to go manual and was fighting stick drift and overcorrecting.

Pro tip: If your equipment is fighting you, you're doing something wrong. You need to find out what it's trying to tell you.

Shantu hit the secondary before it could reroute. Piper and Dr. Selig were on the thing with mechanical cutters and drills near the cockpit. The canopy blew off in six sections, knocking them both aside.

The pilot came out firing wildly with a sidearm. Their pilot suit melted into steaming globs in the corrosive rain. Their flesh was consumed by the heat and chemicals. The sidearm misfired against the pilot's helmet, failing to penetrate.

Piper recovered and was back on the pilot before I could think. All I could do was just stand there and look at what I had done. They ripped the pilot's dissolving helmet off and jumped to Dr. Selig to shove it in the gel of his backpack.

Inside was a young woman with short curly hair. I imagined it was brown, but her face was a colorful scale of acoustic density. She was as beautiful as she was terrified. Trying to see her destroyed hand. But I doubt she could see in this infinite night. Her head was robbed of her hair by the thick sponges of congealed chemicals that burned away her scalp. She seemed to be trying not to breathe her last breath as the scalding caustic atmosphere waited to end her short life.

Piper pulled her out of the cockpit and tossed her aside.

The beautiful young pilot lay on her side. I could feel her trying to make sense of what was happening. The deck's sludge stripped the flesh from her skull, and with her remaining eye, she stared at me. Her skin cracked before more toxic rain robbed her of that too.

I watched her heart beat for the last time.

War is so fucking stupid.

::crying::

25

ANGER

YOU TWO GOOD?" Piper said. "You haven't said shit in like an hour. That's a new record."

I didn't look at Shantu, and he didn't look at me. I could feel him not looking at me, and it was enough.

While Piper and Dr. Selig were doing their due diligence, we had watched a young girl choke to death as her skin had melted off. She didn't even have the luxury to go out on her own terms. I could almost feel the same thoughts going through Shantu's head.

The khanate's force was seemingly eliminated due to environmental conditions and improper preparation.

My feed reconnected and updated. The local resistance was busy trying to contain the elevator shaft's environmental catastrophe. Videos were set to dramatic music, showing people running to their deaths to secure toxic leaks and environmental equipment.

I closed my feed and hoped that kid and his dad made it out.

Maybe that welding helped…

The temperature dropped, and sludge condensed out of the supersaturated air. It grew these ash sponge things that were as mesmerizing as they were corrosive. They corroded straight through the top two decks, leaving a skeletal melted structure of a horrific forest.

"This is why we don't have visors," Shantu said blandly.

I knew his tone. He wanted to talk about things that keep us safe, not worry about how quickly we would die in this environment. Just like that pilot.

The Vanguard Conscript damage control teams alerted us of their demo efforts and the neutralizing foam they were pumping around the decks below us. On Piper's orders, we used the sludge sponges growing on our armor like the ghillie suits of the old ground armies. With the winds dying down, our sensors' ranges increased.

Khanate pods descended with turrets, firing at nothing. It was a show of force. A waste of energy and ammunition. And there were no civilians down here to impress.

It told me where they were and what they had to kill them.

The khanate soldiers emerged. They stood too tall, too proud, and too clean for this caustic muck. Their armor was factory fresh with their electrostatic repulsion fields. They shined like beacons asking for fléchettes.

We didn't fire. We hid monitoring signals.

We did our jobs.

I thought of the two men on the tram and how I could see that despite their poverty, they were still kind. The locals were worried about each other, not themselves. I hoped they weren't on the tram we had crawled through, dead.

This pit of congealed oils and plastics was what the khanate had brought with them. They made everything ugly so they could look good.

FUCK THEM!

If we didn't move too fast, we would be just more crap moving in the toxic abyss. Our armors instructed us on how to move like chameleons, in swaying back and forth motions almost effortlessly on power-assisted fingers and toes. We slithered toward them in the muck face down, using their own scanning pulses to map our way.

I come from the muck. The muck was dangerous if provoked.

From a few dozen meters away, we observed them, letting our sensors gather emissions data.

The baqua moved like abused dogs. Whenever one of the khanate soldiers barked a command, it was usually followed by a kick for motivation. It was cruel for cruelty's sake.

I was learning what hate really was.

The baqua weren't just abused. They were *broken*. Death itself might be a relief, and I was going to have to give it to them. That made me sad for them…

I didn't hate the baqua. They were just in my way.

In the center of the formation, there was a cache of equipment in cases that they seemed to be fixated on. It felt like a bag of money in a room of frost heads.

I wondered what would happen if I put a grenade on it.

I retreated a safe distance down into a depression of a melted deck and let my armor's auto flinger launch a grenade. I could barely hear the *thump* of the detonation.

Instead of reorganizing to target my position as a new threat, they shot the two closest for not shooting a nine-centimeter black sphere out of the air in an environment that is full of black spheres falling from the sky. Even basic sensor packages should have noted my firing position.

Shantu and Piper finished the rest off. Dr. Selig did his salvaging solo, while we provided overwatch.

The arrangement of the bodies told me that several baqua were distracted by trying to protect the warped cases, using a chemical-resistant tarp as hasty protection. I found "IBOTENATE" on a label, next to a timed lock on the latch. We hooked one on to Dr. Selig because it seemed to be a good idea.

The interference died down enough to let us reconnect our feeds… I mean, the battle net. Another barrage was expected.

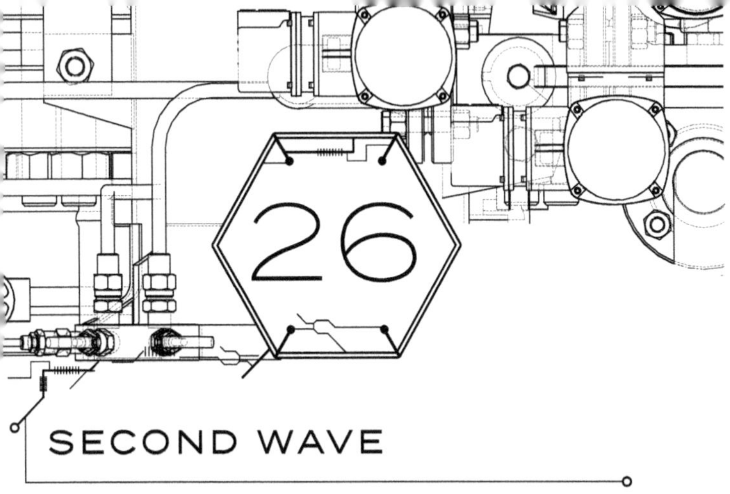

SECOND WAVE

522.295.1941 Human District, Fermi Station

SHANTU AND I got a nap in, and Piper sent Dr. Selig off with our farewells. With the battle net reestablished, we recalled our mules from their parking spot with the guards. The temperatures were letting naphtha and other oils rain from the air. The mules' onboard cooling should be enough to keep the delicate printheads and other systems safe.

We returned to the first turtle and took a bit to help that team. With the mules, we could make a proper fighting position. We built up some barriers and cut their access to the lower deck for a quick outlet for when they need it.

Not if. When.

The Vanguard battle net turned into full sensor coverage. Two khanate drop pods had made it down, so there were at least a few dozen enemies down here.

A second turtle connected and sat on top of something structural. So, we didn't get to cut an escape hatch. The three of us spent our time digging in and building concentric rings of any material that had survived the caustic fallout. Our main donor seemed to be a chemical storage tank that was hit and maybe the reason I was ankle deep in kerosene.

"Hey, Piper. Where does ankle deep in petroleum distillates rank on the weird-shit-o-meter?" I asked because welding in this environment was causing my brain to short out. I thought petroleum products were toxic and flammable, but there wasn't enough oxygen in the bottom of this tube, so it boiled.

Fucking weird.

"I do a point system," they answered nonchalantly. "So, like a two."

"Uh… Okay. What's a ten?"

"I spent six months inside a… You have no frame of reference. Call it a fish the size of a city. It's sentient and a dick. It didn't like one of the other species living in them, but they served some biological purpose, and I didn't know what to do." Their voice was laced with unillustrated frustrations. "The whole thing was a confusing mess on every level. I also had to cover myself with goo to keep its immune system from covering me in shit, turning me into a kidney stone, and pissing me out into the ocean. Every like third day, I was taking a deep dive submersible to recover someone who had let their coating get too thin. I nope-ed out of that."

"So, death by conventional weapons is a one. Noted," Shantu said.

"Good boy. Have a cookie." They pretended to feed him, and he shook his helmet like he was gobbling something out of their hands.

"Oh, fuck both of you," I said.

Piper brought it back around. "Let's call it one point for a hostile environment and another because it's changing. Human-on-human combat, nothing. I'll give another point for the baqua though. Another for them being used as slaves."

"What about the drug addiction?" Shantu asked.

"Still falls under slaves. Operant, classical, societal condition-ing, implants suits—all the same shit. So, like four points."

"We're using brand-new equipment," I added.

"That'd be a point again. *For you*," they said. "This armor is an upgrade for me, but it's like they debugged my other armor. Smoother, faster, and stronger but not a new system. One for an enemy actively trying to kill us. You're at five. If we get shifting allegiances, that shoots it up two points. Random third party takes advantage of the situation would be two points for chaos. But I don't see mercs changing sides much here because the khanate have a long and hard history of killing contractors instead of paying them."

A warning for more shattered tears ended our conversation. We took cover under our shields at our original turtle.

Our local map updated to full detail for the quarter million square meters at the bottom of this shaft. The map was fuzzy past an altitude of two hundred meters. No khanate contacts on the ground. Six other turtles were dark as rally points. Two were orange, showing that they were ready but holding fire.

Shantu picked out a sensor anomaly out of the low fidelity noise. Low fidelity was closer to the raw data that came into the sensor platform. Every noise in the air currents, fluids moving through the pipes, and creaking metal with temperature and pressure changes gets filtered out so only clear signals like a voice, heat signature of equipment, or the bandwidth of a laser gets displayed.

I followed what he was doing and felt like I wanted to vomit.

Take a map, an ordinary terrain map with elevation markers set at a meter. Layer that with the lift's original schematic and equip-ment. Take that and try to track where all that shit went during a bombardment. Follow environmental patterns with wispy swirl-ing glitter. Add a heat map to it. Show the various fluids coming down as staticky rain. Add sound signatures. Not just the wind but creaking metal, splashing fluids, etc. Map the resonance of the damage control teams as the noises they make propagate the superstructure. Sprinkle in the known landmarks, turrets, and detectable personnel. Dial down the highlight for the dead.

It was a fucking mess to look at.

In his feed, he found a signature and tracked it manually. His manual plots showed it moving faster than we could with our armor maxed out. It came to one of the other turrets without alerting the guards. Then the contact came this way.

He sent us the targeting data, and we followed the virtual orb. I kept my sensor probe up on my backpack, so the rest of me could stay behind cover.

The contact stopped short—just behind our cover.

"Wraith is a freak," an amplified voice that I recognized said. "Come out. Easy now."

I returned to the raining petrol and darkness. My sensors resolved the change in the rain, making the figure look like a shadow. I knew the way she walked though, even in her bulky movement assisted armor.

"What do I call you now?" I asked.

"Gunny will do." Takakoa approached and offered me a fist to bump. "I'm taking command down here."

I bumped it.

Her armor was sleek, low profile, and elegant. There was a bulge on her back but nothing like the monstrous backpacks we carried. No shoulder turrets. No sensor probe. Just her rifle, which was a design I didn't recognize. Then I noticed her mule. A predatory-looking thing that scurried up behind her as she held her rifle out. It looked like a mechanical cat with a sophisticated sensor pod for a head. With an over articulated arm, it took the rifle and placed it in the appropriate slot on its back.

Under Piper's orders, we accepted the files with more

battlefield updates and were inserted into Takakoa's battle net. She had a team at one thousand meters and another at two thousand meters. The borders of our map expanded to show sensor bugs, available retreat paths, drone and turret emplacements, and contingency rally points.

The highest team was managing a few dozen drones that were shooting the shattered tears. The drone targeting was impressive. Each shot fired seemed to take out a dozen or more shattered tears in limited chain reactions. Friendly assets were also fighting at various points higher up the shaft. It explained the drumroll of explosions reverberating down.

"I'm impressed y'all saw me coming," she said. "Are your sensor packages rated for it?"

Unrepentant, Piper and I pointed at Shantu, who gave an awkward wave.

"I saw it in the raw data." He rolled back our sensor feed and showed the targeting orb he was feeding us.

"I see your cursor, but I don't see any recognizable signal," she said.

"You kind of have to look at everything at once. Do you want me to build a presentation?"

"No. But I need you on that more than I need another gun." She gestured for a moment. "If the khanate are serious about making use of this real estate to make a staging area, scouts and forward observers should be here. I would like to go hunting. Piper, thoughts?"

"If his role is going to be an analyst, I would like relief and get him on a real data feed, not a disposable point defense platform," they said. "Get me another gun if you can."

"I'm your person." Her head bobbed as she talked to someone in her helmet.

We exchanged glances like we were waiting for our order at the bar.

"The lieutenant says he'll come fight if you can spot contacts in raw data."

"Didn't he punch me in the face?" I asked.

"That was the major."

"Welcome to the team, Stalker. You're on point," Piper said in a friendly tone.

Did they just try to give Takakoa an order?

"Negative. I'm on overwatch," she said, a smile in her voice. She pet the sensor package on her mule for emphasis.

We got moving on our patrol route.

A waypoint and formation shadows appeared in my HUD. I was being scored based on how I got to cover. An animation appeared, showing how I should move to cover and improve my score.

Seriously? This was awkward.

I was in combat below my girlfriend and my best friend's partner. Now, I was watching some computer animation telling me how to move.

"Okay. No, this is a fucking distraction," I said on the open channel.

"What's that?" Takakoa signaled for a halt. "Oohh. Right. You don't have training records. Stand by."

I looked back and watched a blue silhouette gesture behind the gray mound of wreckage. Her hands went from playing with the menus to arguing with an unknown figure.

I was booted from the Vanguard net. Then asked to rejoin without the training bullshit.

Shantu left through a different access point that was guarded by Vanguard Conscripts. I couldn't see or hear the hundreds or thousands of personnel gathering on the other side, waiting to join the fight, but I knew they were there. I could feel them like they were a pressure.

Leaving Shantu, I wanted to ask her if she requested this assignment or if her connection to us made it the logical choice.

I got my chance when she had us take some time scouting the damaged decks full of active sensors.

"Did you pull this gig to come check on me?" I asked, trying to be cheeky.

"One hundred percent," she said with a flat tone. "I'm into you. I'm happier than I've been in I don't know how long. That being said, make no mistake. If you compromise this mission, I'll put you down myself." She took a deep breath. "If I knew you were out here and didn't make an effort, I would be leaving a chamber empty."

Order: One ton of bricks

For: James August Childs

Delivery: My *head*

"Uh…" I said, stunned. "I don't know what to do with that. I…am…processing…"

"Take your time. You good to stay on mission?" she said with amazing command of herself and the situation.

How the fuck does she do that?

"I'm good," I said.

I folded that shit and put it up like a love letter soldiers used to keep in their helmets. When I was ready, I would sniff, and it would smell like her hair.

Right now, I had shit to do.

Takakoa gave orders, and we continued to sweep the lower decks. Here and there, one of us would ping or do an active scan of some super structure. The upper two decks had completely collapsed onto the third. Starting at the fifth deck, every twenty-third deck was a super deck that was all structural to prevent a runaway collapse.

Hours passed until Shantu finally called.

"Sunglasses to Landslide," he said.

I knew he had just made that shit up.

Takakoa looked at me for a countersign that didn't exist.

I mocked wiping my face in frustration and pointed at her. Because that was her name now.

"Landslide. Go," she answered.

He gave some rather detailed instructions about how he wanted us to emerge from the lower decks. Him not being an asshole was worrying.

I made a bit more of a show of readying my weapon than was necessary as a signal to Piper and Takakoa.

They got it.

"Hold," Shantu said.

I froze like I was going to step on a mine.

He spoke in my ear. "On my mark, set velocity at less than two hundred meters per second. Fire here." A dotted red firing line with degree indicators appeared in my HUD. "Target."

I spun and lined up the barrel, using the telemetry from my armor.

"Fire."

BAM.

From the deck, a metal sphere bounced and rolled.

"Recover it!" Takakoa ordered.

I dove more than ten meters toward the sphere, but it bloomed while I was in the air. It sprouted legs, sensors, and other appendages and scurried away. Without turning, she did a graceful backflip to land on it. It closed a moment before her heavy boots crushed it into the spongy, oil-covered metal marsh we were walking in. She squatted on it and wildly flailed her arms to keep her balance on such a small area.

Piper was already diving toward Takakoa's feet with a knife in hand. In an unnatural maneuver, they brought one of their legs back at a right angle to help her balance. The sphere fought to open its shell. I couldn't tell if it was trying to call for help, deploy weapons, or just get away. But the two of them held the tableau until their mules closed.

Then Takakoa jumped.

The sphere bounced up with her, swatting away Piper's knife. Her mule pounced on it like a ravenous fox on a rat. A small explosion ripped off one of the mule's hands, foot, manipulator… Whatever.

"Khanate sensor drone," she said robotically. "Core's intact. Runner inbound."

A green arrow appeared in my HUD. I looked up to see a massive heat signature and had to take a step back against the thruster wash. The blast almost pushed me off my feet.

Then it was gone.

"What the fuck? Was that a missile?" I said, breaking communication discipline.

"Valkyrie. Quick reaction force," she said with a fanboy's admiration.

"Drone?"

She half chuckled. "No."

"But—"

"I know." She was probably cutting me off before I said something I shouldn't have.

The person had to have decelerated at something like twenty g's. Fuck me.

After the valkyrie cleared the battle space, for the whole heartbeat they were in it… Fucking insane. Anyway, after they left, she received orders to link up with a few other squads but to not engage.

"It means they're bringing in conscripts and mercs," she said, "for initial contact. Look at your environmental readout. Most off the shelf HEPS can handle this. Baqua and conscripts fight now. Once they make a solid mess of things, we'll engage." She explained the ugly tactics of using cannon fodder to limit the casualty rates of highly trained military. "I did my time running point. It's their turn."

Takakoa, Piper, and I retreated to the lower decks with two other squads. We found a heavily shielded server room and locked the hatch behind us. Orders were to go dark and stay hidden for thirty hours.

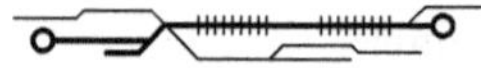

522.296.0400 Human District, Fermi Station

Takakoa, Piper, I, and the other two squads stayed hidden when the tears fell. The acoustic sensors projected that another deck had collapsed.

We stayed hidden when the baqua landed and tried to take their beachhead.

We stayed hidden when other squads were ordered out on scouting missions.

We stayed hidden when the conscript corps gave their valiant charge to retake the lift. Every VAF in the server room stayed silent during the charge.

Eventually, Takakoa shared it with me. "Sorry. You don't get to be an aggie without surviving a charge like that. That's why we're not talking to you. You weren't there with us. Those two"—she nodded to some people I didn't catch—"were at Liddy's World with me."

I shook my head. I didn't know the engagement.

"Starless Nation decided they wanted to take the world just after biocompatibility was verified. Frontier settlers were prepping for the green world packages. Two hundred million starless followed the package in. What. A. Shit. Show. They were starting to strip the mines by the time we got there. We fought nonstop for over a year, just one orbital supply drop to the next. We ended up bringing in the osheran because the biosphere was so damaged."

I nodded. "We have the starliner. Two dozen versus thousands of galunkin. Couldn't disengage without taking a shot up the ass. So, I get it as much as I can."

She did the slow nod people do when hearing a story that mirrors one of their experiences.

The conversation petered out from there. The aggies sedated themselves while I struggled to sleep.

"Shantu shakes his head like that when he wants to get something off his mind," Piper said over a private channel. "You okay?"

"That pilot is still stuck in my mind," I said.

"Sorry. I should have shot her, but I was afraid to hit the tech samples," they said, sounding full of remorse. "She didn't need to suffer like that. That's on me, not you." They patted my shoulder. "Me, not you."

Piper woke me hours later.

I felt the combat-snap-awake. My double tap was in my hand, and I was on a knee, searching for targets, before I realized I was facing green wireframes of friendlies. The aggies nodded approvingly. As my head cleared, I noticed all of them had their weapons pointed away. "Trigger disabled" flashed in my HUD.

I didn't remember putting my weapon on safety.

"Stims?" Takakoa asked.

"I don't think so." I checked my medical log. "No. No stims. They're loaded anyway. I don't like them. We're not there yet."

"Money boy doesn't like to ride the lightning," one of the aggies joked.

"Sounds like drug-seeking behavior," she said, her tone a warning. "I'll be sure to put that in your review."

"Gunny, I don't—"

"Now is when you shut up," a second aggie added.

We switched to a private channel, and she asked hard questions about my drug use. I answered honestly. My recreational drug use phase passed rather quickly after a brief incarceration.

When I started to get uncomfortable, I pushed back. "Where's this coming from?"

"It's the sergeant in me." She took a long centering breath. "The way you kick and fidget in your sleep."

Piper did a snort-laugh. "That's him. He and Shantu both. They're both light sleepers and twitchy."

"Piper, what the fuck?" I didn't quite yell at them.

"You set the channel to private, not secure. Anyway, if you gently rock him when you wake him, he'll be less twitchy."

"Why do you know that?" I asked.

"The starliner. Everyone learned how to wake you without triggering you."

"Please go away." I couldn't boot them from the channel because they had supervisory rights.

"What? If we're going to meet your girlfriend in the combat zone, she gets some sensitive information."

"Thank you, Piper," Takakoa said, her tone oozing with feminine solidarity.

"You're welcome," they said with a verbal smirk before leaving the channel.

What the fuck just happened? Where the fuck was Scout when I needed him to untangle this mess of emotional confusion?

"What's your combat cycle?" Takakoa asked.

"My what?"

"How often are you pulled out of combat to maintain effectiveness?"

"Fuck…" I said with disgust.

"Why?"

"That's a Piper question."

Her military bearing slipped with a giggle.

I sighed and pinged Piper back into the channel. "Piper, how do you determine our combat cycle?"

"Tchaikovsky mapping."

"Ah, thank you, Piper," she said with a clear invitation to leave. They took it.

"That makes this difficult."

"Explain please."

Her voice changed to an almost lecture tone. "Tchaikovsky mapping relies on biometrics and projected opposition to optimize performance to achieve goals. The VAF uses the experiential mentorship method to focus more on unit cohesiveness and individual development. The difference in philosophies is that ours organizes personnel to take advantage of training opportunities, while Tchaikovsky mapping focuses on maximum utilization of available personnel versus goals." She hesitated like she realized she had slipped into a rote lecture. Warmer, she said, "Sorry. It means we're going to have a hell of a time syncing our R & R cycles."

I looked past the next day off. "What's next for us? Never mind this engagement. How do we make this work?"

She let out a deep sigh, staring off. "I'm an aggie through and through. My biggest fear is that I've had my place here for ten years." She looked around and chuckled. "Not in this particular shithole but in the VAF. Until a couple weeks ago, I was worried I'd survive all my wars and get my old ass parked behind a desk. I was looking forward to having my name etched into the VAF Hall of Entry." She gave a laugh that was devoid of mirth.

"What do you want?" I asked.

"What *do* I want? I want to get my people out alive. I want to be buried on Earth. I want to die doing something that matters. When you've been through as many engagements as I have, you start getting worried that something stupid is going to punch your ticket."

I knew she was older than me, but I never felt the gap until now. She had spent decades in shitholes like this, surrounded by people like us.

Was I a good person to get stuck in a foxhole with?

"Like getting suffocated under a fat guy." I had no idea why I said that. Maybe I was uncomfortable.

Thankfully, she snort-laughed. "That happened to a guy in my company when I was a conscript. We were taking R & R on a starliner, and that's what happened. Poor girl was devastated." She laughed like she was holding back tears. "Oh, fuck. Something's wrong with me. I need to laugh more." She turned back to me. "Tell you what. Don't die, and we'll figure everything else out. I might even make an aggie out of you."

There it was again. I'm a Marauder. I don't want to give that up.

I don't know if or how I tipped her off that I didn't like the career advice, but her tone was almost apologetic. "Or you can be my househusband. Cook dinner, take care of the kids, and all that. Honestly, it doesn't matter. Five more, and I'll beat the odds against me."

"What's that?"

"I'm at eleven years as an aggie. At sixteen, you've lasted longer than seventy percent of all aggies. There's a sharp drop off between fifteen and sixteen."

"Oh. Wait."

There was no way she was in her forties. Thirties, sure. Forties, no.

"Math not mathing for you?" Takakoa chuckled. "I've spent a lot of time in a pod. I'm space rated, but I opt for the long nap to get there. I get defrosted every other month during the long hauls to maintain proficiency. By now, I've spent almost a decade asleep."

"Oh." I changed the topic back to hide how dumb I felt. "I don't cook, and I don't know how I feel about kids."

Speaking of issues.

Kids. Just the word makes me think of the child soldiers who I still don't know if I was doing them any favors by getting them to Vanguard versus feeding them fléchettes. They might just live out their lives in long-term care facilities.

She laughed politely. "Fair enough. We'll make something happen. But like my old training officer said, 'Important things are simple, and simple things are hard.' I wish I could kiss you because we're moving out." Her posture stiffened, and she looked around as she shifted gears to go back into combat mode.

She sent me one last private message. "We'll make it happen."

The icon to go dark illuminated. I killed my active sensors and comms. She signed for me and Piper to take ten before leaving the hole.

KLANG!

The breaching charge made my ears pop. The noise vibrated straight through my armor, despite all the fancy noise-canceling tech.

Light poured through the hole, and my visor dimmed to fight the glare. White sand and dust poured through the opening, making me feel like a mummy in a tomb. The first squad launched themselves out. The rest followed with all the rapid coordination I would expect from the best action movie.

Piper and I had our mules do maintenance and tune our armor while we waited.

When we emerged, we emerged into an apocalyptic desert. Glaring white flares hung motionless above us, lifting themselves by their parachutes. We found ourselves in the palm of a mangled skeletal pair of hands reaching out from the white sands of agony.

The display was so surreal that Piper had to nudge me to take a defensive position as we spread out. Sounds of combat echoed from every direction. Sand and shrapnel rained from above in curtains. Light oscillated like an underwater scene but with glaring harshness.

A shockwave decimated our position, burying us in the sand.

My mule pulled me out by my armor's hardpoints. I spun, searching for targets down the sight of my weapon.

The extrapolated strike shadow was an unhelpful big ass cone from the point of impact. The unobtrusive information on likely munitions would have been useful if I knew anything about artillery.

My mule was digging Piper's mule out.

Every shadow was an enemy to my confused brain.

I took a deep breath.

With Piper's mule free, I ordered mine to mirror at my six in a sweep of the parameter. The deck bucked again, and I landed on my ass. My mule pushed me to my feet.

I set my comms to continuous line of sight. "Priority one: point defense! Priority two: recover nearby friendlies!" I shouted at my armor, hoping I was getting the voice commands right.

The gel in the gloves squished as I gripped my weapon tighter. The armor was smarter than me because it kept me from crushing my weapon against my shoulder. On the starliner, I had developed the habit of hugging my weapon to my shoulder so hard that I scraped off the paint. Now, I was glad my armor resisted my unconscious habits.

My mule joined Piper's mule at digging them out.

I took cover near a surviving pillar and took in the battle space. Above, shockwaves ripped through the air, the explosions hidden by floating glaring saturation flares. Curtains of sand and shrapnel fell from the battle overhead.

Imagine your favorite game show host's voice. "In today's episode of *Shit I Wish I Didn't Know*, the analysis of the sand raining on me is roughly three percent human biological material and seven percent baqua."

Not cool…

My emotional circuit breaker tripped. What almost made me a part of that three percent?

Eventually, the mules locked together and pulled Piper from the sand. I watched my mule swivel a turret to gesture my position. Comms were still off.

Piper gestured to where I should go, their relative line and primary and alternate rally points. I took the time to repeat it back. We were on patrol in a hostile zone. No time to fuck up.

Slow is smooth, smooth is fast, and fast is alive.

Deep breath.

I low crawled, relying on my sensors to guide me from one column to the next. No contact. I ran to a mangled shipping container and peeked into one of the many holes and came eye to eye with a baqua.

I kicked off the container like it was going to explode and fired from the hip. My shoulder turret obliterated its helmet visor. The helmet itself seemed to stay intact.

"Max pen!" I screamed, flying through the air.

The turrets sprayed death to a whole squad as I brought my weapon up to my shoulder. The report from my shoulder turrets and their movements gave me a clear signature to target through the container. There was heavy, dense equipment—scores of khanate weapons—in there that I had to target around.

My HUD gave shadows for the equipment that was stopping their weapons.

Laser backscatter burned the air near me. I wished I could thank whoever designed my armor's counter sensors suite. I cut my turret fire, sprinted three steps, and slung my weapon as I slid to a halt. I dropped to my belly and let my armor rocket baby me back in the opposite direction.

Rocket baby is a weird sort of gecko crawl where I must go boneless and let the armor move me with no input to stay under cover. The movement is *not* a natural feeling at all. It feels like going prone and then having four people move your arms and legs like you're doing jumping jacks.

It's weird but better than getting shot.

I set my grenade flinger to airburst sparkling chaff between me and whoever was shooting at me.

Fucking *Liberty's Spear*, a video game, was the only reason I thought to use a grenade as concealment.

I found new cover and took a moment to survey the battle space as some data filtered in from the Vanguard nets. Drones and other aircraft had fought targets in the shaft walls and each other. Counter missiles intercepted larger missiles. Ballistics were dropped on targets from kilometers higher up. Pockets of friendly green were surrounded by an ocean of red.

I raked the chaff, making sure the baqua kept their heads down, and tried to orient myself with the larger picture. But that backfired as a line of baqua charged out of the cloud of sparkling glitter. They were firing wildly, level with the deck.

I assumed they detected my weapon and decided quantity had a quality of its own.

"OPTIMIZE! TURRETS FREE!" I shouted at my armor.

I focused on looking for a secondary explosion—grenades, power cells, something. My armor locked me in as the weapons fire rocked me. The first two dropped. The vibration in my chest each time I fired warned me that this weapon wasn't meant for mortal hands.

My shot analysis showed lines of baqua falling as the ten-by-three-hundred-millimeter fléchettes flew just below its specific heat velocity. Return fire sprayed me with sand and then hammered my shield when my sensor ghosts were eliminated. The green incoming fire solutions showed the armor ablation at negligible. A missile peppered me with shrapnel as it prematurely exploded. Two more went off course as more warnings came.

FUCK!

My armor still wasn't letting me move.

Near me, a second weapon appeared with Piper under it. It chittered versus barking, strafing knees and ankles and tripping the front runners.

The mules fell into line behind us, putting on a laser show of missiles.

The baqua launched grenades as soon as they entered range. We answered with our own airburst grenades and point defense. The torrent broke the charge, but more than half of the baqua were alive, if not completely mobile.

Pro tip: Batteries do not explode in an oxygen-poor atmosphere.

FUCKING NOTHING!

Video games lied. If you shoot a grenade, they do not explode. If they are armed, they burn. Bullshit!

I mean, it makes sense. You don't want your buddy's bandolier talking out the whole squad because he caught a stray. But still, nothing? I'm proud of those shots. I figured I would get one secondary explosion. I'll blame it on the radon I'm swimming in.

My mule reloaded my charge packs and ammunition. Piper and I put down the survivors as quickly and as humanely as possible.

Forty-plus baqua died in less than thirty seconds of pure panic.

That was why I trained, drilled, and ran exercises. Then did it all over again upside down and blindfolded while listening to Krodsyn operas at full volume.

I did not think for any of those seconds. I just did shit.

When the last shot was fired, Piper said, "I want that building. Then do a maintenance check." They highlighted a hardened control building. The sand had filled in so high that I couldn't see the ground floor.

The tough building had shrugged off several hard hits. Sand filled a meter thick. Composite metal bloomed out like a flower where someone had tried to exploit a seam near a window. It was a little more than a scratch, but the window had held.

We had the mules fabricate excavation tools from whatever scraps they could find. They dug down almost ten meters before finding a ground level hatch large enough for my AV.

I had the codes to the blast-proof air lock in our mission packet. My HUD auto translated the constellation some other species used as common symbols instead of numbers on the access pad. The two-meter-thick hatch pulled itself in on giant screws at the corners.

Piper and I, with our mules, were pressure washed with solvents, while unseen fans pulled the spray away. Kilos of oil-caked sand fell from our armor and mules. The chemical-resistant ceramic floor sprouted sprinklers to flush the contaminants away. We were then swept with big magnets that caused my HUD to warp and go fuzzy.

There was a lot of ferrous material sticking to my armor. The thing looked fuzzy by the time it was done.

My HUD translated the pictograms on every screen to "LOCKDOWN: PLEASE CONTACT…"

The impression I got was that this was a reactor facility with all the job safety, electromagnetic, and high-energy posters. I didn't recognize the species in the safety pictograms. It was bipedal, but the arms and legs were too long.

The posters weren't in the holographic hypertext, so this wasn't a mixed-species area.

I stacked behind Piper on the interior lock as the procedures finished.

The interior hatch opened, my HUD flashed red, and I let my armor guide my hand and keep me from strafing Piper as they launched themself forward. It happened too fast. The trained part of my mind focused on the simple icons and colors. Shoot the red. Stay away from the blue.

Piper was a spinning top of death. Our turrets targeted weapons with the precision only machines had. The turrets didn't have the bite to chew through that much armor in that little time, but they could rattle sensors and push weapons off target. Maybe even disable them.

A heartbeat later, Piper stopped on a dime as a medical bot targeted them with multiple turrets holding fire. The pain of a thousand rounds that didn't penetrate my shield washed over me.

"Breathe. Just breathe," I told myself.

In.

One.

Two.

Three.

Out.

One.

Two.

Three.

"Stay on target," I said through gritted teeth. I glanced at my medical monitor. All green.

"Take the wounded and go," Piper ordered the bot.

I stepped out from behind them and raised a weapon at the bot. Two turrets swiveled toward me. Something about threat rating and deference algorithms popped in my head as one turret swiveled back to Piper. I ordered my little grenade arm to extend with a white phosphorus at the tip. All four turrets painted me with active sensors.

I knocked on Piper's shoulder armor to keep them going. They ran off, and I held the standoff with the medical bot. Several moments passed. Then it retracted its turrets. It started with stripping the baqua of their weapons in submission. When it finished, I lowered the barrel a hair off target.

When the medical bot deployed a high-speed circular saw, I flinched but somehow managed to not shoot the damn thing.

Maybe it was testing my reaction. Maybe it was just trying to get its charges out alive. I relaxed my posture a hair. It butchered baqua limbs and sprayed three nozzles of sealant before shoving screaming baqua into body bags and inflating them like morbid pillows. It glued the bags together and departed, looking like a sinister caterpillar.

Piper had me and the mules activate counter sensors with no active scans while we swept the structure. The interior only had conventional firefights not decimated by high heat and chemical erosion.

One of the upper control rooms had been destroyed by an explosive placed on a window. The window held, but the interior partition walls along with any equipment were debris now.

The central hallways had quarters, a galley, laundry, and a single nurse's office with a common rec area on the opposite side. We used the mules as forward and rear guard while we searched the rooms one by one. We were quicker than we were thorough.

"I'm crashing," I told Piper as fatigue and pain caught up to me.

"Acknowledged. We need to repair our armor anyway. Let's go back to the air lock and let the mules scavenge there."

We retreated to the air lock. Sleep was that teasing bitch that would always promise to make it up to you but then would leave you on *read*.

The mules worked on my armor first. Many of the plates were deformed or had significant ablation. Them treating me like a truck needing a hydraulic fluid change was not the way to get me to take a nap.

I took my turn to stand guard. Piper's armor was in worse shape. In more than a few places, their armor was down to the ballistic liner. A human would have had torn muscles and all kinds of soft tissue injuries.

Piper had said something that I missed.

"What now?" I asked.

"Get back to it. We're here to do a job…"

"Save it," I snapped harsher than I had meant.

They were going to get into a spiel about how contracts are agreements, and if we don't honor our agreements, we can't be trusted. Blah. Blah. Blah. But my brain was recovering from the adrenaline crash and was now running on irritation that I didn't get to ride into a nap.

"We're not hunkering down in here," I grumbled. "I'm thinking we find an antenna, get a better picture, and then go make some shit up."

"That may be the smartest thing you've ever said," they said.

"Make some shit up?"

"Yes. You've grown up from the fuck-some-shit-up stage of your life."

I laughed, and we got to it.

With a lot more wire pulling than I really want to talk about, we found the antennae built into the windows. We isolated one, fabricated an adapter, and plugged a mule into it. Voilà. Comms outside a bunker.

"Havok Actual, this is Mike Rock One with Mike Rock Actual." Mike for mercenary. The rest I could make up. "Transmitting in the blind on unsecured equipment. You should have Mike Rock Two with you. Tell Two to quit fucking with me while I sleep. How copy?"

That was my authenticator that I just made up. Shantu would know what I'm talking about.

I repeated the transmission twice with long pauses, knowing they would do appropriately paranoid military things before responding. The background chatter sounded like someone was talking in a crowded nightclub.

"Mike Rock One, this is Havok Oscar." The operator. Not anyone in command. "Negative on that request." Meaning

Shantu must have authenticated it. "Negative data on this net. Voice only. Status?"

"Green. Had to change jackets and could use some more party favors."

The operator continued my theme. "Copy. Green and enjoying the party. Will check on the party favors. No promises."

The background chatter increased for a moment. I had to turn down the volume when it sounded like someone threw the headset in a dryer.

"I don't have time for this counterintelligence bullshit," a gruffer voice said.

The line went dead. No busy restaurant noises. Just static. Piper and I exchanged looks with each other.

"Mike Rock One, this is Havok Oscar Two. We have some kids who have lost their parents in a bad neighborhood. Should be visible from your location."

I looked at Piper, and they nodded. "Copy. Looking for some lost kids in trouble. Over."

"Happy hunting. Havok Oscar Two out."

I pulled the cables from the mules, and they stowed the connectors. We all descended the stairs, and I really didn't want to leave the bunker.

With a deep breath, I pressed forward.

Outside the bunker, we listened for the heaviest concentrations of khanate weapons signatures. Visibility was down to a few dozen meters with swirls of ionized dust, smoke, and ash. We followed our staticky grayscale acoustic sensors, complete with dancing ghosts of unconfirmed contacts.

The rumble in my armor and in the ground told me I was getting close to something that could kill me. The individual weapon signatures resolved into numbered bubbles with approximate locations. After fifty, I stopped paying attention, looked for cover, and signaled to go dark.

This was a shit sandwich too big to eat.

My sensors warned me of large objects coming from above and showed landing shadows of drop pods. I rolled out of the way and pushed along with breaking thrusters. I rallied with Piper in some wreckage. They ordered me to conceal and observe.

The drop pod parachutes retracted into their casings while the corners separated into four separate point defense batteries. The batteries walked away on their skinny legs, almost nothing more than a laser turret with some legs. More waves of braking thrusters. The air cracked with sledgehammers as it tried to equalize electrons.

One of the drop pods exploded, and a white streak of light reached down as if to say "Fuck that thing in particular."

I couldn't tell what class of weapon destroyed that drop pod, but the others seemed to shrug off the death of their companions with indifference.

Human handlers struggled to corral the baqua into something that looked like a fighting force and not a bag of cats. My sensors resolved Vanguard weapons and something that might be a firing line.

The point defense batteries covered their incoming companions. I could feel my organs move as the noise canceling vibrated my armor. I rolled my sensors back and found the Vanguard weapons and the mess of a deployment.

I grabbed for Piper's armor, feeling for the hard link on their hand for their hand.

The hard link is a physical connection to limit our battlefield emissions.

"I think that's the kids or whatever we're supposed to pull out."

They didn't hesitate. They spread out into rocket baby mode, and I followed suit.

Missile fragments bounced off my shield, threatening to reveal us. The khanate point defense was swatting a lot of them out of the air. We blipped our short-range friend or foe identifier before we crested the nearby sand dune.

A flash of red and three rounds deflected off my helmet.

"Stand the fuck down." The sergeant ripped the rifle from the conscript's hands.

"But Sarge, he's got a weapon," the green-as-fucking-grass conscript said.

The sergeant's front heel kicked the conscript in the chest plate, sending the conscript sliding on his ass. "No shit! This is a war zone. If you don't have a weapon, you're fucking dead." He threw the weapon back to conscript and then addressed us. "Do you have a plan to unfuck this, or did you want to die with some company?"

Piper looked at me, the gesture exaggerated with their armor.

"We're on it," I said on reflex with no fucking plan. I used the next round of flash from the batteries to transition from cover to the trench.

"Before you get on it…" He went over some authentication questions that were in my briefing packet. Then invited us to his squad net.

I adjusted the settings for my mule to start resupplying them.

"If anyone so much as uses harsh language in the direction of that mule, I will recycle your armor for ammunition with you in it," the sergeant barked over the local net. "These mercs have a choice to not fucking be here, and yet here they are, so they will have your utmost respect."

Why do sergeants sound the same?

I tuned out his methods of discipline and looked through the roster. This squad was all that was left of an overstrength company. Over ninety percent were dead or missing. More sealant than armor. And I walked in with more rounds than they had between them.

While I was taking a nap two decks down, these people were watching their friends die…

They took the storm of the baqua to the face while weapon-ries fell like rain. They were almost black on everything, down to standoff potshots. I didn't know how they weren't overrun yet.

"Sarge, you're not going to like this," I said flatly. I set the mules to dig up their dead to scavenge armor parts for the paper-mâché they wore.

"Bring me their tags and stack them over there," he grumbled. Piper's mule fabricated a small portable shelter to do armor repairs. The conscript spoke up again. "Sergeant, that's—"

"Conscript Whoever The Fuck You Are," the sergeant barked. The unfortunate conscript's name was clearly displayed on our HUDs and their chest plate.

"What part of my demeanor could have been misconstrued as an invitation to listen to your cerebral evacuation? Sarachek!" He shouted the name with an unnecessary amount of authority. "Sort this banana out."

Cpl. Sarachek picked up the ass chewing. "If you don't have eyes, give me your ammo and filters now because you clearly have lost sight of the situation. They are dead. We are not. We do not have the luxury of being squeamish. We fight on!"

"Over there." The sergeant sent me a waypoint. "If your mules can rig us up some kind of awning with a sloping side so we have a defensive fighting position and not a sinking trench, I would be ever so grateful."

I sketched something into a public workspace. It was a simple load-bearing structure that would hold the sand. I used arrows to show firing position spacing and where I would like egress points. "Like this?"

"That's more than we have now. Don't run your plasma cutters for too long. That's how we lost our mules." His armor seemed to crack. "Maybe shield the cutting. Fuck, I don't know."

I opened a private channel with Piper. "Hey. The sergeant wants to dig in." I sent them my sketch.

"Okay," they said. "You get on it, and I'll keep with the scavenging."

"Why are you being weird and making me do all the talking?"

"Conflict avoidance. I don't have a good history with Vanguard grunts. At best, I'm no better than a mule. At worst, I'm a threat that needs to be eliminated. If they think you're my boss, it's better for everyone."

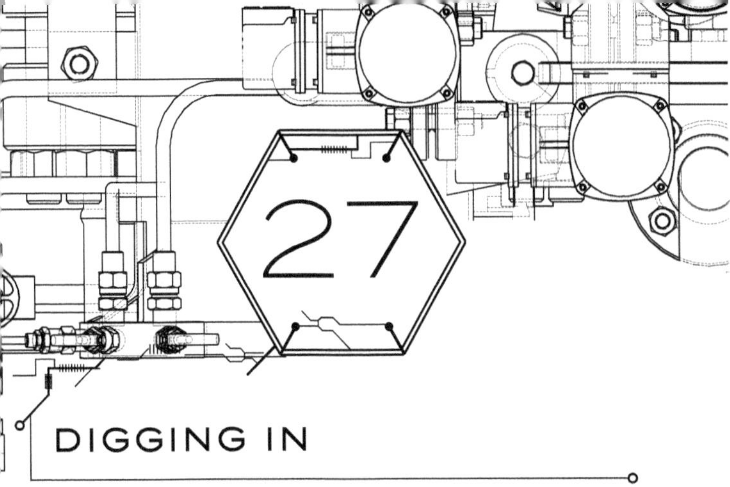

27

DIGGING IN

THE TOP OF the lift had become a white sandy desert filled with toxic gases. The skeletal remains of chemically ravaged decks populated the area. Light was provided by harsh flares that strobed violently. The Vanguard equipment description said the flares were designed to cause seizures in baqua, and some humans were at risk.

Fucking brutal…

Our briefing packet provided the settings to filter the strobing effect out. But horrible battle sounds still stormed around us like we were the calm eye.

Piper and I led the conscripts to a chemical handling facility. The equipment and pipework had largely collapsed as the decks below had dissolved. That was what we were here for—the mess of a metal jungle gym.

"It'll take a few executions for the baqua to come down here," the sergeant said. "They don't like confusing messes, and they're not built for climbing. Poor fuckers. Khanate doesn't just irradiate the rebels. They kill their families, their friends, and their entire circle of contacts. And they do it publicly on the evening news."

I wished he hadn't reminded me how the baqua were treated.

His words were flat and emotionless, but below them, I could feel a rage that gave people like him a purpose. It radiated from him, calming and focusing his people.

Piper and I left him our mules while we scouted the opposite sides of the facility, and the cold part of me came on. Piloting. Marksmanship. Math.

Dissociation.

All the things that let good people commit horrible acts.

I think I know what Javelin felt when she assassinated the galunkin leader on the starliner with a seemingly impossible shot.

The baqua squad never saw me as they wandered into my sensor range. My armor analyzed their transmissions. It couldn't decrypt their signals, but it gave me more than enough targeting data.

It bothered me how much they looked at each other and gestured when they communicated. They took their hands off their weapons too much. It was bad situational awareness and discipline.

Or maybe that was Wraith's and Sgt. Tok's training in me.

I was ten or twenty meters off the deck, in the remains of a structural column. Twenty plus baqua were spread out over fifty meters, walking right toward the facility.

I switched to visual only, and it looked like the bottom of a clogged toilet. Everything was in hues of brown with the occasional bright white streak glaring in. Unaided, I could only see maybe a few meters. I switched back to the grayscale of acoustic and thermal.

I had a clear line of fire for all of them.

As my sensors resolved, they were communicating with short-range line of sight lasers that were getting backscattered all the way to me and over a hundred meters away.

I mapped each one, aiming to penetrate their comms gear. There were two, one in the helmet and another in the left shoulder. If I could destroy their shoulder transmitters and then hit their helmet ones, I could prevent any transmissions from going out.

I didn't know if their comms could transmit in this soup regardless.

I went through the motions, setting the targets on each baqua. I let the armor set the velocity and the number of rounds. Afterward, I took aim and squeezed the trigger.

It was violent chaos for a heartbeat. Then pain the next.

My armor moved so fast I could feel my bones press out of my skin. I longed for Takakoa's armor's hardpoints to keep my joints from squeezing the cartilage out like toothpaste.

I tried to focus on my heartbeat and my breathing through the searing pain.

I was alive.

I FUCKING LIVE!

I processed the pain while looking at the medical menu. I didn't die. I wasn't even injured, despite my skyrocketing heart rate. The portion of me that pilots my meatware assessed the data and turned off the damage alarms as fast as it could.

The baqua fell, writhing in agony as toxic gases boiled in their armor. The shape of their helmets and skulls combined with my angle of attack left too many alive.

I executed an unassisted reload faster and more perfectly than I ever had before. Gabe would have been proud of each one of those shots—clean, penetrating, and merciful.

I don't think I've ever fired that cleanly.

I hope if the roles are ever reversed, someone will spare me the fléchettes.

I never want to watch that girl suffer again.

When we reconvened, Piper told me they used hit-and-run tactics on a squad and an assortment of stragglers. The wrecked facility was now clear and mapped. With its twisted and mangled pipework, it was on its way to become the conscript's labyrinth of horror.

The sergeant had us set our mules to fabricate the components of primitive traps while his people prepared layered fortification with hidden paths.

"Come on, people!" he shouted after them. "Make friends with the terrain, and it will protect you!"

"Do I smell minotaur philosophy?" I said to get his attention.

He gave a slight nod while gesturing into the battle net for the changes he wanted and to approve suggestions.

"Sergeant." Cpl. Sarachek looked at me. "No disrespect." He turned back to the sergeant. "Should I treat him like an embedded lieutenant or what?"

He was referring to a lieutenant or other frontline commanders.

"Sarachek, I'm going to make sure you get your stripe before we go our separate ways." The gruff sergeant almost beamed with pride.

I tilted my head at the sergeant, but he didn't acknowledge the gesture. "What the fuck is he talking about?"

"He's worried you're OI," the sergeant said.

I made a face but then remembered they were staring at a triangle metal helmet, so I gestured for them to continue.

"Operational investigations," he said like I should know what he was talking about.

"Look, I've been on my ship for two years. My correspondence courses didn't include Vanguard military doctrine."

Cpl. Sarachek seemed offended. "Why not?"

"Vanguard is just a port to me," I said, wanting to believe it.

"They've become boogies for the lower enlisted," the sergeant said. "They are counterintelligence and investigate war crimes and whatnot. That one's looking for someone other than me to write him a letter of recommendation. But he needs to survive today before he worries about that."

Cpl. Sarachek took the hint. "Large hostile force at two hundred meters and twelve o'clock from our position. The visibility is less than ten meters. Unknown composition and disposition of force. Inferred that they don't have sensor coverage over us, less sure if they have it outside their own wire. Local data." He nodded at me with his helmet. "Suggests they are staging, and I'm inclined to agree."

"Logic," the sergeant prompted.

The corporal stopped sounding like he was reading his homework in front of the class. "We're not dead. From what I remember from training, the khanate don't engage soft. They're big and strong, and they need everyone to know it. Engagements have tapered off, and those were light compared to when we breached the lift. Khanate infantry wouldn't avoid a fight. Baqua and khanate conscripts on patrol will. If we killed anyone who was worth more than the protein it takes to feed them, they would have come in, forced to engage with us."

A Vanguard all-hands shelter-in-place warning flashed. We exchanged looks. I thought that was exactly what we had been doing.

"Get everyone digging right fucking now!" Piper yelled. They then had our mules collapsing our firing ports with full power lasers.

"What is it?" the sergeant said, checking his weapon and not digging.

"Brimstone incoming!" They pulled a makeshift trenching tool off a mule and threw it at me.

"You heard the lady! If you're not digging, get the fuck out of the way!" he yelled, turning his weapon over and using the stock as a trowel.

I was uncomfortable letting the gendered language slide, but that wasn't the place and sure as fuck not the time.

With our mules, Piper and I did more work in our powered armor than all the conscripts combined. We dug straight down into the biggest mound of sand in our little defensive position.

"What the fuck is brimstone?" someone shouted while digging.

"It's four thousand degrees of fuck your face," the sergeant said.

"I thought it was hypobaric," someone else shouted. "Like a fuel-air explosive."

"That's thermobaric!" another yelled over the frantic panting of digging.

I shoved the sergeant out of the way as Piper and I moved cubic meters of sand from the center of our position, sealing our exit hole.

"Sergeant, last one in the hole will most likely die," they said shortly.

The sergeant started pushing his people into the hole. "FLATTEN OUT!"

In minutes, we had dug a roundish hole that was two or three meters wide and just as deep. Piper and I were on top, while a mule tried to provide some support against the weight of the sand. The last mule buried us.

As sand filled in around us, a message from Shantu popped up. "Friendly fire. If you're forward in your position."

I chuckled.

Man, something is wrong with me.

"What the fuck is so goddam funny?" the sergeant asked, his helmet pressed against mine.

"Let's play a game," I said.

"You better start making sense real fast." His adrenaline-loaded voice wasn't ready for humor.

"Fine. You want to know what our warning was?"

"If I just dug my own grave for no fucking reason, I feel inclined to donate my efforts to you."

I erupted in laughter. "Careful, Sergeant. Shit rolls downhill, and I'm at the top."

That got a few nervous chuckles from down the pile.

"Out with it," the sergeant snapped.

"Our message was 'friendly fire.'"

"Isn't…"

"And if you're forward in your position?"

"The artillery will fall short. In Murphy's name, we pray. Amen," he grumbled mirthlessly.

"Who's Murphy?" someone down the pile asked as the sand kept getting piled on us by the remaining mule.

The sergeant let out a world-weary sigh. "I'm too old for this shit… Murphy is just a grunt who's grunt enough to understand he's a grunt. Someone has fucked up your training by not imparting his wisdom upon you. Remember this: If it can go wrong, it will go wrong. That's why sergeants yell at corporals to yell at conscripts and privates to make sure it cannot fucking go wrong!"

"If we're going to die in this hole, you have to tell me. Are you OI?" Cpl. Sarachek asked.

"That's a negative," I answered. "I'm a merc who likes to keep their clients happy."

"Ha!" someone said. "You owe me twenty credits."

KA-BOOM!

EEEEEEEEEEEEEEEEEEEEEEEEEEEEEEEEEEEEEEEEEEE

I was deaf. The only sounds were my ears ringing.

All I could do was close my eyes and hope as the world around me tried to rip itself apart.

The new ringing in my ears and the drunk feeling in my body told me I wasn't dead yet. When I opened my eyes, my HUD told me it was half a kiloton explosion. The local atmosphere had more phosphorus oxides than it had before. No temperature spike.

My own voice sounded like someone was arguing in the next room. Fuck. I switched over to finger gestures and tried to think of something to message… What would Shantu say?

"Hey! Now I don't have to listen to the sergeant's orders any-more!" I messaged.

The joke landed with the local net filled with LMAOs.

I'll save you how poorly my armor translated the sergeant's speech-to-text. "Joke later. I have three breached armors."

The tram that never hit me in the tube found me in that hole.

I felt cold and weak as my HUD alerted me of low blood pressure and rising heart rates. Below me, two dozen people were stacked on top of each other, hoping that their unpowered armor could support the weight of everyone above them and that the sand above would provide enough thermal insulation to keep them from becoming canned meat in the very armor meant to protect them.

I glanced at my environment readout. The temperature was steadily rising. I knew my armor could ablate some incendiary as long as it didn't get in a joint. But I really didn't want to test it.

I also wasn't currently dying.

"Temperature is rising. How much do you want to risk a face full of thermite?" I asked the sergeant on an open channel.

A moment passed. I assumed he was looking at their leak rates and projections.

"Wait until it levels off," his voice said like he was tired of watching kids die.

We waited.

And waited.

The conscript at the bottom, Cs. Bris, flatlined.

I pulsed my active sensors. His chest plate had collapsed, breaking his ribs and puncturing his lungs. I shared the feed with the sergeant.

"Fuck…"

Inside my mind cockpit, I put my meat systems into idle while watching the temperature climb. I hovered there, barely awake for hours.

Silent.

The temperature finally leveled off at four hundred degrees kelvin. Their armors could heat sink it for a few hours max. The sergeant gave the order to start unburying us. Which translated to slowly and awkwardly shifting back and forth.

"I want to try and seal those armors before breach," he said.

This pile of people grumbled and bitched.

"Lift your foot."

"Move your helmet."

"Sick a hand under there and support…"

Was this how a caterpillar felt?

"Ha! Human centipede!"

"Shut the fuck up!"

"I mean, we *are* ass to mouth!"

My HUD flashed red, and the harsh snap of shattering metal vibrated through my armor. The weight was gone as the hill above us evaporated with a kinetic round. Piper ordered my grenade flinger to use the last of my smoke, flash, and chaff to basically pop against my armor because I sure as fuck didn't do it.

We launched painfully at ninety degrees away from each other.

Hard points were quickly getting on the menu. I felt the sickening sudden loss of resistance, and I knew I had just crushed someone.

But I grabbed the feeling of shock, remorse, and guilt by the throat and threw them in a fucking trunk because I didn't have time for them now.

The matter that made my emotional state irrelevant was the building on treads that looked like it could fire people out of its massive cannon. I was clear of enough smoke that I saw the cool black shadows of heat-sinked armors and a fucking tank pointing its main turret at me.

And I was flying right at it.

My time in zero g helped me control my roll midair. I fired up the lift shaft before I could get my weapon around. My panicked "AAHH!" was enough for my armor to free my shoulder turrets. They peppered two soldiers who stood on either side of the big tank.

The soldiers fired while dropping to a knee. Cool. Clean. Professional.

FUCK ME!

My shoulder turrets ricocheted off the khanate body armor. I got my legs under me so I could change directions when I hit the ground.

I hit the deck, and my armor resisted my barrel drifting down as I preloaded for the next leap. I felt like chewing gum getting squished as I changed directions to a lateral leap and hopefully to get out from in front of the tank's main gun.

I didn't know if my armor was better or if luck was with me, but when I pulled my weapon on target, I strafed the tank's ground escort's weapon. I wasn't getting any more return fire. I ran my weapon dry before I hit the ground.

I hit and rolled. I got to my feet and threw my arm back so my pack could reload my rifle. I had a heartbeat to glance at my map and see the only cover was the hole. One of the rear corner turrets peppered me painfully, but I didn't check to see if the bullets were penetrating. Instead, I aimed and fired at the turret until my weapon went dry again.

While I reloaded, I barked to switch over to full active comms with an active sensor ping. I called for help.

Great. Now the squad escorting the tank knew my position.

The original khanate shooter was taking potshots at me with his pistol as he confidently walked toward me with a sword in his other hand. I sidestepped until his squad was holding fire behind him. I dropped my rifle, and the auto holster snatched it into its socket.

"Piper, I'm about to do some dumb shit… What do I do?" I almost cried in panic.

Fuck you if you think I should be ashamed! I wasn't currently getting shot, and I didn't want to get shot anymore if I could help it. So, fuck me.

"If he thinks he's going to lose, he'll order his soldiers to shoot you," the sergeant's message read.

Fuck me.

"Are you fucking kidding me?! I thought this backward high school fucking pageantry was over!" I bitched on the open channel.

That killed my panic. The ten-year-old version of me rose with the rage of childhood trauma.

I also grabbed that emotion by the throat and threw it into a locker. I'd deal with that later.

With the cooler combat calm washing over me, I sized up this piece of shit. I knew the walk. Completely confident in his own fucking superiority.

Stupid fucker would rather measure his dick than get laid.

His soldiers fanned out to form a firing line. Shithead held up a hand to halt me and tapped his shoulder. I got the message, shrugged off my auto holster, and pulled out my tet.

"How'd it go?" I muttered. "Once more in the breech, dear friend? Fuck, I'm stupid." My chest moved with a laugh I couldn't hear.

"Focus," Piper messaged. "What can you tell me about your opponent?"

I turned off my feed, so I could see the stupid son of a bitch who wanted to have a duel with me because I broke his gun. I then turned off my HUD. No distractions for my fight.

Thirteen soldiers stood behind him with their backs to the tank. Two shoved others apart to show a message scribed in sand that stuck to the tank in ugly common text.

"KILL HIM AND GO HOME, MERC."

I exaggerated a nod to make sure my helmet noticeably moved.

One soldier gestured their weapon at my opponent's back and mocked recoil. I nodded again. All the soldiers then relaxed their weapons and spread out like they were going to enjoy the fight.

Asshole First Class took a dueling stance.

Did he think I was accepting his challenge? I mean, I was, but that was not what I was nodding about.

Piper overrode my HUD settings. "I need their backs. Twenty seconds."

FUCK!

I wasn't really thinking when I maxed out my external speakers. I let out my best lion roar and felt the vibration as I charged. Asshole First Class set his feet for a thrust like anyone running powered armor. The attempt to dodge while striking bullshit turned into me viciously throwing him into the tank, shattering a ceramic coating outside the hard armor.

Asshole First Class popped onto his feet and took a challenging pose.

I casually stood.

Fucking Wraith… So much of his melee training looked just like this. I knew the guard. I knew the stance. And I knew that forward knee would buckle if I did as I was trained. Knees, crotches, elbows, and armpits—the weakest places for humans in armor.

This fight was like a video game, but my whole body was the controller. Small movements turned into large actions with my armor doing all the work.

Metal twisted, ceramics shattered, and I imagined there was a person screaming because I would from that hit. Asshole First Class didn't know how to throw his knee down and rotate his hips to take the hit. So, it bent ninety degrees in a way human knees shouldn't.

Somewhere along the way, my brain gave up on trying to make sense of the overlapping false images. I moved by touch. Mechanisms yielded. Components snapped, and flesh and bone were extruded.

I thought of my AV. It was math and physics. The actuators and springs did not care how mad I was. The world was made of rules, and fighting them was for children.

I was on my back with Asshole First Class, who was trying to decapitate me with his sword. He fought me like we were kids. Full mount, trying to slice off my head.

Amateur.

I got my chin down, and the sword against my helmet did nothing without the thermal activated. I had my hands over his. My armor multiplied my strength as I raised him up with a fraction of the effort it would have usually taken.

He tried to shift his weight instead of grabbing me. He then ignored me whacking his ribs with my tet, still trying to lean on my one arm like hydraulic muscles fatigued. My tet found purchase and opened his armpit seal like a can of cheap calories.

In my head, I drove a blade into an angry egotistical abusive asshole's chest while staring into his eyes so he knew who ended his life.

In reality, when he panicked, I hooked his arm behind my knee and rolled with him to get control of his sword arm. I then took the opening and forced my tet into his torso, ruining the seal.

I remembered the give of the shock gel in my armor. The smooth softness of it. The soreness of my joints and how easy it was to move, like in the water with Takakoa or in low g.

I tried to retrieve my tet but wrenched too hard and ripped his sword arm off.

"Holy fuck…"

I couldn't tell who was talking with my HUD off. Everyone sounded like they were underwater. The voices could have been coming from inside my head for all I could tell.

"Why the hell are we fighting?"

"Pay this fucking guy."

"Worth every fucking credit."

"One, two, three… Fourteen."

"Is the tank one or five khanate tanks with a crew of five?"

"Six if they have the commander."

"Driver, gunner, ECM, point defense, and comms is the tank commander. Plus or minus a column commander."

"Fuck! Give him seven for the tank itself. I don't give a shit."

"Let me get this straight… A tank shoots at this motherfucker, and the tank *loses*?"

I found myself standing with one foot on my opponent's severed arm while his body hung limp from my tet. The burning ruin of the tank and a field of body parts behind me stretched between me and Piper.

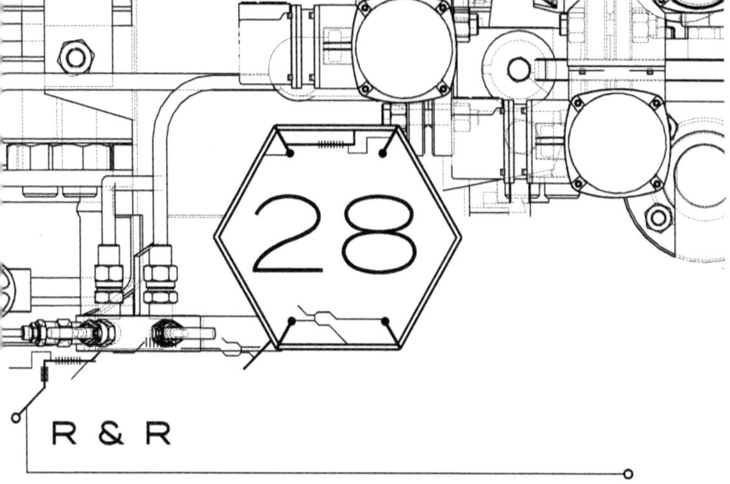

ON THE BATTLEFIELD, Wraith locked down my comms and messaged me. "The official story here is that you slaughtered those fuckheads. I'll have your logs fixed by the time you clear the combat zone. You used them as meat shields to plant a khanate charge on a capacitor near the left rear tread. You didn't need to breach the armor but got it to flex enough to rupture the capacitor."

"Why?" I asked.

"None of these guys get to know I'm here. If I'm not invisible, I'm not doing my job. Take the glory and make the story your own, and Piper will follow your lead. Charge, left, rear, tread. Got it? Wraith out."

That was what we put in our official story.

Yes, I lied. I won't try and justify it with some greater good or dogmatic bullshit. If I had a reason to keep that lie, I would. But I don't, and that's why I'm fixing it here.

I trust Wraith, and that's enough.

I never saw him either, just the changes to the narrative. No updates to the battle net. Just a text-only conversation.

War is stupid.

"Tell the master sergeant to get his people out while we gather his tags," Piper ordered.

The sergeant responded with "My ass…" and a lot of creative and colorful epithets for mercenaries that I couldn't read fast enough.

Being a slow reader might have saved me from being insulted.

The humor evaporated as Piper and I started pulling Vanguard Conscript armor from the sand.

There was some yelling, and "Secure the perimeter!" scrolled across my HUD.

I looked up, and the surviving were in a circle, watching us work. Wide eyes and open mouths stared in all the vivid glory of colorized acoustic sensors. The look of horror behind layers of armor is what will haunt my dreams for the rest of my life.

Not the mangled armor and desiccated bodies.

The look on these kids' faces and how they were unable to respond to the sergeant's orders, locked onto our work of arranging the bodies.

The battle net showed Vanguard forces approaching and no khanate in our vicinity.

Piper and I kept at it while the sergeant organized his people.

The sergeant's text scrolled. "Thank you. This isn't for the connies. This is sergeants' work."

It felt like I just got initiated to some club that there was no turning back from. I didn't see the option to opt out either.

Four conscripts never made it out of that hole. Folks, Lincoln, Li, Adibah. I crushed Adibah and Li when I jumped to engage.

Piper and I dragged the armors while the sergeant chased after his people to keep their eyes forward.

We rotated out through a makeshift hospital.

That battle cost me my eardrums, my armor, and my mule. Vanguard Fleet Medical Services repaired my eardrums without complaint. The real bitch was the one ruptured and three compressed disks in my spine.

I didn't even notice how I hurt myself until I got out of the armor. I screamed and made noises nobody ever wanted to admit making. It felt like getting hit with an electric baton on my back.

The technician and the medic running the skinner supported me with one hand while reaching for their instruments with the other. They relaxed when I could form words and explain what I felt.

"First armor bite?" the technician asked.

I tried to see if there was shrapnel in my ass and screamed with immediate regret.

"How much acclimation time did you get in that armor?"

"I read the manual on the way to the fight," I answered, letting them lift me out of the pile of scrap that was once my armor.

"First time in powered armor?"

"Yeah," I answered honestly.

The medic and the tech exchanged looks.

"If you were one of us, you would be getting fitted for a physical therapy exo, but we can't give you one," the medic said. "I can give you something for the pain and print you a wheelchair or a cane. You should stay out of armor until you get that sorted with a regular doctor. Otherwise, you might end up paralyzed."

"If you can get one fitted with a conditioning mode, it might help," the technician added. "However, nothing is better than physical therapy and time."

"Or hardpoints," the medic added

"Or hardpoints," the tech agreed.

They were patient with me as I tried to be tough and figure out where my new limitations were. I got cleaned up, and they printed me out two walking crutches with the forearm support and sent me on my way.

The hospital room seemed to be an office with a private bathroom. Drag marks leading to the equipment scored the carpeted floor. I left the room and stepped into a lobby that might have been a foyer to an office building before Vanguard turned it into a hospital.

"Monolith?"

I stopped at the threshold and met a short old man's tired but fierce eyes. He had thinning hair. I didn't recognize him.

"You are human…" He glanced at my walking crutches and then took in a deep breath like he was doing something he didn't want to. "My 'scripts have a forty-eight hour pass before they get reassigned. It would mean a lot if you can let them buy you a drink."

He looked like he didn't like the idea. This confused me.

"Why do you look like you want me to say no?" I asked.

"I'm old and tired. The last thing I want to do is babysit a bunch of connies who had their first near-death experience."

I went from confused to befuddled. "Can't you order them to stay in their rooms or something?"

"Come on," the old sergeant said. "I'll buy the first round."

I didn't argue. "I'll need to check in."

I called Piper, and they gave me the green light. Javelin immediately followed up with orders to recover the primary and secondary hard drives and walked me through the purge for my armor. The old sergeant seemed to respect the info sec protocols. I retrieved my tet from the decontamination bin, and he started talking again.

"This war has been a long time coming. I'm sad I'm too old to fight in it."

"But you were just fighting," I said.

He chuckled. "No. This is training. Call it mentorship. I call it the iceberg they send old aggies to die on."

For a moment, I thought the old sergeant had lost all his marbles. "What…?"

"Never mind. You're young, and you'll have to see this war through. In the end, it's your future, not mine." Despite being half a head shorter than me, he stood straight and rigid and walked like a master lecturing his young protégé. "When you become a sergeant or what have you, it stops being about you. At first, it's about not fucking up and getting your friends killed. When you inevitably do, it's about training and managing a bunch of fuckup kids who aren't your friends. Eventually, if you live long enough, you get to meet younger versions of yourself and your best friends, and you try to be the sergeant you needed. That's why I'm buying drinks for a mercenary." The last bit sounded like it was a bitter taste in his mouth.

"Because it's not about you?"

He glanced back at me with a nod.

My back was spasming, shooting electric arcs of pain down my legs. My steps closely resembled a toddler on frost. The crutches kept my ass from the deck.

"Do you want a wheelchair? It's a half kilometer from here to the bar."

"No," I said stubbornly.

The old sergeant shrugged, let me be, and slowed down. "The war with the khanate and the rest of humanity is the norm. The couple of centuries of relative peace is a new concept. Prior to the osheran, armed conflict between groups was so common that it was considered part of the human condition. I think it was only a matter of time before the old mentalities crept back up."

"What?"

"Never mind. Don't dwell on it. Let's try and have a good night."

The old sergeant and I chatted about nothing as we walked. He spent thirty-six years in the VAF until he got too old to maintain his qualifications. Instead of retiring or taking a desk job, he downgraded to a master sergeant in the Vanguard Conscript Corps, where he could coach and mentor the new conscripts. This was the only way to become a legendary master sergeant. There were only forty-six on the station.

I was polite and kept my feelings about Vanguard to myself.

I felt my training and practice sessions aboard *The Happy Marauder* guiding the conversations more than me. This was a conversation with a client. Stow my personal feelings and paint myself in the best light.

I wasn't James August Childs right now. I was Monolith of the FTS *The Happy Marauder*.

At the bar, thunderous industrial metal screamed at me as the vocalist tried to destroy the microphone with a backup of breaking glass and industrial accidents. The synthetic smell of—welding…and…octane?—wafted over my face like someone had shoved my head into a bag. The tableau of dimly lit tables and fistfights were caught one strobe at a time.

I think I liked it…

The old sergeant guided me over to a table, and the sound dampened down to background noise. The tables seemed to be islands of calm versus the club's cacophony. Neat effect.

At the table, two dozen young faces stared off into the distance.

The old sergeant plopped into a chair and tapped on the table pad. Shots found their way from the slots at the center of the table. Someone knocked on the table between us, the sergeant exchanged looks with the stranger, and two more shots came out.

"Look, I'm not religious," he said. Despite the steel in his voice, he sounded like he was going to cry. "If you want that, there's a chapel two decks up from here. I sincerely hope it brings you comfort. But that's not for me. I'm an old man where the young die. I know it's going to be all right because the next batch of kids did not fucking disappoint. Now, grab your drinks, and if you spit them out, I will make you lick it off the table."

The old sergeant nodded over his shoulder. The lights came on, and the music stopped so abruptly that the place could be mistaken for a photograph. There was even a pair in the middle of a fistfight who had stopped mid-swing. Only the vapors in the air didn't respect the reverence of the moment.

An aggie reached between us and retrieved his shot of liquor. Everyone who could stand stood with their shot in the air.

"For the living!" every voice said together like an angry god.

We drank and tapped our empty shot glasses on the table twice.

TAP! TAP!

"For the lost!"

TAP! TAP!

"For the future!"

TAP! TAP!

The whiskey went straight for my head. Then just like that, the lights went out, the music kicked back up, and some fights ended while others resumed.

It was surreal.

"Were you wounded? Or were you…" a conscript asked, rubbing the fuzz filling in her head. The young woman with medium brown skin seemed uncomfortable with the air.

I recognized the voice though. She was in the hole with me.

"This is what it looks like when you have zero training in powered armor and spend five days in combat," I said. "I tweaked something. The techs had to cut me out of it and call it an armor bite."

"Shit! That's a thing?"

"For real…"

The old sergeant pulled his collar down to show fading callouses of where his hard points used to be. "Can't be an aggie without them because that's what happens."

"If anyone starts bugging the master sergeant for war stories, you're buying the round," one of the corporals warned.

"If he gives some clichés like…" The other corporal did a gruff affectation. "'I didn't die.' He should buy the round." The corporal then seemed to recognize the overstep. "I mean, please, Master Sergeant?"

The old sergeant's smile set the mood for the table. "If you want to pay for this old sergeant's drinks, I'll sing and dance for you all night."

This was what leadership looked like. He barked at people he didn't know to keep them alive, and now he was showing them how to turn *it* off. He was being a warm uncle who dispensed advice between jokes and insults, filling the air with laughter.

"Was it you or the armor doing the fighting?" someone asked.

I mused the question for a moment. "It depends on how you break it down. The turrets and sensors are mostly automated, so ten percent me. Any melee was ninety-five percent me. The rifle is complicated. I don't know where to put that line with the barrel targeting assistance, recoil compensation, and live trigger."

"What's a live trigger?" someone else asked.

"A whole bunch of settings that can change muzzle velocity and delay sending the round." I went on to explain what I had learned about the armor.

Conscript Simonetti shit on the levity. "Must be fucking nice. To run around in your fancy armor, shrugging off rounds that killed my squad. Easy to show up and play the hero so you can raise your hourly."

I looked at the old sergeant for guidance.

"There's no rank in the bar," the sergeant said. "If he's got something to say, he can say it."

"You think you're a hero?" Simonetti asked.

"Am I a hero?" I asked to find time for me to think. I felt Shantu's words coming out of my mouth. "No. I'm no hero.

That's the difference between mercs and military. Mercs are dead when they leave port. Fail to complete the contract, we don't get resupplied, something breaks, and we have to decide between eating a fléchette à la mode, eating each other, or seeing the void with the old mark one eyeball."

"Seeing the void?" someone asked.

I didn't break eye contact with Simonetti. "Spacing yourself to avoid starvation. Mercs are already dead. We're fighting to push that off a little longer." I was getting aggressive because I didn't like this little fucker's tone. Or maybe it was the whiskey. "Tell me, Simonetti, are you going to make a career out of this, or are you going to do your time and get the fuck on with your life?"

My aggressive question seemed to catch the angry conscript off guard. "No… I didn't want to do this, but what choice did I have?" He was about to start in on the woe-is-me bullshit.

I didn't care, and my back hurt. "Fuck you and your helpless fucking attitude," I said. "Was your alternative a death sentence?"

Vanguard emigrants who graduate secondary school tend to earn in the top twenty-five percent in the Commonwealth. It was one of the many backburner plans I had before *The Happy Marauder*. But mostly, I was trying to get through the day.

Simonetti didn't get a chance to answer because someone horse-collared me. A punch or a kick hit my stomach, and my breath left me, along with a whiskey-flavored burp. My assailant said something about not talking like that between strikes.

But my world was upside down. Between the light show, the music, and the alcohol, everything was lost to me. I managed to hook one of my walking crutches on an ankle or a knee. Either way, my assailant hit the ground.

My legs gave out before I could find my feet, and an electric bolt shot down my legs.

I flew into a rage powered by agony. I saw a foot, grabbed it, and rolled into an ankle lock. Another blow hit my neck and ear.

I threw my chest back in an ugly wild flail that Wraith would have approved of.

Tendons and bones snapped in both ankles and knees. The bloodcurdling scream that came out of the person complemented the death metal ambiance.

I grabbed for the foot slamming into my spine, but bodies fell on me, pinning me down.

"Easy, easy," a calming voice said as the music faded. "It's over. You've won. Can you let him up please?"

Medics stood all around me, their vests and shoulder lights illuminating the area.

I found myself panting in a cold sweat as my back spasmed. I shook my head violently as my body betrayed me.

One of the medics produced an injector collar. "Sir, it's okay. Bar fights are allowed as long as you stop when we ask. Now…"

Between painful pants, I managed, "I-I'm st-stu-stuck." I nodded to my crutches.

"These are yours?"

I nodded, which triggered another painful round of spasms. I tried to relax my arms, so they could extract whoever from my overcommitted ankle lock.

After they put me back in my seat, I took the shot that sat on the table in front of me. "Now, where was I?"

The old master sergeant shot beer out his nose and across the table.

"What did I miss?" Shantu asked, patting my shoulder.

The lights kicked on as another table initiated the ritual. Piper and Shantu steadied me to my feet.

"For the living!"

TAP! TAP!

"For the lost!"

TAP! TAP!

"For the future!"

TAP! TAP!

"What's going on here?" Piper asked, pointing to their forehead. A motherly green-blue hue came from their frame. They wore a flowing ethereal dress that hid their curves.

I wiped my head and found blood.

The old sergeant still had tears of laughter in his eyes as he caught them two up. I was busy getting the attention of a medic who was not shy with the antiseptic as they stitched me up.

"What the fuck was that guy's problem?" I asked after we got resettled.

"Maybe he thinks mercs should know their place?" Simonetti offered.

"What the fuck is that one's problem?" Shantu said, backing up.

"Never mind them," Cpl. Sarachek said. "They've been a moody bitch since indoc."

Indoctrination or indoc is the early phase of conscription training with all the yelling and head shaving.

Before Simonetti had a chance to protest, he continued. "If one more word comes out of that mouth that isn't a drink order, I will mop the fucking floor with you."

Simonetti didn't know when to shut the fuck up. "I just think—"

He cut that off with an elbow to Simonetti's teeth. "Mercs in the corner, we're going to drink and sing and tell stories until Simonetti starts making sense. Then all bets are off."

The sergeant smiled and raised an approving glass to Sarachek as we shuffled.

"So, what the fuck was all that about?" Shantu asked.

"Don't worry about it. Simonetti here just needed an attitude adjustment." He put a friendly arm around Simonetti, who was fuming while dabbing at a busted lip.

"Then I won't. Who's hungry?" Shantu went a little wild, ordering the menu to try everything, and then chugged a beer.

"Dude, your girlfriend shafted me! At the command post, they put me in a fucking closet with two disabled kids who didn't have any idea how personal hygiene works. Fuck, I was sharing a desk with their supervisor. My heart goes out to the dude. He had the patience of a saint. He had to wrestle them out to take them to the bathroom, and the bigger one would shit himself if he struggled too hard."

Piper flashed an angry red but bit their tongue.

The old master sergeant picked up on the concern that went around the table. "What Vanguard has found is a place for those who don't interact with the world on the same wavelength. In many ways, they're better off. Prioritized job placement and the like."

"Nope. Nooope. We are not talking about the merits of inclusion versus social burden and individual agency. I am in way too much pain for that shit!" I yelled at Shantu to head off baiting someone into one of the arguments he had with Gabe all the time.

"The medics are right there," someone said. "They can give you something."

"Did he tell you how he got his handle?" Shantu said.

"Something about a drop gone wrong?"

"Is that all he…"

Piper and I turned the same embarrassed red.

"Gentlepeople, tonight's entertainment will be brought to you by Sha…" I coughed. "Tombstone The Unending. Challenge: If anyone can wrestle the conversation away from my counterpart here, there will be a bottle of"—I set the table to my account, scrolled through the bar menu, and found the most expensive bottle of whiskey—"Wind in the Black Sail!"

The table erupted in shouting. I started eating chili fries.

"What's the situation between y'all?" the old master sergeant asked, starting on a chicken wing basket while everyone still screamed.

"Uh, he's basically my brother." I nodded toward Piper. "They're a couple. Piper is our pilot and superior officer."

"Then why did it seem like you were on point?"

"Oh! We're rated on everything we do. My ability to embed and be an asset affects my résumé. Piper doesn't need the bump in their credentials the way I do." It was a half-truth but easy enough to swallow.

"How much did y'all get paid to rescue us?" one of the conscripts asked.

"We weren't even there for you," I admitted. "Our mission was to get tech samples and mop up behind the aggies. Then everything just kind of went to shit. Speaking of which, who shot me in the face?"

"Lincoln. His armor breached in the hole."

In the hole.

The grave I crawled out of that others didn't.

Thankfully, Shantu was making a ripe ass of himself and distracted me and that conscript. It set the mood, and the conscripts paired off or hit the dance floor. I cherish the hours of poor attempts at singing and shouting opinions, only to get so far off topic that there was no chance of coming back. I can't tell you what we were talking about, because honestly, I don't know. Some might say it was the drinking. I like to think it was the fact I switched off.

I wish I had their names.

Those who know what I'm talking about, I'm sorry you understand.

But it all came crashing down like an unstable orbit. The table showed images of a past Shantu and I kept trying to forget.

"Sergeant, did you know you brought a couple of blue dots into our establishment?" A man on crutches appeared on the far side of the old master sergeant with two people who looked like Vanguard security.

Is that the ankle I broke?

How long have I been here?

Fuck!

There's a nice pyramid of shot glasses forming in the center of the table.

Shantu would have been removing organs in ascending order of importance if it wasn't for Piper and me.

"Coded as sexual violence." He highlighted keywords. "Your newfound merc friends couldn't join the conscript corps because of their history. They're rapists." He laughed like he had won. "Arrest them!"

The security looked at one another with small hand gestures that said they were looking into the story. Blue falcon here clearly wasn't in control.

I put my lips up to Shantu's ears and whispered, "Calm down and fucking end him."

That did the trick. He took a shot, shook off the burn, and took a deep breath. It was like watching him change characters between takes.

"Sorry," he said. "I almost lost my cool there for a second. Congratulations. A blue falcon has never soared so high."

I had just learned *blue falcon* meant *buddy fucker*.

Shantu continued. "Here's what I know. Firefights are dangerous places. This one"—he pointed at me—"is stone fucking cold. Thus, the name Monolith." He raised a hand to calm the security as he slowly stood and pulled pal'loch from his back. "They call me Tombstone because I always know what to say. In accordance with the Vanguard/Minotaur Nonaggression Treaty of 512, I could kill you where you stand, and they couldn't even ask me to leave until I finished my nachos. And I ordered a lot of nachos."

How the fuck did he work nachos into sounding badass?

One of the security guards frantically gestured as if to check the legitimacy of the claim, while the other stuck his finger to his ear in the universal I'm-on-a-call gesture.

"They're going to find my sponsorship to the Tilled Wind Clan." Shantu lifted his chin to the distracted security. He then rested his hand on my shoulder. "He's my tet, my friend in blood and battle. I trust him with my life. This is a tet."

I popped my weapon out of its ring, and he snatched it out of the air.

"It's the weapon that appears when you need it, a friend."

He then got his feet tangled in my crutches while trying to get out of the corner. The sound of them clattering against everything made it awkward for a moment. He let that moment hang there while I stared at him, wondering if he was going to kill himself with my tet.

We waited way, way too long.

I think he was waiting for the first snicker, which was provided by one of the conscripts at the table. He then picked up like nothing had happened.

"He and I have been through a lot together," he said. "If you look at the case files that you have so helpfully provided, you will find how we spent our childhood at the institute in *excruciating* detail. We spent our younger years being exploited by the very people who were charged with our care. What is a kid to do when their whole reality is being held down and taken advantage of by bigger and stronger kids while the staff are getting rich by streaming it?"

The hairs on the back of my neck stood. There were sounds in the natural world that were the only warning signs before a disaster: hisses, guttural growls, scales grinding, and Shantu's tone right now.

He held up my tet, looked at it, and dropped it. In a motion so smooth they should make barrels out of it, he drew his pal'loch and hooked the crescent moon blade under shithead's shirt and jacket. His opposite hand was at the back of his neck as the armor piercing forward point drew a single drop of blood from under his chin.

The music stopped, and the lights came on, but no one was setting up a toast.

"Would you mind not killing him?" a voice identified as Maj. Lavin asked.

His aid retrieved my crutches and handed them to me.

"Major Lavin, I do believe I would be doing you a favor by ridding you of this individual," Shantu said.

"Trust me. The consequences of his death would be most inconvenient," the major said. The dropped contractions and deliberate language were cues that he had spent extensive time with the minotaur.

"At your convenience, Major." Shantu released the blue falcon, who then tripped over my crutches and landed on his ass.

Maj. Lavin nodded to the security people, and they scooped up the blue falcon. The blue falcon ripped his arms from security's hands in an adolescent display.

Maj. Lavin did a slashing motion across his throat. The music stopped, and the lights came on.

Did they have that on a hot button?

Now that I could see clearly, I worked my way out of the booth to recover my crutches before they ended up across the bar. It wasn't until I was finally standing mostly comfortably that I realized the entire bar had watched me crawl to recover them.

Did I mention I was blowing past drunk and dipping into shitty?

A whole bar of off duty military people watching me crawl to get my crutches.

Not my proudest moment.

I might have been three sheets to the wind at this point, but rapidly switching the ambiance was the coolest, most dramatic thing I'd seen.

"Atten-SHUN!"

The entire bar snapped to with Maj. Lavin's order.

"Private, *you are disrespecting the master sergeant*" came out as a growl.

The whole bar glared at the blue falcon, and I winced.

I don't know why.

The blue falcon tried to argue. "But Major…"

"PRIVATE! Do you not understand you are the only thing between everyone in this bar and a good evening."

"Sir!"

"I am trying to save your life. Stop making it hard." Quieter, he said. "If the merc with a pal'loch asks for your head, I *will* give it to him."

"Shantu, atten-*shun*!" Piper barked in a commanding voice.

I knew those words; I knew that tone.

Never out of Piper.

It could have been an audio clip from Sgt. Tok for all I knew. I wanted to stand at attention.

Piper was flashing an angry red, and their filigree swung with sharp spikes like a murderous rose bush.

The blue falcon was the only one breaking discipline with his laughing. "Your name's Shantu? Like the trash can?"

CLANG!

Unstoppable force met an immovable object.

Piper stood with their back to Shantu, facing Maj. Lavin.

I was hammered drunk at this point, but it seemed like Piper did a ninja teleport to stop Shantu from slicing this guy in half.

"That won't be necessary, Major," Piper said, "if we can get back to the hospitality of the master sergeant."

"Hos-hospitality? I-I thought you guys-es were buying?" M.Sgt. Irons slurred out. "I wuddn'ta drank so much if I was paying. That shit's expensive."

Apparently, M.Sgt. Irons was joining me in the shit-faced

drunk parade. He swayed against the table but still looked rigid at attention.

"I got you…"—I almost fell trying to turn to the master sergeant—"…and you and you…" I was pointing at each of the conscripts at the table, but I got stuck when I noticed several were missing.

"Then I won't let this one keep you from entertaining my master sergeant." Maj. Lavin nodded to security and twirled a finger.

The music was up, and the lights went down again.

I swung, catching Shantu in the mouth with everything I had. The motion sent white hot fire down both of my legs, and they gave out.

I did not recover. I face-planted and stayed there.

"WHAT THE FUCK?!" Shantu burbled out through the blood coming out of his nose.

Piper scooped us up and returned us to the booth. Medics stopped the bleeding and reset his nose.

I didn't feel the crunch, but I had fucked up his face.

"Why'd you hit me?" Shantu asked when the medics were done.

"You're fucking up! That's why! Look at Piper's hand!"

I couldn't see the cut, but two of their fingers didn't display their color and filigree. Piper pulled their hand from the table and flashed an embarrassed orange.

I don't know if the rage was clearing my head or if all this came out like a drunken asshole. "We're on fucking Fermi. We never thought we'd get out of the gut!" I shouted. "I ripped a khanate officer's arm off and beat him to death with it. I blew up a tank and saved these guys. What were you doing?"

Okay. I want credit for remembering to stick to the story while not being able to feel my face.

"I was getting studied by the signals analysis people to help penetrate khanate ECM," Shantu answered, giving me the side-eye.

That's *electronic countermeasures* if you didn't know.

"Fucking right!" I growled. "We made it! We're doing shit that matters with people we can trust, and you're fucking it up." I turned to Piper. "I can't order you to do shit. If you were organic, the healing time and scar would be one hell of a reminder. Keep that in mind when you get it fixed."

The conscripts stared wide-eyed, and the master sergeant smiled proudly.

Shantu looked to be on the verge of tears.

Good.

I spoke to the table. "I was found on James Street. Shantu was found the same day in a Shantu-model refuse collection system. We got into a lot of fights over our names at the institute. That doesn't"—I glared at Shantu—"shouldn't"—I turned my attention back to the table and ordered another round of whiskey—"matter anymore."

The drinks arrived, and I picked mine up.

"It's time to be *fucking* awesome," I said and threw the shot back.

Shantu downed his drink.

Piper shined a proud green.

M.Sgt. Irons raised his drink, and his conscripts followed suit.

ABOUT THE AUTHOR

Jordan Gray is a base-line human aside from decorative pigmentation. Pre-first-contact OId Earth is a dumpster fire social stratification and resource hoarding. Old Earth is a far cry from the Mother Terra described in certain religious texts.

Jordan found comfort with a close group of friends who enjoyed tabletop RPGs. It was during these gaming sessions that the first embers of The Infinite Night began getting stoked. His notions of good and evil were challenged by perspective. How does a person determine how much of a necessary evil is tolerable? The books started to take shape as mental exercise to deal with the mind numbing tedium of various occupations.

Then the day came as one venture failed and priorities changed and breathing life into The Infinite Night became not just possible but a necessity. He hopes you enjoy exploring the universe as much as he enjoyed creating it.